praise for

THE EXPATRIATES

"What I really adored about this novel were the gripping story line and the compelling characters. This novel delivers on every level."
—Elin Hilderbrand, author of *Here's to Us*

"Poignant and compelling...Lee's storytelling is intricate, precise, and rich enough to keep the reader seduced until the end." —THE SEATTLE TIMES

"Gorgeously wrought." —MARIE CLAIRE

"A novel about displacement and belonging... A thoughtful portrait of motherhood's trade-offs, the book also offers sharp insights into the tensions between moneyed expats and the impoverished locals who serve them."
—PEOPLE ("The Best New Books")

"Combines a page-turning plot with intimate perceptions about Americans in Hong Kong." —MORE

NEW YORK TIMES BESTSELLER

PENGUIN BOOKS

THE EXPATRIATES

Janice Y. K. Lee was born and raised in Hong Kong. She received a BA in English and American literature and language from Harvard College. A former editor at *Elle* magazine, Lee lives in New York with her husband and four children.

* * *

Praise for *The Expatriates*

"A nuanced reminder of how shockingly easy it can be to lose everything in a moment and of how to reinvent one's life after a fall."
—*San Francisco Chronicle*

"With meticulous details and nuanced observations, Lee creates an exquisite novel of everyday lives in extraordinary circumstances. . . . How Lee's triumvirate reacts, copes, and ventures forth (or not) proves to be a stupendous feat of magnetic, transporting storytelling."
—*The Christian Science Monitor*

"One chief pleasure of *The Expatriates* is watching how the lives of Hilary, Mercy, and Margaret converge and are changed by that convergence, and how they each metabolize grief. A more subtle yet lingering benefit is getting to know Lee's acutely observed Hong Kong, a city on the cusp of change that must eventually affect the lives of expatriates and locals alike."
—*Los Angeles Times*

"Janice Y. K. Lee's absorbing, poignant novel . . . [is a] nuanced story of the ordinary heroism needed to move past some of life's worst experiences. It's a great read and a testament to the strength and resilience we all have."
—*Redbook*

"Everyone's buzzing about *The Expatriates*. . . . These women and their stories will pull at every string in your heart."
—*Bustle*

"Janice Y. K. Lee nails family drama and gentrified Hong Kong."
—*New York Magazine*

"Devastating and heartwarming, and exquisite in every way, this is a book you'll fall deeply in love with and never want to put down."
—Kevin Kwan, author of *Crazy Rich Asians*

"*Sex and the City* meets *Lost in Translation*."   —*theSkimm*

"Like Jodi Picoult and Kristin Hannah, Lee is a perceptive observer of her compelling characters and brings them vividly to life in this moving novel."   —*BookPage*

"Captivating . . . Lee's women are complex and often flawed, which makes the stories of their strength all the more compelling in this tale of family, motherhood, and attempts at moving on."
—*Publishers Weekly*

"A richly detailed novel that rubs away at the luster of expat life and examines how the bonds of motherhood or, really, womanhood, can call back even those who are furthest adrift."   —*Kirkus Reviews*

JANICE Y. K. LEE

The
Expatriates

PENGUIN BOOKS

PENGUIN BOOKS

An imprint of Penguin Random House LLC
375 Hudson Street
New York, New York 10014
penguin.com

First published in the United States of America by Viking Penguin,
an imprint of Penguin Random House LLC, 2016
Published in Penguin Books 2016

THE LIBRARY OF CONGRESS HAS CATALOGED THE HARDCOVER EDITION AS FOLLOWS:
Names: Lee, Janice Y. K., author.
Title: The expatriates : a novel / Janice Y. K. Lee.
Description: New York, New York : Viking, [2016]
Identifiers: LCCN 2015041269 | ISBN 9780525429470 (hc.) | ISBN 9780143108429 (pbk.)
Subjects: | BISAC: FICTION / Literary. | FICTION / Contemporary Women.
Classification: LCC PS3612.E34295 E97 2016 | DDC 813/.6—dc23 LC

Printed in the United States of America
1 3 5 7 9 10 8 6 4 2

Set in Adobe Garamond Pro
Designed by Francesca Belanger

This is a work of fiction. Names, characters, places, and incidents either are the
product of the author's imagination or are used fictitiously, and any resemblance to actual
persons, living or dead, businesses, companies, events, or locales is entirely coincidental.

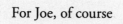

For Joe, of course

Prologue

THE NEW EXPATRIATES arrive practically on the hour, every day of the week. They get off Cathay Pacific flights from New York, BA from London, Garuda from Jakarta, ANA from Tokyo, carrying briefcases, carrying Louis Vuitton handbags, carrying babies and bottles, carrying exhaustion and excitement and frustration. They have mostly been cramped in coach; a precious few have drunk champagne in first; others have watched two movies in business class, eating a ham-and-Brie sandwich. They are thrilled, they are homesick, they are scared, they are relieved to have arrived in Hong Kong—their new home for six months, a year, a three-year contract max, forever, nobody knows. They are fresh-faced; they are mid-career, hoping for that crucial boost up the ladder; they are here for their last job, the final rung before they're put out to pasture. They work at banks; they work at law firms. They make buttons, clothing, hard drives, toys. They run restaurants; they are bartenders; they are yoga teachers; they are designers; they are architects. They don't work. They are hoping to work. They are done, done, done with work. They arrive in January, after Christmas; they arrive in June, after the kids get out from school; they arrive in August, when school is about to start; they arrive whenever the company books their ticket. They come with their families or with their wives or their boyfriends, or resolutely single, or hoping to meet someone. They are Chinese, Irish, French, Korean, American—a veritable UN of fortune-seekers, willing sheep, life-changers, come to find their future selves.

These days, they always come by air, disgorged from the planes that encircle Chek Lap Kok airport. The new expatriates wait in line, somnambulant in the fluorescent light, with their pallid skin and greasy hair, wondering if jet lag will ever be less horrendous. They present their passports, clear immigration, collect their bags, and emerge from the terminal to scatter—disappearing into the Airport Express train; queuing up for double-decker buses, taxis; stepping into the back of black Mercedes sedans bearing the emblem of the Mandarin Oriental, doors opened by white-capped chauffeurs. They are swept away and driven along the highway, so clean, so new, past villages that are just remnants of what was there before all the buildings went up, those giant complexes built to house the ever-burgeoning local population, those people who will be their colleagues, their employees, their employers, their drivers. All the expats disperse, are quickly absorbed into their new home, each quickly becoming just one more face in the crowd.

The new expatriates are tired. They have arrived, but they are not sure to what. The immediate journey has ended, but the longer one has just begun. They rest their heads on the window of the bus, on the leather headrest in the car, on the velour of the train seat, on the way to their bed in Chungking Mansions, at the YWCA, at the Four Seasons, at a friend's house, at their serviced apartment, at the house on the Peak that has been leased for them. They quiet the children, they drink a bottle of water, they drum their fingers on the seat. Hong Kong flashes frantically by. The road stretches long before them. They are exhausted. Their eyes close, and they dream of what lies ahead.

Part I

Mercy

A SLOW-ROASTED UNICORN. A baked, butterflied baby dragon, spread-eagled, spine a delicate slope in the pan. A phoenix, perhaps, slightly charred from its fiery rebirth, sprinkled with sugar, flesh caramelized from the heat. That's what she wants to eat: a mythical creature, something slightly otherworldly, something not real. A centaur. Yes, the juicy haunch of a centaur. Mercy lies in bed, not quite asleep, not quite awake, sheets crumpled around her, feeling the gnawing hole in her stomach, relishing it, savoring it.

The sun streams in through her small, smudged window. By the looks of it, it must be past 11:00 a.m., a time when most people—respectable people, people with jobs—have been at work for several hours and may already be contemplating what they should eat for lunch.

She can hear the muted sounds of the streets below. Sheung Wan, an area too quickly being discovered by the rent-hikers—those young, industrious careerists in their well-cut suits and shiny leather shoes who leave at eight thirty in the morning with wet hair and sheaves of papers shoved in briefcases. They have discovered this relatively cheap neighborhood, a short walk from Central, and have succeeded in slowly gentrifying it. The rent-hikers live among aging locals who view their encroachment with bemused silence. Every morning they pass the crazy charwoman in the lobby who barks incomprehensible Cantonese invectives at them as they walk through, fingertips pecking on their phones, pretending not to notice. These superbly energetic men and women have tried to get the charwoman replaced, started a petition, which was photocopied and slipped under Mercy's door for her signature, but all their efforts have come to naught. The crazy woman stays all day and night, sitting on her plastic stool, bucket and mop beside her, shouting at them and at herself. It is believed she lives in a little room off the lobby, but no one has been able to ascertain the truth. No one has ever seen her do any cleaning, or leave, or come back. It's one of those Hong Kong mysteries, where she might be the landlord's demented aunt, a homeless person who has made the lobby her home, or indeed an insane millionaire who owns the building. All this conjecture and information is conveyed through messages posted in the elevator. Then suddenly one day, a direction to an online message board, to which they all migrate, leaving the wall in the elevator mercifully blank. All that remains of the shrill, slightly hysterical dialogue is a strip of yellowing Scotch tape on the plastic wall.

Mercy is hungry. She should eat. But she wants to eat a centaur's thigh, roasted over a bonfire, turned on a spit by fairies, their sparkly little faces perspiring from the heat. She is certain she will not find this when she ventures out into the small, tight streets around her. They are filled instead with equally improbable things: shiny cow innards; disembodied pigs' heads with floppy ears, stacked up in bloody piles; dried seahorses in burlap sacks. She does not find the food grotesque, instead is bewildered by how one begins to eat such items, existing as they do in such peculiar and indeterminate forms, or indeed, alive, or in quantities that would feed a village.

When she gets up, she determines, she will turn on her space heater to warm the chill of the December air. She will take out a head of organic Boston lettuce from her little refrigerator and pull apart the leaves, soak them for ten minutes, then transfer them into a spinner, where they will be centrifuged, and the sandy water discarded. She will toss the leaves in a wooden bowl with a micro spray of olive oil, a drop of balsamic vinegar, the insanely expensive balsamic vinegar that she bought at the gourmet store, so viscous it drips in a slow, thick stream. A tomato. A Persian cucumber. These will emerge, pristine, from her tiny refrigerator, chilled, perfect. She will slice them thinly and fan them into beautiful patterns, a vegetable mandala, courtesy of the mandoline, a feast for the eyes. She will hand-crumble Parmigiano Reggiano onto the top, and then, from on high, she will brandish the mill and grind coarse crystals of pink salt from the Himalayas into fine, sparkly shavings that will float, like snowflakes, onto the pale green surface of her salad.

She will bring the salad to the table by her bed, which she will have set with a scalloped linen placemat she bought on a trip to Hanoi, with a matching napkin, and a glass with a bottle of Fiji water just next to it, ready for pouring. She lives in a two-hundred-square-foot studio, but she does not have to live like a savage.

Mercy will sit on the bed and take up her instruments: her heavy silver fork and knife, stolen from Gaddi's restaurant on a memorable night in better times. The lettuce, slightly glossed with oil, will yield as she presses the tines of her fork into it, the hole bleeding a slightly darker green as she breaks the cells of the leaf, violent death in its own microscopic way. From there, she will lift it into her mouth, a light sliver on her tongue for an instant before her teeth grind it into a small, slippery pulp that will slip down her throat. She will swallow. She will cut another piece. She will put it in her mouth and chew again. Swallow. Drink water. Drink more water. Spear another leaf. Repeat.

It is important to do things right. Otherwise, when you live alone, it can devolve very quickly. Stand on ceremony. Observe the rites. That's how you get through the day.

Margaret

IT'S A TRICKY PROJECT. The house sits atop a sloping meadow, and the clients want to flatten out the land and make an English garden—totally wrong for the landscape and the surrounding area. It is woodsy and natural there in rural Connecticut, where they are. She wonders why they didn't buy a tidy, flat plot of land near potato fields instead, or a suburban house in Darien—a tabula rasa, where they can put up high hedges and rose gardens in symmetrical rectangles and live out their Anglophilic fantasy undisturbed by the illogical terrain of the hills. They have friends in the area, they said. That is why they bought in Litchfield. But this is not her problem. Her problem is persuading them to listen to the land.

It sounds pretentious or mystical, but it's true: The land dictates what will happen to it. So it is not a problem in the end. A lot of clients try to have their way, but eventually, always, they have to yield. If not to her, then to nature. No one has enough time or money to bend nature to his will. Nature is patient, can wait for centuries.

Margaret leans over the desk, wielding her ruler and pencil. This is the part she loves most, the clean beginning, when it is only her and the land and the blank paper, all possibility, no problems. She has her drawings spread around her. She always starts by hand and ends up on the computer.

The problems come later, when concept collides with reality and human nature.

A stone fruit orchard on the east side of the garden. This will appease them. She sketches in some trees. These clients will buy them mature. So much easier. So much more expensive. An allée of trees will provide shade for an afternoon promenade. It is part of her job to idealize life, to proffer a gracious, perfect existence in its most optimistic aspect. She knows all too well that soon the constraints of reality, budget, and deadline will alter her plan until it's almost unrecognizable. She also knows that this particular project will never get off the ground. This is not a real project. These are friends of friends who forwarded her photos and surveys and asked for her opinion. She's doing this as a favor for her friends, and she suspects that they suggested her so she will have something to do, to fill the hours, to try to still her mind. Still, she loses herself in the work.

They arrived three years ago in Hong Kong, Clarke and Margaret Reade, with their three children. He is with a U.S. multinational, she says if anyone asks, which they always do. The sound of that term always gives her a frisson: anonymous, vaguely threatening, nationalistically contradictory in terms. It reminds her of when she reads in the paper about companies with names like Archer Daniels and Monsanto, names she has only vaguely heard of but that own everything that touches people's daily lives, like toothpaste and children's aspirin and milk.

But here they always just ask, Which one? as everyone here works for a U.S. multinational. They don't see anything funny about the term. And she tells them M_ D_. Oh, yes, they say, do you know John McBride and Suzie? From Winnetka? I think John works in sourcing? So he's up in the Pearl River delta a lot? They natter on and on while she wonders if she'll ever find anyone who understands. So many people here seem hermetically sealed, as if they live in Hong Kong but are untouched by it. They live in an almost wholly American section of the former British colony, now China, and are only inconvenienced sometimes by the lack of good tomatoes or how hard it is to find a really good hamburger.

She looks up. It is noon. A gift when time passes and she is unaware. She has a lunch in town in an hour, and she has to get ready.

It is with a party planner, of all people. Clarke is turning fifty, and she wants to throw him a big celebration but has no idea how to do it and, really, no inclination either.

She showers, thinking about all she has to do. This is the last day of school before the Christmas holiday, they have a dinner party to go to tonight, and then they are leaving for vacation the next day. Suitcases need to be packed, children readied. Dressed, with wet hair, she leaves, bidding good-bye to Essie, her Filipina helper, flags down a taxi on Repulse Bay Road, slides into the plasticky backseat, fastens her seat belt. Loud Cantopop fills the interior of the cab.

"Four Seasons Hotel, please," she says. "Can you turn down the radio?"

He nods. The taxi flag goes down. They career around corners; she holds on to the handle on the side, thighs sliding on the vinyl. Outside, despite the December date, all is green and sky and sea. They drive through the Aberdeen tunnel to emerge on the other side, where gray office buildings crowd the skyline. Margaret is reminded again how life on the South Side is the suburbs and Central, the town.

Priscilla is thin and blond, with a mess of clattery bangles down her sinewy, tanned forearm. They jangle as she lifts her arm to shake hands with Margaret in the cavernous lobby of the Four Seasons. An enormous Christmas tree looms above them. Priscilla's hair is expensively highlighted, with strands of gold.

"Nice to meet you, Margaret." She smiles. Chiclet teeth.

"Nice to meet you too," Margaret says. "Thank you for coming."

"Of course."

They go to the coffee shop, order drinks. Priscilla doesn't know, Margaret realizes. She doesn't know about G. Okay. She recalibrates to this. She doesn't know how she knows if people know her story or not, but she always does.

"Have you lived in Hong Kong long?" asks Priscilla.

"Three years now. And you?"

"Six. Do you like it?" Expats always ask one another that, after they declare their time, often with a searching look.

"I do," Margaret says. "I do."

"Good," Priscilla says. "I hate it when people complain all the time about being out here. They miss the most ridiculous things. Like Safeway or a special type of diaper. I just want to say, look around!"

Margaret is taken aback by the woman's vehemence.

"Sorry," Priscilla says, noticing. "I just think you should try to be happy where you are and not complain all the time. People here have the most extraordinary lives, and they focus only on what they're missing."

"I suppose so."

"What brought you here?" Priscilla asks, gesturing for the waiter.

"The usual. Husband."

"And you work as well?"

"Used to. Not so much anymore."

"What kind of work?"

"Landscape architecture. I design gardens for people."

"How lovely."

"Yes, it can be."

"Hard to do here in Hong Kong, though. No one has any land."

"Yes, but everything's over e-mail now anyway, although I barely work anymore. Although China could be interesting."

"Yes, China, of course."

They both stop to ponder its enormity and possibility, as happens thousands of times every day in Hong Kong, where China's proximity and power is both celebrated and feared.

Margaret tenses, waiting for the next question. She has cultivated a very accurate sense of when it might come in an introductory conversation.

"And children? Have any?"

She looks down at the menu. "I've never been here. What's good? I'm starving."

Priscilla takes it in stride. "The chopped salad, the Hainan chicken. Everything is good here."

"Oh, lovely. Chopped salad!"

They murmur the conversational inanities and order from the waiter.

"So how does this work?" she asks, after they have ordered. "I've never used someone like you before."

"You tell me what you want, I try to make it happen."

"You can guide me, though."

"Of course. This is for your husband's fiftieth, is that right?"

"Yes, in May."

"Any ideas on themes or what he'd like?"

"Half-life?" She laughs, but Priscilla does not. "Mid-century?"

Priscilla has taken out a big yellow pad on which she writes "Clarke Reade's 50th birthday" with a Sharpie. She looks up, all business. Margaret wonders why she always thinks everything seems absurd. Like it seems absurd to write the client's name and event on a yellow legal pad. With a Sharpie. No one else seems to find it the least bit strange.

"Thoughts?" Priscilla tries again.

"I haven't the slightest idea, I'm afraid," Margaret says. "Is there something you can suggest?"

After going over possible themes and venues and dates, they get the check. Margaret opens her bag, unsure of the protocol, but Priscilla waves her away. As they take leave of each other, Priscilla asks again. "Do you have children?"

Margaret gathers her jacket from the back of the chair, where she has hung it.

"Yes," she says. "They're at TASOHK, you know, the American school." She nods, looks away, past Priscilla and her bright smile.

And that's it. She has survived the moment. She walks quickly to the glass doors of the hotel lobby and pushes through to the cool air outside. She gulps and breathes.

Mercy

HONG KONG was supposed to have been a new start—if one could say one needed a new start at the age of twenty-four, which is how old she was when she came, three years ago. It is safe to say that life has not turned out the way Mercy thought it was supposed to.

But she cannot say she wasn't warned. Her mother came home ashen-faced one day when Mercy was thirteen. She wouldn't tell Mercy what had happened, but her father, dependably drunk and abrasive in the evenings, told her the bad news. Superstitious mother had gone to a fortune-teller to waste his money and find out about Mercy's future. Idiot fortune-teller had clucked his tongue at her reading, said he had rarely seen someone whose life would be so muddled. She would have bad luck. Things would always go topsy-turvy. She was not a bad person, but things would never go her way. Understand? Her father poured some more whiskey, face already tomato red.

Korean *ajumma*, busybodies that they were, were all amateur fortune-tellers themselves and liked to read faces. One Sunday, at their church in Queens, she had overheard her mother's friends talking about the composition of her face having no *bok*, no good fortune. Thin, jutting eyebrows, cheekbones that were too sharp, a chin that was so pointy it would cut away all the good. She's pretty, one said. Pretty in a cheap way, said another. That makes it worse. That will invite the bad luck. And the bad men.

Later, she found the fortune-teller's predictions in her mother's underwear drawer. She recognized the characters of her name and opened the red paper booklet. It was written in Korean and Chinese characters, so she couldn't read it, but she took it out and asked a Korean man, a stranger on the street, what it meant. In Flushing, where they lived, it was almost like living in Seoul, there were so many Koreans. The man gave her an odd look but translated a few lines.

"This means, you are riding a fast horse with no saddle. The rider will fall." He hesitated. "And here it says, a crow cannot soar like an eagle." His eyes dropped, and he handed the book back to her. "I have to go."

A crow cannot soar like an eagle.

It was always there in the back of her mind, but what did you do with a fate like that but dismiss it as old Korean folklore that had nothing to do with her?

At Columbia, she had been disheartened to see how hard it was to do well, to stand out. When she got in, she thought, I'll show those Korean ladies who has bad fortune. But it was harder than that. In her freshman class alone, there had been an Oscar-nominated actress, a boy who'd had two poems published in the *New Yorker*, someone who had sailed around the world and been written up in *National Geographic*.

And this is the thing too. In college, Mercy had gone above her station, as she thinks of it in gloomier moments. Perhaps this was part of her misfortune. There was a whole new kind of person there, people she had seen in movies and read about in books. Rich people; really, really rich people. Kids who had drivers, who had never done a load of laundry, whose parents had private planes. Her own parents were not dry cleaners or deli owners, as some curious new "friends" had asked. Her dad had an unsuccessful import/export company with an office that was always littered with samples of ugly, Korean-made poly sports apparel, and her mom, long-suffering, helped out at her aunt's Korean restaurant and told Mercy she had only one child because she could see that life wasn't going to get any better. Mercy never apologized about her family but never volunteered information either.

Mercy never knew why she was included in this new crowd. An

accident, she thought, born of the fact that she was pretty, looked surprisingly good in a forty-dollar strapless dress from Forever 21, was always up for a dare, and that her freshman-year roommate was a friendly, pudgy Chinese girl from Hong Kong, who went downtown one Saturday in October and bought a cherry-red Mercedes convertible and whose parents had a three-bedroom pied-à-terre on East Seventy-fourth Street. Philena was a homely, uncomplicated rich girl who liked to have lots of people around, always, and included Mercy without drama, paying for everything with her black American Express card.

That first year of university, Mercy studied her classmates, the rich ones, a special breed unto themselves. She noted the soft, flabby skin of the boys, their whiskey breath, the petulant way they talked to their mothers, the way things always got sorted for them. They came from all over the world: Abdul, from Saudi Arabia, who went to London every weekend and would sometimes invite a girl from school, who would come back with six new pairs of shoes and a dress from Harrods and a story about a party at Elton John's country house, although privately Mercy thought the whole thing made them little better than escorts; or Cal, from LA, whose father was a director and who hung out with Julianne Moore on the weekends; or the boys from Manhattan, so many of them, with their hedge fund fathers, bony, raspy-voiced mothers, and limitless credit cards. The rich boys were thin-skinned, with a puffed-up bravado that was millimeters thin; if you nicked it, they collapsed.

Mercy borrowed Jimmy Choos from Philena and went to the apartments of upperclassmen (oh, the irony of that term!) in doorman buildings, where you walked in to the heady smell of pot and dirty laundry and the drone of some basketball game always in the background. There were half-empty bottles of Johnnie Walker and Jim Beam on the Corian kitchen counters, props for an always ongoing party. The boys were pigs in the way they lived, whereas the girls were princesses.

The girls burned an endless supply of $60 scented candles from Bergdorf's and did class reading under embroidered duvet covers from Italy. They floated around in weightless cashmere hoodies that felt like gossamer, bought $1,800 handbags without blinking, paid private Pilates instructors a hundred bucks a session, got their pin-straight hair blown out shiny every three days. They went to class in groups and planned trips to Canyon Ranch. Mercy hung out at the edges and witnessed it all. She was the crazy one who'd take any dare, do anything to keep the party going.

Of course, she and Philena had a falling-out halfway through college. Mercy borrowed a silk scarf from Philena's closet and got ketchup on it. Worse, she hadn't asked to borrow it. Worse, she put it back without bothering to dry-clean it. Even worse, it was far from the first time, but it was the first time Philena minded. She usually didn't care. Mercy had exhausted even the lovely and unflappable Philena's vast reserves of tolerance. That was something.

Mercy felt herself hardening in college. She learned the way they spoke, the rich kids: a reflexive irony where the most important thing was to show you didn't care, that you were impervious to others' opinions. But, of course, the hardest shells hid the most fragile selves. Doug, a real estate developer's son from Chicago, took her out a few times, then cried after they slept together. He never spoke to her again. She told people she thought he was gay, which she did think, but it probably wasn't so nice to relay to other people.

She meandered her way through college, going home sometimes on the weekends when it got to be too much or too expensive, helping out her mom and aunt at the restaurant. Her aunt, who had no children and ran a cash business, always pressed a hundred-dollar bill or two on her afterward, although Mercy tried to refuse. Family was supposed to help, that was the rule, and she didn't expect to be paid. Still, her aunt said, "Enjoy. I remember what college was like," although she had no idea what Mercy's college life was like. She imagined her college friends coming in to the restaurant and seeing her, hair tied in a ponytail, apron soiled, carrying trays of *banchan*—spinach, lotus root, marinated bean sprouts, and cold crab—to the waiting throngs or having a cigarette in the back with the Mexican busboys who teased her about being a college girl. Quite a far cry from her black-clad Saturday nights with them. Of course, those friends would never come to Queens, so it was just fantasy.

She toggled back and forth from the different worlds, the subway shuttling her to and fro. Her mother urged her to do premed or become a lawyer, with a desperation that made Mercy uncomfortable. She signed up for art history instead and told her mom that she could still go to law school but she needed some time to figure out what she wanted to do. She figured she was young—she had that luxury.

But that was college. After, the differences became clear. Her friends graduated and got jobs at banks, magazines, PR companies, their way paved by family connections. Mercy applied for jobs, and if she got an interview, she never got past the first round, although her grades were just as good and sometimes better. Her friends moved into one-, two-, in one case three-bedroom apartments funded by their endlessly generous parents. One of her friends, Maria, a girl from Mexico, bought a four-thousand-square-foot loft in Nolita the week after she finished college and spent the summer decorating it before deciding on a career in interior design or art consulting. Mercy went home to Queens, subsisted on temp jobs, and took the subway into the city whenever she could, for dinners in dark West Village restaurants and parties in brand-new condos. She learned to arrive late, not order food, and just toss in a twenty for the two drinks she had.

One night, at a party, she confided to a girl she knew a little that she really needed a job.

"What do you want to do?" Leslie said. She was a button-nosed blonde from Greenwich who was working as a paralegal.

Mercy hesitated. She wanted to do so many things. "I don't know. I'd like to do a lot of things. I'm interested in art. I could work at a museum. Or photography? Or a magazine?"

"Oh, wow," Leslie said. "Those are really competitive fields." She looked skeptical.

"Well," Mercy said, "those are my wishes. I don't know how to make them reality."

Leslie looked sad for a moment. "I'm sorry for you," she said, and she seemed sincere. Then she got up and poured herself another drink.

Mercy felt better, as if she had whispered a secret into a well, and expected no more, but later Leslie e-mailed her with a lead for a job, and she felt that life was okay sometimes.

Occasionally, she wished she hadn't gone to the fancy college with the fancy kids who showed her a different world. She used to go back to Queens and see some of her old friends, still living in the neighborhood, with the same boyfriends, working in their dad's accounting office, or managing the family beauty salon, and though she didn't want that life she knew they were happy. But, then, this was Queens, land of immigrant dreams, and there was an equal number of kids who had made it, walking around in the city with their six- or seven-figure salaries, who got quoted in the paper and whose parents mentioned them with every breath at church, as her mom told her whenever she got home on Sundays. "Jenny Choi, she lawyer now. Big law firm. Harvard Law School. Also has Korean boyfriend from Harvard Law. Probably marry next year."

Sometimes during the day, when she didn't have a temp job and was at home by herself, she went to her parents' room and sat at her mother's dressing table, with its bottles of Shiseido moisturizer and sunscreen, and she opened the precious small jars as she used to when she was a kid. She dipped her fingers in and brought them to her nose, capped in white cream. She sniffed the cool, viscous lotion, and the scent brought her back to when she was just eight and learning what it was to be a girl, a woman. She'd lain in bed watching while her mother sat on the stool, fresh from her bath, hair wrapped up in a towel turban, face pink and moist. Her mother swirled one finger expertly around the jar and tapped five dots sparingly on her face: forehead, nose, two cheeks, chin. Then she'd make circles around them, radiating outward until she had spread the cream all over.

Mercy remembered lying on the bed and thinking that her mother was the epitome of grown-up sophistication and beauty, that all she ever wanted was to become like her mother. She didn't remember when the scales fell from her eyes—when she realized that her dad drank and gambled away most of his small earnings, that her mother was desperately unhappy and it was making her prematurely old and gray, that she wanted Mercy to have a ticket out of this world and was scared to death it wouldn't happen, that her family was not the happy one you read about in books—but she had been happy as a child. She had loved to watch her beautiful mother put cream on her face in front of a mirror.

Where had that girl gone? The hopeful, innocent girl who didn't have to act the clown to keep up. When had it all gotten so complicated?

She began to think about leaving New York after three years of trying to find a career. She had had a string of temp jobs, answering phones at a record label, being a floating receptionist at Condé Nast, where she ran into an old college acquaintance in the elevator, who worked at *Allure* and asked her which title she was at. Mercy had answered, *Glamour*, and imagined the girl going to check the masthead right away. The masthead she was not on. She had lunch in that cool cafeteria and tried to fit in, but none of those jobs ever turned into anything permanent, although they did for other people. Then, also, she had been told to use the service entrance at the Park Avenue co-op where her friend Pru lived, still, with her parents. She had offered to bring takeout Indian from Queens for a group dinner when Pru's parents were in Europe, and the doorman had thought she was a delivery person, although she couldn't remember the last time she had seen a female delivery person. She smiled tightly, holding that stinky bag of curry, and said that she was a friend of Pru's. He hadn't even been sorry, just waved her in without interest. Of course, she made a joke about it when she walked in the door, demanded a credit card and a tip, but it was kind of uncomfortable, as if they all knew it was a little too close to possible. That Mercy was just one step away from doing those types of jobs.

All these things conspired to make her think she should try her luck somewhere else. A few friends had gone to Europe—London, Paris, but those cities seemed too expensive. There were others in Tokyo, Hong Kong, Mumbai, Seoul. She didn't want to go to Korea—her Korean wasn't good enough, and she imagined a country full of men like her dad. She e-mailed Philena, who was working at Goldman Sachs in Hong Kong, and asked what was going on in the city. They spoke English there, right? The silk scarf incident was long forgotten. Lovely, simple Philena, bored of the scene already, invited her to come and stay for a few weeks, and that's how she had gotten to Hong Kong.

In the beginning, it seemed the right move. Hong Kong was more manageable than New York, but it was still a big city—Central, with its close cropping of skyscrapers and the sea right below, with the "burbs," as her friends called the outlying residential areas, easily accessible for beach days and outdoor activities. It was easier to get jobs, although they paid almost nothing, and she started working at a weekly newspaper a few weeks after she arrived. It was a listings and features rag, with a grizzled Fleet Street hack at the helm. "Out to pasture in Hong Kong," he told her over lunch the first day before asking her out. She declined—she had that much sense—but he still let her write articles from the get-go, and she quickly got to know the city. She got her first business cards, although they were a cheesy, shiny white. Her friends from college hooked her into a social scene—young grads from Columbia and other colleges littered the city. People were friendly. She found her cheap apartment and felt that she was getting a foothold. Then the office door was locked one day, the publisher went under, and she didn't have a job again. Then it became a sort of a roller-coaster where she had a job, then didn't, then got another lead. Her longest gig was four months as a hostess at a swanky Italian restaurant in Lan Kwai Fong, but that ended when the parent company folded. She started getting letters from Hong Kong Immigration, inquiring about her status. And it was the same thing, lurching from one near-missed opportunity to another. And then she met Margaret.

Margaret seemed the answer to all her problems. The pay she offered was very high, and she offered it apologetically enough ("I know you went to Columbia . . .") that Mercy thought she could probably ask for more soon. It was not permanent work, of course, but that was fine. And then the disaster happened. The thing with G. And then it felt as if life would never be the same.

~

So now she spends her mornings reading about all sorts of lives in the local newspaper, the romantically named *Far East Post*, where the smaller city items often have to do with men bludgeoning each other with choppers, the local butcher implement, and children falling out of windows when left alone by their teenage mothers. It makes her feel slightly better, reading about all the chaos, as if her own life is not so bad. But when she thinks about her life, really thinks about it, she feels short of breath. Her life! Oh, Mercy! Her life.

She also looks for stories on the Internet, in magazines. *People* usually has one, a dependably sentimental human interest story. Last month, there had been an article about a pretty teenager in Tennessee who had her arm blown off while drinking beer with friends and playing around with a gun. In another story she found, a man had driven his girlfriend's two sons to school, only he had been drunk (at eight in the morning!), and they had been killed in a car crash, because he hadn't put them in their car seats. The man survived, courtesy of his airbag. The mother had been at home, asleep. Or the famous case of the chimpanzee woman. A woman had a chimp as a pet and had sedated it before her friend came over. The chimp had reacted badly to the drug and torn the friend's face off. The victim had to have a complete face transplant, and children on the street cried when they saw her.

Mercy wants to find a story that echoes her own.

These stories always talk about the victim, and how she or he is coping. There are lots of pictures, in *People* magazine, at least, of the victim at home, disfigured or pale, chopping some sort of vegetable

on a wooden board in the kitchen while his or her loving and supportive spouse or family member looks on. There are quotes from
friends about how brave the victim is, how his character has been
strengthened by the tragedy. You can survive a tragedy, given time.
But what Mercy wants to know is never there. The person responsible for the calamity is never mentioned. No one wants to hear about
the guy who shot the gun by mistake, or the drunk boyfriend driver,
or the chimpanzee's owner. The victims are richly sympathized with,
and their guilty, confused perpetrators are erased from the story.
They don't exist. They are supposed to disappear.

What did all those people do?

What are their stories?

She knows her own. She sits at home, eats almost nothing, looks
at her dwindling bank account online, and wonders when she's supposed to start her life again, when she is allowed.

Margaret

HER BODY LIKE VAPOR. Margaret sits in the tub, perspiring from the hot water, her hair pleasantly damp around her face, sweat and steam mingling into one fragrant wetness. The smell: pungent, salty, body, along with the lavender oil she poured into the water. She feels as if she might disappear, melt right into the steam, an intoxicating feeling. After her meeting with Priscilla, she found her way here, of course.

Dr. Stein says she should live life, meet people for lunch, form words so she can speak them, nod her head, put one foot in front of the other. She has to do this to live.

She had seen the building for months, passing by it every time she drove to town. One like many others, a dilapidated structure of many small apartments or rooms, with washing hung outside on bamboo poles, often turning gray with soot. She couldn't imagine why anyone would hang laundry outside in Happy Valley, where the air is thick with dust from the exhaust of passing cars. Sometimes the curtains were drawn back from the windows, and she could see inside various homes: bunk beds, usually metal, a TV flickering, very basic.

A small sign appeared one day, red letters on white plastic, in English and Chinese: FLAT TO LET, WEEKLY, MONTHLY, and a telephone number. She passed the sign several dozen times before she stopped at a traffic light and wrote down the telephone number.

The next week, she took a taxi there—parking was difficult in the tight, scrambly streets, and no one answered the phone when she called. The door was smudged glass with chipped plastic Chinese characters glued on. She pushed the metal bar. A rank lobby with chipped tiles on the floor, torn red vinyl couches along the wall. An old woman sitting behind a steel desk, eating a pungent lunch out of a Styrofoam container, shabby ledgers and an impossibly old phone. A phone that no one answered.

"I would like to see the room," she said, girding herself for the exchange that lay ahead.

"*Mae-ah?*" the woman grunted in Cantonese, uninterested. One of her front teeth was outlined in gold.

"The room." Margaret gestured outside, to the sign.

The woman inspected a piece of meat in her chopsticks and looked away. Complete disinterest in the crazy *gweilo* who was trying to complicate her life.

Margaret clasped her hands in front of her chest and took a deep breath. She remembered the thing she had done when she first arrived, when she had gone to a supermarket in search of corn syrup, something not easily explained if you don't speak the local language. When the first store clerk had disappeared on her, unwilling or unable to help, she had collared another and would not let him go, frustrated. "Find the corn syrup," she had said over and over again, implacable in her consumer's right to do this to a store employee. (Wasn't that his *job*, finding products for customers?) She had raised her voice as if this would make him understand her better. Finally, after wandering the aisles, they had found it. And then the store clerk found his friend and left the store. He had been another customer, a hapless local, not a store employee, abused by yet another boorish foreigner. She still blushed when she thought of the incident. She wondered what he must have thought of her. He probably had not been all that surprised.

This was what bothered her: the presumption of the expatriates in Hong Kong. It is unspoken, except by the most obnoxious, but it is there, in their actions. The way they loudly demand ice in their drinks or for the AC to be turned up or down or for "Diet Coke, *not* Coke Zero," as if everyone thought such a distinction was crucial. The idea, so firmly entrenched, that they could be louder, demand more, because they were somehow above—really, better than—the locals. How did that still exist in this day and age? And it was in her. That was the thing. Every time she spoke louder than a local because he or she didn't understand what Margaret was asking, every time she insisted on her way, was rude, she felt it in her and was ashamed.

So instead she had groveled, beseeched, stayed long enough at the building that the woman realized she was not going away. Margaret had led her outside and pointed to the sign, and the woman had taken her, grumbling, to the elevator, which they took up to the third floor. There, in a glum hallway, she paused outside a steel door that was painted a glossy olive green that was stripping away in long ribbons.

"*Bat cheen*," the woman said in Cantonese, holding up eight fingers. Eight thousand. Outrageous. A foreigner's price. The room was probably full of asbestos and cockroaches.

"Okay," Margaret said before the woman had even turned the key and opened the door.

An iron bed, twin size, or possibly even smaller. A filthy thin mattress, pink, with brown stains. No sink. When Margaret wrung her hands, pretending to wash them, to ask where the sink was, the woman pointed to the miraculous thing in the room: a tub. As if to say, why would you even ask? But a tub in this kind of space was a mistake. Certainly. It was ugly, a small, plastic thing, but was newish, bought in the last five years, installed with the water line coming straight up outside of it. So you wash your hands in the tub. Margaret could not imagine what it had replaced. There were no cooking facilities or closets or anything that most people would ask of a living space. The toilet was behind some plywood painted white. She was lucky. Most of these kinds of places had a bathroom down the hall. It was as if someone had taken a random slice out of a normal living space and this is what had been in that asymmetrical, random segment. But it was perfect for her. She gave the woman eight thousand in cash, swiftly withdrawn from the ATM conveniently located outside, signed some Chinese contract, and got the key the same day.

There she imagined what people would think about what she did if they knew. She imagined they would think she was having an affair, was running an illegal operation of some sort. In fact, her utter conformity, even in isolation, amused her. She had gone out and bought a cheap mattress and pillow and had it delivered. She left the old ones in the hallway, unsure of disposal procedures, and they were gone an hour later. She bought cotton sheets and had them washed by the laundry business just outside—she couldn't bring them home to Essie, too many questions. She bought pajamas from the China Emporium, pale blue with pandas embroidered on the right front pocket, and she put them on and she lay down on her new bed with her new sheets, all brand-new and nothing to do with her real life, and she lay there, arms by her side, eyes closed, and felt at home.

She had scrubbed the entire room, mixing up buckets of bleach and soap and mopping until the mop came away clean. After there was some semblance of overall cleanliness, she went at the corners with a toothbrush. She was thinking about painting the walls. Everything she did there made her happy.

The hours stolen there vanished into some forgotten morass of her life. Clarke had no idea where she was. He thought she was at home or shopping for food or picking up the kids. She could have told him that she had rented a work space or a studio, but she didn't. She squirreled away money by buying groceries at the local market instead of the gourmet stores and was chastened to see how much money that left for her to pay for the apartment.

But this is what she did: She lay on that twin bed, or in that tub, and she lay there without a thought in her head. If she did think, it was about what her life would be if she only had this life, this one room, this one place.

Of course, she had to get more things, eventually. A soap dish, a bar of soap to put in it, a toothbrush, a small tube of toothpaste, a single-cup coffeemaker, a white mug, a package of three hand towels, red, yellow, blue-striped—primary. A small space heater for when the weather turned cold. She bought them at the local Price-Rite, a fluorescent-lit shop in the basement of a shopping mall, with odd items like Japanese scrubbing cloths and purple humidity-absorbing beads. Her small collection of possessions filled her with gratitude in a way that her house full of furniture in Repulse Bay did not. She got to know the neighborhood around her: the flower shop with cheap, bright flowers, no expensive peonies or orchids, just geraniums and gerbera daisies; the steaming noodle shops, with their round tables and stools, chopsticks bunched in the middle like utilitarian centerpieces; the tiny stationery shop; the dress shop; and their proprietors. She bought lunch and ate it in the room. She brought her garbage out with her and threw it in the public bin. She kept the enterprise simple, and so it all worked.

She squeezes the washcloth over her arm so soapy water trickles down in slow rivulets. So theatrical, she thinks, like something you learn to do by seeing it in a movie. "This is how to relax, this is how to enjoy yourself." She rinses out the washcloth, wrings it, and places it over her face, leaning back.

~

She was not supposed to have met Clarke.

She was living in New York when she did, working at an advertising agency. She had been at home when she got a tipsy phone call from two girlfriends who were at a party three blocks away. "Come!" they had said. "It's so close to you. We'll have dinner after."

After putting on lipstick, she made her way over, only to find that the party was an intimate affair of thirty-five, an engagement celebration with family and close friends, in a palatial apartment on Fifth Avenue. Her friends were happy to see her but also busy talking to other people. Having been lured into coming by the promise of dinner afterward, she tried to hover invisibly by the window overlooking Central Park and spent her time trying to figure out who was the host and who were the guests of honor, so she could avoid their field of vision.

Unfortunately, everyone there was extremely kind and concerned that someone was being ignored, so she had to fend off questions from strangers about whom she knew and where she was from.

Sucking down her second glass of wine and cursing her friends, she looked up to find Clarke.

"Are you crashing?" he said with amusement. He was handsome, yes, but had crinkly, kind eyes. Older than she, mid-thirties.

She mumbled into her glass.

"Come on, fess up," he said.

She made a decision.

"Who the hell says 'chaise lounge'?" she asked.

"What?"

Good. She had startled him.

"I was talking to someone and they said 'chaise lounge.' But it's 'chaise longue.' You know? It's French. Means 'long chair.'"

"I'm proud to say I've never said either," he said.

"Americans are so idiotic," she said.

"Aren't you American?"

"Yes," she said, all twenty-six-year-old bravado. "So what?"

He laughed. "You're feisty," he said. "You're lucky you're cute."

For some reason, she didn't bristle.

He joined her and her girlfriends afterward for dinner, at a small Italian restaurant on Madison Ave. They drank wine, and her girlfriends giggled, and the two of them knew that they were going to be together.

He was working at Procter & Gamble in New Jersey at the time, and they married and headed back to San Francisco, where they were both from, and she went back to school for landscape architecture, and Clarke got a job at M_ D_. They had Daisy, Philip, and G in quick succession, building their family.

When Daisy was nine, Clarke's company approached him about a three-year rotation to Hong Kong, where he would oversee Asia Pacific, ex-Japan. It was a big promotion, and along with a substantial raise, they offered him a housing package, a car and driver, live-in maid, school fees for their three children, a country club membership, and two business class flights home a year for all of them. Later she would find that this was a standard package for senior executives, but it seemed dazzling at the time.

He came home with a big folder labeled FAMILY EXPATRIATION, which included a few paperback books written by women who had followed their husbands abroad. They called themselves "trailing spouses." Their author photos were bright and cheery, showing them in front of the Forbidden City in Beijing or sitting in a *tuk tuk* in Bangkok. There was also a guidebook on Hong Kong and a twenty-page printout on the different neighborhoods, schooling options, medical care, and associations that women could join to integrate. There was a lot of talk about the "honeymoon period," when one was busy setting up and settling in, and that one would be fine during this time. Then, after all that was finished, there would be a grief period, where one mourned the loss of one's old life. They cautioned against living in the past, suggested that one canvass diligently for new friends and interests. Going to museums seemed to be a popular suggestion.

The entire thing gave Margaret hives. She was fine with moving to a different country, excited even, but the 1950s attitude toward women was frightening to her. Everyone seemed so earnest and cheery. It made her teeth hurt.

Her job was portable, of course, with the Internet and e-mail, and she had been doing fewer and fewer jobs anyway as the kids got older and needed more help with school. Maybe that portrayal hit a little too close to home.

She and Clarke flew to Hong Kong for a few days to house-hunt and get the lay of the land. The real estate agent, a young Chinese woman whose glasses steamed up in the humidity whenever she got out of the air-conditioned car, clutched a clipboard and had an earpiece permanently stuck in her ear. Her name was Rosacea. Margaret later discovered that the curious English names that locals gave themselves were cause for much merriment in the expat community. She and Clarke found themselves that first weekend at a dinner party where someone insisted that they had known a Pubic Ha and that their Rosacea was nothing special. Johnakin, Zeus, Tweety, Aids—everyone had encountered something stranger. One-upmanship was universal after all. There was a long and animated conversation about names that were one letter away from being ordinary, such as Jackon or Rimy (Jackson, Remy).

"It's sort of a bastardization of an English name," said one American woman.

"'Bastardization' seems a strong word," Margaret said.

"You know what I mean," said the woman impatiently.

Margaret looked around. Everyone was white, and they may have all been American, and even all from the left side of the country. She had thought that Hong Kong would be international and cosmopolitan, but she felt as if she were at a dinner party in any suburb in northern California.

She was dizzy with jet lag and sleepy from red wine, and the hostess, a nice woman from San Diego whose husband would work with Clarke, told her, when she was helping her pour the coffee, "We've all been there, honey. Trying to stay awake in front of the new boss or trying to look good for new friends. Be good to yourself."

"Where are the Chinese people?" she wondered to Clarke later that night as they were getting ready for bed.

"What are you talking about?" his voice garbled as he brushed his teeth. "They're everywhere!"

"But where was that place we were? Stanley? I felt like it was all white people. It could have been Marin County."

He spit foam and laughed. "Look at you," he said. "One day in Hong Kong and already you see the vast schism between white and Chinese here. What do you think you are?"

"You know what I mean," she said.

The next day they got on the plane and flew home to rent out their house, decide what to take. Three months later, they landed back in Hong Kong and began their new life abroad as one more iteration of that species found throughout the farthest reaches of the world: the American expatriate.

It was exciting—this young family taking on the world. Daisy, at nine, was the most upset, but she handled the transition fine. G was just three, not old enough to know anything. Before they left, he would wake up every morning and ask, "Are we in Hong Kong?" She was so in love with him at that age. Two and three, the impossibly sweet ages, where they still smelled delicious, still nestled their head into your neck. They, the bright young family, moved to Hong Kong and started their bright new future.

~

Now she leaves her house. Just leaves. The power of that impulse. Just leave the children. Just leave the house. It will all be here when you come back. Things will roll on without you. Questions will be answered, repairmen admitted, homework somewhat finished. Just leave. Things will be the same. A thrilling idea. One she knows is not true.

She's been saying she's going to the gym but driving instead to her secret room. Her need to leave her house, her family, is growing. Before, she would steal away at nine in the morning, seeing all the kids off, Clarke to the office, but she wakes up and feels as if she cannot breathe, cannot possibly go through all the motions. So she says she has a 7:00 a.m. exercise class and escapes the house at 6:30, kissing warm, groggy children good-bye, making two cups of coffee, one for Clarke, one for herself in a stainless-steel travel flask, making sure the homework is in the backpacks and Essie knows what to pack in their lunchboxes.

She drives in the near-deserted streets and parks in a local lot, where the man knows her by now, waving her in. Margaret loves driving in the open, empty streets early in the morning, seeing the world slowly wake up. She sees both women and men in clothes from the night before, puffy-faced and abashed; industrious runners, sheened with perspiration; shopkeepers, rolling up their steel awnings. She thinks that anyone up at this hour is a saint or a scoundrel, or a little bit lost. She is removed, in her little car, driving, driving, driving, the steering wheel solid between her palms, her destiny so completely linked to her actions: If she moves right, she will be hit by a car; if she moves left, she will drive the car into the concrete wall. These certainties are what keep her grounded. She is in control here.

She goes to her apartment, and sometimes she reads a book or wanders through the Internet—she has begun bringing her laptop with her. She supposes she could just call it an office, but that doesn't begin to describe what this place does for her.

It is a space of her own, just for her, where nothing from her real life need encroach.

This morning, though, she had waited. She had waited with her children at the bus stop in the cool December air. She had held their still-small hands in hers, feeling their frail bones. And they had let her, because they knew she needed it. The preschool buses really get to her. They rumble up the hill, filled with small children and their small, curious faces. On one bus this morning, a little girl had stared out, her blank face painted white and black like a dog, framed in the window. Like a moment out of a surrealist film. Then the bus rumbled past, and the girl with the face paint was gone, vanished. These are the moments that fill her with a temporary, bittersweet gratitude, that she is here, on this gray sidewalk, with her children by her side, an empty day stretched out before her after they have gone to their respective classrooms with their respective teachers, the temperate blue sky above dotted with floating clouds. And her fear that it will all go away, again.

Her children went off to school this morning, she had a meeting with a party planner, and then she came here, to her secret place.

It is here that she allows herself to think. She is in the bathtub. She is naked. She is alone.

She is a woman who has two children. Not three.

She sits in the warm water, embryonic, floating, and wonders how to begin living with that fact as a base.

Mercy

WOULD THINGS have been different had she not gone on the boat trip? Never met Margaret? She thinks about that possibility until the unfairness makes her breathless.

Junk trips were a common weekend excursion. On Saturday or Sunday mornings, boaters congregated on far-flung piers or in the cool marble lobby of the Aberdeen Marina Club or the more basic Boat Club, with swimsuits and towels packed in L.L. Bean canvas totes; PARKnSHOP bags filled with paper napkins and plates, plastic forks and cups; coolers with marinated chicken wings, cold potato and pasta salads, chopped-up fruit, bottles of wine. In this case, the boat trip had been organized for a friend's fortieth birthday, Barbara Chang Miller, a Korean woman married to an American man, with two young children. Barbara had been like a big sister to Mercy. They had met at a Columbia alumni event, and she had taken Mercy under her wing and introduced her to some people, which she had appreciated, since the twenty-something scene was a bit of a goldfish bowl and it was nice to escape it every once in a while to hang out with real adults. Mercy brought a bottle of sauvignon blanc and a linen scarf bought in Stanley Market as a birthday present for Barbara.

It was September but still hot, as it tended to be until mid-October. The boaters greeted one another, finding their respective groups, moving slowly in the damp morning air, hair wet, clutching lattes, children scampering around exploring the corners, as they waited for everyone to arrive. When critical mass was achieved, a phone call was made to the boat to dispatch the tender, or to hire a sampan, and a smaller boat came to take the group to the bigger boat, usually a lacquered wooden junk or a large white yacht rented out for the day.

There were around twenty people—five couples, most with children, mostly American, plus Mercy. She and Barbara were the only Asian people in the group, something she always noticed in Hong Kong, because it was pretty hard to accomplish. Mercy was introduced to Margaret and Clarke Reade, who had three kids who were dashing around the pier. Mercy had never met Margaret but had read about her in the local paper when she had consulted on some hotel garden in Mong Kok. Clarke, Margaret's husband, looked vaguely familiar, but she couldn't place him. She had never met the other families. Mercy was the lone single girl.

They got on the sampan and were taken out to the boat. The boat boy hoisted them on, and there was the usual flurry of activity: the women dumping ice in the coolers, putting away the food, setting up the drinks; the men popping open beer cans and retiring to the top of the boat; children scrambling everywhere, babies wailing, mothers calling distractedly for all to be careful; the chatter and the warm smell of coconut sun lotion.

The driver started the engine, and as the boat gathered speed they settled into their roles: the children, sitting at the front, wind ruffling their hair, noses up in the air like dogs, as they sipped from soda cans; mothers gossiping in the back; the men laughing and relaxing on top.

Mercy found herself sitting next to Margaret, who on first glance seemed perfect. She was beautiful, in that polished, golden brunette way, with the perfectly peaked eyebrows and tawny skin and long, coltish limbs. She had on white knee-length shorts and a raspberry linen tunic embroidered in darker raspberry curlicues, under which she sported a red triangle bikini. From what Mercy could see, she had a kind, handsome husband, three beautiful kids, whom she patted distractedly and lovingly, and an interesting job. Women like her made Mercy itchy. How did she end up with all that? She was older than Mercy, of course, but still, she couldn't imagine accumulating all those things in eight years, or in eighty.

Margaret was one of those women who Mercy imagined didn't recognize a mean person, since no one would ever be mean to her, or snotty, or distracted. She gave off the aura of someone who was someone, someone you should know, or whom it would behoove you to know. She had never known condescension in her life.

She was kind too. She asked Mercy about her work, was lovely about it. When asked about hers, Margaret tried to demur but was pressed and then told of some of the fabulous gardens she had done all over the United States.

She talked to Mercy for a while about hiking and beaches and outdoor sports, hesitated, and then asked if she'd ever want to take her kids out. "Of course, I have a helper, but what I miss is the young people who will take my children out and really talk to them and can get them moving and thinking. Kids in Hong Kong just want to sit inside in the air conditioning and play video games." She told Mercy a story about a neighbor whose child was so spoiled he sat playing video games while a helper spooned food into his mouth. The child was eight.

This is what parents did. They told you stories about children and were outraged or delighted by some odd detail and were perplexed if you were not appropriately outraged or delighted as well. They lived so entirely in that sphere, that sphere of people with kids, that they forgot that people could have no kids and have no idea what they were talking about. But Mercy didn't mind Margaret. She was gracious and kind and wanted to include Mercy in her life. So she said yes. She would come over and do stuff with Margaret's children. She wondered how much she would be paid but didn't ask. She was not good at that sort of thing.

Another mother fretted about being on a boat. "It's like being surrounded by a giant swimming pool," she said. "Your child could go overboard, and if you didn't notice right away . . . ," she said, gesturing at the wake. She sipped urgently at her white wine. Mercy wondered why she would drink at ten in the morning if she was worried about vigilantly guarding her children's safety.

"The Shang in Cebu is the best!" a woman said, talking about her recent vacation. "The beaches in the Philippines are so nice." Living in Hong Kong, the exotic became affordable and everyday. Mercy herself had gone on group trips to Boracay, to Hanoi, to Bangkok, on package tours that cost about US$300 for air and hotel. Even Philena had joined in a few, slumming it in her good-natured way as they caroused in the cheap bars and beaches of Southeast Asia.

The pleasant journey took about an hour, and they anchored near the beach, the boat boy scrambling around the front, hauling the anchor off the deck. It was around eleven, and it was starting to get crowded in the water, some six boats already there. The motor turned off, the boat rocked gently, and the heat gathered in the sudden silence. Everyone turned slippery and loose in the sudden warmth. Children began to jump from the roof.

Mercy joined them. She threw off her tank top and shorts on the roof of the boat, her one-piece swimsuit underneath. She had learned to wear modest clothing around older, married people. She stepped over the low rail, gripped the white surface of the roof with her toes, felt the sun warm her shoulders. Then she leapt. The water enveloped her, harsh and cold, as she plunged. She went in deep, her body a sharp line, then struggled up, frightened. People were always dying on these trips, boozy sunny days when people drank to forget the week. You would read about them in the local paper on Monday: not missed until the boat trip home, or someone hitting his head on part of the boat as he dived, or a propeller accident, or a simple drowning.

She broke the surface and waved to Barbara, who waved back.

"You look like one of those shiny-headed seals," Barbara said.

"Should I swim under the boat?" Mercy called.

"Aren't you frightened?" Barbara shouted. "I would be."

She was, but that's why she always made herself do it.

"Watch for me on the other side," she called, but she couldn't tell whether Barbara had heard her. She treaded water for a few seconds, filled her lungs, and jackknifed into the water.

She went deep, and went down, down. The silence. The loud, echoing silence always shocked her when she was in the ocean. She went deep enough to be sure to not touch the bottom of the boat, slimy and crusted with creepy shelled things. She saw the dark hulk of it in front of her, went deeper. She wondered if salt water was good for your eyes or bad, or neutral. And then came the moment when she couldn't back out, was more than halfway. You decided to go for it or not. She fought the urge to turn back and instead swam for her life. Her head ached. She swam, powerful strokes with her arms, kicks with her legs, head stretched out as far as possible. The beginnings of panic. She swam and swam and swam. Finally, light above, her neck straining to see. She broke the surface and looked up. Air heaved into her lungs. The sun was shining. Children laughing, people talking. Life going on. No one was watching for her. Barbara had gone off, to pack something or follow some child's cry. Mercy ducked her head underneath again and came up new. She swam to the back of the boat and hoisted herself up. She rinsed off with the freshwater shower nozzle, tears stinging her eyes, and dressed. She felt so alone. She thought that she must be getting her period. She must be melancholy for a reason.

People were starting to gather their things to make the short journey to the beach. They waved over a sampan, and the first boatload left. When the boat came back, Mercy climbed in with her beach bag that had her sunscreen and towel. An old fisherwoman was steering the boat. She had a big black brimmed hat and leathery brown skin.

She looked at Mercy, with her tanned thighs and white shorts and orange tank top. Suddenly, Mercy felt very exposed.

"*Joong gok yan?*" the woman asked. "Are you Chinese?"

Mercy shook her head no. "Korean."

"*Hong gok yan.*" The old lady nodded. Then said in English, "You no marry."

Mercy laughed. "What?"

"You no marry." By this time, another couple and their toddler son had come on board—the worried mother, who had been frightened of accidents.

"Yes, I'm not married." She smiled.

"You no marry. No have husband."

"Yes," she said. "Okay."

"Never!" The woman leaned over and tugged on Mercy's earlobes. It was so sudden she couldn't even recoil.

"Okay, okay!" she said, laughing out of shock.

"Your ear say no children." The old woman looked at the other woman. "She have no children. But you never get fat," she said to Mercy, as if by way of consolation.

The other woman looked at Mercy uneasily. "I don't know . . . ," she started to say.

"Oh, don't worry," Mercy said. "You have no idea how used to it I am. It's fine."

The woman looked at her with pity. "Okay," she said. "But this woman shouldn't say that to you."

"Oh, what does it matter," Mercy said. "She's just an old woman on a fishing boat."

The boatwoman pulled on the rope and started the engine. The boat started puttering slowly to the shore. Mercy looked out at the flat horizon and tried to arrange her face in a pleasant expression. When they reached the shore, she got out in thigh-deep water and helped to pull the boat in so she could receive the boy from his mother. She reached her arms out.

"No, thank you," said the woman. "Bill will get him." She waited for her husband to get out of the boat and then handed over the child.

"I'm sorry, what's your name again?" Mercy said, holding on to the boat so the woman could clamber out.

"Jenny," said the woman. "And Bill, and our son is Jack."

"My name is Mercy," she said. She was so tightly wound she didn't know whether she was mad at Jenny or at the fisherwoman or at the world.

They all arrived at the beach and wended their way to the barbecue pits.

Lunch was jovial, lubricated. The men poured out charcoal and tried to light the fire, swearing merrily. "Man make fire," Barbara's husband grunted.

When the charcoals glowed orange, they laid down chicken wire and roasted the chicken wings while drinking bottle after bottle of beer. Jenny was nervous about Jack being so close to the fire and kept talking about it.

Another woman looked at Mercy's wet hair and said, "You are so brave. I haven't swum in Hong Kong waters since I saw a bloody Kotex floating by." The others hooted, and Mercy felt stupid.

"It's so hot," she murmured, twisting her hair back. "How can you not swim?"

"Yes!" Barbara said. "You are all old, afraid people. Mercy is the only one who has joie de vivre. She is young! You should try to be more like her." Barbara was from Korea, and her English was not perfect despite Columbia, but she was the warmest person Mercy had ever met. She invited every stray to her house, cooked them *jigae* and *mandu*, and was the den mother for stray Koreans in Hong Kong. Mercy smiled at Barbara gratefully.

A man from New Jersey with a sharp face said, "What's with the Normals?"

"What?" said Margaret. "What do you mean?"

"I just interviewed a guy from Beijing Normal University. That's different from Beijing University, right?"

"It's more of a teacher's college," said Barbara's husband, who was in Beijing every week for work.

Mercy watched Clarke sip his beer, and suddenly it clicked. She knew where she knew him from.

She had been on an elevator with him, and he had been with another man. Two anonymously handsome Western men in suits. They
were everywhere in Central. She had, uncharacteristically, been
laden with shopping bags, as she had been tasked to buy group birthday presents for a few friends, since she was the only one not working
at the time, and she supposed she had looked like a spoiled princess.

"Women!" the other man had said to Clarke, as he scanned her
carelessly. "Women and their shopping."

She had been stunned. The man spoke as if she were invisible, or as
if she couldn't understand what he was saying. Later she had thought of
all the things she could have said. Like "I went to Columbia!" or "Because you men take all the high-paying jobs." Or something. The idea
that she was entirely inconsequential to the men in a small elevator was
hideous to her at that moment, struggling as she was to find a job, find
her rent money, find her life. She turned red, almost stamped her feet,
struggled to find something to say. And then they got off. She was left
steaming, unfulfilled. And here Clarke was, sitting across from her, as
confident as ever, as unknowing, married to a perfect woman who was
presumably exempt from the assumptions of him and his ilk.

As Mercy looked over at Margaret, something dawned on her.
"Are you half?" she asked.

"A quarter," Margaret said, a little surprised. "My father is, was,
half-Korean—he passed away—but my mom is white. Most people
can't tell."

Barbara piped in, "I could tell right away."

"Yeah, but others can't, really," Mercy said. "Do you speak Korean?"

"Not at all," Margaret said. "I feel bad about it, but I think it's
usually the mother who does it, and my mother couldn't. And we
lived in a very homogeneous neighborhood. My dad basically wanted
to be white. He didn't like growing up Asian in California at the
time. There weren't very many. Do you speak?"

"I understand everything, but talking is hard. I grew up in Queens."

"Have you gone to Korea while you've lived here? It's so close."

"Not yet," said Mercy. "Soon."

"I'll take the both of you," said Barbara. "It is so wonderful now, you cannot imagine. I grew up there, and it is so changed now!"

"We're going soon," Margaret said. "For school fall break, and Clarke needs to go see the office there."

The conversation fizzed on in the hot summer sun. Mercy drank cold beer and listened in on the exchanges. She heard a woman slip up and say something about a helper's "owners," instead of "employers." Then her husband, embarrassed, made things worse by trying to make it academic, saying that throughout history, humans have always enslaved other humans. There was a pause after that statement. Then, being adults, they moved on. Mercy, being not quite so adult, meditated on it for a while, realizing that she would never view that woman in the same way again when she ran into her at the prepared-food counter at Oliver's or in the taxi queue in Central.

Jenny's husband, Bill, noticed that she wasn't speaking and kindly tried to pull her into conversation. He was interested in shamanism, he told her, having studied anthropology in university. He was telling her about shamanism and the place it had in Korean culture. "Why is it," she said with a smile, "that it's always the white person telling the Asian person about their culture?"

When his smile faltered, she persisted.

"No, really," she said. "It's funny, and I don't mean to be obnoxious, but haven't you noticed?"

"Not really," he said.

"I think it's because of the study of anthropology," she said. "It's a Western construct."

As she spoke she knew she was off-putting to him, that she could not engage in the simple interchange most people lived and died by, that the casual, nonmomentous observations were anathema to her. She could also tell, as if she were looking from high above, that her approach was detrimental to her, but she couldn't help herself.

When she'd said this to a friend, he'd said, "Self-important much?"

But she couldn't change. She couldn't talk to people like they expected to be talked to.

"So what do you do, Bill?" she asked.

"I'm a lawyer," he said. There was a brief silence. "And you?"

"I'm a friend of Barbara's," she said meaninglessly. "Oh, and I do a couple of things. I used to write for *City Magazine*, before it closed down, did some restaurant and music reviews, then I was the hostess for Il Dolce for a while, and now I'm looking . . ." She trailed off.

"How interesting," he said. "That must be really fun. You get to go out for a living, right?"

"I guess."

Barbara rescued her with a request for her to open another bottle of wine.

There were times when you were at odds with yourself, when you couldn't carry on a conversation or when nothing you said came out right. This was one of those times, she told herself as she wedged the corkscrew in.

She opened the wine, got up, sat down next to Margaret, and asked her when she wanted her to come over and babysit her kids.

Then later, on the boat ride back, when everyone was on the top deck, wiped from the sun and the long day and the beer, she emerged from the bathroom to find the slavery-remarking man creepily, drunkenly waiting for her, then grabbing her butt and saying, "Your ass is so tight." She looked at him and pushed past. She'd given up wondering what vibe she gave off so men think it's okay to do that to her, but she knew she was always going to be blamed. That was her life.

Margaret

IT ALL HAPPENED because they had planned a trip to Korea that year. For the kids' fall break, and to meet some of her father's relatives for the first time, and also for Clarke to see some of his people in Korea. He told her she was expected to come to a lot of these lunches and dinners, and she was wondering what to do with the children. She didn't really trust hotel babysitters and had been told that most of them wouldn't speak fluent English and wouldn't know what to do in an emergency.

And then she met Mercy on the boat trip.

It seemed incredibly extravagant to bring a babysitter on a family trip, but she was finding that nothing in Hong Kong seemed extravagant. No one cared; that was the other thing. Raising her children in California, she and her fellow new moms had discussed ad infinitum how long to nurse, why women would hire nannies when they were at home, or why children needed their mothers around them all the time, but here those sorts of conversations tended to go nowhere, and women looked blank. She was learning that everything was contextual. Here, as in most of the world outside America, there was widely available help for the more privileged—and mostly every expatriate she knew was privileged—and those sorts of discussions were not interesting, like talking about sliced bread, because it was so taken for granted. It had taken her a while, but now she didn't feel guilty for having a girls' dinner with Daisy's class moms once a week, or going out for dinner with Clarke instead of doing a family meal.

The travel was one of the reasons they had come, after all. To get their kids more international exposure, in an increasingly global society.

The Christmas before, they had gone to India, to Rajasthan. There, at the maharajah's palace in Jaipur, they saw a pair of enormous silver urns, which a former prince had used to transport his own water when he sailed across the ocean to attend the wedding of the queen of England. (He had never drunk or bathed in anything but the water from his beloved Ganges.) Later that day, the children perked up when they went to the firearms section of the museum. It had weapons to crush an enemy's skull, huge poles with spiky iron heads, giant, weighty swords, an archery set. The dusty museum dwelled in shades of ochre and tan, the dust motes floating slowly in the refracted sunlight through the high windows. Philip stood in front of a scratched glass case and read "blunderbuss" from a label about a bronze weapon that Indian soldiers had used—a magical moment when she heard him utter the word and then recollected the term from some childhood book, perhaps Lewis Carroll? "Blunderbuss" echoing through the past and into the present, where they stood, the Reades, with their three children, and they went through the halls, looking at all the artifacts and clothes, including a pair of pants six feet wide for a particularly fat maharajah. Then they went out into the courtyard, none of the children complaining, with this new knowledge inside them, with the bright sunshine, a sun that had looked down on them in California, in Hong Kong, and now in India, and G ran into a flock of birds and they lifted off, flapping their wings, with him behind, mouth open with happiness. She loved him so much, this little man, with his small shoulders and tiny elbows and feet, his stomach still jutting out in the way of toddlers. Her son looked up in wonder at the life swirling and lifting around him, and she remembered thinking, This is life, too good to be true.

Margaret knows now that is not true. She knows that those moments are all false. They are just harbingers of disaster, as if they are there to remind you of all that you have to lose.

Mercy had seemed perfect. Young, but not too young to be responsible. A college graduate with a flexible job. Margaret hesitated to bring it up, not wanting to offend, but Mercy leapt at the opportunity.

"You'll have to share a room with the children," she said, but Mercy didn't care.

"I love to travel!" she said. "And I haven't been to Seoul since I was a baby. I'm sure I'll have the chance to take great photographs. I've been learning how to shoot."

Margaret had her over a few more times before the trip to spend time with the kids, and they loved her. She was energetic and young and thought of great games to play with them, as well as always being available to read a book to them. She was an odd girl, for sure. Once she entered the house and said, out of the blue, "This area, the South Side, must have the highest density of bald white men driving convertibles that I have ever seen." Margaret laughed, but Mercy was intense in a queer and, at the time, likable kind of way.

The first warning was at the airport. Mercy was an hour late, and they couldn't check in until she came. Clarke was livid, but when she showed up, wet-haired (she had taken a shower when so late!), Margaret said only, "What took you so long?" lest the trip start off on the wrong foot. Clarke nodded curtly at Mercy and then had not spoken to her again. They checked in and lined up for security in a thick, oppressive silence, the children uncharacteristically quiet as they absorbed the mood. Mercy had apologized, of course, but didn't seem to have a real excuse, so Margaret spent the whole airplane ride wondering whether she had made the right choice and whether they were now saddled with another child instead of someone who would make her life easier.

At the hotel in Seoul, Mercy was mildly helpful, corralling the children as they ran around the lobby while Clarke checked in, but she didn't stop G from climbing on top of the coffee table and jumping onto the sofa a dozen times while Margaret watched, frazzled, from the reception desk. Philip, eight, could still get remarkably immature if he was tired, and tried to join in, but Daisy sat and read a book. G and Philip were wired from the soda Mercy had let them drink on the plane while Margaret was in the bathroom.

She remembers thinking that maybe she was a control freak, maybe she shouldn't have an opinion on what her kids did every second of the day, but what of it? She was their mother, for God's sake, and she had to have an opinion. She was the only one present enough to know when they had reached their limit on snacks or whether they were too tired to go to an activity. She had to shape their lives, a little this way, a little that, the constant wind shaping the particles of sand that were going to form their lives, their personalities.

So she watched her sugar-addled children jump all over the lobby at nine at night, and then she took them to their room, where Mercy was staying with them—the boys in one bed, Mercy in another, and Daisy on a roll-away. Margaret padded down the hotel hallway back to Clarke in her bare feet and went to sleep, still a little disturbed by the day.

She didn't know how much to tell Mercy. She couldn't tell if she knew anything about children. In the morning, Margaret opened the door to their room to find Daisy and Philip watching television in their pajamas and drinking orange juice from the minibar (the cost!) and G brushing his teeth, precariously perched on an upside-down garbage can he must have dragged over so he could reach the sink. Mercy was sitting in a chair by the window checking her e-mail on her phone.

"Uh, good morning," she said. "Kids aren't ready for breakfast?" She had told her that it would be great if they could be ready to go at 8:00 a.m.

"Oh?" said Mercy. "What time is it?" She was wearing a watch. "My phone isn't working well here, must be the different networks. Had to go to Wi-Fi."

"It's eight fifteen."

"Oops," she said. She was still typing into her phone. "One second," she said. She finished tapping into the phone and looked up. "Good morning!"

"The kids sleep all right?" Margaret said.

"Didn't hear anything. They went to sleep around ten, and then I went down and had a drink."

Margaret's look was misinterpreted.

"Oh, I didn't put it on the room," she said. "I paid cash."

"No! You can't leave the children in the room by themselves! G is only four! Are you kidding?" Her voice rose.

"Oh, really?" Mercy said, startled. "I'm so sorry. I really apologize!" She shook her head. "But Daisy is ten!"

"The whole reason I have you here is so that the children don't have to be alone and I can go to meetings and meals with my husband without worrying about them! Daisy is ten! She is not an adult and can't handle emergencies. That's what you are here for!" Margaret didn't know whether to go crazy or try to stitch everything back together again. Now that Mercy knew the transgression, surely she would be more careful. But the girl was so blank, so odd, sometimes.

Later, they went to Dunkin' Donuts for coffee and a snack—the stores were shiny and new in Seoul and filled with well-dressed customers, unlike back home. Mercy told Margaret that her mother had often left her in her crib to go out at night with other Korean couples. "She said everyone did it. One woman she knew came home to find her baby almost smothered in a blanket."

Margaret watched G eat a chocolate-glazed tofu doughnut with a look of total contentment on his face. Daisy had lobbied for an iced coffee, sure that she was too old for hot chocolate and pastries, and had been talked down to some sort of fruity iced tea. Philip didn't eat sweets and opted for a ham-and-cheese croissant sandwich, an hour after breakfast. Mercy hovered, wanting to make amends for the morning, but Margaret found herself wishing that she would disappear.

"That's awful," she said to Mercy absentmindedly. Clarke was at a meeting, and she had brought the children out to walk around. Seoul was immense! It reminded her of New York in that there was a density to it, which was awesome. On the sidewalk right outside their hotel, there were carts selling socks, cell-phone covers, doll clothes, and kitchen towels, a riotous display of unnecessary abundance. The large avenue in front of the hotel could be traversed underground, and when you descended the stairs, there was an entire underground shopping arcade, which sold trendy clothes, eyeglasses, handbags, pharmaceuticals, anything you could think of.

And the smell! It smelled pungent and not unpleasant, like a thick soup of kimchee and garlic vapors, but it took her a while to get used to it.

"Listen," she said, "I don't have anything until the evening, so why don't we meet back at the hotel at four, and you can have dinner with the kids and put them to bed."

Troublesome babysitter dispatched, she breathed easier and moved into her usual rhythm with her children. She had never known how much she would love, really love, being a mother and having kids, how natural it was to her, how everything else paled in its intensity and pleasure of experience. Clarke asked her every once in a while if she minded that her career had come to a slow halt, but she assured him that these were the best years, the best experiences, she had ever had, that she never regretted it. Although she had definitely grown into it. It had not always been so easy.

She remembers her pregnancy with Daisy so well. Her first pregnancy. The one that changed her into a mother. The metallic but not unpleasant taste of Total cereal in skim milk, which she had eaten religiously every day for breakfast to get all the vitamins and minerals they told you were needed, plus the horse pill of a prenatal vitamin. The websites she lingered over, with pictures of your baby at different stages: the size of a grape, the size of a strawberry, the size of a peach. How she bought maternity clothes at three months, too excited to wait anymore, looking at her reflection in the mirror of the dressing room with a foam pillow tucked inside her shirt.

And she was alone. She remembers this. She stopped working because of an early scare, spotting bright red blood, and when that passed, they decided she wouldn't work after the baby, so she might as well quit. It was summer, and Clarke was at the office a lot. Most of her friends still worked or went to school, and so she spent a lot of time by herself. And she had loved it, never felt lonely, with her child growing inside her, her constant companion. She had gone to movies to escape the heat, eating a small popcorn in the air-conditioned dark; read books in bed; ordered mayonnaisey BLTs with salty fries and a Sprite at diners, where elderly women smiled at her burgeoning belly. She remembered seeing an exhausted-looking woman at the supermarket just lingering at the edge of an aisle while children shouted, "Mom! Mom!" The woman had lifted a finger to her lips to Margaret, *shhh*, as she hid from her children for a moment's peace. Margaret remembers being thrilled by the assumption of their imminent sorority. She joined a health club and swam laps in the pool, afraid to do any other sort of exercise. It was a wonderful, simple time in her life, when she had time to think, and think mostly about herself and Clarke and the baby that was coming. The chlorine smell and echoey, enclosed sounds of an indoor pool could bring her instantly back to those unwieldy, but not unpleasant, last, late months of pregnancy. Those were the final moments of complete peace that she could remember. Then the birth came, like a bomb.

Daisy was born after three hours of pushing, the hardest thing Margaret had ever done. She remembers thinking that it would never end, and the terrible feeling that this was something that had to be done and she was the only person who could do it. There was no way out. Then Daisy came, squawling, as red as a beet and about as attractive, and as the nurse put the naked baby on Margaret's chest, she fell in love. In a desperate, intense, suffocating way. She couldn't stop looking at her, afraid Daisy would stop breathing, or get smothered. She didn't sleep more than ten hours total in the first week of Daisy's life.

The first few months after giving birth, Margaret felt nauseated, as if she were still pregnant. Her breasts, big and alternately baggy or rock hard, leaky and messy. The soft, shifting flesh of her belly—she was not one of those women who sprang instantly back into prepregnancy fitness—being squished into her jeans and marked with angry red splotches where the buttons pressed. Her hair was incredibly greasy, and then it all fell out. She sweat and sweat.

And the baby! Daisy was not a hard baby, but not easy either. All those terrible women she met who expressed pure happiness in their new roles and ignorance of anything as awful as bleeding nipples, or hormonal fluctuations that left you homicidal. The most they would admit to was a slight nod to the fact that it might be a little hard, not sleeping for three months, becoming a new, completely different person, the sheer relentlessness of it, that you would never be able to change back, but then they always follow it immediately with a "It's *so* worth it, though, isn't it? I don't even think about it when I look at Sadie's adorable face."

Margaret, who was used to being above average in most things, couldn't understand the gap. This was the hardest thing she had ever done, and arguably the most important. And no one was acknowledging that it really, really sucked. A lot.

This metamorphosis into that other being, that mother, was excruciating. She noticed that it got better in quarters. Three months, six months, nine months. And then suddenly she woke up and she felt better. She was not back to normal—that baseline had shifted. But she could cope with her life.

Later, people would ask, "Why didn't you see anyone?" And certainly, after the incident happened, she did—it was practically court-ordered. But at that time, with that first child, she never felt that desperation was a good reason to see someone. And where would she have found the time? She didn't have time to shower, let alone see a therapist or have a leisurely cup of coffee with a friend. And then the others came, and they were different and easier, because she had already crossed over into that other country of motherhood.

She thinks about that a lot, how you get used to everything, that the first shift is difficult and horrible, and you live your life because what else can you do, and then one day you wake up and your life seems normal. You start to forget the bad times. You shift into your new self.

At least, that's what she had thought about life and change.

The other pregnancies were less vivid, and she was certainly less careful. She drank coffee with Philip; in the last five weeks of her pregnancy with G, she had a glass of wine every few nights. Of course, there was not the luxury of movie watching and solitude. She had Daisy and then Philip and her whole blazing new life as a mother. Everything revolved around the children. And here she was, in Korea, traveling with them to her quarter home country and feeling blessed.

They spent a lovely day wandering the streets of Insa-dong, where they bought colorful stationery, browsed through secondhand book-stores, walked through art galleries and craft shops, and saw a cart vendor selling fried silkworms from a cast-iron vat—a nostalgic treat for those who remembered when Korea was so poor they couldn't afford meat and insects were an important source of protein. They couldn't bring themselves to try them but bought roasted chestnuts from the vendor next to him, cracking and peeling the soft shells and eating the warm meat of the nut. Margaret carried G when he got tired, and he nestled his head into her neck.

At three, Margaret shepherded the exhausted kids back to the hotel and found Mercy doing yoga on a towel on the floor. "Did you have a good day?" she asked.

"I just walked around here," Mercy said, from down dog. "I'm going to try to meet up with some relatives if I get a chance."

"Great." She paused. "Well, the kids are hungry, since we're an hour ahead. You might as well eat now. I guess you could order room service, or go down to the restaurant? What do you think?"

"It's pretty small in here," said Mercy. "I think we should proba-bly go downstairs."

"Okay, just don't leave the hotel." She felt absurd that she even had to say it but wanted to be sure. The kids were excited to see Mercy, and she took them, chattering, telling her all that they had done, down the hallway and into the elevator.

Margaret went back to her room and got into the shower. She was meeting Clarke in the lobby at five, and they were going to the com-pany headquarters to meet some people and then out to dinner.

In the car, Clarke ruffled her hair and asked about her day.

"It was good," she said. "Where we were was really charming. And I think we're going to meet my great-uncle tomorrow. He had his son e-mail me back with a time and a restaurant. Very sweet e-mail. We're going to have lunch."

"Great," he said. "I don't think I can make it. Is that okay?"

They sat for a moment, quiet, happy, hands intertwined in the backseat. She remembered this moment later as one of the last times she felt totally content.

At the office, she met some people, who all bowed, so she bowed back, feeling her 75 percent Americanness very strongly, and when she went to the bathroom, she saw a strange glass cabinet full of toothbrushes.

"What's that for?" she asked one of the ladies in the office.

"Koreans like to eat Korean food," the woman replied, giggling and covering her mouth, "but it smell very strong. We always brush teeth after lunch. It is an ultraviolet light cleanser, so it sterilizes all the toothbrushes so it is hygienic."

"Oh, wow," Margaret said. She was six inches taller than any other woman in the room and felt incredibly large.

They went out to a barbecue restaurant and ate *bulgogi* and drank beer and came back to the hotel with smoky hair and pungent clothes, and when she peeked into the kids' room, they were watching a movie, bathed and pj'd, and they swore they had brushed and flossed. Mercy winked at Margaret, and she softened. She was charming, in an odd sort of way. She felt sorry for Mercy, although she didn't know why.

The next day, she met her extended family for lunch with the kids, having given Mercy the day off again. It was at a barbecue restaurant (the amount of meat you consumed in Korea was extraordinary) with an outdoor garden and ponds, and they all took a photograph in front of the fake waterfall. It reminded her of old-fashioned family portraits as they seated her great-uncle and his wife in the front center and radiated out, agewise. There was much exclaiming and smiling and broken English and broken Korean. They were about twenty in all, many second and third cousins, who had brought their children, who played with Daisy and Philip and G in the outdoor garden. Margaret showed them pictures of her father and his parents, and they showed her old photo albums of their side of the family. The relatives showered them with presents—a woman's silk scarf for her, hair accessories for Daisy, a tie for Clarke and toys for the boys—and she was mortified that she hadn't thought to bring anything. She snuck off to pay the bill, and when the waiter presented her with the credit card slip, there were stricken faces all around.

"I have to pay!" she said. "So many presents! I no give anything!" resorting to pidgin English for some embarrassing reason.

"You our guest," they said. "You come to our country."

She signed the slip, embarrassed, and finally they smiled.

She looked at a cousin and tried to see her father's face. He had died too early, her father, and she could not remember much about the way he looked anymore. She wanted to feel a connection to this family of hers but knew that if she saw some of them in the hotel lobby the next day, she would be hard-pressed to recognize them.

At the end of the meal, she brought the kids back to the hotel for a rest before dinner. Mercy was there, and she ordered another movie for them.

"We'll go somewhere fun for dinner," she said. "Daddy has to go to a work dinner, so it'll be you guys, me, and Mercy."

And then. And then.

She went to pick them up a few hours later, and she and Mercy took them out to the bustling Myungdong area, just in front of their hotel. It was crowded and neon and loud and had a carnival atmosphere, with people selling remote-control cars and light sticks out of boxes, cart vendors lining the sides of the road, shoe and clothing stores blaring K-pop. The young kids had dyed hair and wore trendy clothes.

"Korea is so consumerist," Margaret had said to Mercy. She remembers this so clearly, the unimportant remark.

"I know," Mercy said. "It's terrible."

Margaret was watching all three kids, and then one kid, and two kids, all at the same time, and assumed Mercy was doing the same.

They were darting back and forth, looking at this display, shouting to one another about that store window. They came upon a soft-serve ice cream cart where the ice cream was dispensed in swirls ten inches high.

Margaret bought everyone a cone, and they sat down and licked them clean. Margaret went to the bathroom inside a Starbucks and came back.

"Where's G?" she asked.

Mercy looked around slowly. "He was just here," she said.

They both looked around, couldn't see him, asked Daisy and Philip if they knew where he was. They didn't.

Margaret started walking around, looking for him. Then she started calling his name. Then, after a few minutes, there was that moment when it tipped into panic and she started shouting his name, not caring if she was making a spectacle of herself. She started screaming at the top of her lungs. "G! G! Where are you?"

The amazing thing was that life went on. Around her, people waited in a line to get movie tickets. A girl in a doorway lit a cigarette. But they were all staring at her, staring at the crazed, shouting woman. They were living their normal, regular life, only they were all staring at her, wondering what was wrong. Suddenly they all seemed sinister to Margaret, as if they were all possible child abductors, or insanely important, as possible witnesses with clues as to where G was: That old man with the salt-and-pepper beard was a pedophile, that young man with the slicked-back hair and the black leather jacket was a cog in a child-smuggling ring, that nice-looking woman must have seen something. But no one came forward, no one bolted. There was no G. It was as if she were in one of those movies where the camera swings around 360 degrees, dizzyingly, relentlessly. She stood and she ran and she turned around and scanned and screamed and screamed.

It was the lack of an answer, his small voice crying, "Mama!" as he came running toward her. The same voice that had once, already it seemed so long ago, triggered irritation in her, irritation that she was to be interrupted in the middle of something, that his knee had been scraped and he wanted a bandage, or that his brother wouldn't share, and she would have to get off the phone, or stop writing down her grocery list. His voice was gone.

Later the technology defeated her. Her phone didn't work. She had just gotten the newest phone, and there was some type of new network it was supposed to work on, and it just didn't. As soon as they had arrived in Seoul, her phone had started acting erratically. She hadn't been getting e-mails, only sometimes texts would go through; the phone would ring randomly and never connect. The idea that something so prosaic could ruin her efforts to find her child made her even crazier. She crouched down on the street, pushing at different buttons, trying to get it to work, trying to borrow a phone from someone else, although she didn't even know the number for the police. Shouting about 4G networks, police, and G, as if they were all important. She was trying to get something to go right, even just a phone call. She was trying to remember how to dial in a foreign country. She needed to get in touch with Clarke. She needed to know if abduction was common in Seoul. She needed so many things. She remembered later that her phone sometimes rang, but when she picked it up, it disconnected, and later, that it was on vibrate, because she must have pushed that button inadvertently. She had her phone in her shaking hands, clutching it with desperation, willing it to connect her to someone who could help, someone who would do something. She screamed at Mercy to go to the hotel and get someone to help. Around her, Korean people stopped and stared. She noticed this too, in a corner of her mind, that they just stood still and stared at her. She supposed they were voyeurs, but also grateful that today it wasn't them, that disaster could press by you so closely in a crowd that you could feel its terrible presence but that you could go home and eat dinner with your family and say a silent thank-you that it had passed you by.

Daisy and Philip were mute, standing close to her without being told, terror holding them rigid. She regretted this later, that they had seen her so unhinged. She thought that Clarke would have handled it better. They didn't cry until much, much later, when they were told to go to bed by their ashen father, and then they cried and cried and cried and couldn't sleep until all of them went silent in the room, Margaret holding Clarke's hand as they sat in chairs overlooking the street where it had all happened. She had spent a few hours in the nearest police station filling out forms with a nice young lady who spoke some English. The added layer of not knowing how to speak or write the language she saw all around her made her feel as if she couldn't breathe, that she couldn't move freely in this world.

She had wanted to stay in the street where she had last seen him, but after five hours, at eleven at night, the other children were falling apart and needed to be in a quiet room. Still, she had put them in their room with Clarke, Mercy a black void among them, not physically there but a terrible presence still, and then she had gone back to the street, where she had stayed until one in the morning, when the streets were empty and she had to admit there was little chance that G would be brought back. She came back and watched Daisy and Philip shift uneasily in their restless sleep, with this blackness inside her stomach. They were still in their clothes. She had no idea where Mercy was.

This is what could kill you about children as you watched them: the way they slept, their open-mouthed unconscious faces, their frail collarbones, their defiant stance right before they cried, their innocence. Their crazy, heartbreaking innocence. It could really kill you, if you thought about it.

She wanted the hours back. She wanted to go back ten hours, to when life was understandable. She wanted to not ever have to go to the bathroom again. She wanted to have a kind stranger lead a crying G back to her, to be enfolded tight in her waiting arms, to be squeezed, to feel the corporeal flesh of him, the shaking, sobbing child. This was understandable. The absence of him was incomprehensible. Most of all, she wanted to erase Mercy from her life. To absent the girl and get her boy back. That was what she wanted.

Part II

Hilary

HILARY PAUSES. There is a stain on the piano's ebony surface.

"Puri," she calls. "There is a water mark here from where Julian left his glass during his lesson."

At some point in her life, she realized that she never says anything directly anymore. She has become a master of indirection, or misdirection. She will say, "Mr. Starr is arriving from Kuala Lumpur at 11:00 p.m. tonight" or "I stained this blouse with red wine at dinner," when she should say, "Please keep the lights on and notify the gate guard that Mr. Starr will be late" or "Send this out for dry cleaning."

Puri, of course, cannot always decode the message, and Hilary will come across the garment, still stained, folded neatly in her closet, or David will complain that the guard didn't let his airport car into the complex without an ID check.

She has noticed how, as she grows older, she is more and more reluctant to say anything directly, even to her husband.

She will tell him, "I haven't told anyone else about that," when she means to say, "Don't tell anyone." When David later says he has mentioned it to a friend, she gets upset, and he will exclaim, in the simple way of men, "Why didn't you just tell me you wanted to keep it private?" and she will retire, injured. He should have intimated, she thinks. Intimated, because they are supposed to be intimate. He should have known.

So she does not say, "Please try to get the stain off the piano." She walks into the kitchen and says, "Puri, I'm leaving now."

Julian is sitting there, having a snack. Usually she would be there with him, but she forgot her lunch appointment and now cannot cancel. He is seven, wary. He comes, once a week, for his piano lesson, paid for by the Starrs, a new arrangement that has already revealed itself to be static and in need of change, but one that she has no idea how to alter. She sat with him during his lesson, as she always does, watching his slender fingers hover over the keys. He is talented. She found Julian in foster care, half Indian, half Chinese, left by his teenage mother. At the table now, he looks up and gives a shy smile, with his light brown skin and beautiful dark eyes, ringed with impossibly long lashes. How odd, she thinks, to not know whether his mother was the Chinese or the Indian half. The system must know, she thinks, but she doesn't want to ask. But this seems a vital part of the equation. He will want to know, she thinks, and he should be able to find out. She should find out for him.

"I have to go out for lunch, Julian. Sorry I couldn't reschedule it. Sam will come to take you back in fifteen minutes, after he drops me off. I'll see you next week."

She thinks he understands her but isn't sure. His English is almost nonexistent, but he is agreeable. He gets in the car to come here, he plays the piano, he eats the snack they give him, and then she takes him back to the group home. She gives him a kiss on the cheek and goes home. Another odd event in his odd life.

Sam is waiting downstairs for her in the car. She gets in, and even in the cooler air, the interior is redolent of body odors. Humors, she thinks. The humors of the body, escaping through those tiny pores, roiling around the interior of the car.

Chinese or Filipino? everyone had asked when she said she was hiring a driver. Sam is Indian, an anomaly, but he grew up in Hong Kong, speaks fluent Cantonese, and knows every street in Hong Kong. She thought he would be happy to see Julian visit, but he is odd about it. Later she realizes that he thinks Julian is a street child, beneath him, a proper working man with a family. She realizes that everyone wants to find his own level.

Sam starts the car, and they go to the club.

Hilary sits, hidden behind sunglasses, waiting for her friend Olivia. Children are playing on the lawn while their mothers sip tea and gossip. A boy falls and cries. His mother goes to comfort him. She is a woman Hilary sees at the club every time she is there: a woman with three children, two girls, one boy. Today the woman is in dark jeans that show her wide hips and bottom and a white wool sweater that is stretched across her large breasts and hugs the shelf of flesh above the waistband of her jeans. The muffin top, Hilary knows it is called, the soft, doughy edge that tips over the waistband of your pants. The woman stands up and returns to her group of friends.

Hilary views the thickening torsos and thighs of her peers with a visceral disgust. How can they let themselves go like that, these women, as if it didn't matter? Even if they did have children, surely it can't be too much work to refrain from shoving éclairs and cream puffs down their throats for a few months? She was a heavy child, but she lost weight, and she kept it off. She looks at their arms, spilling out of their clothes like ham hocks, and the way their faces are cushioned in multiple folds, what she calls carb-face, and is nauseated. They have plates of food in front of them, chicken satay in congealing pools of oil, half-eaten grilled cheese sandwiches, glistening mounds of French fries with violent squirts of tomato ketchup.

They are so cheerful, the mothers, so enamored of themselves and their lives, as if the fact of bearing children earned them some unnamed right to sit in the dappled sun with their warm drinks cooling in the winter air and their disheveled hair and their ketchup-stained clothes. Hilary loathes them. She loathes them so much.

They are so lucky.

A year had passed before she thought anything wrong. She had gone off the pill, but it had been a casual event, after a dinner with a lot of wine, a lot of giggling about pulling the goalie, about whether they were really this old. They had not had a great longing for children; it was more

of a maybe-it's-about-time—they had been married two years. She supposed, they had both not been against it. The irony of their casual decision! She was thirty; they had just moved to Hong Kong. When it
didn't happen, month after month, she got nervous, figured out when
she was ovulating by taking her temperature, made sure David was in
town during her fertile time, as he traveled so much for his job. Sex became a chore, a baby-making effort. But nothing happened.

It has been eight years now, eight years during which she has seen
friends have one or two or three children, or twins, a veritable frenzy
of fertility, pregnancies, baby showers, births, and hospital visits, until they slimmed down and told her again, over lunch, apologetically,
that they were pregnant again.

And yet she doesn't want to go any further. The hormones, she
has heard, make you fat, swollen, moody. She has been reading about
the surrogate village in India—a friend forwarded the article—and
the thought makes her feel faint.

So instead she waits. She thinks sporadically about going to a
doctor, but then that thought is always drowned out by the thought
that surely if it is to be, it will happen naturally. She is frightened by
the thought of pregnancy, by the thought of her body changing. The
body she knows so well and knows how to control so well. It is not
the idea of being pregnant that moves her. She would like a child.
She would like to be a mother.

David follows her lead, is amenable to what she wants. Their relationship has cooled in the meantime, cooled into politeness and well
wishes, but she pushes that thought away, because how many difficult
thoughts can one handle in one sunny afternoon? Perhaps a baby, a
pregnancy, will save them from this gradual decline. But how to get
there? She pushes the thought away again. She sits instead, wills her
mind to go blank, sips at her iced tea, feels the smooth passage of it
down her throat. She waits for her friend.

Hilary is from San Francisco, but not the San Francisco where
everyone seems to be hiking or biking while chugging sports drinks,

or doing some other sort of physical outdoor activity, and then talking about it endlessly. When people find out she is from the Bay Area, their eyes light up and they talk about this hike or that park, and she says, "Oh, I don't know from that." Or they talk about Napa Valley and the vineyards, and the cheese! "I like it," she says. She is not effusive, the way people seem to want everyone to be, full of excitement and vim. She grew up just outside San Francisco, where her parents live still, and she moved to the city when she got her first job in PR.

She spent her early twenties working and then met David at a friend's wedding. Everything according to plan. They married when she was twenty-eight, ten years ago. He was an associate at a law firm with offices all over the world, and he had always wanted to travel and live abroad. She said she would go with him anywhere.

After moving, there was a new vocabulary to learn: "lifts" instead of "elevators," "flats" instead of "apartments"—vestiges of the British colony Hong Kong used to be. Also, instead of a housekeeper, the province of only the rich in America, everyone in her new world had a live-in domestic helper from the Philippines or Indonesia, who took care of all the housework and babysitting for the astounding sum of US$500 a month. They live in a particularly homogeneous enclave of expatdom, Repulse Bay, where half the people they see are white, and more than that are not locals, be they Chinese American or Japanese or Filipino. In this particular corner of Hong Kong, newly arrived Americans bump into one another at the supermarket and talk of their sea containers, arriving soon with their belongings, how to find a travel agent, how to get a driver's license. The husbands get up in the morning, put on their suits, and take taxi-shares or minibuses or are driven to work in the tall, shiny office buildings in Central, while the women putter around the house before getting ready for their tennis match or going in to volunteer at the library, since they mostly had to give up their jobs when they moved. It all feels a bit like *The Truman Show*.

Still, even within this sphere, Hilary soon came to see the very fine distinctions.

There were the new expats, who signed up for courses on Chinese cooking at the MacDonnell Road YWCA, took the train to Shenzhen to buy fake DVDs and cheap dinnerware, went to the Art Village to have paintings copied cheaply for their apartments ("A funny Lichtenstein for the bathroom is so cute, don't you think?"), and did first vacations in Phuket. Then there were the intermediate expats, who went to Bhutan to trek and Tokyo to eat and eschewed the touristy. They had favorite hikes. They threw out the IKEA furniture and bought real antiques. They had some local friends, a Mandarin nanny, and preferred to eat at restaurants secreted away in office towers. They started small businesses, like children's clothing or jewelry design, all made in China, and sold their wares at the holiday gift fairs that sprouted up in hotel ballrooms around December. And then there were the old Hong Kong hands, who had racked up ten, twenty years in the colony. They were mostly in Hong Kong for good, sometimes had given up citizenship in their former countries. They owned their homes, always bought on a dip in the property market, didn't talk to newcomers, and smiled blankly when people brought up newbie topics like schooling and medical care, as if they had mentioned something as unspeakable as their bathroom habits.

Of course, there were the international lines as well. The Japanese were a discrete group and rarely mingled, playing baseball and soccer together every weekend at the municipal athletic fields, with their neatly packed bento lunches and peculiarly named sports drinks. The French and Koreans were a bit more porous, the English perhaps a bit more, and the Americans most of all, although, after a few years of socializing strenuously with everybody, people tended to slip back into their national identities. It was just so exhausting to have to explain what a state school was, or how football and soccer were different. After a few years, even the most well-meaning Americans found themselves calling only other Americans and doing Super Bowl breakfasts (due to the time difference) and Thanksgivings at the club with other families. You found yourself somehow more American than ever.

Hilary has become firmly ensconced in her new life, one she slipped into frighteningly easily, as David's career flourished in Asia over the past eight years. He is now one of the most senior attorneys at his firm. Hilary has servants—a domestic helper and a driver—a membership to a country club, where she plays tennis with other sun-visored ladies, and afterward, showered and dried and clad in cool summer shifts, they order Greek salads and salted French fries and sip pinot grigio as the sun sets and their husbands work and they gossip and complain and otherwise act as if life has always been this way.

~

And now there is Julian.

She first saw him a few months ago while on a tour with the American Women's Association, which she joined back when she was new to Hong Kong. She had seen a flyer for the association at the American Club. There were photos of smiling women eating Chinese food, holding a bake sale, at a costume party. The aura of nonjudgmental acceptance drew her in. She stuck with AWA over the years, taking part in some of their activities, and was on their e-mail list. She decided to sign up for an introduction to Hong Kong Social Services, where they learned about different situations and how they might volunteer and be useful.

They saw an orphanage, or what they called a child-care center, as well as a small group home. The child-care center was in Kowloon, in a massive concrete building. Hilary found herself on a tour with five other well-meaning American women clutching Starbucks coffee cups. Amid the powerful scent of Dettol—disinfection was a religion in Hong Kong after SARS—Belle Liu, the bespectacled representative who sported the inexplicably mannish cut of so many local women, explained the different areas in the blunt, accented English Hilary often found startling, the locals not yet having adopted politically correct terminology.

"This for the retard children," she said, gesturing to a padded room where two boys in helmets rocked back and forth while a woman read a newspaper in the corner.

"Sometimes mother will not come back for one year," Belle said, "and we don't know if the child is abandon or not."

"Is there a cutoff date for when you would find the child a new home?" a woman asked.

Belle went into a lengthy explanation of government regulations and the forms the women were supposed to sign when they left their children. However, she said, very few complied. They were mothers, after all, and most could not bring themselves to give up their children if they weren't made to. They imagined a future when they would be better off, have more, and reclaim their child. So then the children languished in legal limbo, unable to be put in the adoption pool, unable to go home. Like many locals in government administration, Belle was very excitable about rules and regulations and following them to the letter.

Another room had five baby swings and an equal number of foam seats for infants who could not sit upright yet. There were no children in that room—down for naps, Belle explained.

The women were kind, the furniture and equipment were clean, the endeavor was wholly adequate, and yet, of course, the whole building reeked of sad desperation. Hilary walked through the fluorescent-lit, linoleum-floored hallways in a daze, looking at all the abandoned, luckless children.

She went to the bathroom, an institutional affair that smelled strongly of bleach and urine, and closed the stall door. When she pulled down her pants, they were stained with blood. Her period, again. The earthy, rich smell rose and sickened her. Her stomach dropped.

She sat in that stall, her head in her hands, for ten minutes, listening to people come in, urinate, pull on the toilet paper, flush, wash their hands—the mundane sounds of the lavatory. She breathed carefully, modulating the sound so that people knew someone else was there but not so loud as to disturb them. Someone from the tour came in to check on her, and she said to go on without her, she would find them.

She looked at her bloody underwear. This had to be a sign, she told herself. Just like the signs other people are always going on about of when they recognized their child. Getting your period in an orphanage had to be a sign.

She had taken a class in college about feminism and medicine. In it, she learned that the whole terminology around menstruation—a failure to conceive, a shedding of the lining—was negative and misogynistic and old-fashioned, teaching women that their sole purpose in life was to have children. The lining of the uterus was not shed; it was cleansing itself to make way for a new lining. Back then, so far away from the idea of having children, the whole premise had seemed impossibly academic and precious. Now she wants to find that book again and read it. She wants to find a way to redefine what is happening to her, to own it.

And then she saw Julian.

Of course, his name was not Julian then. She decided to call him Julian after all the arrangements had been made. That seemed an enormous encroachment into his life, already, naming him.

The group went on from the child-care center to what was called a group home, a smaller institution that housed only eight boys. Here, their guide explained, they had a smaller setting. The government outsourced child care, so children would end up in a child-care center, a group home, or foster care.

Julian was doing homework in a room with older kids. He stood out because he was not Chinese but, instead, that beautiful brown mix. She tried to talk to him, and the guide told her that he was wonderful at music. Sick with the knowledge that she was not pregnant, she rushed into something impulsive. "I'll find him a piano teacher," she said. Belle Liu nearly had a conniption, what with all the regulations that would violate, but Hilary simply kept talking, and the kindhearted woman finally could not bear to see Julian miss a chance at something he would never otherwise get.

"I don't know," she kept saying. "I don't know."

And she didn't say anything more, and Hilary knew to just shut up and come back and do it later. Julian's paperwork had recently come through—a small miracle, the woman said—and he had been released into the adoption pool, but his chances for adoption were close to nil because of his age and because of his mixed race. Normally-developing babies had a 100 percent chance of being adopted if their paperwork was done, but after a year or two, the children's chances dropped steeply. Julian went to school near the group home and walked there and back. He had already started on the life he would lead if no one were to intervene.

~

He has been coming to her house for just a month. She usually picks him up early, so that they can have a snack. The first time, she made him lasagna herself, Puri clucking over the mess Hilary made in her own unfamiliar kitchen, spilling tomato sauce on the countertop, opening every cupboard door in search of the Pyrex pan. But he barely ate it, pushing it around the plate until it became a huge, gloppy mess that looked unappetizing even to Hilary.

Puri stood over him with a satisfied expression on her face. The ma'am was not supposed to go in the kitchen. That was her domain.

"*Sik mae?*" Puri asked him, motioning to her lips with an imaginary spoon. She spoke some Cantonese, from her time with a local Chinese family.

"*Chow faan,*" he said. He liked fried rice. Even Hilary knew what that was.

So now Puri makes him the food he likes, that she knows how to make from her previous job. She makes pork fried rice, spring rolls with shredded carrots and turnips, vinegary chicken wings; once she made an entire steamed fish with head on. The house smells like a Chinese restaurant on Julian's days, all soy sauce and deep-fried Mazola, but she does not say anything, because he devours the food while Puri looks on, gratified. This is a child who does not know what to do with a carrot stick, or celery filled with peanut butter, or a cream-cheese-and-jelly sandwich. She might as well give him hay.

Hilary usually sits opposite him, always, stunned by the silence in her, unable to say anything but the most cursory social greeting. He has to learn English, she says to herself, he has to learn English. But who will teach him? She has given him an English name. What next? What next? Isn't there some sort of manual?

But he doesn't make it easy either. He is usually reserved, but sometimes, suddenly, clownishly friendly, as if the women at the group home have told him he has to close the deal, although she knows that must just be her own projection. She does not know how to handle him when he is like that; she is too close to his desperation and confusion and is overwhelmed. But she does not even know if it is desperation that drives him. She has no way to read what he thinks, what he feels. She has nothing in common with him except what she has the will to build, and that will, it seems, is not strong enough.

This complete flouting of all common adoption wisdom—that she is allowed to take a child home, a "test-drive" she thinks of it sometimes, the thought bubbling up in her head before she can suppress it with horror—is an incredible, under-the-table thing that has somehow happened because everything is personal and the head of the AWA really, really likes her because they went to the same university and so she vouched for Hilary to the department head, whom she has known for sixteen years. It is terrible, it is scandalous, and yet Hilary cannot come to a decision. She can tell herself that she is giving her time to a child who needs it, a volunteer sort of thing, and that she doesn't have to go the whole way.

It is also, she tells herself, because she finds herself already too surrounded by people who depend on her. Given fifteen minutes in the same room, Puri will tell her of her family in the Philippines and their various medical ailments, their debts, their divorces, all of which Puri—and, by implication, Hilary—is responsible for. Puri will weep and all but rend her clothes. Their lives in that country are operatic: epic tales of affairs and jail time and abandoned children and mistresses and sickness and thirteen-hour bus rides. Hilary adjusts her bangles and makes sympathetic noises, but she cannot understand what Puri is talking about. She pays Puri triple the usual rate and hopes that recuses her from further responsibility. Puri is short, squat, with a farmer's build. She is not honest, but she is clever, and from what the expatriate women say, you cannot have both.

Puri bangs around when Hilary is in the kitchen, asks loudly what she is looking for. She cannot stand to have intruders on her territory. She inhales sharply over Hilary's cooking, signaling her complete disbelief that someone can have so few skills. The ma'am is not supposed to cook.

And Sam. Sam, the driver. Sam is a trial: proud and angry and a ruinously bad driver. He has dented their car twice, parking, and rear-ended someone at a red light. But she cannot fire him. He has not done anything really bad, she tells David, who shakes his head at her indecision. If I ran my office the way you run this house, he says before he leaves for the morning. The statement lingers. What would happen? she thinks. What would happen?

When Julian came into their lives, the few people they told assumed they were going to adopt him. And she thought so too. Once she and David took him out for dim sum on the weekend, an awkward outing, both parties not knowing how to move it forward, how to take the next step, paralyzed by the notion that it might be a mistake from which they would never recover. She cannot understand all the other families around her, the ones who add to their families with such single-minded, deliberate simplicity and assurance.

"I just knew," they say. "As soon as I walked into the orphanage and saw Mei, as soon as I did, I knew that she was mine. She looked at me and I looked at her and we both knew."

"How?" she wants to ask them. "How did you know?"

But, of course, no one ever asks that. They tell their stories all in the same way: how they filled out their applications and waited and waited, the sudden call, the hastily booked flight, the anonymous hotel room they bring their new child to, the formula bought on the fly. The children never cry, because it never did them any good in the orphanage. Then they have tantrums. These adoptive parents have a network, and they help one another. They know their children when they see them.

They seem wholeheartedly good in a way that she cannot understand, because she is in some way bad, or selfish, or ignorant, or unwilling to believe, because she cannot recognize her child when she sees him. They believe her to be one of them, but she is not.

"You'll know," they say.

So she looks at Julian and tries to know. But all she can see is the questions. What if he hates her? What if he tries to run away? What if he has some genetic disease that will waste him away before he turns thirteen? What if—and this is the big one—what if she can't love him? She knows these are selfish questions, not the kind she is supposed to be asking. She is supposed to care about his well-being, about how his life will be, but she cannot shake off her commitment to herself. Sometimes she thinks that is what the nine months are for, so that women can get to know the person inside them, that it is a mingling at first of self and child, and then after the baby is born, that is when you can become the selfless, generous mother you are supposed to be. She doesn't have that yet, she thinks. Maybe nine months of getting to know him is what she needs.

And then, just when she and David seemed to be moving to some sort of decision, there was a spate of articles in the paper about a family who was essentially giving up their adopted child. Facts were murky and hard to come by, but the family was Dutch, and the child, Chinese. They had adopted him about three years ago, and they wanted to give him back. There were outraged letters to the editor, saying that adopting a child was not like buying a pair of pants—you couldn't return him when he didn't fit. There were racial overtones, of course, the privileged white minority and the beleaguered local community.

She read each day's developments with a heightening sense of dread. She was implicated in this, she knew it. There was some lesson being taught, but she didn't know what it was. Was what they were doing worse than this family? They were essentially trying out Julian, without adopting him, bringing him home, interacting with him, seeing if this could work. At brunch at the American Club, a woman brought it up, quite aggressively, and so now she doesn't mention it anymore. Another thing to be ashamed about.

David lets her drive the process. He is supportive enough, but she knows he thinks she is being crazy about the whole thing, that it will just happen if they relax. Or that they can adopt. He is noncommittal about either situation, which seems to her a strange reaction to something so momentous, but she doesn't push him on it. He seems to dissolve into the workday and come back spent. Whether they're driving to a restaurant or taking turns in the shower in the morning, the complaints and discontents of their marriage have reached a granular level that surprises her with its mundane primacy: He never recaps the toothpaste; he never lets her know his schedule, then acts surprised when she is not available or is miffed when there's nothing for him to eat. They bother her in a deep, distant way, as if they are coming from far, far away. Marriages are mysteries to everyone, she supposes, most of all to the people in them, if they are not paying attention.

Hilary sits and waits for her friend—her chronically late friend, who has told her she needs to see her—so that they can have lunch. She sits and waits at the table, seeing the white surface of it made gold by the light, with the sounds of shouting children and bursts of laughter and women's chatter surrounding her, and wonders how she can feel so closed off from it all, how she feels as if she's in an echo chamber, apart from everyone else, excised from the collective experience of a cool winter afternoon.

But she remembers. She remembers having moments when she felt lifted with gratitude. It was dizzyingly gratifying to feel that you wanted nothing more than what you had at that moment: a hot latte with a full head of foam, and a newspaper filled with facts you were about to learn, a man sitting next to you who wanted to be there.

Those moments are there in her past, glimmering like small flames in the far, far dark of her memories. Maybe she has to go back to go forward to get there again. Maybe that's what she needs to do.

~

Olivia arrives, finally. Forty minutes late.

She is Chinese, striking.

"Hello, darling," she says. Never an apology for being late. People wait for Olivia. She takes off her sunglasses and waves them around. "Nice day for December, isn't it? I love that you can sit outside in Hong Kong year-round. Nowhere like it." The sky is crisp and blue, the blue-green sea meeting it in a flat line. She is wearing tan wool trousers and a brown chunky-knit sweater.

"It's wonderful today."

"Let's get some drinks." She waves her hand to the waiter. "Hello, Kevin," she says. "Chrysanthemum tea."

Hilary asked Olivia once why she didn't speak Cantonese to the staff. Her English is perfect but stiff, as if she is elocuting, not talking.

"I do when I'm with family and other Chinese," Olivia had said, surprised. "I'm with you, and I think it would be impolite."

"Like you were talking about me to them or something?"

"I suppose," she said. "I haven't really thought about why, just do it naturally. Sometimes I don't even know what I'm speaking unless someone comments on it."

The tea comes, and Olivia pours Hilary her cup first. This is something Hilary loves, how everyone is so polite here at the table. They serve others the choice bits first, would never dream of eating before a guest, never drink the last of the wine, fight to pay the bill. An admirable trait of Asian culture, but then you are horrified when you go back to the United States and it's a free-for-all and every man for himself.

"My mother would faint, us sitting outside," Olivia says. "She always says that you should retain warmth. After I had Dorothy, she didn't let me go outside for a month, literally. You know, the confinement period, when they make you eat foul broths and teas and you can't wash your hair."

"This is for you," Hilary says, and gives her a shopping bag tied with red ribbon. "Belated birthday. Open it later, though. I hate it when people open presents in front of me."

Olivia is a citizen of the world, one of those effortlessly cosmopolitan people. She has lived in London, New York, Paris, but prefers Hong Kong to all else. She has been to every restaurant, every spa, every good hotel. She can hold forth on where to get the best massage in Morocco, a good driver in Italy, a yoga teacher in Bali.

She is not beautiful; she is sophisticated looking, with good bones, matte skin, perfectly arched eyebrows, long, thin fingers that are always buffed and filed, nothing as vulgar as nail polish. "I do think all those women who spend all that time getting manicures are insane," she once said to Hilary, who burst out laughing. "But you spend so much time on grooming!" she said. "Your haircuts, your clothes, tailoring your clothes."

Olivia just blinked, unmoving. "I do not," she said simply. "That is different."

Hilary admires her a great deal. Olivia's very presence seems to suggest that alternatives exist.

"So I went to Burberry this morning because I had to pick up something that had been altered, and a shopgirl was there who used to help me at another boutique—you know the salesgirls move around a lot. She had just done a stint over at Tsim Sha Tsui at the Louis Vuitton, and she told me the most screamingly funny stories!"

This was another Hong Kong peculiarity. Olivia is Chinese, local-born and bred, went to a Cantonese girls' school and then to the American school before college in California with Hilary. Yet she has English mannerisms and speech.

"Like?"

"You know, no one we know ever shops over there, it's all for the mainland people. Have you ever been over there? Nathan Road, Canton Road, Tsim Sha Tsui, with all the big luxury boutiques?"

"No, I barely buy that stuff over here."

"But she said it's like a zoo. There are children having tantrums, eating McDonald's, licking the mirrors! She said once she went in to clean a dressing room and someone had peed on the floor! Peed! They're really animals!"

Hong Kong people are like the landed gentry in England, beset by pesky, redolent immigrants, Hilary thinks. People like Olivia are disdainful of their mainland counterparts, who sweep over the border in overwhelming numbers with their fat wallets and arriviste ways. She makes fun of how they buy up baby formula and Ferrero Rocher in enormous quantities—these have become currency in the mainland for some reason—and thinks of them as not quite people.

But it seems Olivia wants to talk to her about something else.

"So I wanted to ask you something," she says, bringing the cup of tea up to her lips.

"What?" Hilary asks.

Olivia puts the cup down.

"If you knew something about a friend, something that was important, would you tell her, even though it might hurt her?"

Hilary looks at her. Olivia is fiddling now with the fork, unable to look up. It is odd to see the unflappable Olivia visibly nervous.

"What kind of thing?" she says slowly.

"You know, important stuff. Stuff that might change their lives."

"Is it," Hilary says slowly, "to do with me?"

"Yes."

"I don't know," Hilary says. "I don't know."

There is a pause.

"I think you should know," Olivia says gently.

Hilary looks away, at the horizon, where the sea meets the sky. She makes a decision and looks up at the kind eyes of her friend.

"Not today, please," she says, making the kind of statement that makes her wonder if she knows who she is anymore. "I can't hear anything life-changing today. I have a dinner party tonight."

~

When she gets back home, the salad she somehow managed to eat a jumble in her stomach and mind, Julian is gone, and Puri is furiously chopping something in the kitchen, and the table is already set, ready for the caterer. She is having a dinner party, but she doesn't really have anything to do. She thinks of the tired jokes that Hong Kong housewives make, when complimented on their food at dinner parties: "Thank you, it's homemade—meaning made in my house," or "Thank you, I'm a great supervisor."

She wants a drink, but it's only three in the afternoon. Puri is in the kitchen, so she goes in and makes herself a vodka tonic, trying to seem like it's perfectly normal to mix yourself a cocktail in the afternoon.

The fact is, the helpers see everything. They see the fights, they see the messiness. They hear the arguments, are witness to the silent, toxic aftermath as they pour the coffee and clear the breakfast plates. They know which vase got thrown, because they clean it up in the morning. They know when sir gets a call from a strange woman with an unknown, hesitant voice, or comes in at 3:00 a.m. when the ma'am is in America, or when the teenage children throw a party when their parents are out of town and hand them $500 to "clean up" and keep their mouth shut. They know so much.

So why does she care? Hilary ponders this as she goes to her desk and takes her first sip. Ah, that warm thrum of the alcohol traveling down your body and hitting your stomach. She doesn't care so much, it's just that you can't walk around naked or eat peanut butter standing in front of the fridge in front of someone who's not your family. That's the price you pay for having live-in help. Boo hoo. Poor her.

Hilary sips at her drink and wonders how many calories she is taking in. It's not the alcohol she's worried about: It's that she is always looser, more lenient with herself after a few drinks. A small bag of potato chips, a slice of cake out of the fridge. It all adds up.

Her body, her body, her body. This is what she thinks about at night, lying on the sheets, after David has gone to sleep and she can hear him breathing. She imagines her old fat distributed uncomfortably over her, lying, puddlelike, on her bones.

She is thin now, but in an unnatural way, with pudgy arms and thighs that would not slim down no matter what she did. But she has kept off the weight for thirty years, something her mother praised her for. After her childhood episode with being the fat girl, she made herself be uninterested in food. Ate to live, didn't live to eat. Nothing tastes as good as thin feels—isn't that what the ads said? David once came across photos of her as a child, and he couldn't believe how big she had been, even though she had been a little girl and still cute, though she could tell he didn't think so. In college, she read a story by Andre Dubus about a fat girl who lost weight, got married to someone who worked for her father, and got fat again, and then the husband found her disgusting. She read it fast, furious, her face hot. She threw it down as soon as she finished, as if it were pornographic. In class, she didn't participate in the discussion, as if to do so would let others see what she had been. She saw herself in that story but didn't like to think about what that meant. Of course, she would never let herself get fat again.

The thing was, she and David had never fit. They were mismatched. She had never known why he asked her out. When she saw photographs of his ex-girlfriends, they were sharp-cheeked blondes with shallow blue eyes, mean-looking brunettes in small, tight dresses. She asked him once, early on in their relationship, "Am I a different kind of girl for you?" and he replied, not without affection, "You're the kind of girl I marry."

He was handsome, in a seamless sort of way, especially in a suit. He was better looking than most of the other guys she had dated. She had not had a very serious boyfriend before him. Everything had just fallen into place. Right time, right guy, right age. And now they have been married for ten years.

They are having the dinner tonight for a new person at David's firm, someone who just made partner in San Francisco and then was relocated here. David told her that the promotion had been contingent on the understanding that the man relocate his family to Hong Kong for at least three years. Having been here so long, Hilary doesn't understand why anyone is reluctant to come to Hong Kong, with all its advantages. There's also an old friend of David's, from California, who is passing through with his wife, another couple from Tai Tam, and the Reades. A comfortable mix of people.

The menu: Three canapés: sesame salmon tartare in phyllo tarts, Peking Duck spring rolls, mini cheese quiches for the vegetarians—vegans had an obligation to declare themselves in advance. Then a chicory salad with roasted garlic and goat cheese tumbles, and the main course: Chilean sea bass with an olive tapenade and mashed turnip, cappellini primavera for the vegetarians. For dessert, warm caramel tart with burnt-sugar ice cream and coffee or tea. A nice Italian pinot grigio and a red cabernet from Australia. Leafing through menus at her desk, she often floats above herself and sees the woman she's become, eerily similar to her own mother, someone she thought she would never be. She knows that canapés have to be easily eaten in one bite, knows how much and what kind of wine to order for different crowds, has different sets of china and linens to set different moods.

The money has always come from the women in the family. Real estate, so quaint an industry in new-age San Francisco, but all those tech titans needed office space and places to live. It seemed quite natural to have David sign a prenup. "It's the family custom," she said at the time, nervous. It was true. Her father had signed one as well. Of course, her father had gone on to make his own fortune in real estate, then technology investments. "You should be so lucky," her mother said. She had sized up David pretty well when they first met for lunch at a pier-side restaurant. "He knows how to eat an oyster, at least," she said after he'd gone to the bathroom. She had always been a snob.

David was as good about her family and the money as he could be expected to be. But it was always there, especially when they talked about buying a house or a car. David was a lawyer and earned a good living, but they lived as well as his boss and had a nicer car. She supplemented their housing allowance to get a bigger place, and they bought a Mercedes, new, in Hong Kong, where cars cost twice as much as they do in the United States.

Hilary doesn't care about money all that much, but that's probably because she's never been without it.

Her mother was once a great beauty, but all of a sudden her face caved in, her body ballooned out, her hair frizzed, as if beauty were an all too temporary gift, perhaps from a witch or a fairy, to be cruelly taken away somewhere between your sixtieth and seventieth birthdays. Or maybe you just stopped caring. Not her mother. Hilary cannot reconcile her mother now with the one in the photos and in her memories. Lissom, shiny waves of mahogany hair, large brown eyes, always in a fitted sheath or silk blouse, immaculately pressed pants with a thin leather belt. Slim, slim, slim. This is the chant she grew up with. Of course. When she sees her mother after a long period, like at the airport—she still picks her up, dutiful daughter that she is—she is always shocked for a moment at the stranger who is waving at her, that stoutish matron who looks wrinkled and untidy, tired from the long flight.

How uncharitable, she knows, but what can you do to suppress your thoughts about your mother? Her mother mentions it sometimes, as she pushes away from the dinner table: "The metabolism goes, you'll see," and "I never thought I'd look this way." Once, when they were standing together in a restaurant bathroom in front of the mirror, her mother said, "When you get older, Hilary, there will come a day when you don't recognize yourself in the mirror. You will feel like the same sixteen-year-old girl, or twenty-five-year-old, or thirty, but an old woman is staring back at you." Hilary was uncomfortable with the confidence, but she nodded and quickly dried her hands.

Her mother comes once or twice a year, usually at Christmas. She is due to arrive in a few days, and they will spend three days in Hong Kong and a week in Bangkok, where her mother loves the Chatuchak Market and the food. Her father is ill, with dementia, and this is the only time her mother leaves him.

If she had a child, maybe she would understand her mother better.

She finishes her drink, goes down to find CK already setting up the ice bucket and the highball and wine glasses. CK is a freelance waiter and bartender, a Chinese man who has found a living working the expatriate dinner party circuit. He has been at her house so often he doesn't need any direction, just comes in and starts placing the glasses and folding the napkins. She sees him at every third event she is at, at other people's houses, always in his impeccable white shirt and sporting a steady smile. Once, leaving a party very late, she saw a man waiting at the bus stop and, startled, realized it was CK, in a black tank top and baggy pants. His deference was gone, and he seemed decades younger as he talked in Cantonese on his mobile phone and gesticulated with his other hand. His voice carried over as he talked easily, loudly. Where was the exaggerated bow, the ingratiating smile? Her heart sank as she thought of how he put on his face for his job, but was it really any different from a disgruntled accountant complaining loudly to his wife over dinner, then smiling and making a sycophantic comment to his boss in the elevator the next day? Wasn't everyone just trying to make a living?

"Hello, CK," she says. His name was Cheng Kiang or something like that, but of course he told all his Western clients to call him CK. Whatever was easier for them.

"Hello, Mrs. Starr," he says, smiling.

CK and Puri have a funny relationship. Now they are friends, but they had it out the first few times about whose responsibility it was to clean the glasses. Puri, no fool, said it was his job. He said his job was outside the kitchen. Now they have come to a compromise: He brings the glasses into the kitchen and puts them neatly in the sink for Puri to wash. Everyone saves face.

The cook and his assistant have arrived and are clearing space on the tiny counter. The kitchens in Hong Kong are small and uninviting, as the mistress of the house is never expected to be in one.

"Hello, do you have everything you need?" Hilary asks. She stumbles over a box of pre-prepped entrees.

"Are you all right, Mrs. Starr?" asks the cook. He is of an indeterminate race—Tibetan? half-Indian? half-Chinese?—but speaks perfect English. He has been here once before, but she doesn't remember his name.

"Fine, it's nothing." She waves him away. She is more deliberate after a drink.

She dials David, gets his voice mail. "Tell me your ETA, please," she says, and hangs up.

"I'll have a glass of the white," she tells CK. He pours with a flourish and hands it to her. She sits down on the couch and crosses her legs, cool in the flurry of activity around her. Another Saturday night. Another dinner party.

She remembers one of the first ones she was invited to in Hong Kong. A woman, unpopular, it later turned out, leaned over to her and said, "Out here, you're not a real woman unless you have four kids." She left, back to New Jersey, a year or two after Hilary arrived, but she thought of her sometimes and her casual, unthinking cruelty.

She hears David arrive downstairs and gets up to greet him.

"You look nice," he says. She looks down at her black dress with filmy chiffon sleeves to cover the upper arms she is sensitive about. "Thank you," she says.

"Everything set?" he asks. He smells like alcohol, or maybe it's her.

"It always is," she says. When did her marriage shift so that the simplest comments come to seem like snipes? She doesn't remember, but it has, indisputably, shifted. She remembers Olivia's face hovering over the glass of hot tea.

"Okay," he says. "Great. I'm going upstairs to freshen up."

She looks at the retreating back of her husband as he goes up the stairs, a slim, handsome back in a gray suit. She spirals up, out of her body, so that she is looking down at the house, at the husband and wife, having a dinner party, like paper dolls, or those Sims characters in that computer game that used to be popular. Sometimes she feels so old.

Part III

Mercy

MERCY SITS in the restaurant, sipping coffee. She had actually had something to do today. She remembered when she got up from bed to fix the salad she had been thinking about. On her computer, a reminder popped up: "Lunch with Sandra Parnells, Conrad hotel."

Mercy avoids old friends, as they're too concerned about her, or not concerned enough, and she can't abide either. But this was a complete stranger, a friend of a friend, who e-mailed her a few days ago as she was new in town—a woman who followed her husband to Hong Kong and is now looking for a job. Pleasant enough, but Mercy watched the woman slowly realize that Mercy is not someone who is going to be helpful or useful or anything. Her face recalibrated; she was waiting for the lunch to end. So Mercy helped her out: She said she had to run, let Sandra pay for the salad Mercy had picked at, and then watched her leave.

Now she is sitting in the hotel lobby restaurant, nursing a coffee, loath to return to her rabbit warren of an apartment. When she does come out and see people, the outside world, it seems unbearably bright for the first fifteen minutes, and then she adjusts and can imagine herself living again. But this is dangerous to do too often, to imagine things changing. Suddenly she recognizes someone from across the room. He is a Chinese boy to whom she never spoke in college. He didn't run in her crowd, was a bit FOB—fresh off the boat, as the immigrants call one another—but they had a few classes together. Nerdy, but would be handsome if only someone taught him how to dress. She can tell he recognizes her by the way he keeps looking over.

Finally he stops on his way out. He is tall, wears a double-breasted navy suit with a purple tie. Terrible, cheap shoes. He has a backpack. Still nerdy.

"Columbia, right?" His voice still carries a slight Chinese accent. She nods.

"You had an interesting name. Not the usual Asian name . . ."

"I still have it," she says. "Mercy. You're . . ."

"Charlie," he says. "Charlie Leung. I work here in Hong Kong. You live here now?"

"For a couple years."

"What do you do?"

She hesitates. He sees it, rescues her. "Sorry, I shouldn't ask."

"No, it's okay," she says. But then can't think of what to say.

"Well, I'll see you around," he says.

"Yes." She waits, but he bows a little bow, formal, how odd, and turns to leave.

She has never seen him around in Hong Kong, which means that he must not go to the same places she and her friends do. Maybe more of a local. Hong Kong is so small that if you go out enough, you will run into every expat at some point in the same five restaurants that people frequent. The restaurants change, but the scene never does.

Next table over is a man at lunch with a redheaded woman, a business lunch that has seemingly stretched into something longer and more meaningful.

"I'm in a bit of a pickle," the woman says cheerfully, sipping her coffee, and Mercy can almost see the man's face soften, fall in love. It seems so easy, so ubiquitously available: love and happiness. It happens every day. Later she will see the man with his wife, a different woman, and realize, with a sense of relief that is almost palpable, that the world is complicated indeed. That everyone has secrets and despair and romance in them. It makes her feel better.

Another man comes and sits down at the bar and orders a martini. He is in a suit but somehow looks louche. Three thirty now, when all the responsible work people have long ago gone back to the office and the stragglers are the housewives who have had a second or third glass of wine, the freelancers who have no meetings, nowhere else to be. A man in a suit at the bar at three o'clock is a man to avoid.

He scans the room; his eyes alight on Mercy.

"Hi there," he says. "Do you want a drink?"

Of course she says yes. Of course she sits down with him. She may not eat, but she drinks. Falling into another bad decision. It feels like coming home.

~

Men. Men are a disaster for her.

"You are a pig," she said to one obnoxious man at a bar who had propositioned her in a particularly crude way.

"And you are a chick who loves bacon," he said back. And she laughed, because she thought it was actually a pretty funny thing to say, and then she spent the night with him, which was a pretty stupid thing to do. She sees him sometimes in Central during the day and ducks her head or goes into a shop to avoid him. He never seems to see her. She doesn't know if it would be worse if he pretended not to know her or actually didn't remember her. Or if he tried to be nice.

Another guy once said, nodding toward his beer, "Do you know how to take the head off the foam?"

"No," she said.

He swirled a finger around his ear and stuck it in the white foam. It dissolved instantly. He grinned.

"Am I supposed to be charmed?" she said. "Impressed?"

"The oil in the earwax makes it go away," he said.

She got up and left.

But all too often, she didn't.

Even when she was younger, she always liked the wrong men. In high school, all her crushes turned out to be gay or those boys who were unattainable. The one guy at college she had really, really been into had lately been in the news for being fired for writing an incredibly misogynistic e-mail, about his colleagues at the New York investment bank where he worked, that had gone viral. All this makes her very uncertain about her judgment.

She doesn't understand why men seem to treat her as if she doesn't matter, as if she's someone to spend a few hours with. All around her, she sees her friends in relationships; boyfriends who call to see what the agenda is for the weekend, who plan trips, who want to get married. She meets the guy at the bar who wants to have sex for a few weeks.

And so, today, she sits down with David and proceeds to get very, very drunk.

They sit so long, they see a couple come in to have an early dinner with their three children. They look Indonesian or Malaysian, and the children range from five to ten or so. They have three maids trailing them, in matching uniforms. The mother, in head-to-toe designer wear of the most glittery kind, and the father, in a shiny Adidas tracksuit, sit down and both bring out their phones and start tapping on them. The five-year-old boy plays on an iPad that one of the maids holds up for him, like a human tripod. Another maid massages hand cream onto the hands of the middle girl. The maids stand up, as if they are not allowed to sit. Everyone in the restaurant is staring at them.

"Unbelievable," says Mercy.

"Happens all the time in this part of the world," David says.

They have ascertained that they are both American, both sarcastic, both a little bit bitter. She notices the ring on his finger but is careful not to ask. Nothing inappropriate has happened. They are just two strangers having a drink in the afternoon. It makes her feel grown up, this possibility of a married man, an opening into a world she has never contemplated before. They segue into flirtatious back-and-forth.

"Like, really, what kind of name is Tucker?" she asks. "Or Chet? Only white people have those names."

"Korean names are odd too, like Yumi or Yuri."

"Those are Japanese names," she says.

"I knew a Korean girl named Yuri!" he says triumphantly.

"I'm sure you did," she says drily.

"Hey, now," he says.

"Hey, now," she repeats, mocking him.

"Now you've hurt my feelings," he says. "Don't you feel bad?"

"Not at all."

"Want another drink?" he asks.

"Better not," she says. "Drinking at four in the afternoon. You must be a dissolute kind of guy."

There's a pause. All this sparring is going to lead to something, or not.

"Well," he says, "if you're not going to have another drink with me, I do have a dinner party to get to."

"It's been a pleasure," she says.

He gets up to go but lingers.

"I guess I'll see you around?"

"Maybe." She's not that desperate.

He considers, says it. "Where do you hang out?"

A better man would have asked for her number or e-mail, but she's not used to better men.

"I know the bartender at Il Dolce, so I'm there for drinks sometimes." A little crumb laid for a trail to follow.

"Okay." He leans in for a kiss on the cheek. "Lovely to meet you, Mercy." He smells of the cigarette they shared outside and the Macallan he's been drinking.

She sits at the bar, with a lovely fizzy feeling in her stomach. Maybe this man is the way out, maybe this is the sparkly path to the future. She knows it's the alcohol talking, mostly, but that's okay. She's had her fill of the past. She wants to break out of the mold everyone thinks she should be in. Everyone thinks for her too much, has their nose in her business, tells her what they think she should be doing. On rare occasions, something good happens to her, like two years ago, between jobs, when she found out she had enough miles for a free ticket and booked a flight to Italy just to get the hell out of the hole she was in, and people thought she was extravagant or foolhardy. One friend, Tracy, who everyone said came into a $10 million trust fund when she turned twenty-one, sat her down and told her she had to think about her career. "You can't just go to Italy whenever you want," she said, this from a girl who had gone to Italy twice in the past three years, plus India and Thailand and Australia.

"Why not?" Mercy asked, wondering why Tracy cared.

"It's irresponsible. You don't know where your next job is coming from. And . . ." It was unseemly, was what Tracy wanted to say but couldn't. But she couldn't understand how difficult it was for Mercy to sit in her tiny apartment day after day and do nothing.

"You can't just get job after job," Tracy said. "You need a plan." As if plans were so easy to come by. Or careers. "You're getting older," she said. As if Mercy didn't notice that all around her, people were getting promotions and getting important, or getting married, or having kids, or moving to other places. As if she were unaware. As if.

"You went to Italy," Mercy pointed out. "Last summer."

Tracy paused. "It's different," she said. She wasn't embarrassed in the least.

Tracy is different from Mercy. It is just a fact to her. This is the dissonance. Mercy thinks she is like her friends, and they think she is different. It was not so apparent in college, but now in postcollege life, in real life, it is obvious that they think she is different. If she believes that too, that she is different, it seems like giving up, and then where does she go from there?

The trip to Italy didn't pan out. She couldn't find a cheap enough hotel and had to factor in traveling money and realized she couldn't swing it, and then when she tried to get the miles back, it cost so much to put them back in her account that she hesitated, and when she called back two weeks later to do it, it was too close to the date and she lost all those miles. Of course. But, she thinks. But. It was almost worth it to have had that giddy day of possibility when she booked the trip, imagining the wonderful things she might do, the small, tiny espressos she might drink standing up at small cafés, and the old stones and fountains she would wander around and look at. It was almost worth it.

Mercy walks home, pleasantly drunk in the crisp December air, swaying a little, dreaming of a higher authority—one that sees all the injustices meted out to her, that sees all the good things she tries to do, no matter if they don't work out or no one notices—and that she will be found to be correct: Everyone will see that she has suffered more, been given less. How unfair, they will say. There will, finally, be justice.

Margaret

SHE IS OUT of the bath now, skin moist and flushed, wrapped in a Portman Ritz-Carlton bathrobe from an old trip to Shanghai. A trip from another life. She has wrapped her hair in a turban, so it can dry slowly and comfortably, the heat from her head trapped and steamy inside. The small space heater in the corner is sputtering out some warmth, and she is making a cream-cheese-and-olive sandwich. She takes out the cream cheese from the small box refrigerator she bought a few weeks ago, which reminds her of college days. The cream cheese is thick and white and comforting as she slides her knife out of the container. She spreads it across the thick multigrain bread. She slices the olives and studs the cream cheese with the bits, fingers slippery with oil. Her mouth is watering. What a marvelous combination, the smooth creaminess and the salty oil, paired with the heartiness of the bread. Food is good. She has to remember the good things, the small good things.

And tonight, a dinner party. She has to get home, to make sure the kids are packed for vacation and to get ready. It's at Hilary and David Starr's. She knew Hilary as a child back in California. Their mothers were friendly. Hilary was very chubby, one of those flaxen-haired girls with porcelain cheeks, a rotund Dutch doll of a girl. Then suddenly one fall, maybe sixth grade, she came back to school with her cheeks caved in in a funny way, her arms and legs still largish but her waist tiny. Margaret remembers going to Hilary's house one day, maybe in fifth grade, and seeing a schedule pinned up above the desk. In tidy, round letters, it spelled out a stringent schedule:

3:30 Arrive home

3:45 Snack and unpack

4:00 Homework

5:00 Outdoor time

6:00 Dinner

7:00 Finish unfinished homework

8:15 Shower

8:30 Reading in bed

9:00 Lights out

Margaret came away with a deep sense of wonder that someone her age could be so methodical and disciplined. She didn't admire it— already she knew the beauty in ease, the greater cachet in *sprezzatura*— but the disconcerting sense never left her that Hilary was a deeply formidable person, one who would win over her genetics (she would have liked to see that diet and exercise plan) and whatever else stood in her way and never look back. There was something unnatural about the way she looked, like a fat person turned skinny, never natural, but she had won. She was no longer the chubby girl.

Hilary went on to do well at school, but she never was able to shake that plodding image, that of a workaday bee. She and Margaret were never good friends, just nodding acquaintances who were polite to each other.

Margaret hadn't seen her in years, maybe decades, until they ran into each other at the airport. They had both been going to Thailand, and they ended up at the same resort as well. Their mothers had lost touch, so they hadn't known the other also lived in Hong Kong.

She had been amazed at how quickly she could summon memories, pictures of them together, once they recognized each other. It reminds her of when she was going to her high school reunion and looking through the names of the attendees, and thought bubbles sprang up unbidden—old reputations, the gossip about someone: "pretty blonde, short legs, though," "brainy, chess club, Stanford," "opportunist," or "comes too quickly," the last the malicious gossip about a handsome football player who had killed himself when he was thirty. Could everyone be summed up in a few words like that? Hilary was "fat girl turned thin, type A." She supposed she was something like "pretty, easygoing, lucky," or had been.

She and Clarke had drinks with the Starrs during the trip but didn't really keep up afterward in Hong Kong, and then it became a little awkward when they saw each other in town, or at parties, as they had both accepted they wouldn't go any further with the friendship. But then after what happened, a phone call. Hilary called to say how sorry she was about G and wanted to see her. They had lunch, and now they had a passing sort of friendship where they saw each other and made polite noises about doing it again and sometimes coming through.

So, tonight.

She cleans up her snack and gets ready to leave.

Back at home, Clarke has returned early, is there before her. He kisses her.

"Good day?" he asks.

"Yes," she says. They are still always careful around each other. She wonders when that will end, if ever. They've both read the literature—the majority of marriages break up after the death of a child or something like what's happened to them. It's too painful. But they have the other kids, and the memory of what it used to be like. Maybe that is enough.

"We have that dinner," she says. Before, she would call his assistant and have her remind him, or send an e-mail, but she never bothers anymore.

"Yes, it's on my calendar," he says. "David and Hilary."

"Right."

Clarke gets along with everyone, but they both don't love David. Hilary is fine.

They both remember when they first met them together, on that trip to Thailand. There was a New Year's Eve party at the resort, and after the children went to bed, things got a bit wild, with a lot of drinking and middle-aged people going crazy on the easily available drugs. David was on something and started grinding with some man. It wasn't even that she thought David was gay or that she cared; it was just a little factoid about him that she kept with her. Just a little thought bubble in her head when she saw him put a jacket over his wife's shoulders as they left a party or if she saw him swimming at the club. It was not unkind, more of a "people contain multitudes within them" feeling.

They kiss Daisy and Philip good night. Their children sit, watching a movie, as Essie reads a book next to them. This used to be one of her favorite moments in life, leaving clean, fed, contented children behind as she and her husband went out to enjoy each other, but now nothing is easy, nothing is pleasurable. She can't let it be—it would feel like a betrayal. How can she be sitting in an air-conditioned restaurant in a comfortable chair enjoying a grilled fish and a glass of wine, or lying on a beach chair with a good book, while G might be starving or worse in some barn in rural Korea? How can she let herself?

They drive to the Starrs' in silence. It is only fifteen minutes away, but she lets herself think that the silence is a friendly one, nonreproaching, comfortable. She touches Clarke's cheek while he is driving, wonders what he is thinking. He looks over at her and smiles. They have learned to do with so much less.

At the Starrs', everything is perfect, the house warm and inviting with scented candles, lamps giving off muted light, jazz playing softly. Hilary achieves this by being stringent in everything in her life, from her diet to her house. There's the usual mix: South Side investment bankers and regional company heads and Mid-Levels ad execs and their wives, all American. When she first moved to Hong Kong, she thought she might make friends with the different nationalities she saw all around her. Her children's friends were Danish, Japanese, local Hong Kong. But after a few strained meals, she saw how it was easier to stay with your kind. So, although she loathed the concept, she embraced the reality and became friends with the same people she would have known back in America.

She accepts a drink from the smiling bartender and turns to talk to a couple who are visiting from California, faces starry with jet lag.

"You're from San Francisco," she says politely. And the conversation starts. Another night in Repulse Bay.

Hilary

An odd mix that never gelled. The Reades, whom everyone knew. Poor Margaret. They were trying to live, but how could they? She seemed tentative all the time now, as if she was trying to lead a normal life but had forgotten how. Hilary had never seen her cry, but she imagined that she must cry all the time. And the new couple, who were moving here. The wife, what was her name? Molly? She was asking about tennis, so she might be an addition to Hilary's team. She would e-mail her about it.

Then the couple from out of town, David's college buddy, who was the most boring person she had ever met. She sat him next to her, because he was the visitor (and, of course, the newcomer was on her other side), but he tried to talk to her about basketball, and she had been so bored.

She lies in bed, thinking about what transpired at the dinner. Nothing, really. Just the usual talk about children and families and where people were going for the upcoming holidays. It turned out that the Reades were going to Phuket the next day and coming back via Bangkok, and they would overlap with her in Bangkok when she was there with her mother. So they'd made plans to get together. Her mother would be glad to see Margaret. And all this not to think about the fact that David has disappeared. He said he wanted to go out with his friend, but the wife gave his friend the stink eye, and they declared they were going to hit the sack—jet lag and all. But David insisted, said he was meeting someone afterward. She was pointedly not invited, so she pretended she knew and was okay with it.

So here she is, lying in her bed, with an almost empty glass of wine on the bedside table, teeth freshly flossed, Bio-Oil glistening unattractively on her face, slubby pink floral pajamas. Hardly a temptress who knows how to keep her man, let alone bring a child into her world.

Because, of course, that's what Olivia wanted to talk to her about. Hilary's not an idiot. She knows, little bit by little bit, that David has changed here in Hong Kong. He is absent from her because he works so much and she has less and less to do with his life. She doesn't know what his life is like when he leaves home, and home is where he spends two or three awake hours, max, getting into bed at night, showering in the morning. He's been staying out later, smelling of booze when he gets home. (Oh, the irony! They could be drinking together.) Being evasive about where he's been. It's not like he is actively doing something wrong, like having an affair or nurturing a drug habit, but he is on the verge of tipping over. She can sense it. Olivia may not have seen him actually with some girl, but he's probably been seen in bars in the company of other women, without his wife present, without a chaperone. There, that sounds about right, in a Jane Austen version of the world. Disporting himself inappropriately.

This is the Hong Kong curse that expat housewives talk about in hushed voices: the man who takes to Hong Kong the wrong way. He moves from an egalitarian American society, where he's supposed to take out the trash every day and help with the dinner dishes, to a place where women cater to his every desire—a secretary who anticipates his needs before he does, a servant in the house who brings him his espresso just the way he likes it and irons his boxers and his socks—and the local population is not as sassy with the comebacks as where he came from, so, of course, he then looks for that in every corner of his life. The rental buildings are littered with the ghosts of ruined marriages: a husband who left his wife and kids for his assistant, an ebony-tressed Chinese sylph who is already pregnant; a man who was lost to the seedy, red-light pleasures of Wan Chai and the paid hostesses who found his every utterance completely fascinating, or sometimes to a more interesting, engaged female colleague, a welcome relief from the woman he faces at home, complaining about his travel, his schedule, his lack of time with the kids. So why not change it up? Why not trade up? Or down, and have some fun?

Hilary and her friends have all sat next to a sheepish father introducing his children to his sexy young fiancée in the safe, public, but judgmental environment of a restaurant. He is worried, solicitous of both his children and the woman but usually more of the latter. He is also proud and newly virile. He pulls out the woman's chair, asks if she likes her food, hands her her dropped napkin as if demonstrating to the children that this is the proper way to treat the new person who has ripped their lives apart. Sometimes the woman is nervous, smiling too much and asking loudly about what the children like to do and saying how she would love to do it with them. Other times the woman is removed, arms crossed, sunglasses, skimpy dress. They'd better learn, these brats, that he belongs to me now. This is what I have to offer. You can't compete. This kind of woman is usually very young and attractive and so very foolish. She thinks that the battle is a matter of weeks or months and that a victory is a victory forever. If the children are adolescent, the girls are defiant and silent, the boys more approachable. The young ones are heartbreaking, that is all. If you were to feel bad for the man, and the expatriate housewife usually emphatically does not, you would feel bad only because you would know that he knew, on some level, what he was doing to his children.

Of course, there are always two sides to every story. Sometimes the woman who's been left is crazy, or horrible, or mean, and everyone understands why. But it does seem that she is always left worse off and the man just starts his life anew, with a younger model of a wife, sometimes a slightly smaller apartment, but that his new life pretty quickly looks like his old one. While the woman often starts working again, depending on what kind of financial arrangement they've come to, and has the kids and her work, and usually soon comes to look harried and gray-haired, so that when her ex-husband comes to pick up the kids, he can see the stark contrast between what he's left and what he has now and congratulates himself that he's made the right decision. To add insult to injury, in his fervor to not mess things up again—because it was so painful and he never wants to go through that again or put anyone else through it again—when he has more children, he vows to really do things right this time, so he pitches in to an unimaginable extent, does more with the kids, since he was always working before and now he knows that he needs more work/life balance, so the new family gets the benefit of this new and improved man, and the old family gets to see it all. It's terrible.

In the eight years she's lived in Hong Kong, Hilary has seen this happen to at least ten women she knew pretty well. She counts them on her fingers: Manda King, Tara Connelly, Kathleen Li, Padma Singh, Sheryl Wu, Jenny Harrison, Lorraine Greenspan . . . there are more, but she can't think of them. A ghostly procession of marital destruction. Of course, marriages break up back home as well, but because Hong Kong is such a fishbowl, you view the carnage from a front-row seat. There's Jim with the new wife at the American Club! There's poor Sylvia waiting for the elevator at her new office with a lunch box—she had to take a job and can't afford to eat lunch out anymore. Some women move back home, but that's a struggle, because the husband won't usually let them take their children so far away. Some enter into the strange netherworld of clubs and unsavory older men, who usually prefer their women younger but will entertain an older one the later the hour. Some migrate to the outlying islands, to *Truman Show*–like Discovery Bay or hippie Lantau, and change accordingly.

Once Hilary was approached by a heavyset woman with long, frizzy hair at IFC Mall. "Hilary!" the woman trilled, happy to see her.

"Hi," Hilary said, reflexively.

The woman understood but was still taken aback. "I look different," she said sheepishly. "I've gained some weight."

And then the woman's face shifted, and Hilary recognized a vestige of Tammy from the tennis team. She had been the captain of

the A team, a five-year veteran of Hong Kong, when the newly arrived Hilary first met her. She had her husband, Garth, and two
children, Mark and Melissa. Two years later, it turned out that Garth
had another family in Shenzhen, the mainland city that neighbored
Hong Kong, with a former club hostess, who had borne him two
additional children, and that he was living a double life, shuttling
between the two on his commute from Hong Kong to China. Mainland women had the reputation of doing anything to secure their
futures and to have the opportunity to marry an American and move
to Hong Kong or even—oh, the glory!—to the United States. The
whole affair came out when the doorman of the apartment building
Tammy lived in rang up to say there was a Miss Chan there to see
Mrs. Brodie. Tammy, not expecting anyone but used to deliveries,
was going through her e-mail when their helper, Gina, came to the
bedroom saying that the woman was asking to see her.

She emerged to see a pretty young Chinese woman in her twenties with a fierce look on her face. She was wearing red plastic shoes
and a fake Hermès scarf. She had come on the train from Lo Wu,
then the MTR to Admiralty, and then a taxi to the South Side. Gina
later told her helper friends, who told their employers, that the girl
showed Tammy pictures of Garth with her and their children, in
their apartment and at restaurants in Shenzhen, and demanded that
she be able to move to Hong Kong. It seemed that Garth had been
putting her off, and she was sick of it. She had been waiting for three
years, and she wanted her children to be educated in Hong Kong—
her oldest would soon be three—and she wanted to have the life that
was due to her and her children as the family of an American citizen
and resident of Hong Kong. She had finally managed to get a visa to
Hong Kong—mainlanders were not allowed unlimited entry—and
now she was here to settle matters.

Tammy's initial response was not duly recorded, as the Chinese
woman quickly became very aggressive and threatening. Her English
was not very good, and translated through the grapevine through a

Filipina maid, her words and the events that transpired were not crystal clear. There were some broken items, as the woman declared that everything in Tammy's house also belonged to her. She demanded to know how many bedrooms they had and how much the rent was. She wanted to know what kind of car they had and what Garth's salary was, as she suspected he had been lying to her.

Tammy, who had been an alpha-expatriate woman, a sort of middle-aged mean girl in tennis whites, heading up school parent committees and chairing charity balls, did not know what to say to this woman who was walking around the house inspecting all her things, but when the woman started going through her closet to see her jewelry, she wrapped her arms around her and tried to restrain her. Thrilled, Gina—who had never seen such drama, even back home in the Philippines—screamed as the two came wrestling out of the master bedroom and did the one sensible thing she could think of: She called the driver, who was downstairs washing the car. He came up and saw three shrieking women scratching and pulling one another's hair and, terrified, called his employer, Garth, who was having a coffee at Cova in Prince's Building with a colleague. Garth took a taxi home.

Apparently—this had entered into expatriate lore—he separated the two women (who must have been tired by that point) and sat them both down on the sofa. Tammy demanded that her high school boyfriend turned husband, whom she had known for more than thirty years, kick this woman out of their house and out of their lives. For God's sake, this is where she and their children lived, and this woman had trespassed on their private property. He looked at her and said, anguished, "I can't."

She started screaming then, started screaming and wailing: Hadn't she followed him here to this godforsaken place where you couldn't get a proper iced coffee to save your life? Hadn't she never complained about all the travel he had to do, all the work, during which apparently he was fucking around with this whore? And hadn't she kept herself up, looking good, and what the fuck? What the fuck? She was going to tell his kids what a shit they had for a father, what a terrible person he was, and he was never going to see them again, and she was going to take all his money. Garth sat there, taking it all, and the woman—he called her Lily—also sat quietly, perhaps afraid and understanding, finally, what she had started.

"There are children involved," he said, meaning his children in China. And that set Tammy off again.

"Your children are Mark and Melissa! The ones who are at school right now, with no idea what you've done to our family. They are going to hate you forever. You are never going to see them again."

Finally, "Tell that whore to get out of my house," she said. You could only rage for so long before you physically gave out. And this Garth did, he asked Lily to leave. But he walked her downstairs, and he gave her some money and asked their driver to take her to the train station. Tammy did not know this. The two may have even awkwardly touched hands. The driver told the helper who told her friends and so on. And Lily tried to speak to the driver on the way there, perhaps to get more information, or to gain an ally, but his English wasn't good and neither was hers, so they couldn't communicate well.

What happened after was good for nobody.

Garth had four children with these two women, and he couldn't give any of them up. Some of Tammy's closest friends swore up and down that if he had come back to her, begging forgiveness, promising to never see the other family again but only support the kids financially, she would have taken him back, but he couldn't leave two children, even if he was willing to leave the woman, which was unclear. So Garth was in a giant mess ("What was he thinking?" was the thrilled whisper heard around the American Club that spring). Tammy wrote an explosive e-mail, in which she luridly detailed all his transgressions with bizarre misspellings and breaks in logic, that she then forwarded to his boss, colleagues, and employees. As a result, he was told he should move to the Shenzhen office so he would not be a distraction to other employees of the toy-manufacturing-outsourcing company of which he was a vice president, and then one must assume that Lily got at least part of what she wanted—she got Garth all to herself—but in China, and not the Hong Kong apartment or residency or schooling she had so yearned for. Tammy had a nervous breakdown after the e-mail went viral, and she dropped out of sight for a few weeks. People said she went to rehab or an ashram or a yoga retreat, but no one really knew, and her best friend wasn't talking. The kids were in high school and middle school, and Tammy's mother came to take care of them for a while. Melissa, a tenth grader, started going out to bars in Wan Chai, and when people ran into her, she was with older men and reeked of smoke and worse. Mark's grades went off a cliff and never recovered. Collateral damage, the housewives said, all because of one man's penis.

When Tammy returned, she handled the divorce quickly and cleanly and then proceeded to get extremely fit. She ran like a maniac, did yoga almost daily, played tennis with even more vigor and enthusiasm, and lunched and dined with her friends frequently and publicly, as if she was showing the world that she would not be cowed by what had happened. She looked fantastic. Garth was no longer in Hong Kong, so people didn't have to make the choice between them, which was convenient. She lived her life as normally as she could until one day, in the middle of a match, she got frustrated when an opponent contested one too many points, and she threw her racket down on the court, got her gear, and disappeared for the second time.

Later she surfaced in Lantau. Perhaps the ashram's lessons had kicked in a little late, but they kicked in. Hong Kong was too small to ever disappear for long. Lantau was an island a ferry ride away, filled with expats who eschewed the materialistic, shiny world of the main island. It was grotty and small, and people kept beehives and made their own jam. And there she was, at IFC, on a trip to the mainland, as it were, smiling at Hilary and all but unrecognizable.

She was perfectly normal, asking how David was, saying that Melissa had just graduated from the University of Vermont and that Mark was operating a food truck in Portland. She seemed happy and asked after other women who had been on the tennis team with them. Hilary just couldn't get over how different she looked. They parted, professing intentions to e-mail, to call, to have lunch, both comfortable in the knowledge that none of those things would come to pass.

Hilary is a little bit older now, and she thinks that Tammy may have finally got it right. Who gives a damn? Just make yourself happy. She was a miserable person before all that happened, she really was, excluding people from committees and throwing cocktail parties to which a few people were never invited, and now she seemed happy. She didn't seem to work but lived simply. But who knows. She might be miserable and spend her evenings plotting revenge, but to Hilary's eye, she had made the best out of an impossible situation. Could you spend the rest of your life being angry? She supposed you could, but it was never good for you in the end. When everything you thought was yours was taken away, and the foundation of your life shifted so you have to start from zero, you might find out who you really are. You might come up against that dark, immovable wall of truth. And that is probably the most frightening thought of all.

Hilary shifts in her bed, takes a last gulp of her drink, looks over at the absent spot beside her, and thinks, where on earth is her husband?

Mercy

THIS IS WHAT she smells when she comes out of the bathroom from her shower: a thousand stale exhales, humid with alcohol and cigarette smoke. This is what she sees: the man in her bed, his bottom half covered by the sheet, snoring. She sits down in her chair, wrapped in her towel, wondering what to do next.

It happened so quickly. She went home from the hotel and showered and took a nap. When she woke, at ten, she wanted to go out for something to eat, and something had pulled her to Il Dolce, the mere utterance of the name several hours ago suggestion enough. Maybe something might happen. She was talking to Richard, the bartender, on her second glass of sauvignon blanc when he walked in, the man from the afternoon at the hotel bar. David. The night accelerated into strobe lights and chaos. From bar to restaurant to club, he shouted his life story at her: a wife, no child, an orphan (she couldn't remember whether he was an orphan or there was one in his life), disappointment, no solace at home. Then to her house. Messy coupling, not finished, dizziness, spinning ceiling. She looks at the sleeping man: this new and different animal, older, married, complicated. Different from the pale, anomic twenty-somethings who usually inhabit that space.

Her phone buzzes. Her mother is texting her: "What r u doing?"

"Getting ready for work," she writes back quickly. "Text later, already late." It's Saturday, but her mother doesn't know her work schedule, or even what she does exactly. The best thing about texting is that it makes phone calls obsolete. She doesn't need to worry about her voice quavering or her eyes tearing up on Skype. She hasn't had to talk to her mother in months—all communication is through texts.

Her mother doesn't know about what happened, about the incident. Her mother doesn't know, and her father is a bastard. She wishes she could tell her mother what happened. But she is afraid of making the fortune come true. By acknowledging what happened, by articulating it to the universe, sounds, words that can never be called back, it will become reality. She is indeed the unluckiest girl in the world. How will her mother react, to find that what she feared most has manifested itself? She can imagine the sharp intake of breath, the quick silence afterward while her mother tries to conceive of how she might best help her child. Because that's what mothers do—they protect their children, no matter what. Mercy knows that in the matter of mothers, she has been blessed. Her mother, unhappy, still loves her daughter.

Of course, Mercy might be surprised. Her mother has always told her that Koreans are a hardy people, that what she and her family survived, with the war in Korea and then immigrating to a country where they didn't speak the language, Mercy would never understand. "You think your life difficult," she says. "You don't know. In Korea, our lives so hard." But this is not a high school misunderstanding or a lack of a job. There has been a disappearance, a crime, probably a death. There was *fault*.

Mercy hadn't known those Reade kids very long, but they had liked her, and she had liked them. When she had gone out to where they lived, she had been amazed. They lived on the South Side, an area you got to by going through the Aberdeen tunnel, through a mountain basically. When you emerged, it was all sea and sky and rich suburb. She had passed by there before, on trips to Stanley or to Shek O Beach, but she had never gone into a high-rise with glossy marble floors and doormen and lobbies and gyms with gleaming new equipment. They had playrooms with colorful padded walls and what seemed like hundreds of toys, as well as a sparkling blue swimming pool outside with fancy deck chairs. Mercy grew up in a tiny two-room apartment in Queens, and she still remembered the day in elementary school when she realized that sometimes a family lived in an entire house. That not everyone lived in a room with a hot plate and Korean blankets on the floor.

Still, the Reade children were lovely. Not spoiled or entitled at all. She had an easy rapport with them. Daisy looked up to her. (She was too young to know otherwise, the way you idolize your high school teachers when you're young and sometimes, when you come back for reunions, you realize a few are drunks or so very sad.) Philip liked how she was amenable to everything he wanted to do, and G, well, G was just the most scrumptious boy, a little love of a child. She was never one of those people who adored kids—she had babysat at Korean church gatherings and viewed children as cattle to be herded, mostly—but G was so sweet, slipping his hand unexpectedly into hers a mere five minutes after she arrived at their house the first time. There was no guile or fear in him. He expected to be loved, because that was all he had ever known.

And now he is somewhere she cannot imagine. That is, if he is not dead in a ditch somewhere. The fact that it was both her and Margaret watching the kids gives her a little bit of comfort. Except that Margaret went to the bathroom, implicitly giving her all the responsibility in that situation. And she was watching all of them— really she was! G was out of sight for five seconds, maybe ten, when Margaret came out, wiping her hands on her pants and asking where her child was.

She tries not to think about that day, she really does. She doesn't see how it will help her. It is, indisputably, her fault. That much is clear. But it's also indisputably just shit bad luck. She remembers trying to disappear, not knowing where to go. She couldn't help, couldn't speak Korean, couldn't do anything except be the villain. At the police station, each new officer arriving to speak with her had a rebuke on his face, not only for her crime but for the fact that she couldn't speak

Korean—a useless girl. She was a disgrace to her country, and a care-less girl who brought disaster to those around her. She answered all the questions for the report, and when it became clear that she could go home, she didn't know what to do. Out of the question to return with the Reades—a more terrible situation she could not imagine. So she got a taxi to the hotel, getting there ahead of the Reades, stuffed all her clothes in her bag, and then asked the concierge for a recommendation for a cheap hotel. She was directed down the street to a *yogwan*, a local inn, where for fifty dollars she got a room not much bigger than the length of her and a bundle of thick, colorful blankets to be spread on the floor as a bed. Every Korean family had a set of these blankets, and after she spread them out, she lay there, cold, feeling a scratchy, un-clean blanket over her, wondering what on earth she was going to do now. Every time she blinked, she prayed that she would wake up from the nightmare she was in, and every time she opened her eyes, the hor-ror remained the same. The homeliness of the room seemed just right. A person like her should never enjoy anything nice again. The enor-mity of her guilt and her pain and the awfulness loomed so large it blocked out everything in her mind, so that all she could do was think about breathing another breath.

There was an old vacuum flask in the room, so she went down-stairs and filled it from the hot water pot in the lobby, just to have something to do, just to feel something. She was grateful for the sim-ple gesture the woman in the lobby made, helping her to work the lever. This is a person, she thought, who doesn't know what I've just done. The woman's nod and smile were like a salve to Mercy, who didn't expect kindness from anyone ever again after what had hap-pened. She sipped the hot water, felt its warmth trickle down her throat, shivered, and wondered if she'd ever feel warm again.

Somehow, at some point that night, she fell asleep. When she woke, she felt fine for a few seconds, and then the memory of the day before came roaring back. She washed up and tried to figure out what to do next. If she returned to Hong Kong, would it seem as if she were running away, and a fugitive? She had to stay. She also had to let the Reades know where she was in case they needed something else from her. Finally, she went downstairs, borrowed paper from the desk clerk, and wrote a note saying that she was at the *yogwan* and for them to call her if they needed anything. Then she walked to the hotel and dropped it off at the front desk.

She never heard from them, and she spent three days waiting before she paid her bill and took the bus to the airport. She left them another note, saying she was leaving, and sat, dry-eyed, for the entire three-and-a-half-hour flight home. She still hadn't cried. She hadn't been able to eat for three days, drinking only the hot water from that flask, and she felt empty. She soon became used to that feeling.

That was about a year ago, give or take. She was never able to tell her mother, and her friends found out through reading about the incident in the paper and putting two and two together. They e-mailed or called and came to sit with her. Most were ham-handed, only muttering inanities like "That's so intense" or "Wow" until she wanted to beat at them with her fists. A few thoughtful ones brought food so she could eat. From these friends, she felt only their acute sense of relief that such a thing had not happened to them, that they were only the cars cruising by and seeing the pileup on the highway. She imagined what they said to one another afterward, how they talked about her, until she couldn't bear it and stopped answering people's e-mails. Then she started combing through magazines and the Internet for stories like hers, and what happened to the person who didn't *commit* the crime—that wasn't her—but was somehow responsible for it happening. To wit: the drunk-driver man, the chimp owner. These shadowy persons, she came to find, were never there. They were erased from the story as if they had never existed. They were inconvenient and culpable, and no one wanted to hear about them.

So it's come to this moment, when she's sitting here in her chair, damp from the shower, looking at a man in her bed, a married man she first laid eyes on a mere twenty-four hours ago. And there's this feeling she has, this good, tingly feeling, that this is her first step out of this netherworld, that this might be forward motion. She doesn't know how or why, but it's the first good feeling she's had in months, so she's going to hold on to it.

The man on the bed stirs.

Let it not be like a bad movie, she prays, where the man groans and rubs his head and asks where he is and is ashamed and wants to leave and it's so awkward.

Instead, he lies very still after his initial entry into consciousness, like a cornered animal, thinking what to do next while being watched by his predator. Then, wonderfully, magically, he sits up without embarrassment, naked, shaking off any vulnerability he might have had when he first woke, and looks straight at the young girl, sitting on the one other piece of furniture that can be squeezed into the room, arms wrapped around her legs, staring at him.

"Good morning," he says genially. "What's for breakfast?"

Margaret

THE FAME. That had been unexpected. Fame, infamy, whatever you called it. The police had said that publicity was good, and so she had allowed herself to be photographed, she had agreed to news conferences, she had stood up and pleaded for her child to be returned to her, with a Korean translator by her side. She and Clarke had been on all the local and news channels, the local ones making much of the fact that she was a quarter Korean, although she had never felt more foreign, and that Clarke was a Yale graduate, because Koreans loved brand names. For a few days, every newspaper, every news broadcast, had mentioned their story, which was what they wanted, with the photo of G plastered everywhere. There had been articles bemoaning the breakdown of Korean society and the rise of crime and all that was wrong with the modern world.

The abduction had also made the news in Hong Kong, because of their Hong Kong residency. But later, when it had all quieted down, the unwelcome development was that she was now known in Hong Kong, recognized, when she went to the supermarket to buy bananas, or to town for a doctor's appointment. People, mostly women, stared at her for a beat too long, or nudged each other surreptitiously when they saw her. She supposes it is a little bit like being a celebrity, when so many people know you and you don't know them at all.

At dinner parties, mostly, people were prepped in advance, she assumes. This happened to Margaret, they were told, so best not to talk about certain subjects, like children, or traveling to Korea. But it was amazing what people said nonetheless. A woman she knew only slightly tried to be provocative and knowledgeable and said it was great that the case got so much attention, and that it was probably because she and Clarke were so photogenic. Margaret stared at her and wondered why she always had to be the bigger person. She wanted to scream at the stupid cow and tell her to shut her fucking mouth forever, but she just nodded, and then she got up and walked away. Later the woman said to other people that it was understandable, of course, but Margaret Reade had become so uncommunicative that it was hard to get through. The number of people walking through life with sub-par emotional intelligence was incredible.

She knows what it's like to be them, though, to have tragedy slip by your door so closely you can feel its chill. She *was* them before. A child drowned at a birthday party, a raging bacterial infection that could not be checked—tales told in whispers in case saying them too loudly would summon misfortune to your doorstep. These things happened, and people knew, and people went on living, because what choice did they have?

She has woken up early today, as she usually does, to a still house. The dinner party last night was fine, no one too obtrusive or obnoxious, but at one point she caught Clarke's eye and they smiled at each other, chagrin-filled smiles, as if to say, here we are. She was seated next to Hilary's husband, David, who was drunk at the beginning of the party and got progressively worse. He was drinking whiskey when everyone else was sipping wine. Hilary ignored him; everyone ignored him. Then he disappeared at the end of the night, saying he had an appointment. Poor Hilary. Margaret hadn't known that Hilary's marriage had gotten to that stage. Last she knew, they were thinking about having kids, and having some difficulty, but she hadn't really heard anything more.

It's good to go out sometimes, good to go out and interact with new, different people. Someone once told her that if you keep pretending it's normal, it'll become normal at some point and you won't even notice when it happens. She's still waiting.

But now they've come home and gone to bed, and now there goes the blare of her alarm clock. It's been over a year since G disappeared, and Clarke had brought up the idea gingerly: what to do for winter break, do you think we should go away, the kids could really do with a holiday.

Tickets to the tropical Thai island of Phuket have been bought, a beachside hotel has been booked, a connecting door for the two rooms an absolute must. Because that's what normal families do, she supplies in her mind. They go on vacation. Because it has been so long, because there is nothing left to do that she can think of, because she is worried about how much time Daisy spends in her room, because staying in a quiet town over Christmas seems terrifying, because her therapist says she needs to metabolize the grief and try to live life.

She goes downstairs and checks on the children. They are still sleeping, and their suitcases are lying open, mostly packed but still needing the last-minute things: the toothbrushes, the toiletry kits. She hovers over them, watching their breath coming in and out in small bursts, their small faces at peace. Philip still shares a room with G's bed, empty for a year now.

She has packed her and Clarke's bag already. Packing for hot places is easy: swimsuits, flip-flops, shorts, all taking up barely any space. Back in her bedroom, she adds sunscreen, a camera, to the bag. Clarke is starting to stir. She goes in to take a shower. The house starts to move: She hears Essie start the coffee machine, Philip going to the bathroom.

Margaret's frighteningly efficient travel agent, Rosalie Chan, arranged this vacation. She is the type who, if she asked a question on e-mail and did not get a response within three hours, would keep e-mailing, asking if you had gotten her e-mail. She constantly scours her computer system for cheaper fares for her clients and books one type of ticket as a placeholder before exchanging it for a cheaper one, ad infinitum until the ticketing deadline. She is efficiency and diligence personified. Margaret, used to more desultory service types, marvels at her energy. She met her only once, years ago, in her rickety office building in Central on Wyndham Street, and it was awkward and strange, and they mutually implicitly agreed to continue only on e-mail. They have a sort of magic rapport online and none in real life.

Rosalie had, of course, asked some unanswerable questions when Margaret told her to look into a Christmas break in the Philippines or Thailand. What room configuration? What activities? She had just found a business-class seat to Phuket that was just a hundred dollars more than coach; did she want it for herself and Clarke and they could put the kids in coach? Of course, when she sent the itinerary through, G was on it, because how could she have known? And Margaret, of course, didn't take his name off—how much could she be expected to bear?—and when they get to the airport, there is his name, and the Cathay Pacific check-in attendant is asking where is G, and Clarke is staring at her but not saying anything because, of course, he understands.

What she can't stand, also, is how many "of courses" there are in her life. The sympathetic women murmuring "of course" all the time. How do you tell your travel agent that you lost your child, literally lost him, more than a year ago, and that now you're going on vacation? Of course, it's impossible.

The check-in woman tries to say their seats are canceled because G is not there and they are on a special group ticket—another side effect of Rosalie's superb efficiency in getting them the best tickets for the cheapest prices is that they are usually immutable in their classification and resistant to any sort of change in plans or attempts at spontaneity. Somewhat like Rosalie herself, Margaret has thought on more than one occasion. Clarke sorts it out by raising his voice and demanding to see the manager—typically American behavior, which is amplified in an unusually distasteful way in Asia. When he does this, when *she* does this, to be really honest with herself, the usually dormant 25 percent of herself that is Korean raises its head and asks why a big, rich white man is shouting at a poor, small Asian person.

Clarke waves at her to get the kids away so they don't have to listen to their father angrily explain their situation to yet another person. The manager, a thin young man in his thirties, listens, bewildered, to the insane story he is being told.

They sit on the bench and wait for it to get sorted. Airports must get this all the time, she thinks. Like hotels or other clearing spaces, there must be tragedies and romances and happy endings every single day. Criminals on the lam, boys pursuing girls, families separated and reunited. The departure halls and detention rooms must be filled with tragic stories, the arrivals lounge with unbelievable happiness.

The boarding passes get issued finally, and they go through immigration, but Clarke is still fuming. In all fairness, he probably is angry at her but had to take it out on the airline clerk because he can't yell at Margaret. Later in the lounge, where they go because Clarke travels so much he's a VIP, he sits next to her and says, "Margaret, I understand why you did it, but come on! That was so much worse than it needed to be. Daisy and Philip are upset now."

And they are. Daisy's reading on her Kindle, and Philip is playing his DS, but their faces are tight and withdrawn.

"I'm sorry," she says. Because that's all she can say. She can't say it won't happen again or anything that will help the situation. She can just express her feelings of empathy for what her husband is feeling. Clarke sighs and heads over to the noodle bar to get a bowl for a late breakfast.

After the short flight, they are greeted in arrivals by a smiling young man holding a wooden sign with their name in one hand and a tray of cold, damp towels in another. Escorted to the car and offered water, they settle in and set off for the hotel. They have been to Phuket once before. It was their first vacation after they moved to Hong Kong three years ago. Margaret once heard a woman deride the island as the "expat starter vacation." They stayed at an American chain hotel on the beach. This time, they are staying at a French chain hotel on the beach. She didn't want to go to the same hotel.

"There is no way forward in these countries," Clarke says, looking at all the young men sitting outside. "What are they going to do with their lives?" Margaret looks at the people talking, drinking beer, some animated, some resigned, and thinks, This is life. These people are living. They are not waiting. But, of course, some of them must be. Just as they cannot see her and what she is doing, how she is not living.

She shakes it off.

In a bright voice, she says, "No matter how many times it happens, I can't believe that we can be in one place in the morning and then in another country in a few hours. And they speak a different language and eat different food. Isn't it amazing, guys?"

Daisy nods, still reading her Kindle. Philip is looking out at the streets.

"Do you think we can surf?" he asks his father. "I want to try surfing."

"Sure," Clarke says. "I'll try it with you."

"What do you want to do, Daisy girl?" Her mother ruffles her hair.

"Maybe snorkeling?"

"Let's see."

They arrive at an enormous thatched-roof lobby, then are brought into a reception area overlooking a wide reflecting pool filled with lotus flowers. They can hear the sea and smell the humid tropical air. They are seated on red Thai silk sofas and given a fruity drink and more hand towels while Clarke registers at the front desk. The first time they did this, Philip put his feet up and said with satisfaction, "This is the life!" and they laughed, and then G did it and they laughed again. Clarke looked on with pride, seeing the life he had provided for his family: Thailand! And in such style! Margaret thinks, she will not do this for the whole trip. She will not think of the last time they were here and when G was here.

They go to their rooms and get their luggage, unpack, and change.

This is when she really feels like she's on vacation: when she changes into a sundress and applies sunscreen to her kids' faces. It's so visceral:

the smell of coconut sunblock and the feel of the white lotion, the light cotton of your dress on your pale body.

She unpacks the children's clothes and puts them away, finds their toothbrushes, stands them up in a cup in the bathroom.

Is the change from three to two that different? There's that funny equation that people talk about when they're having children. The first is the hardest. The second is hard because it impacts the first so much. Then some say you don't even notice the third. Others say you're going from man-to-man to zone defense, that funny football analogy. But what is the reverse? Going from three to two means it's simpler in terms of management. Two parents, two kids. Two girls, two boys. Simple. With a ghost in between.

They leave their room and walk down to the pool. The paths are wide and paved, and they pass housekeeping golf carts and smiling employees who greet them in the traditional Thai way, palms pressed together as if in prayer, murmuring, "*Sawadee ka.*" Large palm trees sway overhead, providing shade. There's that disorientation that happens the first day in any resort—not knowing how to get from your room to the breakfast restaurant, to the pool, to the health club. By the end of the vacation, everyone is at home, familiar with the layout, just before they have to leave.

By the pool, they acquire loungers, towels, cold drinks. Margaret sits under an umbrella someone has set up perfectly so she is in the shade, sipping an iced tea, with a hat and dark sunglasses, the very picture of relaxation. But this is what she is actually doing, if anyone looks carefully: She is closing her eyes, trying to conjure up a picture of G. It is so difficult. She is getting panicked, heart racing, that his picture won't pop up when summoned. It is so hard now to get a visual of him. She has a picture of him in her bag, but she doesn't want to cheat. So she lies there, eyes fluttering, finding it harder and harder to breathe, feeling this sick sense that she is losing him all over again.

How can she not picture her child on command? So then she tries to picture Clarke and Daisy, and Philip. She is relieved to find they don't spring instantly into focus either. So then she tries to think of a photograph, and then she can imagine all their faces. So this is how it starts. You remember the child. Then you remember the photograph. What comes next? These generations of memories. They fade.

Her children step carefully, lightly, into the pool, as if they know how fragile everything is, and of course they do.

~

It was hard, almost impossible, to know when to leave Seoul. In the beginning, they thought they would stay until they found him, because what was the alternative? And then, when days turned into weeks and weeks turned into a month, she started worrying about Daisy and Philip, how they were just sitting in a hotel room. Her mother came over, and their extended family in Seoul had been wonderful. Once they found out what happened, they came to the hotel every day with expensive melons and chocolates and offered to take Daisy and Philip out so they wouldn't be bored, although it made her too nervous when the children were out without her. So sometimes they would just take them to their homes, but communication was difficult, and the children were frightened. But she knew she couldn't lock them in a hotel room forever. She tried to get the international school in Seoul to let them go to classes, but although they were sympathetic, they were unwilling to admit her children for an unknown amount of time.

"It would be very disruptive to our community," said the administrator, "and of limited use to your own children."

In this new world, everything was so raw, so blinding. The first time she took a shower, her mother forcing her, she soaped her skin and told herself, G is gone, G is gone. She washed her greasy hair, fingers slipping over her roots, and thought, G is not here, he will not be here when I emerge from the bathroom. She put on new clothes, realizing, I don't know where G is, and I don't know when I'll know. Everything looked new and meaningless. She looked out the window of her hotel room and saw a beautiful moon against the dark buildings and wondered if she would ever find any pleasure in anything ever again.

In the meantime, she started working on a comprehensive description of what G had been wearing that day. It had been unseasonably warm, and he had on warm-weather clothes. What drove her nuts was that she knew the T-shirt and the shoes but she didn't know which exact shorts he had been wearing. He had a few pairs that were very similar. He had two pairs of elastic-waist khaki pants and a pair from Target that had a button. He liked the elastic-waist pants more, because his little fingers were not yet very dexterous. His fine motor skills were not very good, and she had been told to let him play with pens and chopsticks to strengthen his hands. She didn't know which ones he was wearing, because she couldn't remember which ones she had packed. She wanted to call and ask Essie what was at home, but imagining the conversation exhausted her. She knew the T-shirt. It was yellow, long-sleeved, with the faded image of a green dinosaur eating leaves off a tree with I'M A VEGETARIAN on top in green letters. He had loved it, wearing it whenever he could. The shoes were velcro Weebok sandals she had bought online, and they were no longer available. She had printed out a picture of them from the website, with the "No longer in stock" message, because she wanted an image of them. Because this is what she can do. She can write things down or print things out so she has a record. She can make lists of what is missing. She can do these things so she doesn't have to think of what she cannot do.

She then became seized by the idea of getting a duplicate outfit, so she scoured eBay and found the T-shirt, used, for $3.99 (although it was a 5T, not a 4T). Then she paid $35 in shipping to get it to Korea. She brought it to the police station in triumph.

"This is the T-shirt he was wearing," she told Mr. Park, the sergeant who had been appointed to be her point person. He carefully took a photo and said he would add it to the file. She asked whether it would be helpful if she found the shoes he was wearing at the time, and Mr. Park looked at her sympathetically and shook his head no. The T-shirt was enough.

She had already given them the photo of her extended family at the restaurant earlier that day, but G was on the periphery and barely visible, even when she blew up that part of the picture. She became obsessed with the fact that she hadn't taken any photos of the kids later in the day, and her with an eight-megapixel camera on her phone! Perhaps if they had had an accurate photo of what G looked like on the day he disappeared and they had released it to the public quickly, someone might have recognized him. And then she wanted to document Daisy and Philip, but she wanted to do it without frightening them. She knew if she told Clarke, he would discourage her, so one night, before they got in the shower, she asked them if she could take photographs of them.

They submitted in a way that frightened her. They didn't want to, but they did, because they knew it was important to her and that it would be futile to say no. They seemed a little bit like abused children. She was causing them more trauma.

But. She couldn't help herself. So, a catalogue of moles.

She had been thinking about if she found G two or three years later and he had changed a lot. What if she was unable to know for certain if it was him? Yes, of course, DNA, but in the immediate sense, the first moment when they showed him to her. She wanted to know right away. Children change so much. How to be sure? She came up with this. A mole catalogue.

She stood Daisy and Philip in the bathroom in their underwear and took photographs of their arms, their inner thighs, anywhere they had a birthmark or irregularity or mole. And then she labeled and filed them on the computer she had had Essie send to Seoul. Daisy had a large mole on her left inner thigh, and two close to one another on her right back shoulder. Philip had a scattering of them on his right arm, above his elbow. He had a scar above his right eyebrow. She had the photos on her computer, backed up, and in hard copies.

Of course, the ones she needed, she didn't have. She couldn't remember the details of G's body. He must have had moles, but who
noticed those kinds of things on a third child? She pored over old photos on her computer, trying to see what spots he had on his face, things
that would not change even after years and years. But everything
seemed so mutable, so temporary: eyebrows, hair, even the shape of his
face. He could get fat, he could be unrecognizably skinny, depending
on what type of environment he was in. He might be with a family
who had just wanted a child and got him off the black market and
spoiled him rotten. Or he might be in some terrible place, a surly street
urchin or worse. She can only bring herself to read snippets of what
happens to children who disappear, glancing off the terrible surface of
what might be. Her therapist tells her to stop thinking about it.

But sometimes she'll read in the paper that in China and India,
children are kidnapped and maimed so that they become more compelling and effective beggars. In other countries, kids are taken for
their organs, but those are usually the older ones, older than G. There's
the sex trade, of course. This is what she has to digest. G, her one-
eighth Asian child, who actually could pass for Asian. They would
never have taken light-haired Daisy, who looks white. Too much trouble, a foreigner's child, too much media attention, potential for international conflict. But Daisy and Philip look white. G looks Asian.
Only G had that one recessive gene pushed to the fore, that stubborn
Asian DNA strand that burst when he was made, so that while he's
recognizable as her child—only one person has ever asked her if he's
adopted—he looks quite recognizably Asian. So he has dissolved into
the fifty million other Korean people on the peninsula.

After she photographed Daisy and Philip and they went to bed,
quiet and submissive, she realized that she was damaging them further and they needed more normalcy. She booked a flight for them
to go back to Hong Kong the next day with her mother so they could
go back to school. She and Clarke stayed on.

That was when she weaned herself off the anxiety medication. The

Korean doctors had been liberal with prescriptions, but she wanted to stay sharp, be ready for whatever came her way. She only took an Ambien when it was two in the morning and she couldn't stand it anymore.

Then, after six weeks, Clarke went back to work. She couldn't believe it, but he said, "You'll be here. I'm not doing anything that you can't do. And we need to see our other children. Make sure they have a parent there, even though your mother's there. They are suffering as well."

And he left her, fuming, in the hotel room. What was it about men? They didn't feel things the same way. How could he leave the country where his child was lost? Now the person she saw the most in the world was Mr. Park, a gentle man with glasses who handled her with extreme delicacy.

She remembered sitting with him in the police station, as she did almost every day. It was getting cold, November, December, and the building was not well heated. He apologized for the temperature and said the government saved money on heating.

"At home," he said, "we have the floor heating, the *ondol*. It is very effective, and we eat and sleep close to the ground."

She wondered what he went home to every night, whom he lived with, if he had children. She asked him once about his family, and he told her in a way that indicated he was making a sacrifice by telling her, so she didn't delve into the personal again.

They shared coffee every day. Once, sick of the terrible brew they had at the station, she made an impulsive purchase at Hyundai Department Store on the way to the station. When she came in bearing the espresso machine, the policemen were struck dumb and then all in unison said they could not accept the present, government regulations and all. She insisted, said it was for her as well, as she was there every day, and then she set it up and made everyone a cup, foaming the milk she had brought and stirring it into paper cups. She and the policemen sipped the good coffee together in silence, each lost in his own thoughts.

The police were very polite and concerned but completely ineffective. She didn't go ballistic on them, because she didn't think it would help her or G. But it was incredibly frustrating. Every day brought new leads: phone calls, e-mails from people who thought they'd seen G. But they never led anywhere. Seoul was blanketed with closed-circuit televisions, but there was a blind spot where they had been, and when they studied the adjoining ones, they couldn't see G anywhere. One store's camera had been broken for a week and was getting fixed that day, so the whole system had been down. This is the direction where they thought G must have been taken. They told her of another case where a boy had been taken and they had been able to trace his path with different security cameras. It had taken them a few weeks, but they had traced him to a village an hour outside Seoul, reachable by bus, where a mentally disturbed woman had taken him as her child. He had been shaken but healthy when they found him. She had treated him well, he said, but had insisted that she was his mother. He was seven years old, so he knew it wasn't true but was frightened of challenging her, so he had played along and stayed with her in her house, afraid, but even more afraid of what lay outside.

The police were very proud of this case, but it didn't seem that they were having the same luck with her child. They apprised her of all their work, but nothing ever panned out.

Clarke flew back every ten days or so, but there was never any progress to show him. He brought the kids with him the first few times, but they got upset when they had to leave her, so they decided it was better to let them stay in Hong Kong.

After three months, he took her by the hand while they were eating dinner at the hotel. "Come back home," he said. "We have to live our lives. We can return whenever they find something. We can't destroy four more lives. Philip and Daisy deserve a chance."

She felt a white-hot hatred for him then that swept through her so violently she felt it physically. She snatched her hand back and didn't speak to him for the rest of the night. He left the next morning in silence.

In Korea by herself, Margaret got into a rhythm. She'd wake up in the morning around six and go to the hotel gym for an hour.

She'd run on the treadmill, watching the television. She got to know the other regulars at the health club, as many locals used the hotel facilities as their gym. An old white-haired man stretched with his young trainer every morning, a few businessmen in their forties, a few pretty young housewives. They nodded to each other in the morning. Afterward she went upstairs and showered and put on comfortable clothes to go to the police station. She walked over—it took about fifteen minutes—and checked in with the police. Initially they had asked her to stay at the hotel and they would contact her with any leads, but she had been politely persistent, and now they let her stay around the police station with her laptop and access the Wi-Fi. How could they say no to someone like her? It was sterile, with white linoleum floors and fluorescent lights and that peculiar Korean smell she now recognized, from the accumulated smell of a thousand bygone boxed lunches. It was comforting to her now.

She would ask for any updates. They would show her a few badly translated e-mails or phone messages that had come in during her absence—"I know kidnapped child in Suwon!"—and say they were following up. That she was allowed to stay was against all protocol, but they found a way as long as she didn't ask too many questions or interfere with their work. They knew it was hard for her to stay at the hotel.

Lunch was at one of the many small restaurants in the neighborhood. She learned that one o'clock was the regular lunch hour, so she went at noon so there was no wait. She ate *ddukbokki*, *bibimbap*, *naengmyun*, trying all the different foods by pointing to the menu pictures and what other people were having. She felt as if she were connecting to her Korean roots a little bit, having a tiny taste of what it must be like to live in Korea and be Korean. She ate salted sprouts brushed with sesame oil, cold marinated crab—although she got food poisoning so bad she thought she might die later that day, lying on her bathroom floor—the gelatin-like *mook*, the *kkagduki* kimchi, the endless warm soups. She came to crave room-temperature barley tea with her food. It helped her digestion and soothed her stomach.

After lunch she would go back to the police station for a few hours. Around four, she would head back to the hotel and do laps in the pool. It was important to be physically active so that she could sleep at night. She usually ate dinner at the hotel, where all the staff knew her by now, watched TV, answered e-mails, and surfed the Internet, and was usually in bed by ten. Her life shrank down and became ascetic, which meant that she felt like she was focusing all her energies on finding G.

But he remained lost. The police shook their heads and complained about the dissolution of Korean society.

"Before," Mr. Park said, "it was a good society. But now too much money and the Western values have come, and the children want to eat hamburger, and the adults only interest themselves. They don't care for the other people." He told her amazing stories: of people who were sick of taking care of their elderly parents with dementia and drove them out to the countryside and abandoned them, knowing they could never find their way back; of young parents neglecting their baby to go play a computer game in which they nourished a virtual child, only to come back to their apartment to find that their actual child had starved to death. "This society is no good now," he told her. He recommended that she watch Korean television dramas. They were very popular around the world, and she could begin to understand the problems of modern Korea. He gave her the names of a few and also where she could download them. He highly recommended one drama in particular and underlined it, with exclamation points surrounding it.

She started watching and, despite the melodramatic acting and bad lighting, found herself quickly sucked in. *Winter Sonata* was the story of a young man in search of his father who falls in love with a girl in a small town. The girls in the show were always running after buses and scolding their love interests in a coy, flirtatious way, and the men were unnecessarily brooding, but there was something viscerally compelling about the people and their interactions. She watched episode after episode in a trance. She downloaded the entire series onto the Korean smartphone she had bought and watched it at the police station, on the subway, at the gym. Even now, whenever she hears the piano music of the opening credits of the series, she is transported back to those months in Seoul, cold mornings on the subway, the intense monotony of those days, the sick feeling she had the whole time.

Her mother found her a shrink from San Francisco she could talk to on Skype. Dr. Stein and Clarke seemed to be on a team, trying to get her to move forward, but she couldn't. She didn't tell them about the hours she spent on eBay, trying to find the sandals G had been wearing. This mindless searching for an artifact that was without value to anyone else was what made the hours go by as she sat in her hotel room at night, searching the Internet for anything that might help her find her child. She regretted not learning Korean, regretted that the most important parts of the Internet were off-limits to her. Koreans were the most plugged-in society in the world, and they had many, many more forums like the ones she read in English about missing children. They were the relevant ones, but she was stuck reading about missing children in Maryland or California when her child was missing on another continent.

She checked in with the embassy once a week, talking with a nice woman, Gerry, from Atlanta, a divorcee with two children, who tried to be helpful. Gerry moved every two or three years for her job with the State Department and had lived in Morocco and Shanghai as well. Gerry invited her over for dinner one weekend night, and Margaret went, because she couldn't stand another night in the hotel room watching television and scouring the Internet forums or eBay. Gerry lived in an old neighborhood, a far cry from the windowed skyscrapers of downtown, where Margaret was. Gerry's apartment was one of four in a two-story house, and spacious. But when you stepped inside, it was like stepping back into America. Everything was from the United States, courtesy of the State Department courier, which shipped things for free regardless of size or weight. Whereas most people who lived overseas had local-brand strollers or televisions, Gerry had everything straight from Amazon. It was the oddest experience, having dinner in a house in Seoul and being served Crystal Light and Duncan Hines chocolate cake, as if they were sitting in Atlanta, two miles from Target.

"People expect me to be so international," Gerry said, "but to be honest, I get so homesick, I just want American stuff around me."

She was not in touch with her ex-husband, and he didn't keep up with the kids or pay child support.

"I'm here, carting his children around the world, and he has e-mailed me twice in two years," she said. "You'd think he'd care a little more."

She was abashed, then, remembering why Margaret was in Seoul, and tried to apologize.

"No need," Margaret said. "It's just nice to have a normal conversation sometimes." And it was. This was her odd, staccato life in Seoul—the weird, empty evenings, the blank spaces—while she was waiting, waiting.

Korea turned cold in the winter, a vicious cold she had never before encountered. The wind sliced against her face and went into her bones, even as she bundled up in a newly bought winter coat, scarf, hat. She bought wool long johns and undershirts. She thought of G in his T-shirt and shorts, and her blood froze inside her.

This was when she developed a taste for being alone. She could glimpse her life as it might have been, if she had not married, if she had not had children, if she had been an entirely different person. She could see how your life came together, how you cobbled a life out of moments and routines. She started eating the same lunch at the same restaurant, a beef broth with a bowl of rice and a cup of barley tea. She ran five miles every morning. She watched television alone at night. She could see doing this for a long time. And that was when she decided she had to go home.

There were Daisy and Philip. They cried when they Skyped on the computer. They stopped short of pleading with her to come back to Hong Kong but wondered aloud when G would be found, when they would come home together. They told her about their days at school, the projects they were doing, the sports they were playing. She had two children trying to live a life in Hong Kong, and she was in Seoul, Korea, searching for a child who had disappeared. She was doing nothing in Korea. All the leads had dried up. The media were no longer interested in her story. She was like a hamster on a wheel, running, running, running, with no end in sight.

So she took a flight home one cold January day, having the concierge book her the ticket, because she didn't want to talk to Rosalie, the travel agent, telling the police she'd be back every two weeks, and making them promise to e-mail her every day (which they did, religiously, and if they didn't, she'd e-mail them until they replied), and then she went home, without G, something she had sworn she would never do, something that had been unimaginable five short months ago. She sat on the plane for the four-hour flight, alone, and ate the chicken and drank ginger ale and felt her eyes dry out in the airless cabin.

She hadn't told the children or Clarke she was coming, so she came inside the house, strangely the same after all this time away, saw Essie, who started weeping the moment she opened the door for her, left her suitcase on the floor in the hall, and went upstairs to see her children: Daisy getting ready to go to soccer, Philip doing homework. They saw her and ran up to her, and she hugged them as they clung to her side. She dug her fingers into their hair as if to anchor herself. They didn't ask about G; they didn't want to hear the answer. She didn't have an answer to give them. She didn't even know what the question would be. So she did the only thing she could. She just wrapped her arms around the children she had, pulling them toward her with as much strength as she could muster, and tried to feel as happy as she could to be back home with them.

And time keeps flowing. Here she is, in Phuket, Thailand, on Christmas vacation about a year after her baby disappeared, sitting by the pool. Here she is, reapplying sunscreen on her daughter's face and reading a magazine in a beach chair. This is what she has learned in the past year: You go through the motions of life until, slowly, they start to resemble a life.

Hilary

SHE WAKES UP with knives in her throat, hot with fever. Pops three Advils, boils water, adds salt and cold water, gargles, staggering from bed to kitchen to bathroom to achieve all this, while Puri stands there as still as an Easter Island statue, staring at her employer, completely useless. It hurts to speak, so she doesn't. Finally Hilary lies down in her bed, towel under her head for the sweat.

That's when she notices that her husband is still not home. And then she remembers that her mother is arriving today at 11:00 a.m.

She texts Sam the flight details and tells him to pick up her mother at the airport. Then types out an e-mail to her mom, explaining that she's sick and won't be able to go to the airport to pick her up. Then she realizes that Sam and her mother have very little chance of recognizing each other and, groaning, gets up and finds a piece of paper that Sam can use as a sign and writes MRS. MARJORIE KRALL. She's writing with a regular pen, and it's not dark enough. Cursing, she goes downstairs to find a Sharpie. Then she rewrites MRS. MARJORIE KRALL in thick black strokes and hands it to Puri to give to Sam when he gets in.

"I'm sick," she says, in case Puri has missed this fact. "I'm going to sleep. Please answer the phone and the door and don't get me. And please bring me up a pitcher of water and a glass."

She goes upstairs and falls into a deep, dreamless sleep.

When she wakes up, she is surprised at how quiet the house is. Usually Puri is wrestling with the vacuum in some corner of the house or listening to tinny music through earphones. It's past ten, and she feels much better, the Advils having kicked in. She gulps down a glass of water and wonders whether David has made his way home and gone out again while she was sleeping. There are no clothes strewn on the floor. She feels his toothbrush. It's dry. So he never came home. This is new.

She calls him. There's no answer, so she texts and e-mails him: "Where are you?" An even tone: no reproach yet, leaving the door open for fury. She'll decide the tenor of her response when she sees him, based on the level of his dishevelment, drunkenness, remorse. Such are the negotiations of marriage.

She walks into the kitchen to see Puri at the stove making chicken soup and is filled with gratitude.

"Thank you, Puri!" she says.

"Yes, ma'am," Puri says without turning around. "You are sick."

When she is spooning up soup and sweating, she looks at the clock and sees it's just past eleven. She dials her mother, who should be in the car.

"Did you get in okay and the pickup was okay?"

"Yes, all fine. How are you doing, dear?"

"I have a fever, but I took Advil, so I'm okay right now." As she goes through the expected questions and responses, she wonders if she should tell her mother that her husband went out last night and didn't come back. If she doesn't, of course, her mother will find out, and it'll be worse than if she had told her. Then again, if she tells her now, it will cast a pall on the beginning of her mother's visit. She decides to stall.

"Okay, I'm here. Can't wait to see you."

She has an hour or so until her mother arrives, so she goes upstairs to her room and gets into bed and logs on to her laptop.

She found this other, online world by accident when she was looking for a way to get rid of some old furniture she was throwing out. A website for expatriates in Asia: www.expatlocat.com. The name was a bit confusing, but the site was marginally helpful. She posted a message on "Odds and Ends" saying that people could come and take pieces that she described: an old coffee table, three lamps, an ottoman. She was taken aback by the aggressive responses. People demanded photos, demanded to know where she lived, asked if she would deliver the items to their homes. She wanted to respond, "These are free!" but instead she never replied to any of the messages. She told Sam to get rid of the furniture instead, and it all disappeared without a fuss.

Poking around the site, she found advertisements and a tab labeled Message Boards. When she clicked on it, a list of topics popped up: "Dating," "Friendship," "Moving to Hong Kong."

She is not at all current, but current enough to know that online forums, in the age of all that is possible online, are almost laughably antique. Still, that is why she likes them. This website has something quaint and old-fashioned about it, in the context of all this Internet insanity. The graphics are nonexistent, just lines of text, some under-lined, some indented, some bold, and that's as complicated as it gets.

She posts on two communities: expatlocat.com and citypeople.com, which is based in Los Angeles and is more lively, because people all over America post on it. There they talk about popular TV shows and cur-rent events, household income, and BMI. The tone is more ironic; peo-ple are feistier, less provincial. People often post their height, weight, and HHI and ask, "Do you hate me?" But the Hong Kong one is more relevant, and she's there most often.

She is always astonished by how loose people's networks are, how they are so trusting and willing to meet strangers based on a few elec-tronic exchanges. People who have just moved to Hong Kong post on these boards and arrange social get-togethers. They seem to have no compunction about the fact that the only connection they have with these people is through the Internet. She knows that her mother would be horrified; in her world, it's families, schools, workplaces. She also knows that no one in her world would ever be caught dead on an on-line forum. So it's perfect.

She pores over the forums and has become familiar with people who post frequently, whose handles are JamesBond and taiwanmum.

People complain about their help, or wonder whether to leave their boyfriends, or ask where to buy an air-filtering machine. No question is too personal or inane or random for this place. Anonymity is so comforting.

When she registered, she filled the blanks with fake information. Her online name is HappyGal, something that would set her teeth on edge in real life, but online, she figures, she could, she should, be a different person. In her bedroom, with her laptop on her bed, she signed up to become someone else, a gray, amorphous collection of 0s and 1s traveling through space to join a virtual community that has become a large part of her day.

HappyGal is younger than Hilary, twenty-seven, and she is originally from Oregon, although they used to live in California. Her husband works at an accounting firm. She likes to run and hike the country trails, which she's had fun discovering. She is blond. This is important. Hilary has always wanted to be blond.

HappyGal has a helper they just hired, whom they pay HK$2,000 over the minimum wage, and the helper works only five days because they value their couple privacy. She and her husband live in the Mid-Levels. It's like a smaller, scaled-down version of Hilary. Someone she might have been, in a different life, or maybe even this one, if she had made some different decisions.

Hilary has read a lot of the archives, so she knows the history of a lot of her fellow posters, and she has become one of the regulars. Taiwanmum is shrewish but clever. Texas4Eva is one of those irritating, newly arrived Americans who take umbrage at everything that is not shiny and happy, as she thinks everything ought to be. She complains about the injustices in Hong Kong—how helpers are underpaid, how the minimum wage is outrageously low, how pollution is ever-present. Her outrage is not shiny and happy, though, which many other posters have pointed out to her. Hilary wonders if she knows Texas4Eva in real life, if she's had lunch next to her at the American Club. Still, they have formed a sort of community, a society of people who recognize one another and know one another's personalities and quirks. They are merciless to newcomers but chummy with one another.

The etiquette of the online forum has to be learned through weeks, probably months, of lurking. Also, the tone. Hilary read thousands of messages before attempting to post one of her own. People were very extreme, punctuating their sentences with exclamation points and bobbing yellow smiley faces that winked or stuck out their tongue. It was like on Facebook, which Hilary goes on sometimes, and whenever someone posts a photo of themselves, all their friends post profuse compliments, say utterly ordinary women are "gorgeous!!!!" or "stunning!" On the flip side, people become enraged easily and insult one another with a vehemence that would never exist in a face-to-face encounter. There are dozens of posts where people try to explain why they are right and the other is wrong. Whenever Hilary sees this type of exchange, she wonders at the futility and hopefulness of these people, that they actually think they can change someone else's mind, that others will acknowledge their correctness. They must be young. She was that way too when she was young. If only it is explained enough, they think, surely everyone will understand, everyone will come around to their way of thinking. It is exhausting, being so hopeful. She remembers.

She signs in. HappyGal, password: honkers, all lowercase.

She enters the forum "Misc in Hong Kong," her usual haunt, where a dozen or so people post regularly.

Taiwanmum is online, posting about a new dim sum place in Kowloon: "Very good food and reasonable price. The chef from Four Seasons."

"That seems unlikely," Hilary types. "And how do you even get there?"

"Ah, HappyGal, welcome," blinks back the response. "There's this thing called public transport. Not everyone sits around in their air-conditioned mansion in Repulse Bay and refuse to go to Kowloon."

Hilary is surprised. She has always written that she lives in Mid-Levels.

"I live in Mid-Levels," she types.

"OK, your mansion in Mid-Levels," Taiwanmum pings back.

Hilary has been getting more paranoid lately about being found out.

"How long have you lived here again?" comes a question from Asiaphile, an intermittent poster, known for peppery remarks and not suffering fools.

"A year and a half," she writes.

"All sorted out?" Asiaphile writes, not unkindly.

"Are you a man or woman?" she responds.

"Touche."

"I'm home sick today, be nice," she types. She clicks off to another thread.

And then she sees it. Her story. Right there on the forum for the other thirty or so regular readers to see.

"I know a woman," it begins. "She is so rich and has a huge house. She can't have kids and is maybe trying to adopt and has a kid she is 'trying out,' like a ball gown she can return." The user ID on the message is HappyValley, a neighborhood in Hong Kong.

The casual cruelty takes her breath away.

She scrolls through. The subject line is "Should anyone be able to adopt?" Off-topic, yes, but not unusually so.

"Is this a friend of yours?" someone asks.

"More of an acquaintance. She runs in different circles."

"Sounds horrible!" exclaims Christy3.

"Well, they have different rules for rich people, don't they?"

"I'm sure the HK government wouldn't allow this. They have such strict rules," writes MadHatter.

"Yes, my friend wanted to adopt and had such a difficult time. She ended up getting a child from Russia."

They are in this peculiar situation in Hong Kong, of living there but not being local, and being privy to the regulations of their own countries and of Hong Kong, and sometimes of China. Hong Kong orphanages give preference to local Chinese families and also prefer to place Chinese children with Chinese families. If there is a half-Indian or half-Filipino child, they will go to families with similar backgrounds, and once there was even a white child, and she went to a white family. It is their policy, and they adhere to it with much vigilance. It is surprising that Julian is with her, given his half-Indian, half-Chinese background, except that mixed-race children are much harder to place in Hong Kong. She's been assured that this, in conjunction with his relatively advanced age, will make it much easier for her to adopt him.

She reads the thread. The last post was from an hour ago. Her heart pounds in her chest. Who could have written such a thing? Enough people knew about Julian, although she and David tried to be discreet. But who would write about her situation so meanly?

The doorbell rings. Her head is a mass of white noise from what she's just seen. But her mother has arrived. Her mother has arrived. She hears a sudden burst of activity downstairs. Puri is probably taking her mother's luggage, bringing her a cup of tea, and asking her about her flight, all the things that Hilary is supposed to be doing but can't right now, can't because she is sick and feverish, can't because a website splayed her life out on the screen, and can't, simply can't, because, because, her husband is simply nowhere to be found.

Mercy

CAN YOU SUDDENLY be summoned into adulthood? Mercy wonders. Is it the same as being promoted and suddenly having to pretend you know how to be a boss, or getting your period or having sex and suddenly being on the other side, knowing what it's all about? She is suddenly an adult. She is sitting here with a man who has a wife, and he is on the precipice. This is what they must mean by being an adult.

He is sick of it, he says over fried eggs at the Flying Pan. He is sick of the wife and the nagging and the baby talk and just all of it. He doesn't have the life he wants. He wants to change. He wants to evolve. He has the manic, unbridled energy of someone who has just made a foolish decision. Who better to do it with than me? thinks Mercy.

He tells her, this is the first time he's done this. He's never cheated on his wife, except he says it more delicately, says, he's never "been with" anyone else since his marriage. She wonders if anyone calls what they're doing cheating, or if they always make it into something more noble in their mind. She also knows to wonder whether it's true. She's not that stupid.

She listens, is the vessel into which he can pour all his frustrations and fantasies.

"So," she says finally, "you're having a kind of a Jerry Maguire moment, huh, where you're taking a stand and going off on a new path?"

He laughs.

"Don't you need to go home?" she asks.

"You know, my mother-in-law is coming today," he says, ignoring her question and looking at his watch. "In fact, she's probably already here. And she and my wife, they're going to hang out here, and then we're all going to Bangkok, which we do every fucking year, because the mother-in-law likes that weekend market and she buys all this crap and ships it back to the United States, like she doesn't already have enough shit."

"Listen," Mercy says, "I understand you're going through some serious stuff right now, but you need to back off a little bit and calm down. You are being way too intense." How interesting to be the sane one.

"I'm not a bad guy," he says. "And actually, Hilary is not a bad person. We've just really grown apart, and I'm angry because I haven't had the relationship that I want for a while."

Are all older men this conversant in Oprah language? Mercy finds herself thinking. She can't imagine any of her contemporaries talking like this.

"And I work all the time, and all she does is sit around and mope. You know, her family's rich, and she thinks that entitles her to bitch and be sad all day. And she's gotten us in this situation with this boy, and this poor kid, he doesn't know which end is up. He doesn't know what we want from him, or what to do. It's totally crazy."

It turns out that the Starrs have a pet child they take out and walk and water every once in a while. What is wrong with these people?

"Are you serious?" she asks. "Isn't that against the law or something? I thought that the government didn't even let you look at a child until they decide to give it to you."

"The rules don't apply to certain people, babe," he says. "You are so naïve."

She pauses. "First," she says, "don't ever call me babe. And second, are you still drunk?"

"Is that why you think I'm still here?"

"I guess," she says. "I would think that you would have to go home at some point."

"You would be thinking wrong," he says, wagging a finger at her. He sops up some runny egg with a torn-off piece of toast. "You don't eat, do you?"

She has not eaten any of the pancakes he ordered for her. She feels light inside, clean.

"And what of you?" he says.

"What of me?" He asked, she thinks—he's not a terrible person. Perhaps there's more to this than a man coming off the rails.

"You know," he says, "don't be coy. I've just laid out my life in front of you, and you haven't told me anything."

"I didn't know we were sharing so much."

"Come on," he says. "Throw me a bone."

"I'm not your escape hatch," she says. It's the only smart thing she's said all morning. "Your bad behavior doesn't mean that you get to blame it on me later."

He looks up, startled. Maybe he's seeing her for the first time. "I'm not doing that," he says.

"Good," she says. "Then we can have a conversation."

She reaches over and covers his hand with hers. "Are you ready?"

Margaret

AT THE LUNCH BUFFET, picking up melon and prosciutto with silver tongs, Margaret hears a familiar voice. She looks up to see Frannie Peck, whose kids go to TASOHK as well. They greet each other,
and Frannie asks if they want to get dinner at the seaside restaurant
tonight. There is no gracious way to demur, so Margaret agrees, and
they both go back to their tables.

After a few hours by the pool, Margaret goes back to their room,
where Clarke has booked her a massage in their private garden. There,
amid frangipani and bougainvillea, an embarrassment of tropical lush-
ness, a quiet, dark-haired woman spends ninety minutes moving Margaret's muscles around, in an air temperature that miraculously seems to
be the same as her own body's.

It is so indulgent and gorgeous and the masseuse so docile, so servile
(she won't even look at Margaret as she sets up the table), that Margaret
spends the entire time—lying on soft terry cloth, her face looking down
through the hole cut out of the table onto a thoughtfully placed bowl
with a floating lotus flower—feeling absolutely awful.

Is it any wonder, she thinks, that expats become like spoiled rich
children, coddled and made to feel as if their every whim should be
gratified? These trips to islands where the average annual wage is the
cost of a pair of expensive Italian shoes cast the Western expatriate in
the role of the ruler. The locals are the feudal servants, running to
obey every whim. These small empires, these carefully tended para-
dises of sand and palm, shelter the expatriates from the brutal realities just outside the guarded gates.

The woman softly asks her to turn over onto her back. She drapes the towel decorously over Margaret's torso, all the while looking away. Margaret wonders where she lives, probably in some disheveled bunkroom in a hotel dorm with other staff. What must she think of the cool, stiff hotel rooms she visits for her work, with their Bose stereos and private plunge pools? They must seem a strange, alien fantasy land. Margaret saw staff quarters in another hotel once, when she went for a tour of the organic garden, and there through a fence, where the foliage had not grown quite thick enough, she saw some ramshackle buildings with laundry hanging out to dry. She asked what those buildings were and was given an abashed answer by the gardener, suddenly embarrassed after proudly showing off his work. Do you live there? she asked before she could stop herself, and he crumpled into an impoverished island native, transformed from the career horticulturist he had just been. She was ashamed, of course. What else could she have been—an apologist for the way things were and how she could not change them.

She drifts off into a light sleep and is wakened by the sound of the woman getting her things together.

"Finish," she says softly. Margaret sits up and wraps a towel around herself, hair falling disheveled around her face. She is drowsy and disoriented.

"Thank you," she says. "That was wonderful."

She moves to the bed and dozes until she hears Clarke and the children at the door.

They come in with excited stories of crabs and sandcastles—they are still young, these children, these remaining children of hers. They are tentative with their happiness, as if afraid it will upset her equilibrium. It makes her sad that their emotional calibrations are so accurate and so attuned to hers. Any overt happiness immediately tips over into guilt and anger because G is not here, and what right do they have to any happiness? Still, she cannot ruin their lives as well. She smiles and listens to their stories, absently patting Philip's head as she urges him to shower so they can get ready for dinner.

Frannie Peck is one of those small, pert blond women who get married, have two children, and, essentials accomplished, then proceed to live their lives with maximum efficiency, going to Pilates and Zumba on alternating weekdays and running bake sales and school fund-raisers with cheery aplomb. Margaret would think no more of her, except that she remembers driving past her one day going in opposite directions on Repulse Bay Road, when the traffic was slow, and seeing Frannie behind the wheel, shoulders shaking as she sobbed. She was alone. This one image gives Frannie unexpected depth for Margaret. When they meet down by the beach, she is wearing a white sundress on her compact body, freckled shoulders rosy from the sun. They send the children to the beach to play while they order dinner.

"Did you have a good day?" Frannie asks. She has one of those unexpectedly raspy voices.

"Really relaxing," Margaret replies.

Frannie's husband, Ned, kisses Margaret on both cheeks, a European custom that has, for some reason, been hijacked by every American expatriate in Hong Kong. Margaret is quite certain that none of these people ever did the two-cheek greeting prior to stepping on Asian shores, and it's funny that they all adopt it without question.

Is it cynical of her to think this way? As she's grown older, Margaret has developed the bad habit of sizing people up immediately and passing judgment. This person is a small person, she can tell from the wrinkled brow when the person asks about a mutual acquaintance, worried whether she has been one-upped without knowing. This one seeks validation and so is always rushing about doing a million things that don't add up to anything. Another person doesn't understand why she's not relevant. With the exception of that one weeping moment Margaret witnessed, however, Frannie Peck remains a cipher. She seems like a wide, shallow plate, holding nothing except the reflection of others.

Frannie tells an amusing story about a previous vacation, in Sri Lanka with another family, where the villa had been so remote there was no Internet and no cell signal. The husbands all went nuts without access to their e-mail, but the wives refused to let them leave, so they compromised by hiring a driver to drive the two hours into the city with a bag full of phones they had turned on so they would pick up the e-mails when in reach of a signal.

"You should have seen these men," Frannie says. "When the car returned, they rushed it like tweens at a Justin Bieber concert."

So the dinner goes on, with lazy gossip and glasses of wine to soften reality. The children eat satay and pad thai, and the adults eat spicy prawns with basil and marvel that they are on a beach on the Andaman Sea doing such a thing.

The hotel has set up paper lanterns on the beach, maybe a Thai custom, maybe something they do for tourists. It doesn't matter, because they are beautiful. A hotel staff girl is with Daisy and Philip, helping them light their wicks and puff up their lanterns. Daisy and Philip stand on the sand, backs to their watching parents. They each hold a lantern and hold it up high, as if it were an offering. Soon the lanterns float off their hands and sail toward the dark night. There are dozens of lanterns in the sky now, burning off their tiny light, drifting away until they are no longer visible.

Daisy turns around with a bright face. "I made a wish, Mama!" It's uncharacteristic, her use of the babyish "mama," and it makes Margaret suddenly tear up, not wanting to guess what that wish might have been. She thinks, Where is G now? His family is here, in this burnished pocket of paradise, on this sandy beach, lighting lanterns, without him. If he could see them now, would he feel betrayed? She looks at Daisy and Philip standing, watching their lanterns soar, and feels dizzy from the hole in her heart.

Hilary

HER HUSBAND'S GONE AWOL. And her mother is here. Could there be a more awkward set of circumstances? Phone calls to his cell go unanswered—she's been trying for an hour. She's also been checking expatlocat.com to see if anyone else posts to "Should anyone be able to adopt?" and refreshing her e-mail box. She is thinking about calling the police—there has been a spate of crimes where bar hostesses spike drinks and clean out ATMs—when an e-mail from David blinks up on her computer screen.

"I need some time to think things through," he writes. "Will be in touch." Then, as an afterthought, "Not sure I will make it to Bangkok."

After she gets this e-mail, like a bomb, like a bad joke, in her inbox, she sits at her desk, tapping her forefinger on the matte metal of her laptop like a nervous metronome. Her mother is taking a shower—she can hear the water running—but she'll be out soon, and Hilary's going to have to say something.

It occurs to her that it's odd she's more worried about what she's going to say to her mother than about what has happened with her husband.

It's not as if they have had the most loving relationship lately. More . . . cordial. Definitely platonic, except when she tells him the time is favorable, and they dutifully have intercourse. She has felt his waning interest in her as a person, but coming as it did with her own diminishing engagement with his life, she hadn't really minded.

But this is bold! He has written an e-mail, with words that cannot be taken back, words that are a proclamation! She hovers, her hands over her keyboard, waiting. But of course, nothing happens. She does not reply.

The feeling she has is most unexpected. The oddest thing. She feels no distress or worry. Instead, she senses a dim, faint feeling that rises from some unknown place in her heart, rising slowly and blossoming into something that she might call relief.

The shower stops running. She hears the door open and close. Her mother will be in her doorway soon, asking what the plan is, what they will do. What will she say? What will she do?

Part IV

Hilary

IN THE SPRING, the odors come. The outdoor tiles are wet in the morning with accumulated moisture, and when you sniff, there is a sharp, moldy tinge to the air. It means the heat is coming. The early hours are cool and wet; the sun burns through by midday, and you can practically see the steam rising from the sidewalks. And through it all, a pungent, damp smell of rich, rotting soil, the plants growing at a furious rate, the insects *crick*ing and mating loudly, the very atoms in the air whizzing about, suffused with new heat energy after being dormant all winter.

Hilary had thought she had spring down to a science. On a certain day in March or April, she would sniff the air, feel the towels in the bathroom, then say the words: "Spring prep." Puri would know to bring out the dehumidifier units, pack the woolens in crinkly tissue and cedar, and switch the HVAC units to cool, a procedure that takes all day and is not easily reversible. The assault against the elements begins.

But this year, there are moths—dozens, maybe hundreds of them, a new and disturbing development that Hilary has never experienced before. "They might as well be locusts," she tells Olivia over the phone. "That would just make this year perfect. My annus horribilis."

The first one rolls out of one of her sweaters as she is pulling it out on an unseasonably cool day, causing her to shriek loudly, although no one else is in the room with her. It is large and very much dead, with a body that is fat and inelegant, so unlike a butterfly's. She panics. So much cashmere, so much wool at stake! But as she pulls them out,

Puri's meticulous work undone in a matter of minutes, her sweaters are, oddly, unscathed. It reminds her of that scene in *The Great Gatsby* where Daisy is covered in Jay's shirts and she starts weeping because they are so beautiful. Instead, Hilary sits in her humidity-controlled walk-in closet, surrounded by expensive knits, and wishes she felt like crying instead of the constant dry pricking behind her eyeballs that feels like torture.

Soon she grows used to the moths, or as used to them as she ever will. They just blunder around, blind in their mindless fecundity, reproducing like mad, feeding on what, she doesn't know. She finds them on the carpets, in the bathrooms, in the kitchen cupboards. Puri sweeps them up without emotion and deposits them in the trash can in the kitchen, so when Hilary goes to throw away her used coffee filter or an empty carton of juice, she steps on the pedal and is given a small heart attack when the lid opens and she sees the layer of dead insects on the bottom.

She has, of course, called the exterminators, but unless she is willing to move out for a week, all they can do is recommend mothballs and giant planks of cedar, which she buys from them in great quantities, and now her house smells like a chemical factory and she has a headache when she wakes up every morning.

This is the salient fact: She is alone. She is alone in a king-size bed in an enormous house, with no husband and no children and, instead, a domestic helper and a driver.

David is still off on what she likes to think of as his petit midlife crisis, although there's nothing petit about it. It's been more than three months. Why she thinks of it as petit or grand mal, with the attendant link to seizures, she doesn't know, but whenever it balloons up in her consciousness, which it does actually less and less frequently these days, it comes in those words, sometimes italicized: *petit midlife crisis.* Will it evolve into *grand mal*? Will this be permanent, will their lives be forever changed? Would she be willing to take him back?

More important, does she get to have her own midlife crisis? she wonders. When does she get to go completely off the rails? But the thing is, he's beaten her to the punch. If she does it now, who will be the one left behind, to witness, to suffer? There's no one—a tree falling in the woods with no sound. For this, for making it impossible for her to do what he has done, she hates him.

And yet, all this has brought David into sharp relief, made him into a real person, full of jagged edges and surprises. She had thought of him as someone or, if she's honest, something, a husband, who would always be there, and the fact that he has changed what she had thought of as an immutable fact brings her, sometimes, an ineffable, odd and painful pleasure. Good for you, she thinks, before it cuts into her again, the knowledge that her life is changed in some irreversible way. You were the brave one, she thinks, the one to make the bold, life-changing move. You rejected the life we had, the tepid approximation of happiness. You thought you deserved more. You did something. She is envious of that.

Her mother was a surprise. She took the news with aplomb, did exactly the right things. She didn't try to comfort her with anodyne words or hug her or tell her everything would be all right. Instead, she moved forward with a brisk practicality that was perfect.

They went ahead to Bangkok, without David, and they decided to share a room and upgrade to the Joseph Conrad Suite in the old wing of the Oriental. They had stiff drinks by the Chao Phraya River, watching the fat catfish surface, looking for bread crumbs. They meandered through Chatuchak Market and bought rattan baskets and brass tableware, fingered dusty ruby beads, and otherwise pretended that life was normal. Hilary managed to breathe through it, survive the trip, and come back to a cold, empty house. Her mother left the day after they returned to Hong Kong, although she had offered to stay longer. Hilary knows that leaving her father for long periods of time makes her mother nervous. She pities her mother now, having to take care of her husband, worry about her daughter, worry about the fact that she might never have grandchildren.

Her mother asked, gingerly. She usually never did, but one late night, as they nursed coffees after Thai food, she asked how that all was going.

"I mean, I know, now, it might be different. But what was the status before all this nonsense?"

Hilary had thought that trying to have children would kill her, but this new wound, on top of the old one, was so painful she squinted as she tried to explain to her mother.

"We have been trying, and also, you know, with Julian, who you know about."

"You have to do right by Julian," her mother said. "But the situation is obviously different now." She was never a supporter of the entire exercise to begin with, and now it lay in tatters. When Hilary asked if she wanted to meet Julian, she shook her head. "Only when you decide everything."

"I know." Hilary didn't know how she was going to begin to explain it to Julian and the administrators. Obviously, she wouldn't, for a while, and he would continue coming.

"You still don't want to do fertility?" her mom asked. "You know, just if you want to have a baby, regardless of what happens with David. Melissa Bissinger's daughter has these beautiful twin girls, and we know the doctor in San Francisco."

"No," Hilary said. "I don't know why I don't, didn't, want to. I just feel like it should happen on its own."

Her mother looked askance at her. "And it didn't." A pause. "And it's not." They both don't know which tense to use.

"I know."

"And you're thirty-eight now."

"I know."

Her mother stirred her coffee.

"It's funny, you know, Hilary. Life happens, and sometimes it happens so slowly that you have the time to get used to it. That's the mercy of it. You may wake up one day and be older and be fine with not having children. There's no reason why you absolutely have to have them."

"Thank you, Mother," she said, with no inflection, although she had not meant to sound ungrateful. It was so hard to speak when you didn't know what you were trying to convey, let alone what you were feeling.

"You were and are one of the great joys of my life," her mother said.

Hilary flushed. In the annals of her reserved family, this was tantamount to her mother throwing off her clothes and shouting her love for her child on the streets.

"Thank you, Mother," she said again.

And that was how that holiday went.

She has been seeing more and more of Julian, going to visit him as much as she can. She is lucky. The woman in charge of his group home is kind, wishes for him to be adopted, so turns the other way when Hilary shows up again and again. Hilary knows not to push it too much, but she is growing attached, longing to see his face, hear his accented English. Sometimes she goes like a stalker just to watch him get off the bus, carouse with his friends in Cantonese. Boys are like puppies, she realizes, climbing on one another, poking, scrambling around one another.

He is here today, and after his lesson, she asks him if he'd like to go out for ice cream, even though it's a cold spring day. They get in the car, and she tells Sam to go to Times Square, the vast mall in Causeway Bay. There's an ice cream shop there.

Once they arrive, and she's walking through, holding Julian's hand, she realizes she's made a mistake.

There is so much stuff. There is so much to look at, so much to buy—all the accouterments of a privileged life. There's a luxury-handbag store with purses that cost a year's pay for Puri; there are sneaker stores with hundreds of styles, electronics shops with phones and iPods and computers. Julian is seven, old enough to covet. He stares, wide-eyed, at all he doesn't have.

They order ice cream. He just wants chocolate, shies away from all the bewildering choices, and has to be pressed to order toppings or to get two flavors. Hilary has seen three-year-olds order complicated mixed concoctions—half bubble gum, half mint chip, with marshmallows and rainbow sprinkles—with the confidence that comes from being loved and cossetted, their desires listened to and often granted. Watching Julian eat his chocolate ice cream with the rainbow sprinkles she insisted on, she feels awful for him. She must, she must, make a decision, even without David.

He is quiet, as always, and she talks to him in a constant, soothing torrent of inanities: "Piano is so great for you, you have such an ear, are you enjoying the ice cream?" He listens, is aware, but doesn't try to respond.

Later, when she drops him off at his group home, he is clutching a bag with a new pair of sneakers, which she is sure will bring her a reprimand from Miss Chiu, the woman in charge, about how she should not buy Julian gifts, that they are confusing to him and unfair to the other children. But this fifty-dollar bribe, this small token, how can she not give this offering up to the universe, if not to absolve her, then to lessen her burden of guilt?

Mercy

"THAT WASN'T FLYING. That was falling with style."

The phrase is knocking around her head, surfacing at odd moments in the day: when she's making her bed in the morning, waiting in line for a coffee. It's a line from *Toy Story*, the movie, when Woody is denigrating Buzz Lightyear. She caught it on a lazy Sunday at home a week ago.

She doesn't know why that phrase keeps coming up, but it has some resonance. Because she's feeling kind of good. She feels good, and she keeps waiting for the other shoe to drop. Is she flying, or is she falling?

David comes by once or twice a week, on weekends, when he's off work and has some time. She doesn't think there's anyone else. He seems to work an awful lot, and when he does go out, it seems to be with colleagues and mostly men.

He'll text, the buzzer will ring, and she'll let him up. He comes with a bottle of wine, and they'll spend time at her place before going out and walking along Hollywood Road until they get to a restaurant. They'll sit and have a meal, the two of them, looking out at the passersby.

And when they do, she can't help it, she thinks: Everyone out there thinks I'm normal. They think we're a couple. They think that this is all mine. It is thrilling and dangerous, and she allows herself to think it in small doses of outrageous happiness.

She wonders if she was just the girl in the bar, the girl to start the

ball rolling. If she could have been just any girl. She knows enough—
barely—not to ask, but it is consuming her a little bit, as it would.
She wants this to work, doesn't want to self-sabotage, but she is who
she is, right? Who would she be, what would the world be, if Mercy
Cho didn't screw things up by saying and doing the wrong thing?

If some other girl had been sitting there, in the lobby lounge of
the Conrad hotel, on that December Thursday, would she be sitting
here with David now?

But there is this now, this little window, where things are sus-
pended in a magical way, where she is not the mess that everyone
thinks she is and she has a life and a boyfriend. And when she's with
him, she's okay! She's funny and charming and not a nightmare. She
feels as if she is juggling all of this, her new selves, and waiting for it
all to fall apart.

"How are you supporting yourself?" he asks tonight as they're finishing off a piece of mud pie. She is magically able to eat again, not
feeding the emptiness inside her by fasting. She must have gained five
pounds already. This morning, she had a cheeseburger for breakfast.

"I get jobs here and there," she says. "I do a lot of different things."

"Do you need any money?" he asks. It is so unexpectedly kind her
eyes fill with tears. It has been so long since anyone has cared enough
about her to ask something like this, and to have an older, mature person consider what she might need, as opposed to her throng of twenty-
something self-absorbed friends, is disconcerting and an awful kind of
pleasure.

He is living at a fancy furnished apartment in a hotel, where you
can rent by the month. She hasn't been invited over yet—a fact that
seems to get larger and larger in her mind every time they see each
other. It's as if they exist inside a bubble, and she is afraid to pop the
bubble, so she treads lightly.

Tonight they finish another bottle of wine, on top of the one they
had at her place, and are feeling drunk and sedated. They drink wine,
not cocktails, and so the way she's drunk has changed, for the better.

No longer are there large segments of the evening that are blank, where she remembers only flashes of frenetic laughing, screaming, running; now it's a smooth, continuous slip into a shifted reality, rather enjoyable and very grown-up.

So she never asks about his wife. She never asks about other women. She never talks about anything she thinks will break the bubble. Inside this bubble, everything is okay. Inside this bubble, she is a whole person. And for right now, that's enough.

Margaret

WELL-MEANING WOMEN throng the room. They are in yet another hotel function room learning about and supporting yet another good cause. Building schools in Cambodia, supporting the Philharmonic, recycling food from local restaurants to feed the hungry. A school mom whose daughter is friends with Daisy bought a table, and, having refused her last three invitations, Margaret thought she couldn't refuse again. Taking a shower, putting on makeup, finding high heels, she thought, Here I am, going out into the world. She took a breath before entering the loud, echoey ballroom. But you have to start somewhere.

When she first arrived in Hong Kong, she went through that rite of tribe forming, the social ritual she hadn't engaged in since high school or college. It was different from moving to a place where everyone already knew one another and you were the new person. It was more like college, because expats were always arriving and leaving in waves. A new crop, a new class—you met one another at coffees and gym classes and school meetings, and you sized one another up. The signifiers were so important: Are you wearing Dansko clogs or Jimmy Choo mules, are you a salon blonde or do you leave your hair in a ponytail, do you live in jeans or gym clothes or are you always in a suit? Do you want to talk about nannies or Rwanda? For the Chinese women, it was, Are you local, mainland, Taiwanese, or first-generation ABC? For the Americans, it was, Are you East Coast, West Coast, city, suburb, boonies? Are you finance, corporate, small business, or artist? Are you a teacher, or are you an entrepreneur? Do you belong to the Country Club, the American Club, the Cricket? Are you an expat without a club? Against clubs? People found their own kind and broke off into their own communities.

During a long reception hour, in which she hangs back against a wall and wonders why she arrives so accursedly promptly to everything and why she didn't come when the lunch was starting instead of the reception—she is rusty at gaming these things—she watches all the chattering women gesturing with one hand and sipping sparkling water with the other. Finally a waiter comes through the room ringing a bell, indicating that they should go in. Margaret finds her way to her table, where she is seated next to Mindy, who is such a Mindy that Margaret wonders at the power of a name. Mindy has just arrived from North Carolina, where her husband worked at a furniture company. Now all the manufacturing has gone to China, and he has come to oversee production.

"It was that or find another job. His whole family has worked at the same company for generations. Of course, he's in China all the time," she says. "Chaana" is how she says it, with her gentle southern twang. "A lot of the time he spends five days there and is only back on the weekend. He oversees the factory to make sure they're doing things right and there are no child-labor issues." She says this with the wonder of a blond girl who has spent her entire life in the same one hundred square miles of North Carolina and suddenly finds herself on the other side of the world, with a Filipina housekeeper and shops on the street that sell vats of furry, dried deer penises.

"It's hard," Margaret says. "The thing is that everyone here is in the same boat, so the women become one another's family."

"You know what I miss? Good iced coffee!" Mindy confides. "The coffee here is terrible. Even the Starbucks tastes totally different."

"It's the water, plus the milk is not as good here," Margaret says. "You know what I miss most? I miss Target. And how crazy is it that it's all made in China, shipped to the United States, we buy it and bring it back? That carbon footprint is insane!" Mindy's eyes light up.

This exchange, this expat back-and-forth, so familiar to Margaret, is not unsoothing to her. She's done it so often that she's on autopilot.

Mindy smiles at her, relieved to find someone saying all the things she needs to hear, and Margaret wonders how to signal that they are going to share this time at lunch and have a perfectly pleasant encounter but that this is not going to go beyond that. Margaret wants to say, I look like someone you might be friends with, but I'm not. There's a hole inside me, and I can't fill it with other people, although I wish I could. Newcomers all radiate the same desperation: to make friends, put down tenuous roots, survive in this new environment. She doesn't worry about Mindy, though; there are plenty of people for her to be friends with. She knows she will see her in a few months with three other friends, in their Lululemons, doing a boot camp class on the beach, or having lunch at Zuma, all of them with their 1.6 kids at home and possibly a dog. Mindy will at some point put two and two together and realize that the woman she was talking to at that lunch in the first year of her arrival was *that* woman, the woman who lost the child, and whenever they run into each other, at the supermarket or the American Club or the Mandarin Hotel, her expression will assume the same semiapologetic, stricken, sympathetic look that Margaret gets from every other woman.

She looks around the table during a pause in the conversation with Mindy. Every woman there is well exercised, watches her diet, has two or three children, a husband. They all have shiny hair, and they are all wearing sheaths and daytime dresses perfect for the occasion. No one is breaking the rules of the ladies' luncheon. They radiate well-being and privilege, and yet she is among them, so who is to say what's behind any woman's smiling face? She butters a roll and eats it.

On her other side, a woman introduces herself. "I've seen you at school," she says. "You are Daisy's mother, right?"

"Yes," she replies.

"I'm Courtney's mom."

"I've heard of Courtney." She smiles. She has heard not great things. "Yes, I hear about Daisy as well."

"What is your name?" Margaret asks.

"I'm Diana Robinson," she says. She has a brittle smile, which she breaks out now. "I've been meaning to call you," she continues.

"Oh?" Margaret says.

"I'm not sure if this is the right occasion to talk. Do you think we could have coffee later?"

In another life, Margaret would have acquiesced, but she's no longer apologetic for not making herself available to others.

"I have to leave immediately after lunch, so I'm afraid I can't. Don't you think we can speak now?"

Diana leans over. Margaret can tell she is enjoying this a little bit. "It's about our daughters. Courtney has told me some disturbing things." She pauses.

"Yes?" Margaret says. She has no patience for the drama of the middle school mother.

"Apparently Daisy has been going on websites that are inappropriate."

This does shock Margaret, although she tries not to let it show. "What sort of websites?"

"It's nothing crazy, just she seems to be preoccupied with different kinds of problems. Like she's shown Courtney pro-anorexia websites, cutting, stuff like that." She stops. "Also, child-loss websites."

Margaret's sudden fury surprises even her with its intensity. "What?" she says, so loudly that everyone at the table stops their conversation and swivels their head toward her.

Diana nods her head. "It's not *pornography* or anything"—she whispers the offensive word—"but it's odd, and I think you should have someone talk to her. That is, if you don't have someone already."

"So let me get this straight," Margaret says, feeling as if her head might explode from the restraint she has to show, trying to keep her voice from rising. "So you are telling me that my daughter is exploring the Internet, about issues that lots of girls face, and that she is somehow corrupting your daughter? It seems rather harmless to me. Unless you'd like to explain to me how it's not."

Diana backtracks immediately, having misjudged so disastrously. Perhaps she thought that Margaret would be grateful, that she would thank her for watching out so vigilantly for her child. That they would become best friends, that she would have the famous tragedy victim by her side and they could navigate the tricky world of motherhood together.

"I think that every mother would want to know what her daughter is up to on the computer. I mean, we can't be too careful these days," she says, looking around the table for support. "Sometimes you have to stop things before they get out of control."

Ginny, the woman who sponsored the table, looks aghast at the drama that is transfixing the rest of the group. Margaret takes a deep breath. She is not going to lose it today, on this woman, at this table.

"I think you're overreacting," she says simply. "Oh, look. The video is starting."

Margaret turns deliberately around so that she can watch the screen. As the video starts, she steams. She knows this woman, this kind of woman. She thrives on her children's social lives, the drama, as if she is living it herself. She doesn't separate her life from her children's, living through them, like some sick parasite with no life of its own.

But slowly she starts to watch the video instead, coming out of her head. It is the usual charity video fare, with images of children set to a sentimental song. There are two songs that are particularly popular and, she supposes, appropriate for these types of films. It grates to hear the same melody designed to elicit tears over and over again. Still, the videos always affect Margaret, and most women at these gatherings, as they're supposed to, until they open their checkbooks and assuage the guilt of having their own well-fed, lovingly cared for children at home. The charity is about providing art access to children in low-income housing in Hong Kong, and their bright smiles, their bright eyes, set to a crooning ballad, bring tears to Margaret's eyes. It's like crying to a Barry Manilow song.

The head of the charity, a Chinese socialite with an indecipherable pan-European accent, gives a speech. Afterward they are given time to eat the main course. Margaret gets up to go to the bathroom and runs into Frannie Peck, putting on lipstick. She hasn't seen her since Phuket.

"How are you?" she asks, kissing her on the cheek.

"Good. Enjoying yourself?"

Margaret shrugs. "It's a good cause."

Frannie winks. "I know. These things give me hives as well."

Margaret is reminded of the time she saw Frannie crying behind the wheel of the car. People surprise you all the time.

"How do we escape?" she asks, grinning.

"God, I don't know. I'm here with Winnie Leong, whose husband works with mine. Who are you here with?"

"Ginny McGrady."

Hilary comes into the bathroom.

"Hilary!" Margaret says. "I haven't seen you in months! Thanks so much for that great dinner before the break. How was your holiday? Sorry we didn't see you in Bangkok, but it got so complicated."

Hilary looks uncomfortable. "Okay," she says. She looks at Frannie, still fixing her face at the mirror. "Oh, you might as well know," she says in a low voice. "David's having a midlife crisis, and he seems to have left me."

"What?" Margaret says, shocked. "What are you talking about? We just had dinner all together!"

Frannie leaves unobtrusively.

"Sit down," Margaret says, and pulls up a stool.

"Oh, I'm fine." Hilary reconsiders her words. "Well, not fine, but I'm surviving. I breathe, and I put one foot in front of the other."

"I'm shocked," Margaret says. "Did you have any inkling?"

"No. It was right after the dinner, actually. He went out and . . . never came back." Hilary laughs, a short, regretful bark.

"Really?" Margaret can't believe that David Starr is capable of something that requires such emotional range. "It's really uncharacteristic, isn't it?"

"Yes," Hilary says. "But the older I get, the more I think that people are just unknowable, you know? And life is just full of, I don't know, surprises? Shit?"

"I know," Margaret says.

"Of course you know," Hilary says. "I'm sorry."

"There's enough shit to go around," Margaret says, and she laughs. Hilary laughs too, and they sit in the little velvet sitting room of the hotel bathroom in a companionable silence until someone comes in and breaks the spell, and they get up and shake themselves off.

They go out, and the lunch is a little more bearable, and Margaret can make it through until the serving of the dessert, at which time it is deemed socially acceptable to get up, thank your hostess, and leave.

It's the first time she has gone out socially in ages, ever since they got back from vacation three months ago.

When they got home from the break in January, they entered a cold and quiet house. Essie had gone home to the Philippines for home leave and was not due back for several days.

The children disappeared upstairs, and Clarke went up to take a shower as she opened the suitcases and put the dirty clothes in piles in the kitchen. She started a load, hearing the rhythmic lull of the washing machine, inhaling the scent of too-sweet detergent, pleasantly alone in the room.

She was thirsty, dehydrated from the flight. In the cupboard, there were two glasses that a wealthy, impractical family friend had given to her and Clarke as a wedding present more than a decade ago. Fabulously expensive, they were paper-thin crystal highball glasses that shattered at a sideways glance. They started out with twelve, and after more than ten years of living and moving and children, two remained. She got one, filled it with cold Pellegrino from the fridge, and gulped down the cool, refreshing, salty bubbles. Bubbly water, an acquired adult taste, she thought.

Suddenly the relief she had let herself feel only in small dribbles came crashing in. Her tension, her worry, her relief, and still, of course, her sadness, made her unable to stand, and she made her way to the table, supporting herself with the hand that was not holding her water. She collapsed onto a chair, letting herself feel the immensity of what she had avoided on the vacation. She had avoided something that would have destroyed her as surely as if she had stood in front of a bus. How could she live, knowing that one more thing would have sent her sailing straight over the edge? One fragile child, two fragile children, three . . . The infinite variety of things that can go wrong with one life, multiplied by five.

They had gone to Bangkok after leaving Phuket, for a few days in the city, and they had gone to Chatuchak Market, the big weekend market. Philip wanted to buy toys, and Daisy was interested in a rattan bag. In another life, Margaret might have wanted a brass lamp or candlestick holders. There was so much humanity in that market—so many people, so many stories—that Margaret felt overwhelmed from the moment they got out of the taxi. It was hot and loud, and she was clutching a colored map that detailed odd sections, like the location of the "Crime Suppression Police." Whenever they left the safe confines of the hotel, she felt uneasy, as if she were swimming in the ocean. She preferred to take small, measured outings and come back to the safety of the known, but the children and Clarke were antsy after five days on the beach and wanted to get out into a city.

The buzz in her head grew louder as they got out of the cab and walked to the entrance of the market. Clarke walked ahead, looming over the locals with a straw hat he had acquired on Kamala Beach. The kids found a food stand selling satay. "Can we have some?" Daisy asked. Margaret hesitated; it looked dirty. Cholera, malaria, typhoid—fatal diseases crowded her mind. "Sure," Clarke said, short-circuiting her paranoia, and bought four chicken satays. She ate one, because if everyone else died of food poisoning, she didn't want to be left behind. Then later she regretted it, because if everyone got sick, who was going to take care of the sick children? This was how she thought.

They bought bottles of water and walked on. She was always the one consulting the map and trying to find out where they were. "Just follow the clock tower," Clarke had said easily. As if it were that simple. She looked at wood carvings and silk sarongs and ugly T-shirts, all the while keeping an eye on Daisy and Philip, and the map, so she would know where she was. She was carrying her large handbag, with all of Clarke, Daisy, and Philip's extra items that they just handed off to her without thinking, including the half-full water bottles, and her shoulders hurt, and she wanted to scream. Sometimes it was just about the bag, she thought. Men strolled through life with a wallet in their pants, and women were saddled with children, the map, the bag, the half-empty water bottles. Resentment fired up through her body, flushing her cheeks, suffusing her with sudden rage.

Was it that men were heartless? Or without imagination? How could Clarke tell her that she needed to move on? How could he say that life should go on? It is unimaginable, but because she cannot lose him and Daisy and Philip, she has to pretend to agree, to try to do this thing that seems as ludicrous as flying. And sometimes it feels like flying, or walking on water, as if she is doing something so against the laws of nature, so against the very reality of being a human being, that if she looks down, or up, or anywhere but a spot a very short distance ahead of her, she will fall, and fall, and there will be no bottom to where she can go.

And then, surfacing from her thoughts, she realized: She could not see Philip. She could see Daisy and Clarke ahead, looking at some bags, but she could not see Philip. Her hair stood on end, and she felt electrocuted.

Calm down, she told herself. Calm down. You'll see him in a few seconds.

But she didn't. After ten long seconds, she screamed Clarke's name so that he would stop. "Clarke! I can't see Philip!"

Clarke stopped and grabbed Daisy's hand as he came back to her. "When did you last see him?" he asked, calmly.

"Just now," she said. "And I looked at the map, and when I looked up again, I couldn't see him. I've been watching him like a hawk."

"I'm sure he's just down one of these alleys," Clarke said.

Daisy was speechless, Clarke's brow furrowed; all of them were frozen by the unsayable. But it wasn't possible. But anything was possible. God wouldn't let it happen again. But why would God let it happen the first time?

They fanned out, shouting, "Philip! Philip!" Margaret found herself thinking that at least Clarke was here this time, that she wasn't alone.

They found him, of course, but it was a long six or seven minutes, and Philip was a mess, even though he tried to pull it together. Ten was still young. Found by a kind couple from Singapore, he had been crying and screaming, but it was amazing how far away from them he had gotten in that short time. In those moments of emergency, Margaret had felt her heart stop and start several times over, had to fight the urge to crumple to the floor and give up, had to remember to breathe, had to open her eyes extra wide, because she felt the world going black.

Afterward they went back to the hotel, and Clarke got on the phone to book them on the next flight home. They ate dinner at the hotel restaurant and flew home the next day.

So that was their Christmas holiday, the first without G, and that was how that went. Now school has been back in session for a few months, and she has been hiding at home, taking walks and escaping to her room in Happy Valley.

She gets home from the lunch right before Philip and Daisy come home on the bus. She asks them about their day and asks to sit with Daisy for a bit while she has a snack.

"I went to this lunch today," she says, "and a lot of the moms were talking about computers and websites and how kids are getting onto the wrong websites." She lets that sentence sit for a while.

"I know there's a lot kids want answers to, and it's easy to Google everything these days, but talking to me or another adult is probably the best way to get accurate information. There are a lot of crazy people on the Internet. Just as you wouldn't get advice from a random person on the street, you shouldn't trust everything on the Internet. Anyone can say anything, you know."

Daisy looks uncomfortable, buries her face in a glass of milk.

"I'm here, honey," Margaret says. "I am. You can talk to me about whatever you want. Is there something you are curious about or want to know more about?"

Daisy shakes her head, her face still in the glass.

"I love you." Margaret bends over and kisses the top of her head. "I'll leave you alone now," she says.

She goes to her office and looks at menus that Priscilla has sent over for Clarke's party. They have decided on a new private kitchen in Wong Chuk Hang that can fit 40 to 150, since Margaret has no idea how many people there will be. Priscilla has wisely gone ahead and reserved the space, having correctly gauged that she is not going to get a lot of answers from Margaret in a timely way. Margaret appreciates it, writes the check with a sense of relief that someone is taking charge and making decisions so that she doesn't have to. After paying a few more bills, she picks up the paper.

There's a section that fascinates her. It's called Mainland News, and it's a column of brief news items that are maybe two or three sentences each. They are odd and horrifying, gathered from regional newspapers, so she doesn't know how reliable the reports are. Still, they are compelling and very peculiar. On any given day, there might be a report on a girl who was molested by her teacher, with the odd detail, such as a girl's description of his "chalk-tainted fingers"; or a woman who had been held as a sex slave in a dog cage by a policeman and had escaped naked; or how job applicants were refused opportunities because they had pimples or were shorter than 160 centimeters; or other oddities of life in China. And of course there are many, many stories of child abductions. This morning, there is one of a woman being arrested for trying to sell a boy at a Nanping bus station, and another about a teenager being reunited with his family ten years after he was abducted and sold to a farmer in rural China. Whenever she reads these small blips of news, she thinks of the family behind the story, compressed into this one square inch of newsprint, and how it's impossible to ever know the truth.

When her children find her there, it is six, and dinner is on the table. An hour has gone by, and she doesn't know how. They come and tell her that dinner is ready.

When she gets to the kitchen, she feels even more removed, as if she is visiting her own home. The food there is unrecognizable in an odd way, as if her recipes have been refracted through a wavy glass, which they have, in a way, and come out into an alternate universe. Essie is wonderful, but she is from the Philippines and not native to spinach salads and grilled salmon, so they always come out a little tweaked, with too much honey in the teriyaki or not enough dressing on the salad, so it's dry and tasteless. She is making approximations of the dishes. If Margaret lived in the United States, she would be cooking, her dishes would be her own, and her children would know how they were supposed to taste in their own home. She picks at the salad now, discovers a stray cocktail onion, randomly added, and puts her fork down in defeat. The children eat their salmon and chatter about the news at school, how someone is having a laser tag party, how a girl was giving away candy on the bus to make friends. Essie is telling her something about the washing machine. It's all white noise. Clarke calls, Daisy answers, and he says he'll be home by eight and to leave him some salmon. She floats above herself and sees herself, an American woman in Hong Kong with her two children in the kitchen, eating dinner. A phantom child, missing, hovers at the edges.

Doesn't every city contain some version of yourself that you can finally imagine? In southern California, near where she went to college, it was driving barefoot in some old station wagon through a cool, damp night, drawling surfer boy by your side, going to Ralph's to buy beer and aluminum folding chairs for a beach bonfire. The feel of the car pedal ridged smoothly against your sand-buffed foot. In New York, where she was a young working woman, it was walking down a chilly fall sidewalk with a soft paper cup of hot coffee in your hand, multicolored scarf wound three times around your neck, on your way to work in a Midtown skyscraper with steel elevators. Paris, sitting knees-up on a windowseat with a glass of red wine, looking out at something very old and beautiful. That was the thing about this strange afterlife here in Hong Kong: She doesn't have a version of herself without G. She doesn't know what the image is of what she is supposed to be. She cobbles one together, enough to live out the day, but she needs a more permanent, whole version, one with a possible, all-encompassing life, a picture, so that she can begin to try living again.

Hilary

"LAVENDER," her mother says.

"What?" Hilary says, absentmindedly scrolling through the *Examiner* website, looking at local San Francisco news. She is on Skype with her mom.

"Lavender is as good as cedar, and smells better."

"Oh, for the moths?"

"Yes, apparently it's the new thing, or maybe it's the old thing."

"I'll give it a try. Nothing else is working. In an oil or dried, like potpourri?" She clicks over to expatlocat. Clicks on Message Boards. Time to see if the troll is back.

Her mother talks about lavender, and she scrolls down the headers: "Husband traveling too much?" "Looking for dog groomer," "My baby prefers the helper to me!" All the usual travails of living in Asia. She finds the thread with her story, clicks through, sees no new posts, breathes a silent sigh of relief.

"Mom, I have to go," she says, glancing at the clock. "I'm supposed to go on a walk with Olivia."

She meets Olivia at the base of Tai Tam Reservoir Road, where they will perambulate through the country park. Hong Kong is full of these parks and trails, green and wooded, a surprise to newcomers. Olivia brings her two dogs, Xena and Filly, golden retrievers, unusual for Hong Kong because of their size. It is only because she has a garden at home that she can keep them. The air is crisp and sweet, a perfect March day.

They kiss on the cheek. Olivia drinks elegantly from her water bottle, face shaded by an enormous visor. "So how are you?" she asks.

"I feel beset by the world," Hilary tells her. "I have these moths at home. It's like a plague of locusts, and they're constantly dying everywhere. And this thing with Julian. And David . . ."

"Yes, what has become of our David?" Olivia raises an eyebrow. She has never mentioned the time she almost said something over lunch at the club, but her complete lack of surprise is a mild rebuke in itself.

"Apparently he's been seen around town with a young girl."

"So unimaginative," Olivia says. "Why are they always so predictable?"

"Have you seen him?" Hilary asks.

"Absolutely not! And I would freeze him out if I did!" Olivia is outraged at the suggestion.

"I know he and Sebastian are friendly, and they have the work connection."

"I've told Sebastian he's not allowed to speak to him."

They walk on in silence. Ahead of them, the dogs sniff a bush. The road becomes steep, and they breathe a little harder.

"And this thing happened," Hilary says. She hadn't been sure she was going to tell anyone about it, but she wants to tell someone, to get the stone off her chest, to quiet the clanging in her head.

"A thing . . ."

"A text message."

"Oh, from whom?"

"From David. But it wasn't meant for me."

It had dinged into her phone at a quiet moment.

"I came so hard I'm still jelly."

David has never texted or e-mailed her, except for that one e-mail when he said he wasn't coming to Bangkok. It had been something of a principle. He always calls. Spouses should talk, not type, he had said. She had found it old-fashioned but kind of charming.

So what kind of Freudian slip makes a man text something like that to his estranged wife, whom he never texts on principle? Does he hit the Write button and then type his wife's name in by mistake because he has been thinking of her? Does his girlfriend's name also start with an H? Do you try so hard to avoid doing something that you automatically do it? Does he even know what he's done? Or is he such jelly he can't even think straight. This, she thinks with sardonic distaste at his sudden discovery. A man, revitalized, with a new life found. Their sex had become dutiful when they realized having children was going to be a bit more difficult. He had always been game, but she had felt it hanging over them.

The text had come in on a Saturday afternoon, so she had been left to conjure up an entire day for him and this woman. Breakfast, back to bed, lunch, then maybe he went to the gym and wrote that text from there?

Olivia is suitably horror-stricken, and yet, she says with a little bit of admiration, "Jesus. I never knew David had it in him."

"I know!" Hilary knows exactly what she means. And the fact that she can feel this makes her think that the marriage was so over that what he did was not so bad.

"Do you hate him?" Olivia asks. " 'Cause I feel like you don't. At least, not enough."

Hilary hesitates, opens her water bottle, sips some water. "I don't know," she says. "I kind of hate him, but I'm envious of him too, in a way. If you know what I mean. It's like the moment you decide to leap, you leave everything behind."

"I do know what you mean," Olivia says, adjusting her hat. "You're too kind, though."

They walk on, the only sound the panting of the dogs.

"And what's happening with Julian?" Olivia asks.

"Nothing," Hilary confesses. "But I think it's going to happen. It's time."

"That's big!" Olivia claps her hands. "Have you told the orphanage anything about David?" She pauses. "Never mind. That's one of those things that you realize are impossible once you think them through."

"So I haven't," Hilary concurred. "Because, yes, what would I possibly say?"

"Awkward," Olivia observes.

"Yes."

"So that's that," Olivia says. "Onward!"

They walk on, talking about idle gossip. Olivia tells her what's going on in the local Chinese scene, where a scion of a wealthy family has been found having an affair with a pretty karaoke girl and he claims he's really in love and wants to leave his wife and two daughters. "He bought the mistress Van Cleef," Olivia says, "and the wife got Chow Tai Fook!" Chow Tai Fook is the less expensive local jeweler. And that was the outrageous thing, not the fact that he was having an affair.

Hilary has always marveled at how locals talk so unromantically and practically about affairs, how the women tell one another that Angie Chan got an apartment for her fortieth birthday, that property was better than jewelry; that Melissa Wong made a million dollars last year day-trading. Olivia is one of them, but she is rare in that she goes outside their circle to be friends with someone like Hilary.

When they reach the end of the walk, Olivia gives her dogs water and hugs Hilary.

"I love you," she says. "You're a good person, an amazing person."

"Thank you," Hilary says. "I wish it were true."

"I'm worried about you," Olivia says. "I'm taking you out to dinner tonight. You need to get out, and not just in the daytime. No good you moping over a solitary bowl of soup."

She demurs, but Olivia is insistent.

Hilary goes home to take a shower, turn on her computer, watch over the message boards as if the answer to her life were there. The problem is, she doesn't know what the question is.

She and Olivia go out to a trendy Japanese *izakaya* restaurant filled with twenty-somethings, and over the course of the meal, it comes to light that Olivia's husband saw David at the airport this afternoon and he's going to be in Tokyo for a few days on business, and now Olivia, after several cups of sake, thinks they should go and check out his apartment.

"They won't let me in," Hilary says.

"Of course they will," Olivia insists, and Hilary knows she's probably right. Polite receptionists will always succumb to loud, obnoxious foreigners.

"But why?" she asks.

"Oh, come on," Olivia says. "You have to be curious?"

"Yes, but not enough to break into his apartment."

"We're doing it," Olivia says decisively, and waves for the bill.

In the apartment lobby, they pause.

"Should I do the talking?" Hilary asks.

"Yes. I'll go to Cantonese if we need it."

They walk over to the reception desk.

Hilary explains to the smiling woman in uniform that she needs to get into David's apartment.

"You are Mrs. Starr?" the woman asks.

"Yes," Hilary says.

"Do you have any identification?"

Hilary shows her Hong Kong ID card.

"But you have not been living in the apartment . . . ," the woman says delicately.

"No," she says. "I live in the U.S. I'm moving over soon, but David came over first. I'm here to look for apartments. David was going to leave me a key, but I know he had a last-minute business trip." She knows this is a common enough situation, when a man comes to work in Hong Kong first and the wife comes later. She also knows she is talking too much, explaining too much. What is it that people say about lying: Say as little as possible?

Still, a key is handed to her. It's that simple.

In the elevator, she gets a fit of the giggles. "Wasn't that ridiculously easy?" she says. "Too much, right?"

"You look trustworthy," Olivia says. "She knows you're not going to rob the place. Ah, privilege of the white middle class."

"That woman doesn't know about enraged, estranged wives, then."

The elevator doors ding open. The carpeted hallway is quiet and dimly lit. They find their way to the apartment, 1501.

She opens the door. "Breaking and entering," she whispers.

"We're just entering," says Olivia, ever practical.

Hilary hits a light switch. A neat, anonymous living room greets them, stuffy from lack of air circulation. They venture into the middle of the living room, letting the door close behind them.

"What if he comes back?" Olivia says, giggling.

"No, he's in Tokyo for two days, he said."

"We could sleep here!"

"I think we're going to find more going on in the bedroom and bathroom, right?"

"And the kitchen."

Olivia goes to the kitchen and opens the fridge. She gestures for Hilary to join her in looking inside.

"Typical," she sniffs. "Revolting." There's a stained pizza box and a few cans of beer, some Pellegrino.

On the counter there's a half-drunk bottle of Glenlivet. He always liked a Scotch when he got home. Hilary opens the cupboards—unused pots and pans and spotless dishes. No one is nesting here, that's for sure.

She goes into the bathroom, now unabashed. A razor, a contact lens case, a toothbrush, and a tube of Sensodyne lie next to the sink. She sniffs his toothbrush, feels it for dampness. Opening the medicine cabinet, she finds nothing but Q-tips and a bottle of Advil. Where is the girl? No tampons, no hairspray or brush. If he has a girl, she's treading lightly on his life.

I came so hard I'm still jelly.

He wrote that to a ghostly girl whose presence haunts her.

She shuts the medicine cabinet and goes into the bedroom. Olivia joins her there. They look at the neatly made bed, the spotless sheets.

"The desk?" Olivia asks.

Hilary sits down and opens drawers. Empty. There are a few papers from work on the desk. She opens the closet door, sees a few suits hanging, shirts still in plastic from the dry cleaner. She runs her hand along the sleeves of the suits.

"It's so depressing," she says. "Is this enough for him? Is this what he wants? What is he trying to build?" And then she is weeping, quietly, shoulders rocking back and forth as she sobs.

Olivia comes over and puts her arms around her. "Clearly he has no idea," she says. "And it's not anything that you want to be part of."

They leave quietly, a bit abashed now, riding the elevator down in silence, not looking at each other. They take taxis and go home, disappearing into the night.

Mercy

MERCY AND DAVID are at the beach on a cool, temperate day. They took a taxi to Repulse Bay, a popular tourist beach on the south side of the island. They have walked the concrete promenade to Deep Water Bay and back, smelled the potent combination of seawater and dog urine, watched the joggers and the dog-walking helpers. Now they settle on the sand, a few feet from a lifeguard station.

Behind them, hordes of mainland-Chinese tourists swarm the few shops, the dilapidated temple at the end of the beach. Guides holding flags raise them aloft to herd their charges.

"Awful," David says, speaking of the crowds.

"It's changed a lot," Mercy says. "There didn't used to be so many."

Silence, but not uncomfortable.

"The beach is man-made, you know," Mercy says, having gleaned this fact from some guidebook when she was writing a piece on Hong Kong beaches for the magazine. "And they widened it a while ago because it was so crowded."

He scoops up some sand, pebbly and coarse. "It's pretty terrible sand," he says. "They could have brought in better."

She peeks at him from under her cowboy hat, worn to give her a jaunty, devil-may-care attitude. They are sitting on a woven straw mat, the kind that folds up into its own bag. She has brought a six-pack of beer and some potato chips in a supermarket bag, and when he asks for water, she doesn't have any. She looks around and sees that the other people have coolers and Tupperware containers full of food, and she feels inadequate. Or maybe just young. He doesn't seem to mind, just pops open a beer and lies down on the uncomfortable mat, propping his head up with the towels they have brought.

He's still somewhat of a mystery, David, all sharp edges, and she hasn't had the courage to unravel him any further.

The sun is bright, though, today. It's a crisp March morning, and she can feel the winter slipping away.

"Weather's great," she says, just to say something. He nods under his baseball cap, his fingers lying on top of the beer can.

She gets up to walk along the shoreline. It's a man-made beach, but there is still life. She sees small fish darting around in the waves, spots a bleached-out crab shell. She thinks of making seafood stock, how you boil the shells of shrimp and crab until the liquid becomes something briny and flavorful, and looks out at the roiling cauldron of the ocean, housing all that life. So she goes back to David, who may or may not be asleep, and taps his shoulder.

"I'm pregnant," she says.

She found out earlier in the week, lying in bed, waiting to drift off into a nap, when the thought clanged into her head, causing her eyelids to spring wide open.

She hasn't had her period in a while.

She sat up, all drowsiness gone, and raced to her phone, where she pulled up the calendar and did a quick calculation. Five and a half weeks.

She sat down on the bed. She was usually pretty regular, but she has never really noticed when her period comes and goes. She wasn't on the pill. David used a condom most times, except when he didn't. He had trouble getting his wife pregnant, or she wasn't able to get pregnant, so he never really thought about it, he said. Life is shaggy, unpredictable, and who has time to be a hundred percent safe all the time? Certainly not Mercy.

She took the elevator down and walked to the nearest Mannings, where she perused the aisle where they sold ovulation kits, pregnancy tests, and condoms all together, in some frenzy of family planning and unplanning. With the test in a small bag, she walked home, wondering how the next fifteen minutes were going to change or not change her life. She wasn't scared.

When the line showed up, she took a deep breath and looked in the mirror. She held the test next to her head and looked at the mirror image. Her face, flattened against the glass. Here I am, she thought, a pregnant girl. Do I look like a commercial? Should I be radiating happiness or worry? What is this image?

Following the test, she thought, abortion, but after that, nothing followed. She had always abstractly thought of abortion as a right, as a reflexive action, but now, with the idea that there was a baby, her baby, inside her, she felt unexpectedly protective. A tadpole, a little bunch of squiggling cells that would become the chubby-cheeked cherub in the baby formula ads that she suddenly notices plastered all over double-decker buses and billboards around Hong Kong. She has a baby inside her.

Being pregnant feels like another irrevocable step toward becoming an adult, like the first time she got her period and tried tampons and when she went out, she looked around at school and wondered how many girls had tampons inside them. Now she looks at all the pregnant women and is amazed that she is one of them.

It's been three days, and she's been sitting on this information, not knowing what to do with it.

She looks at David, who looks as shell-shocked as one might imagine.

His nose is already turning red in the sun. He is fair, she thinks. Our baby will be a mix of my Korean skin and his fair English skin, or is he Irish or German? She doesn't even know.

"Wow," he says. "Just . . . wow."

She doesn't know what else to demand or expect, so she just pops open a beer and takes a sip before she remembers she's pregnant. He doesn't tell her not to drink. She wonders what sort of sign that is.

They sit, and he doesn't say anything else for a long time. She doesn't drink any more beer, just puts the can down in the sand. She's afraid to look at him, to say anything, not wanting to cede any ground or give him any indication of where she's at. He should give her that, she thinks. He owes her that. He should give her a hint of what he's thinking.

Finally he says, "That's quite a big load to drop on me."

"Well, I've been carrying it around for a few days, and I didn't know how else to tell you." She suppresses the urge to apologize.

"As you know," he starts. "As you know . . . I was trying to have a baby, with my wife, for a long time."

"Yes," she says.

"And we were never successful. And I got tested, and they said I had low, you know, fertility, with the sperm and all, which was just one of the issues, because Hilary had her issues too . . ." He looks abashed when he speaks his wife's name. "Which is why I never took that many precautions when we . . ." He trails off again. "Anyway, it's clearly not impossible."

"Clearly," she says.

He looks at her, surprised. Maybe that came out a little more abruptly than she meant it to.

"Be a good guy," she says.

"What does that mean?" he asks.

"Just be a good guy." *Don't be an asshole. Don't be like everyone else.*

He raises his eyebrows. "I want to be a good guy," he says. "So I'll just say, we will figure it out together. And I will be respectful of whatever you want to do. But you also have to give me a little time to figure out what I feel about this. It's a lot."

"I know," she says.

"Do you want to stay?" he asks.

"I guess not," she says.

As they gather up their things, she wonders at how she can ruin even the smallest excursion. Maybe she should have waited until they had relaxed, enjoyed the beautiful day. Instead, she blurted it out in the first fifteen minutes. Other people must have better ways to deal with things like this, better ways to lead their lives. She can sense, in a murky, shapeless way, how small decisions lead to big effects. If she were able to manage the small things better, her life would be better. But she is powerless to change the way she interacts with the world. Things just happen the way they do to Mercy.

They flag down a taxi from the beach, and he drops her off at her building after a halfhearted offer to have her come over, which even she is too proud to accept. He leans over and kisses her on the cheek. "Take care," he says. "I'll call you, okay?"

She nods and slides out. She comes into her apartment lobby to see her mother, sitting on a plastic stool, looking tired, a big ugly suitcase next to her.

"Mercy!" her mother says.

"Mom?" she says.

Her mother is here. Holy shit.

Margaret

THEY'RE HAVING BREAKFAST when Clarke tells her he wants to invite David to his birthday party. The birthday party that is no longer a surprise, since she casually mentioned it to him by mistake a few weeks ago, something about the Careys being in Thailand on the date and not being able to come to the party. He blinked, said, "Great."

"Oh," she said. "Oops."

Now he wants to invite David Starr. He tells her this while buttering his toast.

"I don't want to," she says.

"Is it my party or yours?" he says lightly. He can be surprisingly obstinate about some things.

"It's your birthday, but it's my party," she says, smiling, still, a little bit.

"You're serious, aren't you?" he says.

"He did a terrible thing to my friend!" she tries to explain.

"Oh, are you and Hilary friends now?"

"You have to choose sides, you know."

"Actually, you don't. And actually, we don't know what happened. And it would be awkward if I didn't invite him. We have a lot of mutual friends, and we do some work together."

Margaret watches her handsome husband wipe his mouth with a napkin.

"I know what happened," she says.

"Let's talk about it later," he says, giving her a kiss on his way out the door.

Priscilla has worked her magic, chosen a caterer, talked about

lighting, flowers, music, specialty cocktails. It's going to be big. Over
a hundred people, more like a wedding. Names she got from Clarke's
secretary and had Margaret vet, because Margaret hadn't been able
to generate anything by herself.

Later, when Margaret checks her phone, it won't swipe open. It
works only every fifth or sixth time, and then not at all, presenting
her with a black screen no matter what she does. Being without a
phone makes her feel as if she doesn't have an arm, so she decides to
go to the store to get it fixed.

But every single day is filled with little traps. She decides to switch
handbags, from a black one to a brown one she hasn't used in a while,
when she discovers a little red plastic dinosaur in the side pocket.
And an old dusty lollipop. They were treats from the doctor when
they went to get G's shots the year before. A punch to the heart. She
sits there on the floor of her bedroom, again, with the contents of her
bag strewn around her, and clutches this cheap plastic dinosaur and
the lollipop and tries to recalibrate her life so she can live it for the
next five minutes. Then blinks, gets up.

She goes downstairs, where the newspaper is waiting. She reads it
with another cup of tea. Today in the Mainland News column, a
story of a boy who was kidnapped as a child and then found his way
home through Google Maps. A picture of him with his newly found
parents, with awkward positions and tentative smiles. Now in his
twenties, he had been adopted by a family who loved him, but he
always remembered the landmarks in his old village, and he tracked
down his family. In China, this must happen every day, children
going missing, being kidnapped, abducted. In a country of a billion,
what is a child a day?

She wonders if his parents will be a disappointment. If he will love
them, or if he is too ensconced in his new life to have room for them.
She went to a lunch for an organization dedicated to the rehabilita-
tion of sex workers in India a few years ago and was told that many
girls go back to sex work after being freed, because it is the world they

know and all their friends are there. It's too hard to go out and forge a new life and easy to fall back on the old one. This organization is trying to help them stay out of their old trade by teaching them a new one: making bras and panties. They showed photos of brightly colored underwear and the young girls who made them, and Margaret couldn't help but wonder if there was any other clothing they could have made, something not so suggestive, like hats, or socks, or scarves.

She closes the newspaper. The house is quiet, with Essie dusting or mopping or whatever she does to keep the house immaculate. Oh, yes, she was going to go get her phone fixed before being derailed by the handbag. She drives to the mall and goes to the phone store, where they sell her a new phone and try to persuade her to add another line to her account.

"No," she tells Jingo Wong (another odd name!). Does he know his name alludes to extreme patriotism? "No, thank you."

He swipes on his own phone, but not before she sees a photo of him with his girlfriend. They are wearing matching furry white hats. A glimpse into another person's life—and all the attendant love and heartache therein.

"If you get the new number, you get the cheaper price for the phone," he tells her helpfully. "Can start the new contract."

But she can never even think about altering anything about her cell phone account. She remembers teaching her children her telephone number. "Six two eight eight . . . ," G would say, as if it were a magic incantation, so pleased with himself. She imagines him chanting the number now, in a small, windowless box, remembering it for when he can call it, for when he is older and can do something about his situation. She told him about country codes, but how much can a child be expected to know? Still, she cannot ever give up this phone number.

She worries sometimes that her inability to move on is just narcissism, that she cannot imagine her child not needing her. Everyone always talks about the resilience of children, how they adjust to new lives, how they survive, and she sees this sometimes, has seen it, in small moments: when Daisy was lost for a few minutes when she was five, and how she hadn't cried out, how she had slipped her hand into another woman's, believing she would take care of her; or how they settle into new situations so quickly and don't look back once their parents are out of sight. This is how you can tell the survivors, she supposes. But while she wishes G is happy, she cannot imagine such a thing.

She thinks about what she would say to him if he came back. She knows that the children who come back talk about how they are afraid their parents don't want them anymore, that they are defiled, or that what they had to do to survive will be held against them.

"I love you," she would say. "I love you no matter what happened, what you said, what you did, what you thought. I understand. I understand. Mommy loves you no matter what."

Her eyes fill whenever she thinks these thoughts, and she feels secretly ashamed, as she is being indulgent or maudlin, definitely, or again, narcissistic somehow.

Jingo comes back from ringing up the sale on her new phone. She thanks him and leaves.

The mall fills up with office workers looking for lunch. She is hungry but leaves the mall so she can go to her favorite Vietnamese place on Stanley Street for pho. Margaret lines up with everyone else and is given a number. Soon she is led to a table already occupied by three other people. She sits down, points to what she wants on the menu, and waits.

Around her, people chatter away in Cantonese. This is a local place, and she is the only nonlocal. The food is good and cheap, and she loves coming here. When the pho comes, she dumps in the tiny red peppers and the sprouts, inhales the pungent steam of the broth. She eats quickly, sweat beading on her temples as the peppers fire up in her sinuses and her mouth starts to burn. Simple things: taste, smell, heat. She takes a sip of water, sits back, her hunger sated. She is sitting with a twenty-something man and two women, who must work together. They chat animatedly, dropping in an English word here and there, taking no notice of her. It feels good to be totally anonymous. She pays the bill and leaves.

It's time to go home, to be there for when Daisy and Philip return from school. As they come in the door, shedding their backpacks and scuffed sneakers, she hugs them, gets them a snack, and watches them drink milk and eat, her babies.

Daisy gets up and surreptitiously signals to her mother to follow.

"Mom," she says, "I think I got it."

"What?" Margaret says. "Got what?"

Daisy huffs with frustration. "You know, the thing. Remember the tea?"

Oh. Margaret vaguely remembers going to a tea for mothers and daughters the previous spring, at which adolescence and sexuality were discussed. She had still been reeling and barely functional, but she had gone for Daisy, so she could be there with her mother.

"You mean your period?"

"Yes! I have this kind of brown stuff coming out."

"Oh, sweetie," she says. "Does your stomach hurt at all? Like cramps?"

"A little last night, but I didn't know why."

Margaret pulls her into her bathroom. "Here." She reaches down to the drawer and gets out pads and liners. "Why don't you start with these? You can let me know if you want to try tampons, but try these first."

Daisy takes the packages and, looking uncomfortable but relieved, hugs her mom.

"Thanks, Mom," she says.

"Go experiment with them," Margaret tells her.

Her daughter leaves.

Margaret remembers when she was fully engaged with everything, before everything happened. Moms talked about everything and gave one another advice on what to do, what stage was coming up for their kids. She realizes now she has no idea what is going on with sixth-grade girls, what other things are going on.

When Margaret first got her period, she remembers, her mother showed her the pads and told her to rip the outside part off, wrap it in tissue, and then flush the cotton down the toilet. She did that for a while before she realized that no one else did. These are all our little mysteries, she thinks.

Her phone buzzes on the counter. Her messages are coming in now on her new phone. There's an e-mail from Mr. Park of the Seoul police.

"Please call," he writes. "I need some information from you. There is new development."

Her heart stops.

Hilary

HILARY IS LIVING her life more and more online. With the message boards, Facebook, and e-mails, she doesn't need to go out for social interaction. And if she needs anything physical, she sends Puri and Sam out to get it, often with photos printed from the Internet of the exact kind of coffee or the brand of bread she wants, so they don't bring back the wrong thing. She pores over adoption boards, infertility boards, expat boards; it is as if she wants to hear advice only from people she has never met and knows nothing about. Maybe she will migrate her life to a virtual world, where she will exist only as finger taps on a keyboard, a ghostly being made up of pithy comments and occasional snapshots. Anyway, she only really ever goes out to see Olivia now. Without work, without a husband, she has faded into the background. She never realized how much of her life was lived through David, through being married and being a couple. When she thinks of whom she would want to see, she cannot think of anyone, save Olivia. And apparently no one is very interested in seeing her either, as her phone remains silent and her e-mail inbox fills up only with sale notifications and reminders of club dinners.

She has heard of people being dropped after divorce or separation, but it's still surprising to her. It's not as if she thought she had so many friends, but it is shocking to realize that the world she thought she had constructed around her was so tenuous. Perhaps it's because she doesn't have children. She's seen the close bonds that women with children form with one another, and that's something she's been shut out of completely. What is left? she wonders. Family. Is that it? And hers is so small. Her mother calls her dependably, in between taking care of her father, who descends ever further into dementia. And also, she's been thinking about what a husband is. David used to be family, but now he's the enemy. She understands now the thin line between love and hate. Casual bonds are flexible, can be attenuated without destruction. Not so the fierce close ones.

When she got on Facebook for the first time, she was struck by how these hordes of middle-aged people had taken on this medium that seemed to be for the young, and made it their own. They posted photos of their thickening, graying selves with self-deprecating comments, boasted about their work achievements, introduced babies and grandbabies, corralled people to reunions. Scrolling through her two hundred friends, she is amazed by the affection she feels for all these people who represent so many different times in her life.

Is this a sign that you've given up? When you spend all your time thinking of the past? She's made the mistake of contacting people after going through their photo albums and feeling a brief, unreal intimacy. She writes inappropriately close things like "Remember in high school when we skipped science third period and went to Union Square?" and she gets back a puzzled, reserved response like "Hilary Krall, I haven't seen you in so long. You look great." And she deletes the entire exchange out of embarrassment, because, of course, they hadn't spent hours remembering shared time and feeling close and they probably think . . . what do they think? The truth, most likely. That she's in a bad relationship and in a bad place and looking for something, anything, that might get her out. People post pictures of their best times, but it's not so hard to see past the smiling faces.

Funny how people really don't change that much. She sees one woman who was always quirky and alone, even in high school. A misfit, to use an unkind high school word. This woman's loneliness and her growing madness are so palpable it's uncomfortable. It's all there in her page full of unanswered questions to friends and family, reminiscences of past injustices, unfocused shots of her pet birds, her disheveled bedroom. Hilary clicks through a photo album, tries to compile an acceptable life for this woman, cannot.

How is it that life is so fragile? It's not just life itself, and mortality; it's more how a perfectly conventional-seeming life can collapse in a few short weeks. Several months ago, Hilary felt she was leading a normal life, and while she isn't really mourning the loss of what was, after all, an imperfect life, there is still grief for the person she once thought she was. She feels vulnerable, a newborn trying to fashion a new life in the wake of all that has happened. She is moving toward the future but uncertainly, and without grace, she feels.

A moth blunders onto her screen.

She freezes.

"MOTHERFUCKER!" she screams, so loudly she surprises herself. It feels good. "MOTHERFUCKING MOTHERFUCKER!"

She remembers that Puri has gone out, to "market," as she likes to say, using the word as a verb. Hilary is alone at home. She can scream as loudly and as long as she wants.

She screams it one more time, slamming down her laptop on the beastly, wormlike insect, smushing it between the screen and the keyboard. Then she puts her head down on her arms and starts to cry, big, gulping sobs that shake her body and wrench her lungs, wet the desk beneath her elbows. Has she cried before this? Of course, she hasn't. It was a point of pride between her and her mother over Christmas break in Bangkok. Their family didn't show feelings like that. They were stoics, proud in their impassivity.

She sobs on. Has something been taken from her? She doesn't know. Was it a life she wanted? Did she want the husband, the child? Or was it something she had just been programmed to think?

Something showy about crying like this, alone. She starts to feel foolish, crying so loudly, and tries to stop. She succeeds, sits on her chair, feeling the stillness, feeling her body heave up and down as her breath regulates.

Julian.

She wants to see Julian. She is a better person when she's with him. She's thinking of others. He gets her out of herself. Julian.

She opens the computer, wipes off the remains of the moth with a tissue. Then she clicks her way back to the thread about her and Julian and begins to write. HappyGal to the defense.

Mercy

BEING WITH HER MOTHER makes her thirteen all over again. But her mother has changed too. Their relationship keeps teetering and swinging back and forth, unsteady, reshaping itself with every awkward exchange.

This is not a normal visit. Her mother has not left the United States for at least twenty years. Mercy thinks she probably had to get a passport to come here. So some planning happened.

Her mother has left her father, it seems. Something about gambling debts, and the theft of her nest egg, her *gae-don*, the Korean women's tradition of lending money to one another at monthly meetings, and also something, muttered darkly, about other women.

What a mess. This is what she comes from.

That first afternoon, when she gets out of the taxi, her mother asks where she has been. But that is just one small blip of maternal concern, a flare struck and gone, it seems, forever. If it's possible, her mother seems even more lost than she is.

They go up together in the tiny, rickety elevator with her mother's suitcase.

"This is where you live," her mother says in Korean, standing uncomfortably close to Mercy, because the suitcase is taking up half the elevator.

"I know, it's not nice," she says.

"When we immigrated to Queens, our apartment was very small, and we didn't have our own bathroom," her mother says. The elevator doors open, and she leads her mother down the tiny, narrow hallway lit by fluorescent lights. She takes out her keys and unlocks the door.

"Ta-da," she says as she swings it open to her studio, her messy bed, with clothes strewn all over it—remnants of her rejected dressing choices before meeting David this morning.

"Very small," her mother says without emotion.

"Only one bed," she points out.

"It is big enough. We can share," her mother says, with finality.

Over coffee later, after her mother has showered and changed and they have made their way to a little café down the street, Mercy asks, tentatively, how long she is here for.

"I don't know," her mother says. "Things are strange at home."

She sips at her plain coffee. She never ordered latte or cappuccino, or the fancy drinks.

"I flew through Seoul," she says. "On Korean Air. Incheon Airport is so modern!"

"I know," Mercy says. "It makes JFK look third world."

"Things have changed so much in Asia," her mother says. "I wonder what it would be like if we had stayed in Korea. Before, America used to be the best place, but now I think it is not so good."

"I miss America," Mercy says. And she realizes it is true. That there is no reason for her to be here in Hong Kong, with her married lover—Can he even be termed a lover? The implied constancy is not there—and a baby, or, rather, an embryo and all the messiness in her life. But she can't go back now.

"I bought the ticket through Mrs. Choi at church," her mother says, putting down her cup. "And she says I can set the return date whenever I want. It is very flexible. And I can stop in Seoul on the way back. But I wanted to rush to see you. You are never home, and you never return my phone calls."

"Sorry, Mom," Mercy says.

"So, do you have a job?" her mother asks.

Mercy's silence is her answer. Her mother rips off a piece of the almond croissant they are sharing—powdered sugar is sprinkled on her chin. How disappointing for her mother, she thinks, to have a daughter like her, but how used to it she must be. Just as Mercy is used to men being disappointing, having had her father as a model. She and her mother—they are lost in these patterns, unable to kick out into another, freer, better life.

"Hong Kong is very expensive, isn't it?" her mother asks.

"Yes," she says.

"I'm staying for some time," says her mother, "so I help you with the rent."

When Mercy went to college, she met not only those wealthy aliens; she also met other Korean Americans from different parts of the country. She understood the Queens Koreans, how most of them came from struggling families, dry cleaners and deli owners and ministers, but there was a whole other breed, like the Korean American kids from Beverly Hills or Bloomfield Hills, or the wealthier suburbs of Long Island. Their parents were doctors or real estate developers or just businessmen more successful than her dad. It wasn't the wealth that bothered her, though; it was the fact that their parents seemed so normal, and they assumed that other Koreans were just like them. They complained about overbearing mothers, fathers who were disappointed that they hadn't gone to Harvard, grandmothers who were a pain. It was this assumption that her family was like theirs, that her parents were together, a team, and that they had the time or the inclination to care about where Mercy went to school or how she led her life.

It wasn't that her mother didn't love her but that she didn't know how to help her, being in a terrible relationship herself.

"Do you think I can get a job here?" her mother asks.

She feels a panic open up inside her. The world she has so carefully been trying to hold together, the fragile bubble, seems on the verge of collapsing.

"I don't—" she begins, but someone is tapping her shoulder.

"Hey," says a young man behind her.

She twists around, looks at his face, trying to place him.

"Charlie," he says. "From Columbia. We saw each other a while back at the Conrad?"

"Oh, yes," she says. "Great to see you." The day she met David.

He looks expectantly at her and then her mother.

"Oh, this is my mom," she says. As they shake hands and exchange pleasantries, she gets the feeling she often does, where she floats away, above herself, and observes the scene. She feels a deep pleasure at the fact that this scenario, this snapshot, is so normal. Here is a girl who lives in Hong Kong, whose mother is visiting, who is introducing her mother to another acquaintance, an old college friend she has run into. She sees it happening all over town, all the time, and always feels on the outside, like that will never be her, and all of a sudden, here it is, happening, although everything on the inside is so very different. She's so different, and marked, but this instant makes her feel normal. In a sudden moment of insight, she wonders if everyone feels this way.

"Maybe I'll see you around," Charlie says. But he lingers.

Her mother sees the look on his face and excuses herself to go to the bathroom. After all, this is a boy/man with a suit and a briefcase. A man with a job.

"What are you doing this weekend?" he asks suddenly.

"Oh," she says. "Um, well, my mom just got here, and that was a bit of a surprise, so I have no idea."

"There's this party at my friend's house," he starts.

"Oh, yeah?"

"A bunch of kids from Yale are throwing it, but they're pretty cool." She has almost forgotten that this is how people her age talk, having sequestered herself for so long.

"Great," she says.

"Wanna go?"

A party for twenty-somethings. This is what she should be doing. Not hiding out from having been implicated in a hideous crime and getting impregnated by a detached married man. She feels the gap sharply, suddenly. Maybe this is why she says yes. Maybe this is why she gives Charlie her e-mail address and phone number. He walks away smiling, and she remains, feeling that she has duped him and it is all going to come crashing down. Her mother comes back, smiling, saying that he looked like a nice boy. "Chinese men," she says, "are better than Korean men. They treat their women well." And Mercy is back to where she started, feeling like a fraud, that she is the architect of her own awful destiny.

But it's as if fate helps her to make bad decisions. Because her mother is here, it is easy (and truthful) to tell David that she can't see him for a bit. After the news, he clearly needs a bit of a break as well.

"She didn't come because . . ." He doesn't finish the thought.

"No," she says. "She has no idea. Just a coincidence."

"Okay," he says. "Okay. Buzz me when she leaves."

And she hangs up and suddenly feels, can it be? Free. She feels a bit freer. She's burst from one situation into another.

So then she's free to go to this party with Charlie, which delights her mother, because even with her track record, she is still Korean enough to think that a man can save a woman. Especially someone with Mercy's destiny, who needs so much saving.

So Charlie wants to pick her up, which is really nice, but her mom is staying with her, so she meets him downstairs in the lobby at nine.

"You look nice," he says.

"Thanks," she says. "So do you."

"Do you want to get something to eat before we go?"

So they go to a bistro nearby and get a table outside, because the night is not too cool, and start with cocktails. The chairs are tippy, and the table's marble top is stained with red wine. She's been here before, with David, and feels awkward, but none of the waiters recognize her, and she begins to relax.

She thinks just for a minute if, if, she should drink, but this baby, this tiny accumulation of cells inside her, is so minuscule and so easily ignored, such a thought and nothing else, that after the first sip of Tanqueray and tonic, she manages to forget about the whole thing entirely.

From then on, it's a typical twenty-something date. Lots of cocktails to get loose and happy, a big meal, he pays, no awkwardness, and they get into a cab at eleven and go to the party, which is at some guy's parents' place, which means it's an enormous apartment with lots of rooms with pictures of the absent parents, who have gone to Colombo for the weekend. There is a strobe light strung up and a rooftop where people are dancing with lit cigarettes in one hand and beer bottles in the other. Lots of her friends are there, and they scream with happy drunkenness to see her.

"Haven't seen you in *sooooo* long," they say, and hug, giddy with alcohol. They are so drunk they forget to ask how she is, which she likes very much.

After this happens for the fourth time, Charlie pulls her aside. He doesn't know her situation. "You're popular," he says, his face flushed and happy.

"You're handsome," she says.

And then they kiss.

The night flashes by, in corners of rooms with beds with multiple couples making out, staggering to bathrooms to fall on the toilets, spilling vodka as she pours some more. When she looks at a clock, it says 1:00 a.m., then it says 3:00, and they're at another club, Charlie by her side.

"Where were you?" she tries to ask.

"I'm here," he says. But he doesn't understand what she's saying. She's saying, "Where were you before all this other stuff happened, where were you when you could have saved me?"

But then she falls asleep, and when she wakes up, she's in his apartment, and it's ten in the morning.

Luckily, her clothes are all still on. And his are too. He lies, disheveled, snoring lightly.

She gets up and almost throws up. There was a *shawarma* pit stop at some point last night, and the garlicky meat stink in her mouth is nauseating. She goes to the bathroom and finds some mouthwash. Gargles. She looks at herself in the mirror, mottled pale skin, sunken eyes, greasy hair. The bathroom is small and humid and messy, a boy's bathroom, with hairs stuck to the shower wall and mold in the grout. She sits down on the toilet and pees. It smells sweet, like fermented juice, residue of all the alcohol.

Bad decisions.

She wipes and gets up to look at herself in the bathroom mirror while she's washing her hands. Poor, pregnant, hungover Mercy.

So many bad decisions.

Margaret

MARGARET IS DREAMING. G is nuzzling her, she can feel the solid, sweet shape of his head on her arm, rubbing as he used to. She used to call him her kitten, the way he would purr up to her and rumble with the simple pleasure of being near his mother. She would press his temples with her two palms while kissing his forehead, squeeze his butt cheeks, rub his chubby, perfect stomach with its adorable knot of a belly button. There is nothing like children to bring out the animal in you.

She picks him up and hugs him, smelling him, then wakes up, with the hard plastic wall of the airplane on her cheek. There is a little drool on her mouth.

It is a dream, and she is awake, and she is on an airplane, although Mr. Park said she shouldn't come yet, that it might all be nothing, but of course, as soon as she heard there was anything, she had to go to the airport right away.

Clarke had come to the phone after his assistant got him out of a meeting, and she had been sobbing. He hadn't been able to understand her.

"They think, they think, maybe . . . ," she had managed to say. "Maybe, a boy, the right age . . ."

"Oh, my God," he said. "When can we go?"

She had told him she would go first, because Mr. Park had said it would take a few days to get the boy to Seoul, but he had needed some more information from her, and he shouldn't have called her so early, but he knew she would want to know, even if it turned out to be nothing. A rural village, a single woman who suddenly had a child, a nephew she was raising, she said, because her sister had died. A suspicious neighbor had finally called the police, and it turned out the child wasn't the woman's and that she didn't have a good explanation as to how he had come to her house. He was the right age, around five or six, and his Korean wasn't too good, and his English was much better.

She had booked the black-eye, the flight that left Hong Kong at 1:00 a.m. and got in at 5:00 Korea time. Clarke would be on the first morning flight. Luckily, the plane had been half-empty, and she got a window seat with no one next to her. She had left a message at the police station that she would be arriving the next day, so Mr. Park would expect her. He had told her to wait in Hong Kong, but how could she have?

The Hong Kong airport at that midnight hour had been spooky, with carpet-cleaning machines whirling and dark, empty shops. She had nursed a cup of tea in the food hall, waiting for the flight to board. Around her, tired travelers checked e-mails, read newspapers, drank beer. She moved to the gate area and sat down. When the call came, the travelers all gathered up their things and traipsed to the gate, almost zombielike in their slow, sleepy gait.

Her body is awake now, immediately, when she realizes where she is. She is tingly, alive, painfully so. Her son might, might, be on the other side of this flight. She will fly across this ocean, go to this different country, check into the hotel and take up vigil again, so that she might feel his body nestle against hers, smell his sweet breath.

The cabin is dark. They switch off all the lights after takeoff, and most passengers are sleeping before the plane even gets off the ground. She was so wired that she thought she would never fall asleep, but it happened without her knowing. She is grateful for the rest. She looks at her watch: 3:00 a.m. She slept for a couple of hours and now has a few more hours of flight time.

It's been seventeen months. Seventeen months since October break when they went to Seoul and G was lost. Seventeen months since she has seen her baby.

When they land, she and her fellow travelers are regurgitated, rumpled and disheveled, into a giant hallway. She goes through immigration and out into the still-quiet arrivals hall, it being a mere six in the morning. Outside is freezing—early spring can still be cold in Seoul—and her breath puffs out as she walks to the cab line. This city is the color of smoke—all gray concrete, cinder-block buildings, and morning sky—but turns into neon frenzy at night, with pulsating lights and the red and white streaks of passing cars. She gets a taxi to the hotel and lies back, exhausted, against the vinyl seat, seeing the flat gray of the Han River, the billboards announcing new electronics, and pretty girls advertising Korean shampoo. Stripped trees line the banks of the river, bare silhouettes until suddenly she sees one with a nest on it. She allows herself to imagine the return trip, with G beside her, surely looking a little bit different, certainly quiet, subdued, but back with her, back next to her. Will this vision come true? Will this gift be given to her? She doesn't pray. She has prayed so much she is exhausted and not sure if she wants to believe in it, just as she doesn't want to say she doesn't believe in it just in case God is vengeful. How many bargains has she struck with the world in these past seventeen months? How many deals has she made with the devil or whoever she thinks might sway destiny? Too many that have come to nothing.

Mercy

MEETING CHARLIE FOR sushi at a small place on Jervois Street the next day, he is cheerful, ebullient, a puppy eager to please.

"I thought you were one of those girls who only like to go out with white guys," he says, grinning. He assumes all is well, can't read her hesitation. She is out with him, hence she must be into him. He is that young. When do boys catch up to girls? she wonders. Maybe never.

"I don't really have a policy," she says.

"But you dated mostly white guys in college, right?" he asks.

"I didn't date all that much," she says. "More like hook up. Nothing serious."

This boy is earnest and sweet. He wants a girlfriend. "You're not drinking," he says.

"I'm hung over," she says, which is true. She wonders if she's already scrambled the cells of her unborn child.

"Did you have fun last night?" He pours himself some more sake from the small porcelain flask. He knows enough to order it cold.

"Yeah," she says. She spent the day with her mother, making Korean *banchan* from the groceries her mother had bought from the Korean market in Tsim Sha Tsui.

"What did you do today?"

Parrying his questions is so easy it's like child's play. "Such a boring topic!" she declares. "How's work?"

And instead of saying, "And that's not boring?" he starts telling her about work.

She listens. It is not unpleasant, being here with Charlie, having small pieces of fish set in front of them at intervals. This is another life, one she should be having.

But still, Charlie is so . . . unsophisticated. He didn't hang out with her crowd in college and is so unknowing it makes her cringe sometimes.

His parents are middle class, his father a math teacher at a high school and his mother a lab technician.

"How'd you find your way to Columbia?" she asks.

"Recruiters came to my local school. I never thought about going abroad, thought that was only for rich people, but this woman said I could apply for a scholarship. Some tycoon families in Hong Kong give aid to local students, and that's what I got, because it's hard to get financial aid for international students."

"You must have done really well in school," she says. "Did you get a full ride?"

"Yes, full scholarship. But we still have to pay some items, like the airplane and all the things I need for living."

His English is still a little bit foreign, with a bit of an accent that surfaces from time to time and grammar that can be off. He doesn't get some jokes, doesn't know anything about American television from the eighties and nineties, doesn't understand colloquialisms but can speak pretty good English, so he seems like a blurred facsimile of an American.

"And you are from New York, right?"

"Queens," she says. "Not Manhattan."

He's not surprised. He doesn't expect anyone he knows to be from Manhattan.

"Big Koreatown there," he says. "We used to go for Korean food sometime. Love the *bulgogi*."

She debates telling him about her aunt's restaurant. Maybe he's been.

"And Chinese," she says. "Lots of Chinese places. And Irish pubs."

He looks blank. "Irish?"

She doesn't explain. "But yeah," she says. "My dad was in 'business'"—she makes quotation marks in the air—"and my mom worked sometimes, so I needed a scholarship too."

He nods.

"You know Philena, right?" she asks.

"So rich," he says, dunking sushi in the soy sauce. He puts the rice side down in the soy sauce, incorrectly. You're supposed to put the fish side in. "Her family owns all the buildings in Causeway Bay."

"Did you know her before?"

"No, no," he says. "Just meet in the U.S. And sometimes see her here but not much."

"I was her roommate for a few years," she tells him.

"I know," he says.

So he knew of her then, even though she didn't know about him. Her crowd was known at school as the fast crowd, the party crew, the cool ones. She remembers her old boss at the listings magazine telling her, "You may be twenty-five and think you know everything, but I am forty-three, and I am here to tell you that life is high school over and over again."

After dinner, she wants to go home, but he doesn't want the night to end. He suggests a drink.

"How about the Mandarin?" he says. It is not far, so they walk. She's getting more and more antsy, not wanting to be there, walking next to the perfectly nice young man she can sense is wondering whether or not to take her hand. Thankfully, he doesn't.

They get to the bar, all smoky mirrors and dark velvets, and he orders a gin martini and she orders a club soda. The alcohol, mixing with the sake he's already had, makes him voluble, and he tells her about his family and childhood.

"My parents live in a three-hundred-square-foot apartment," he announces. "I live in a flat that is twice the size of theirs."

"How does that make you feel?" she asks.

"I don't know," he says, wheezing. His eyes are glassy, and he is starting to slur. This is reason enough to drink, so you don't have to see others being idiots and have to tolerate them.

"They must be proud of you," she says. "I think my parents are proud of me, and I don't even have a job."

"Proud because of Columbia?" he asks. "You were at Columbia, right? Not Barnard?"

"Yes," she says. "And it's not the same thing." She expected him to join in as she said it, being such a familiar chorus, but he looks at her blankly. They teach a lot at Columbia, but what they can't teach is irony and sophistication. What poor Charlie doesn't realize is what potent currencies they are. All his hard work and intelligence are only going to take him so far.

"My parents didn't even dream I could go to college in America," he says. "I had to make it happen. I had to tell them it was possible."

"And now you live in an apartment that's twice the size of theirs," she says.

The bartender shakes the martini and uncaps the flask, pouring the clear liquid glinting with slivers of ice into a chilled glass. He sets the remainder down next to the glass and replaces their nuts with a fresh bowl.

"Amazing service," she says. She is starting to hate Charlie. It is a relief to feel this, as she has spent such a long time worrying that people hate her.

He takes a sip. "My parents act like they are not as good as Americans or British," Charlie says suddenly. "So when you ask how I feel about the fact that I live in a larger place than them at the age of twenty-seven, I guess I feel that you have to believe in yourself if you want to succeed."

Callow. The word floats into her head. Charlie is callow. Unknowing. Naïve. Earnest. And if she can see him for all those things, what does that make her?

They end up back at his place, an enormous apartment complex of tiny flats in Pok Fu Lam, filled with young professionals, a dorm of sorts for the financial sector. After he paid for the drinks, they got into a cab, and she did not disagree when he told the driver his address. His building has a health club, a swimming pool, and a dining room you can rent out for dinner parties. He shows her all the facilities with pride, as if he owns them.

He is starting to sober up.

"Want to go swimming?" she asks.

"The pool is closed," he says.

"That's not what I asked," she says. "I said, would you like to go swimming?"

"Sure." He nods. He tries the door. "It's locked," he says.

"Who has the key?" she says. This is what she's good at: breaking rules, behaving badly. She can take the lead.

He doesn't know, of course.

"Where is the office?" she asks. "One where there's someone on staff all night?"

He tells her.

"You stay here," she says. "You look drunk. It won't work with you there."

She goes and charms the young, bored security guard into giving her the access code with a story of how she has left her phone by the pool. He offers to escort her, but she manages to push him off, saying he has to keep doing a good job guarding the building.

Charlie is sitting on the floor with his back against the wall when she comes back, checking his BlackBerry. She inputs the code, and they go in and turn on the lights. Their sounds echo around the walls, the humid air redolent of chlorine.

"How did you get the code?" he asks.

"Years of experience in bad behavior," she says.

She can see him thinking about what they will swim in, so she strips down to her bra and panties. She looks down. Her stomach is still flat.

"Now you," she says.

He tries not to look at her. This makes her like him a little bit more.

"Okay." He shuffles off his pants, unbuttons his shirt. Soon he is in his boxers. At least he is in boxers. She had thought of him as a tighty-whitie guy.

The water is bracing, perfect. It moves against her skin like cool velvet. She forgets how wonderful it can be to be in water, weightless. She comes up like a seal, hair plastered to her skull, to find Charlie watching her.

"You are very beautiful," he says.

She melts a tiny bit more. All his annoying traits—his lack of irony and sophistication, his tendency to overstate his accomplishments— seem dissolved into the cool water. Unclothed, he is a tabula rasa, without his annoying FOB tics or telltale sartorial mistakes. He has a lean body, with muscles that ripple just under the skin. The handsomest of Chinese boys are—she hates to say it, but it's true—almost feminine, with big, moist eyes and dark, thick hair. Charlie is handsome unclothed, almost beautiful. He needed this, to be without any identifiers.

Later he will ruin it by buttoning his shirt up too high, by wearing jeans and white sneakers when they go out for brunch on a Sunday, but right now, in the pool next to her, glistening and wet and practically naked, he is Adonis, sculpted out of a smooth alabaster flesh that feels almost perfect. Here she can take him as he is, as he was when he entered the world, without complexes, without issues, without all that hard-won knowledge to hinder him.

This is why she urges him to unclothe completely, why she slips out of her bra and underwear.

"I've never skinnied before," he says.

"Skinny-dipped," she corrects.

And they take off their last remaining slips of clothes, feel the water envelop them totally. It is intoxicating and sobering at the same time (certainly for him). The erotic charge of being naked with water's shifting cover is so strong, Mercy feels her body prickle with anxiety, with anticipation. She closes her eyes and dives to the bottom, just to hover, weightless, as if she is going back to some primordial, preexisting state. When she surfaces, there is Charlie, waiting.

When they sleep together later, she will be surprised. He is skillful, assured. People are different in different realms. The boy who sat across from her in class and questioned the TA with a knowing erudition; whom she would see later at a college mixer, leaning against the wall, social anxiety palpable, stripped of all confidence in this different arena. Even as they are intertwined, all skin on skin and exposed nerve, she imagines him practicing on bespectacled girls, eager to shed their virginity, their innocence, to enter the adult world.

What is this new creature, this boy/man who transforms into something else every time he turns in the light, every time he emerges in a new world? Is this someone who is for her? Is this how someone becomes yours?

She doesn't know, so after he has fallen asleep, she wriggles out carefully from under his arm, all the time looking at his face, lit in the bent light from the living room, so at peace, his scent already a little familiar. She goes home at 2:00 a.m. to her mother, sleeping in her bed, her insides clanging with confusion and, yes, this, her baby.

Margaret

SHE GOES to the hotel, and luckily, the room is available, although it's only 7:00 a.m. They remember her from before, and the hotel manager escorts her to her room, only barely stifling his curiosity about why she is back in Seoul. The room is cold, and she turns up the thermostat before pulling back the bedcovers and huddling under the comforter.

The black-eye is so draining she actually falls asleep for an hour and wakes to find that it is already eight thirty. She calls the police station, dialing the number from memory. Mr. Park is not there. She hesitates, then calls his cell phone. When he answers, she can tell from the announcements and ambient noise that he is just emerging from the subway. He is also exasperated.

"Mrs. Reade," he says. "I told you it was not certain. It will still take some time. You should have waited for me to call you."

"I couldn't wait," she says. "You should know."

He sighs.

"Okay, I will call you when I get to the station."

She gives him her room number at the hotel, lies down on the bed again, and turns on the television. There is a Korean morning show on, the kind with impossibly good-looking hosts and people doing funny tricks for their fifteen minutes. The sound of the show helps, the tinny music, the relentless upbeat voices. Her brain is distracted. It reminds her of when she went to a dentist and he wiggled her lip while he administered the novocaine, and it helped a lot with the discomfort.

So part of her mind listens as a woman comes on in *ajumma* clothes, clothes for a middle-aged housewife. Then music starts, and a pole descends from the ceiling. She starts to strip off her dowdy clothing, to reveal an impressive body in a gold bikini. This being Korea, the bikini is still quite modest. She starts a routine on the pole that is reminiscent of Olympic gymnastics, spinning around horizontally, with her arms splayed straight. It is very impressive. The presenters talk all through her performance, oohing and aahing.

She looks at the clock: 8:50. If time passed any slower, she feels, it would be going backward.

He doesn't call until nine thirty. She jumps when the phone rings.

"Mrs. Reade," he says. "There is no news to report. The boy is still answering questions."

"Aren't there photos?" she asks. "Or can I go there?"

There is a pause. She always feel brash and impolite in Korea, as if she's always asking for more.

"I will call you back," he says.

Clarke has e-mailed, saying he will arrive around two. She starts to feel stirrings of hunger but doesn't want to leave the room in case Mr. Park calls, and she's not sure her cell phone will work properly, so she orders coffee and some pancakes from room service.

The phone rings again while the food is being delivered.

"Mrs. Reade," Mr. Park says. His voice is gentle. "There has been mistake," he says. "I am so sorry."

Her heart plummets so fast, so deep, that she feels dizzy from the altitude change within her.

"What?" she manages to say.

"I'm so sorry," he says. "The child has another family that has claimed him. It happened very fast. They are the correct family."

In one corner of her mind, she can still hear the tinny sounds of the television. In another, she is aware of a black hole that she must avoid at all costs. She is teetering on the edge of it, peering down, wondering how she will prevent herself from falling. She does this by feeling a sudden surge of virulent anger toward Mr. Park.

"But WHY?" she cries. "WHY did you call me and tell me there was a chance? Why did you get my hopes up?" She begins to sob, wildly and openly.

"WHY?" She bangs the phone down.

She screams, screams again. It feels good, so she keeps doing it. The phone rings, and she ignores it. Her throat is raw and her voice giving out, so then she crawls under the blankets and climbs into a little ball at the bottom of the bed.

She cannot live; she cannot not live. The child, the children. She almost forgets how to breathe. The stifling air inside the blankets makes it even more difficult. She embraces the difficulty, the suffocating feeling, the frantic scrabble for oxygen. She almost passes out and then has to throw off the blankets before she does.

She lies there quietly, breathing deeply, the cold air.

There is a knock on the door.

"Mrs. Reade," says a female voice. "Mrs. Reade. Is everything all right?"

She almost giggles at the question but succeeds in choking the laugh down.

"Sorry," she calls. "Everything is okay now."

A pause. Then the knock again.

"So sorry, Mrs. Reade. Can you open the door? I just need to check."

She lies for a minute, and then gives in to the inevitable, what she has to do if she decides to stay in the room, stay in a world where people do normal things and, thus, have a chance to get to normal herself. She gets up and opens the door to a pretty young Korean girl in her twenties.

"I'm fine," she says. "Sorry about the disturbance."

The girl bows. "So sorry to disturb you. But our other guests were worried. I will leave you now, unless you need something."

"Thank you," she says.

She closes the door and goes back to the bed and lies down, in the fetal position.

What had Dr. Stein said to her back in those first days? "Your pain is so raw and intense. It's like nerves that have been sheared off, and you are feeling wild, vibrant pain with no painkiller. I know it is unbearable. I know you cannot accept this new reality. I promise you: You can survive this, you must survive this, and time will make it bearable. You will be able to live. Time will help you."

She remembers this. And how to cope. When you feel the grief about to hit you like a tidal wave, you breathe deeply. You decide whether you're going to let yourself go there, or whether you're going to get up and write a grocery list instead. You go through the motions of life and wonder that you are able. When you want to kill yourself from the pain, you write down everything you are grateful for. You go for a walk. You look at the children you still have. You hum, so the silence doesn't overwhelm you.

So it wasn't G. The main thing.

She must call Clarke, she remembers. Another thing. So he won't get on the plane. But when she dials, he has already turned off his phone, is on the plane already. She hates this window of inaccessibility, so unusual in this day and age. The children are at school. They didn't tell them anything, not wanting to get their hopes up. They think she is here to do legal paperwork. So she is here, in this hotel room, by herself, with nothing to do until Clarke gets here. Then they can fly back together.

People go back to work after tragedy; people need something to do. If she hadn't had Daisy and Philip, what would she have done? They had given her a lifeline with which to tether herself. And she wonders, as she has before, if she has selfishly had her children to give her joy, to give her life a facile meaning she never has to question. Who would question someone who spends her life taking care of her children? Isn't that the very meaning of life? She remembers reading a story in the paper about single women in Vietnam having children as they got older. One of them told the reporter it was so that she would have someone to take care of her in her old age. The bald practicality of the statement had taken her breath away. But wasn't that what everyone did, they just dressed it up in prettier words?

There is a burst of applause from the television. It startles her back into the moment. She checks her watch. Ten thirty.

She decides to go to the department store so she is surrounded by people and light. She puts on her shoes and hesitates over her coat until she remembers she can get there through one of those underground tunnels.

At the store, she goes to the basement, where they have dozens of food stalls and stands. She buys a cup of coffee and a brioche and sits down to eat. It's still quiet, being a weekday, and just a few people are sitting around her.

Remember this, she thinks. The hot, fragrant coffee. The buttery, flaky bread. Feel these. Taste these. Stay here.

Later she goes up to the top floor, where they have children's clothes. She buys a coat for Daisy, a pair of pants for Philip, and goes back to the hotel.

People are different in hotels. She always has to get into a bathrobe and climb into bed when she's alone in one. It's because the bed is the focus of the entire room. There's rarely room for a couch or somewhere to sit, so the logical thing seems to be to get into bed. She lies to one side, by habit—she has become used to Clarke and various children sharing her bed, something the children had done while young, which had been resurrected full force after the incident. Before, when they were infants and toddlers, she remembers waking in the middle of the night to find one, two, sometimes three children in there with them, with their stuttered, nighttime movements, often sitting bolt upright in sleep and then falling down again, their shallow, quick breaths while dreaming. Sometimes she would stay awake to watch them, lying there with their small, solid bodies, sprawled insensate, completely vulnerable, and kiss their temples, their sweaty scalps, smell their sweet breath. Then she would steal away to one of their beds so she could get some sleep.

She drifts into sleep and is woken by the sound of the door being opened. Clarke comes in. He smiles when he sees her, full of hope. Her stomach drops all over again. When he sees her expression, his face falls.

"So?" he asks.

"No," she says.

He sits down on the foot of the bed and holds his head in his hands. She puts her hands, palms flat, on his back, delicately, as if they might hurt him.

Her husband is a good man, and this whole thing has affected him in a way that is so vastly different from the way it has affected her that it has almost destroyed their marriage. They have taken turns comforting each other, but he has been the one to keep the family together, to try to make it whole, to encourage her to move forward. That is the way it usually is, it has been explained to her, but it is still unsettling to see how he tries to pretend that everything will be okay. She cannot imagine it, even as she sees how it has to be that way for Daisy and Philip. In some of her more interior moments, she even admits that she is being the selfish one, while he is the one with the harder job.

He turns. His eyes are rimmed with tears. "I just . . . ," he starts.

"I know," she says.

He reaches for her. There is still this. This has remained. So far in the back of her head she has never articulated it out loud. But a faint whisper. Maybe another will come. Maybe.

Mercy

HER APPETITE has returned with a vengeance, a cacophonous hunger that surprises even her with its ferocity. Pregnancy is hollowing her out with cravings. Her days of eating lettuce slicked with oil and vinegar, just to fill the hours, are but a distant memory.

She and Charlie are at a new, hot restaurant she has chosen, a week into whatever it is they have going.

"This salmon has been harmoniously raised," Mercy says, reading off the menu, raising an eyebrow.

"What?" Charlie says.

She tries to suppress her irritation and fails. She pops a piece of bread in her mouth.

"It's funny," she says. "It's funny that it says that the salmon is harmoniously raised." I'm being didactic, she thinks, and then thinks, Charlie doesn't know what that word means.

He looks at her, shrugs his shoulders.

"You wanted to come here," he says, but he's not bothered.

"Because it's ridiculous, you know? Like when they say the tuna is line-caught? Do you know what that is about?"

"No," he says, buttering a roll.

"Because all these people are crazy, and they want to know where their food came from, or how it was raised, in what kind of environment. Like when they say the tuna is line-caught, it means that they didn't fish with nets, because dolphins get caught in the nets and die, and people don't want to think that there is collateral damage or side effects from when they eat their seared yellowfin with cilantro mustard."

He never picks up the thought and runs with it.

"Like *Portlandia*. Have you ever seen it? The whole locavore, crazy liberal thing? And this salmon. It's such bullshit. Have you ever heard of the salmon farms and the color wheels? The people who raise salmon have special feed that will dye the flesh, and the supermarkets and buyers can choose the color they want on a color wheel, and the fish farmers tweak the feed. It's like our idea of what color salmon should be, that orange with white stripes, or the idea that tuna should be that dark red. It's like a giant conspiracy of our own stupidity."

She might as well be speaking Greek.

"I have no idea what you're talking about," he says.

"Because you don't read the *New Yorker*, or the blogs that I do," she says. "You are not interested at all in the same things. How can you not know anything about this stuff?"

She hates hearing herself even as she speaks.

"I do have a job," he says.

Here is a man who is buying her dinner at an expensive restaurant she chose, who is kind to her, who is good in bed. And yet she is the one who feels annoyed. Oh, and here is a man who has no idea she is carrying another man's baby.

When that thought comes to her, she folds the menu and puts it down. She was starving, but now her appetite collapses.

"You know, you are so American," he says. It is a neutral statement, she thinks, but he says it in such a way that she doesn't know what he is talking about.

"I have no idea what that means," she says, trying not to sound combative.

"Americans are so involved in small, meaningless details. Asians are practical. I thought you were more practical, but when I hear you talking about organic salmon and stuff like that, I see you are a lot more American than I thought."

"Oh," she says. Of course he said organic salmon, which was missing the entire point. "Does it bother you? Do you like it or not like it?"

He throws his hands up. "I don't like it or not like it. I prefer not to spend time thinking about such stupid things!"

Stung, she asks, "What do you prefer to think about?"

He sips his drink. "Things like work, if I'm doing well. Whether I should stay in this field or whether I should do something else. I'd like to find a girlfriend who could become a wife"—his gaze is steady on hers—"stuff like that, which is important, which will impact my life. Not whether the salmon is the organic or not."

"Do you think about stuff like that all the time?" she asks, wonderingly. "You have to have some moments of silly thoughts."

"I guess," he says, in a tone that means he doesn't.

"You live in a world without irony," she says.

"You are always bringing up that word," he says with exasperation. "Irony. Or meta. You are always saying things are meta. I have no idea what you're talking about."

This is not going the way she planned. She thought that tonight she would tell him about G. Not about the baby yet. Baby steps. Ha ha.

"Sorry," she says. Time to reset.

He is exasperated, she can see. Not the best way to start.

They order. He orders the salmon, without any apparent irony. She orders the pesto pasta. He gets a bottle of wine, although she says she will just sip at her glass.

"You don't drink much," he says.

"No," she says.

Silence.

"How is work?" she asks.

"I had two almost all-nighters this week," he says. "One for a Chinese electronics company that's about to IPO and also a Malaysian food company. I got home at four in the morning and had to be back at the office by eight."

"Ouch," she says.

"It's like this for everyone when they start," he says. "You work hard and pay your dues."

"So I hear," she says.

"Are you looking for a new job?" he asks.

"Yes, and my mom is too," she jokes.

He smiles. "That must be difficult," he says. "I can't imagine living with my mother, although a lot of people here live with family until they're married. That doesn't work for me. Not with my parents. We're too different."

Mercy is reminded of those marriage manuals from the 1950s that get passed around via e-mail or Facebook every once in a while: "When your husband gets home from work, don't nag him. Ask him about his day while bringing him a drink and his slippers." The slippers part always reminded her of a dog.

"So I wanted to say," she starts, then thinks she should wait a bit, maybe until the appetizers come, so stops.

"Yeah?" he asks.

"Nothing."

"Oh, come on. You can say what you want to say," he says. "You should feel comfortable with me."

"Except we just had a quite uncomfortable exchange."

"That?" He looks surprised. "You think that is uncomfortable? That's just us talking and figuring out who we are in relation to each other."

Sometimes he is surprisingly fluent in English and in emotions.

"Oh, well, I'm glad you think that."

His appetizer comes, asparagus spears drizzled with a reddish oil.

"Do you want some?" He pushes the plate to the center of the table and asks the waiter for two small plates so they can share. This small generosity makes her eyes fill.

"You are crying?" he says, incredulous. "What is going on?"

"I'm just . . . emotional," she says. "Sorry."

"Don't apologize," he says.

" 'Cause there's something I want to tell you." *I'm pregnant.*

"Okay."

"I don't know if you heard what happened to me a year ago.

Something bad happened. And it was my fault, and I've been trying to deal with it this whole time. Which is why I'm not working, and why I haven't gone out or seen people in so long. But you probably don't know, because we didn't know each other back then, so you wouldn't have noticed . . ." She's blabbering out of nervousness.

He reaches over, takes her hand. "I know," he says. "It's a small world, and everyone hears about awful things like what happened to you with the child. In Hong Kong especially. It must be very hard."

"Yes," she says, relieved. "It's so hard, and everyone is focused on Margaret and her family, as they should be, of course, but I feel like my life has been ruined too, and I'm not allowed to say anything or do anything, except be sorry and fade away. I don't know why I haven't moved back to the U.S., but I feel like that would be running away and I should suffer and . . . I don't know."

"I'm glad you told me," he says. "I've been waiting for you to tell me, but I didn't want to ask."

"Thank you," she says.

He doesn't say, "What happened?" or "How did it go down?" or "Do you ever talk to the family?"—all questions she has been asked by other friends, not out of empathy but more out of an unseemly, almost prurient, interest. There are those advice columns that tell you to respond, "Why do you ask?" but that's just such an aggressive thing to say to someone who is purporting to help you that she can never bring herself to say it.

"Terrible things happen all the time," Charlie says. "You just got to keep living your life."

"You are nice," she says.

"I think Asian people are better at this sort of thing, suffering," he says.

She almost laughs but realizes he is serious. "Oh?"

"Yes, of course," he says. "Americans are very soft."

"You like to make generalizations about Americans versus Asians."

"Americans like to say things like that, tell people about themselves," he says with a smile.

"Whoa, this is so meta."

"Like that," he says. "This meta thing is so American, and I don't really get it."

They laugh, and she thinks, Can it really be that easy? Then remembers the other thing. And feels sick again. What would it be like, she thinks, to live life without guilt, without worry, without feeling fraudulent? What is it like to be like Philena, to traipse through life protected by attentive parents and endless bank accounts? She wishes she could have that, just for a little bit, maybe just to see her through this time in her life when everything is going wrong, and even the things that are going right are going to veer off course at some point because of the other things. How fast will this guy flee when he knows everything? She would guess pretty fast.

"What did you do today?" he asks.

Today she tried to make an appointment at a public hospital, but since she's not a permanent resident of Hong Kong, they told her that she will have to pay the nonlocal rate. Since the local rate is around HK$100 a visit and the nonlocal rate is ten times that, this is a big deal for her. She hadn't known that only permanent residents got the cheaper rate, since everyone always talked about how cheap health care was in Hong Kong. She also found out that the birth was going to cost HK$100,000 or almost US$12,000, at least as a nonlocal. Since all this is unsayable, she smiles and says something about updating her resume and browsing online.

She actually finds the whole thing weird. The fact that Charlie is willing to put up with a girl who is unemployed, ostracized, and odd just because she happens to be rather pretty and compatible with him in bed makes her question everything about the world. Why does it work this way? Is this the way everything works? What sort of value system exists that that's okay?

"Do you know Eddie Lai?" he asks. "He's from Columbia as well."

"Name rings a bell," she says.

"Do you want to have dinner with him and May next week? You know they just got married. They're having people over to their house, like a dinner party," he says.

She sees it happening, this coupling, how she is being presented to society as Charlie's girlfriend. She has been witness to it, all through college and after, but it's never really happened to her. She's always been the girl to hook up with at parties, to go out with a few times, but never anything lasting. Is it really this easy? How is it that she's never been privy to it before? It's seductive, this image of newlywed bliss, the starter apartment in Mid-Levels with the IKEA furniture and the expensive groceries from the gourmet supermarket. Acting at being real adults, having dinner parties with other couples. It is so close she can practically smell the California cabernet and the chicken with garlic cloves roasting in the oven—the beginner meal for young couples playing house.

She's been with boys who are cheating on their girlfriends. She can tell the affair is even more amazing for them, the forbidden making everything heightened, double the pleasure, like a drug they snort and then fall back, hit over the head with ecstasy. In the morning comes remorse, but still, the intense pleasure is worth it for them. Damn couples, she used to think, even the illicit sex is better for them than for single people.

So if this is what it's like, she wants to enjoy it, but she can't. Because she's Mercy Cho. Because things never go right for her.

"There are a couple of long weekends coming up," Charlie says. "Do you have any plans?"

"My whole life is kind of a long weekend," she says.

"True." He grins.

"It's Buddha's birthday, right?"

"Yeah, and May Day, and a few before," he says. "I've been thinking about going away."

"Oh, yeah?" she says. "Where?"

"I don't know. I want to go to a beach and drink cocktails with umbrellas on them."

"That sounds nice," she says.

"Want to go with me?" he asks.

"Oh!" She is surprised. This she had not expected.

"I just thought . . ." He is embarrassed, a little shy.

"That sounds great," she says. She cannot even go on to say "but . . ." as she intended, because he beams and grabs her hand.

"Good," he says. "My treat."

Later she wonders what she should have said. "But I'm pregnant." "But my mother is here." "But why me?" All things she is thinking. Anyway, she will have several weeks to mess things up with him, so it doesn't really matter. Sometimes she lets herself imagine what would have happened if she had met Charlie before she met David. Would her life have spooled out in this wonderful, unimaginably effortless way? Girl meets boy, boy likes girl, boy pulls girl out of her awful life. But then she reminds herself that's a fairy tale, and of all people, she should be the last to believe in fairy tales.

Part V

Hilary

How is it already May? May and June are going-away-party season and pack-up-for-summer season. The expatriates have renewed or not renewed their contracts. They have quit or found something back home. The factory has closed, or HQ has downsized the office. Elderly parents are ailing, and they are needed. Some have just become fed up with life in Hong Kong and decided to pack it up and leave. There are homesick wives who tell their husbands they've had it with the air pollution and the unsafe food standards and take off with the kids, leaving their spouses to work and send money home. This sometimes works and sometimes doesn't: The wife comes back to Hong Kong, or there is a divorce, or the man returns home and finds another job.

If the expats are staying for another year or two, the moms take the kids and go on home leave, staying at their parents' or in-laws' houses, camping out at others' homes through the summer.

So in May or June, when the kids are finishing up with school, the packers are called, tram parties are booked, and many, many boozy lunches and dinners are had at the American Club or the China Club or some fancy Italian restaurant in Central.

Hilary sits at the kitchen table with her laptop, sipping coffee and going through her e-mails, finding out who is leaving.

It's a bit like the end of college, when you bid farewell to the friends you've made before going on to the next stage of life. You might see them again, but never in the same normal, everyday kind of way. Hilary has gone to so many of these lunches she knows the format like the back of her hand. First a bottle of champagne and a toast to the departing friend, then the presentation of a group gift arranged by many, many e-mails sent around beforehand, a gift statistically most likely to be from Shanghai Tang—a frame or perhaps a wine stopper—but not before a card is surreptitiously handed around so everyone can sign. There will also most probably be a photo album compiled of many pictures of group outings to Shenzhen to buy fake DVDs and have clothes tailored, dinners at the China Club, girls' nights out at Flow, family days on the American Club lawn, joint vacations to Bali beaches. It's akin to a college yearbook, she supposes, a way to mark several years in one's life, when one has inevitably changed and grown in ways that are hard to see until you find yourself back in the United States trying to explain to people what life was like in Asia and finding out that they care not one whit. But you will have this album to flip through, and a wine stopper. And that memory of the people who were there with you.

That's the shock, and the surprise, to a lot of repatriates: No one back home cares. There's an initial, shallow interest in what life is like abroad, but most Americans aren't actually interested, at all. They're back to talking about the divorces going on at work, or how the neighborhood pharmacy is going under, or how highway construction has added forty minutes to their commute. They don't want to know about the trip to Hoi An and how Vietnam has changed immensely, or how Beijing's pollution is so thick that when you were there, you had to wear a handkerchief over your face. America is so vast, and there is so much to see, just in the fifty states, these people tell you—it's like you never have to leave. This insularity will seem shocking for the first year back, when reentry is difficult, when you miss the ease of Hong Kong, forgetting all your complaints from when you were there, remembering only the good winter weather, the amazing dumplings and cheap taxis, but all too soon most everyone slips into the warm comforts of America, so convenient, so uniform, forgetting there is anything outside its borders.

There's a moment in all these farewell parties when the person leaving is alone, drying her hands in the bathroom, waiting at the bar for a drink, and she foresees a moment in her new old life. Perhaps it will be the still, frozen Thursday-night light of a mall refracting through the window of a TGI Fridays as she's surrounded by old high school friends in this most American of venues, chosen out of what they choose to call nostalgia but is usually something deeper and more fraught, the uneasy push-pull of the giant frozen cocktail, the greasy blooming onion—the all-encompassing and smothering embrace of America. Or she'll see another moment in her imminent future, when she's looking back into the past: Washing dishes in the waning light of a Columbus, Ohio, kitchen, sudsy hands gripping greasy dishes, a woman will summon up a startling picture of herself, a moment in Hong Kong when she was walking across the lobby of the Mandarin Hotel in a fitted sheath and expensive stiletto-heeled shoes, the kind she has no use for anymore, on her way to meet a friend for lunch, or walking through the streets with her toddler on her hip while her helper, her servant, trailed behind, carrying the diaper bag and various other accouterments of daily life she hadn't had to bother herself with. What a life it was! What a life they had all had! While many of them had complained the whole time they were stationed in Hong Kong, it is only after they leave, when they are ensconced in their old lives with no change visible for decades ahead, that they will appreciate the wonder of what they had experienced.

At the farewell parties and back at home, they will take a moment to see themselves with their present friends, their old friends, their new friends, their new old friends, the past meeting the present, endlessly echoing back and forth, and they'll see their future, so close, bumping into the moment, and frighteningly the same, and they'll wonder if their past, their time away in the Far East, was just that, a dream.

As Hilary sits at the kitchen table, she hears the piano playing. She is waiting for Julian to finish so they can go out together. Miss Kim, the Korean lady she found to teach him, says she is happy with his progress, but Hilary has no idea whether he is good. She doesn't care that much if he is. The tinkling melody, not unpleasant, soothes her.

She is going to adopt Julian.

It was not some big awakening, some blazing moment of truth. Like so many things in real, unromantic life, it came in a slow accumulation of small tasks, almost unconscious. She filled out some forms. She sent e-mails to the few people she will need recommendations or information from. She asked the accountant for copies of tax returns and the consulate for legal documents. In this way, she came to realize that she is adopting Julian. She has not told him, but she is clearing away the brush in front of her to see what lies ahead. The social worker has told her that while she cannot request a specific child, if she starts the application process and says she is okay with a mixed-race, older child, the odds are very good she will get Julian, as the adoption pool in Hong Kong is very small, under two hundred, and he is likely the only one who fits that description. The odds of his getting adopted are almost nil. In the last year there were fewer than three hundred adoptions in all of Hong Kong. Most were infants adopted by local families, a small percentage by foreign, and a very few are within families. Hilary wonders about the stories behind that last, small statistic.

There have been moments when she isn't sure, but she plows on, filling in David's name as the father, listing her academic and medical history. Maybe this is all it is. She does not think he will deny her this, after all he has done.

After the lesson, she will take Julian on a walk. This is the second time they have done this. Sam drives them to Tai Tam, and they walk slowly through the park and talk to each other in stilted English.

Miss Kim closes the music book and smiles. "Good job, Julian," she says.

Hilary looks at her, this woman with her lovely, always beaming face, and wonders what she makes of the situation. The orphan, the woman always alone at home, the piano lesson. A job where you go to other people's houses all day must unearth some odd situations.

Miss Kim takes her leave, and Hilary asks Julian if he'd like to go.

They get in the car, equipped with water and some oranges, and ride out to the beginning of the walk. It is one she does often with Olivia.

They get out, and she helps Julian on with his backpack, one she has given him. She grabs his hand, and they set out. It feels strange to hold his hand, but she keeps doing it. It will feel normal, she thinks, she just has to get used to it.

A couple comes out and smiles at them, seeing what they see—a mother and her child. Hilary is suddenly giddy with happiness.

"What is?" Julian asks, pointing at the road where there are splotches of white powder.

"It's snake poison," she tells him.

He shakes his head. She pulls out the notebook she has gotten into the habit of bringing and sketches a snake. "Snake." She draws a skull and bones. "Poison." Then she puts X's in the snake's eyes to signal its death.

He nods.

There is so much he needs to learn, it's overwhelming. Immersion, she keeps thinking, she's going to have to immerse him in English. She reads stories about immigrant children going to America at thirteen and having to go to a school where they don't understand a word. They survive; some thrive. She knows it's possible, but how to give a child a whole new world?

"I'll take you to the Botanical Gardens one day," she says. "They have a few snakes there." She draws a cage with snakes behind the bars. He seems to understand, but who knows.

This planning for the future, this evocation of things to come, gives her a frisson, not unpleasant. She grows bolder. "And in California, in America, where I'm from, there are lots of zoos, and they have lots of animals. We'll go see them together." She squeezes his hand.

"Do you know California?" she asks. She draws America, fails, pulls out her phone and finds a map of the United States.

"Here." She taps the West Coast. "That's where I'm from," and she points to herself. "We can fly there together." She makes her arms wings and bobbles them back and forth.

She has not explicitly told him that she is going ahead with the adoption, but he knows. When she goes to pick him up, his fellow orphans crowd around him, speaking rapidly in Cantonese. They give her the thumbs-up sign and grin widely. She usually leaves quickly, uncomfortable with the implicit longing in the other children.

It's odd, because he already feels like he's hers, separate from the others, especially since they look so different from him, being Chinese. "Which one of these is not like the other?" is the refrain that goes through her mind when she sees him at his home.

After the walk, she takes him to the American Club to have a snack. He has never been. On this warm day, she brings him by the pool and sees the scene through his eyes—these privileged kids splashing in the water outfitted in every possible contraption a diligent mother can strap or pull on: rashguards, water wings, water fins, goggles, colored zinc. There is so much *much* here. What is fifteen dollars for these women to spend on flippers or a safety vest for their beloved, the vessels for all their dreams and hopes? The children stagger in and out of the pool; the mothers hover over them, clucking from the side about rough play, calling out about one child hitting another with a noodle. The dizzying scene is rife with privilege.

Hilary sits with Julian, their silence surrounding them like a bubble enclosing them from the chaos outside. The sound track of a pool filled with children: happy shrieks, a crying toddler, a mother's shout of warning, splashes of water.

Some boys Julian's age come in through the side door, herded by one mother. Julian looks at them, all matching in their school uniforms on their way to get changed for their swim lessons. They chatter easily with one another, poking and cavorting like puppies.

"Toilet, please," Julian says.

She takes him to the bathroom and waits outside.

After a long while, he comes out, followed by the other children, changed into their swimsuits. They look at him and giggle. She feels hot anger surge up.

"What's funny?" she says to the boys.

They ignore her and start walking to the pool.

"Excuse me," she says, and taps one boy on the shoulder. "Was something funny?"

"No," he says. "What?" He looks confused.

"You were all laughing when you came out."

As she speaks, she knows she sounds crazy, that the boys don't know what she's talking about, that it's likely it has nothing to do with Julian, but she cannot help herself.

The boy shrugs and joins his friends. Next to her, Julian is looking down, his eyes brimming. She is stricken.

"What's wrong?" she asks.

He doesn't reply.

She leans down. She has read this is what you do with children, get down to their level so they can relate to you better, so that you're not so giant and unreachable.

"Julian," she says, "you know you can tell me anything. And you can tell me what's on your mind."

He doesn't say anything.

"You tell me anything," she says slowly. Even as she says it, she feels the impossibility of what she is saying. Does she really think an hour here and there will forge a relationship where he feels he can tell her anything? They don't even speak the same language. She has to hurry up. It has to happen soon. He looks at her, eyes wet, trying not to cry. She hugs him fiercely.

"Do you want to get something to eat?" she asks.

He nods, and they go inside to the restaurant.

They sit down, and he looks around. All around, children are eating pizza, spaghetti, club sandwiches.

"They have Chinese food," she says. "Chow fan, wonton noodle?"

"Maybe I have the pizza," he says uncertainly.

"Want to look at the buffet?" she asks. They walk over and look at all the dishes. There is the usual international spread: a curry, a roast beef, a baked fish, sushi.

"Why don't we do this, so you can try everything," she says. They take plates, and she tells him to point at everything he wants. Soon his plate is laden with a smorgasbord of different foods.

When they sit down, though, he picks at everything.

"You don't like?" she says.

He shrugs.

Just then, the boys from the swimming pool come through the door, hair wet, freshly changed from the pool. They swarm the buffet, grabbing plates before their mothers can even get a table.

"I get dessert," Julian says.

He gets up so quickly she is behind him when she sees him stand next to one of the boys who is getting a piece of chocolate cake. In her mind, she is tut-tutting the fact that the boy is getting dessert before a main course when she sees Julian jostle him, quite deliberately. The plate teeters and falls, chocolate cake lies crumbled all over the floor. The boy lets out a wail and glares at Julian.

"You pushed me!" he shouts.

Julian painstakingly ignores him and takes a plate. He cuts himself a slice of the chocolate cake.

"You pushed me!" the boy shouts again.

Hilary is behind them, aghast and yet somehow exhilarated. She puts her hand behind Julian's back to guide him back to the table. They walk back together, side by side, unhurried and deliberate, and sit down. She sees the boy run to his mother and talk to her excitedly, pointing at Julian. The woman rises and comes toward them, a pleasant-faced woman in her thirties.

"I'm sorry," she says. "Michael told me that your"—she hesitates— "your child? Pushed him? And that's why he dropped the plate?"

Julian looks down at the floor, face a mask.

Hilary smiles at the woman. "I'm sorry?" she says. "What?"

The boy has joined his mother now. "He pushed me!" he says, still indignant.

"There must be some mistake," Hilary says. "I don't think Julian pushed you."

"I dropped the cake because of him!"

The mother looks beleaguered. "Why don't we just get another piece of cake?" she suggests. She takes her child's hand. "Sorry," she says with a backward glance. "You know kids."

Hilary sits with Julian and finally dares to look at him. He stares back at her, expressionless, waiting for her reaction.

She blinks, then smiles, breathes.

"Eat your chocolate cake, sweetie," she says, heart beating fast, fast, faster. Is this what it means to feel alive?

Mercy

HER MOTHER has had a job of sorts for several weeks. She's been helping out with a catering company run by an American. Her experience at Mercy's aunt's restaurant has come in useful, and she has been hired as a quasi manager, to communicate to the other mostly Chinese staff what is expected. Why they think she can do this when she cannot speak Cantonese at all is a good question, but she talks in her Korean-accented English and seems to be doing fine. She likes her coworkers and likes having a place to go.

There is a big party this week that they are doing in some warehouse in Wong Chuk Hang, and her mother wants her to work. She moves around the tiny studio, getting ready to go.

"Shirley pays a hundred dollars an hour, and I'm sure she'll pay you more—Columbia graduate!"

Her mother prattles on about the food and the preparation and the work to come—a kindness to her daughter, who she has recently come to realize has ruined her life.

All that jazz, as it were, came to pass, just as predicted. Two weeks ago, Charlie commented on her burgeoning waist, saying she had gained weight. The thing was, he said it in the loveliest way possible, saying, "Look! I'm taking good care of you. You have gained weight!"

She wasn't able to quash the look of horror on her face.

He misunderstood. "No, no," he said. "It's good. I like it. You were too thin before."

When she couldn't speak, he said, "What's wrong?"

And then it all came out, inelegantly, spastically, horribly. She kept seeing his face, uncomprehending at first, then horrified, then, finally, finally—and she couldn't forget this—disgusted. The memory of his look makes her insides curl with embarrassment and self-loathing. When she visualizes it, she makes an involuntary grunt of horror. This good man, this good guy, was disgusted with her. She kept apologizing and apologizing for not telling him sooner, but it didn't matter. There was something so final about being pregnant with someone else's child. It's almost comical. Only the most evolved or self-aware or confident man would be okay with it, or someone who was infatuated beyond reason, and that would be someone who had aimed way above his station. Charlie was none of these, she knew, and so she could not blame him or fault him or even wish that he had acted differently. He had acted in an eminently reasonable way, and she had been a bloody, bloody fool to spool it out for even a week. Now she imagines him telling all his friends, the newly married Eddie Lais, with whom they had had a perfectly lovely dinner, with the new wife being super friendly to Mercy, the work colleagues, other Columbia people. Her news spreading slowly, sickly outward, like an oil stain on the fine cotton tablecloth of common decency. Now she is known for something else, other than having lost a child, and it is this. A new kind of pariah.

And also, she thinks he had already bought their tickets to go away. So now she has cost him thousands of dollars as well.

So she does what she always does when her life goes awry. After all, she's an expert. She puts it out of her mind and tries to move forward. Her prenatal visits are ongoing. She e-mailed David, delicately, about the cost. He e-mailed back immediately that she should send him all bills, then after the first two, he said she shouldn't have to submit forms like an expense report and then just transferred HK$75,000 into her account (almost US$10,000) and said she should let him know when she needed more. So there's that. It sits in her account, more money than she's ever had at one time. Maybe he sent it all at one go because he doesn't want a lot of contact with her, although he always signs his e-mails saying he'd love to see her and hopes that she is feeling well. He never gives a date, though, or any other indication that he cares about what's happening with her. That should be a sign in and of itself.

She also told her mother, who took the news in the oddest way. She told her in halting Korean, and her mother took it in slowly. Then she hugged Mercy and, shaking a little bit, let her go to see the tears in her eyes. "I will have grandchild," she said. "I am so happy." Nothing about ruining her life or who the father is. She just let her be.

Actually, no one has asked her what she's going to do, whether she will keep the baby, any of the questions she would have thought natural. She knows it's getting late now to have an abortion, and she's felt no urge to have one. It's funny how she and her mother have both assumed that she's going to have the baby. It's not that they're religious about it, or because of any sort of dogma, other than she does feel like she's having a child, and the idea of not having it seems wildly improbable. She is pro-choice, always was, but this, her own body, is making the choice for her.

She hasn't even Googled when the last possible date would be, although she has gone onto several pregnancy websites and looked at what babies look like at different months. At the last appointment at the government hospital, she asked when she could get an ultrasound, and the doctor said since she was young and healthy, she wasn't lined up for one. That was when she decided to go private. After a little research, she ended up with an appointment at an obstetrician's in Wan Chai. Her first one is today, and she didn't tell her mother because she doesn't want her to ask if she can come.

"I'll ask Shirley if she need extra help for the party," her mom says.

"Okay," Mercy says, just to get her mother out the door.

After the door shuts and she is finally, blessedly alone, she showers and lies down on her bed, wrapped in a towel. Looking down, she opens up the towel to see how her stomach rises in a gentle peak. She sees the up and down of her breath. She sucks in her stomach, sees it go flat, then suddenly lets go in a panic, feeling as if she is squashing her baby, although she knows that is not possible at this stage. The websites say you might feel little flutters inside at this point, as the tiny baby starts to move around. It might not even be a baby yet. It might still be an embryo. She hasn't gotten all the terms straight.

Her wet hair is warm against her scalp, and she feels water drops sliding off her face. Outside, a garbage truck beeps its slow retreat.

She gets up, dresses, leaves the apartment, and finds her way to the doctor's. In the lobby of the office building, a brass plaque, Wan Chai Obstetrics, announces the name of her new doctor, a Dr. Henry Leong. The elevator has fancy brass buttons covered by a sheet of plastic that is sprayed with disinfectant every hour, or so a notice claims. Hong Kong: still disinfectant mad, decades after SARS.

The doctor's office is pleasant, with fresh flowers and up-to-date magazines, although most of them are in Chinese. Private, public, private, public—the refrain keeps going through her head. Why does money have to make everything so much nicer? The receptionist hands her a clipboard to fill out and asks her to pee in a cup and weigh herself on the scale next to the desk. Mercy's the only one in the waiting room until the door buzzes open again and a woman of about thirty comes in with her husband.

Mercy fills out the form and eavesdrops on the new arrival, an Englishwoman who is discussing with her husband their upcoming babymoon.

"Angie said Bali was great, but the food is terrible. I think Thailand is a better bet."

"Okay," her husband says, scrolling through his phone.

"And there's a really lovely hotel in Phuket called the Andara. Bit expensive but think we should splurge since it's our last vacation as a couple."

"Is it on the beach?"

As they make their way through the inanities of travel, Mercy finishes up and places the clipboard on the desk, then weighs herself.

The woman watches her and exclaims, "I can't believe how they have you weigh yourself out here in front of everybody!"

Mercy looks back and lifts an eyebrow, which she regrets instantly, as it then gives the woman a chance to talk to her.

"Do you know what you're having?" she asks, smiling, friendly. Perhaps she wants to make friends, mommy friends, and form a playgroup.

Mercy shakes her head, unwilling to talk, unwilling to unveil herself as a fellow native English speaker for fear of further intimacies. Better the woman thinks she is local, unable to converse.

But then the receptionist asks, "How much you weigh?" forcing her to speak.

"A hundred thirty-two," she says softly, so the woman can't hear her, but of course she does, so when Mercy sits down, the woman pointedly starts talking to her husband again.

"Listen," she says finally, "I'm having kind of a terrible day."

The woman nods curtly and continues speaking pointedly to her husband.

Mercifully, her name is called, and she goes into the waiting room. The nurse takes her blood pressure and leaves her with a cotton gown to change into. Mercy takes off her clothes except her underwear and folds them neatly. She lays them on the surface next to the sink. She wonders if she should take her underwear off as well. The one time she got a massage at an expensive spa, courtesy of the ever-generous Philena, she wondered the same thing. She sits down on the crinkly paper.

A knock on the door.

"Hello," says the doctor, a soft-faced, aristocratic-looking Chinese man, in British-accented English. Outside, his credentials had been displayed prominently on the wall—Edinburgh, some other vaguely posh-sounding school.

"Hello," she says.

"So." He scans her file. "The date of your last period was approximately January 24." He takes out a little wheel. "So that puts you at"—he spins it—"almost four months. A Halloween baby." He looks up. "You took your time getting here. Most of my patients are here the moment they miss their first period."

"Well," she says, "I was being seen at the public hospital up until now."

Behind the clear glass of his spectacles, a recalibration. Swift, but Mercy is an expert at recognizing these sorts of social calculations.

"I see," he says. "So you've been taking good care of yourself." It is more a statement than a question. "Folic acid and prenatals?"

"Um, no," she says. "I'm not so good at that kind of stuff."

"I see," he says again. "Well, while you're under my care, that *stuff*"—he repeats her word—"is nonnegotiable. You must start taking the pills, although you should have been taking them from day one. Actually, it's already too late for the folic acid, but you can start on the prenatal vitamins. They may cause a little constipation, because they're rich in iron."

"But does everyone have a perfect pregnancy?" She can't help asking. "I mean, I'm sure lots of your patients don't know they're pregnant for a while, and have acted"—she pauses here, not quite sure what she's going to say— "I mean, acted like they weren't pregnant."

"I don't know anything about that," he says.

She's been here only three minutes, and she's already alienated this doctor. She feels exhausted.

"I'll take the pills," she says.

"Are you feeling all right?" he asks.

"Yes, fine," she says. "But this is all kind of new."

He looks at her. "Yes, it's a big change. You're going to be a mommy."

The stern, aristocratic doctor using a word like "mommy" makes her uncomfortable. He wheels over a large machine and starts tapping at a keyboard. His hands are as soft and white as flour, a gold wedding ring on his pudgy finger.

"Have you had a scan yet?"

"An ultrasound? No. The public hospital didn't offer them."

"Scoot down here." He taps on the bottom of the chair. When he sees her underwear, he gives an exasperated sigh. "You have to take off your underwear," he says. "The baby is still small, so we will give you a transvaginal scan."

She gets off the chair and takes off her underwear, adding it to the pile. It looks sad and wrinkled.

He puts a condom on what looks like a giant dildo and holds it up and says, "I'm going to insert this, so don't be surprised." He glides it in as she breathes deeply. On the screen, black and white pixels glitter and wobble.

"There's your baby," he says, pointing with his free hand to what is recognizably a baby, with a head and body.

"Oh, my," Mercy says faintly. "There it is."

"It's around ten centimeters now. Starting to grow." He rolls a mouselike ball on the keyboard around. "I'm just taking some measurements." He rolls and taps. "Everything looks good. You are young, so this should be routine. Too many women getting pregnant too old."

Mercy is so rapt she can't even take offense at what the man is saying. She can't breathe. Her thickening waist, just now becoming apparent, is housing a baby, a human being, something that will come into the world in just a few months. There's a man she's just met who's just inserted a plastic dildo inside her and is showing her something she cannot comprehend. The baby wriggles on the screen.

"It's so weird," she says. "I can't feel the baby, but it's totally moving."

For the first time, the doctor looks at her with what looks like approval. She has finally reacted in what he deems a suitable way.

"Yes, it's moving all around. Next time, I'll probably be able to tell you if it's a girl or a boy. Sometimes I can already tell at this stage, but you have a shy one."

"I can't believe it," she says.

The rest of the exam goes in a blur. Dr. Leong never asks her about a husband or the baby's father, making her wonder if he knows about her. She's paranoid, she knows, but Hong Kong can be that small.

She thanks the doctor, and he leaves. Slowly she gets dressed. She's seen her baby. She is holding three printouts of the baby's image. The baby is real.

When she goes out, she goes to the reception desk to pay.

"Appointments are $1,200 each visit, and here's the schedule of payment, including the hospital costs," the receptionist says. She is a chubby young woman with a plastic name tag that says her name is Minky. She hands Mercy a sheet with the costs. There's a separate line for multiple births.

The bottom figure is alarming, but less so now that she has $75,000 sitting in the bank.

"Triplets!" she says to the receptionist, eyeing the multiples section. "Expensive!"

"Yes," the receptionist says. "You are lucky to have only one."

Someone just called her lucky. Tears pool in her eyes, blurring her vision as she signs the credit card slip.

Margaret

IN HER STUDIO. She is hidden. She has been here every morning this week. Outside, traffic sounds, people's voices.

Clarke's party is imminent. Priscilla has earned whatever exorbitant fee she is probably charging and has done everything, as promised. At some point, she figured out who Margaret was, and her dealings with her changed. She became softer, never got exasperated when Margaret didn't return e-mails or failed to make a decision. She took over and did everything. She started e-mailing Margaret directions, like had she found a dress, did she want to book a hairdresser or makeup, and when Priscilla didn't hear back, she would just e-mail that she had booked one for her and that they would be at the house at this time. For this reason, Margaret now loves Priscilla.

Now that Clarke knows about the party, now that it's no longer a surprise, there is even less pressure, and she has even shifted the question of whether David Starr should be invited over to Priscilla via e-mail. So, Priscilla crisply informed her later, an invitation went out per Clarke's wishes, but David has not RSVP'd yet. Hilary has RSVP'd and called to ask if she could bring a friend, another woman. Of course, Margaret said fine. Apparently David is still out on his midlife crisis, something that may solidify into reality. Margaret views all this with the dim, myopic view of someone watching slow sea creatures through a thick glass, creatures in another world, where emotions run high and people behave badly, as if they have all the room in the world to make bad decisions and they won't be punished for them. Or maybe it's the other way around, and she's the creature behind the glass, watching normal people behave normally.

She asked Priscilla to coordinate with the children about doing something for Clarke, a speech or a song or some sort of entertainment, and apparently they have something planned. She has given Priscilla whole ownership of the party, not feeling bad because she knows now that Priscilla knows about the situation.

Clarke's parents flew in a few days ago and are staying at a small hotel in Stanley. They have been to Hong Kong once before, after her mom left after her extended stay, and they filled in for a month or so, getting the children's lives back on track. They are nice, from a small town an hour out of San Francisco, but they were overwhelmed by Hong Kong—all the foreign food and the maids and the taxis—and they were not much help. They went to a round of parent-teacher conferences on their behalf when Margaret couldn't make it out of Seoul and Clarke was on a business trip, and they tried as hard as they could, but they are limited. They have decided to stay a few days, and then leave. They don't want to be too much trouble. Margaret told her own mother she didn't need to come, that it would be better if she came another time.

Margaret slips into the bath with her headphones on and plays music so loud it shudders through her head. This is the closest she can get to the comfortable numbness she craves.

Dr. Stein has asked her to make friends. To do things with people, to get close and share intimacies.

Friends. What an odd concept. She had them before, of course, but in her old life in California and through her children. When she moved to Hong Kong, being involved with the kids' school made her busy and made it easy to meet other women. There had been a flurry of coffees and lunches, a few walks and girls' nights out. It was so easy that she was lulled into thinking she had lots of friends. And in a way, she had, in the way that doing a favor for an acquaintance and

sending a thoughtful e-mail segued into friendship. If you call someone a friend, they'll become one. Something like that. Since everyone
had live-in help, getting someone to go out with you for dinner was
easy. It was so easy that the women often organized girls' trips to other
countries, like forays to Vietnam to buy art and get embroidered linens
and lacquerware or to Bangkok or Seoul to get skin treatments. She
did not do anything like that, but she had seen how she could have
gotten there in a few years, when her kids were older.

Dr. Stein, her face small and concerned in the reduced Skype
window of Margaret's laptop, said, "Go out for lunch. Take a walk.
Work. Do something."

Margaret assented but then realized she had no idea how to get
back into work mode or whom she would reach out to to have lunch.
She never even got back to the Litchfield people on that spec project
her friends had sent her way. She had zero desire to call someone to
have lunch. The truth is that once you have three kids and a husband, you don't really need friends. She didn't, at least. They were a
perfect unit, a self-sufficient ecosystem, like those green plants in
glass spheres that produce oxygen and water and feed themselves forever in a perfect balance of waste and sustenance. Until fate came
down with a giant, destructive swipe and shattered it forever.

But friends. Back to the point.

"How do I do that?" she asked Dr. Stein.

"You've been out a few times to lunches and things, right?"

"Yes, but those have been more"—she searches for the word—"general.
I could leave when I wanted."

"You need to make connections with people. You have Clarke
and Daisy and Philip, but you need to go outside as well."

"Why?"

"You need to start living as normal a life as possible. Live as
though it's normal, and slowly it will become so."

Who would she call? Frannie Peck? Hilary Starr? Any of the well-meaning class mothers who dropped off food and ferried her kids to the birthday parties and soccer games she couldn't face? Can't she just stay here in this room that has become her sanctuary?

Even as she sinks lower into the too-rapidly cooling bathwater, she knows she cannot. The children are at home, Clarke too. She forgot to tell Essie that the washer repairman was coming, and Essie may deny him entry and cost her the appointment fee. There is a FedEx package to be picked up that will probably not make it to the door. She forgot to call to make the appointment for Philip's haircut, and he will be shaggy for the party. And she has to make friends.

Life presses on her from all angles, and she is not ready to accept it.

When she emerges from the bath and puts on clothes, she feels fortified, a little, as if she has acquired a small buffer for what is to come. Which is Clarke's party. An onslaught of friendly strangers, eager to connect and gladhand and drink and breathe unwelcome intimacies into her ear. These are the people she is supposed to be friends with, the people who will give her normalcy and support.

Back home, Margaret moisturizes her skin and walks around naked to let her skin dry so she won't stain her new dress. She bought it last week in town, a gossamer purple shift with silver sequins, knee length, a bit flapper. When she pulls it out, Clarke whistles.

"Great dress," he says.

She smiles. She wants this to be a good night for him.

"Are you excited?"

"It'll be fun," he says. "Thank you." He is almost dressed, knotting his tie. "Are Daisy and Philip ready?"

"I'll go check." She goes downstairs, pulling on a thin cotton bathrobe. She had bought it outside her little flat, and the memory of that moment, alone, purchasing this item, stays with her as she descends the stairs. She finds Daisy wrestling with a blow-dryer, a new development for her growing girl.

"You want help with that?" she asks. Daisy nods, and she stands while Margaret combs out sections of her hair and dries them smoothly. She looks at her daughter in the mirror, her arms and buttocks thickening ever so slightly—a sign of the impending storm to come.

When Daisy was six, a scrawny girl with twiggy limbs, she had been into gymnastics. Once she sprang into a handstand and a shower of glitter, sequined barrettes, and pink plastic beads fell out of her pockets. Margaret was filled with wonder and gratitude that this strange unicorn being was hers. Having a girl meant sparkling rings and fake jewels twinkling from every crevice of your house, the chemical smell of nail polish, the high, sweet pitch of her voice. She loved it so much, and she sees the end of this era coming—the chaos waiting to erupt onto Daisy's skin, the scramble of hormones to make her moody and silent. She aims hot air at her daughter's hair and wishes for time to stop, for just five minutes. She closes her eyes to stop tears.

"Mom," Daisy says. "Mom."

Margaret opens her eyes.

"Mom, don't."

It's a plea. She can see that Daisy needs her to be steady, to give her ballast.

"It's okay, darling," she says. The hot air blasts onto her hand, feeling almost like a burn. She shifts the blow-dryer. "Do you want French braids?"

"I'm not six, Mom," Daisy says. "I'm just going to wear the new headband I got."

"Okay."

She goes to check on Philip, who's reading a book on his bed.

"Do you know what you're going to wear?" she asks.

"It's fancy, right?" he says without looking up.

"Yes, so a collared shirt and a blazer, please. Long pants."

"It's so hot out, Mom!"

"It's your dad's fiftieth, Phil. I'll find you a good shirt." She goes through his shirts. Many don't fit anymore. "You are growing so fast," she says. Next to Philip's drawers are G's clothes, untouched.

She leaves them alone. She picks out a shirt and hands it to him. "Get dressed," she says.

She goes back upstairs.

"How do you feel?" she asks Clarke.

"Old."

"You look good."

"Thanks." He pulls her in for a kiss. "Hey," he says, releasing her and looking at her face. "We good?"

"Yeah, we're good," she says. Working on good.

"Mom!" she hears from downstairs. "An airplane's gone missing. Turn on the TV." Daisy does have a highly attuned ear for disaster. Maybe Courtney's mother, from that benefit lunch, was onto something. This is a change wrought by what happened. Before, Margaret had been surprised by her children's lack of empathy or understanding. When she had wept at a news story or while watching a documentary, they had asked her why she was sad if she didn't know the people or if just one person had died. Their smooth, guiltless countenances had struck her speechless.

She and Clarke turn on the television but can't find anything—just soccer matches and financial talk. They go to the computer and read of a Malaysian plane that never arrived at its destination.

"Oh, no," she says. "Those poor families."

"It's just disappeared," Clarke says.

They pause, and then they silently agree to move on. This is how it is, Margaret thinks, when it's not about you or your family. You have a horrified moment, your eyes fill, you say a silent prayer, but it's possible, even likely, that you will smile in the next hour. But now she feels grateful for the disaster slipping past her, leaving her unscathed. These are the small mercies she waits for now.

Hilary

HILARY HAS INVEIGLED Olivia into being her date for Clarke's party.

"Think of it as charity," she said. "I really don't want to go by myself."

"Why are you going at all?" Olivia asked.

She doesn't know why. She feels like going out, she supposes, having been a hermit for several weeks.

"I don't know," she said. "But tonight I want to put on a pretty dress and go out and have a glass of wine."

"You expats have so many of these parties," Olivia said. "Welcome parties, going-away parties. It's like you never left college."

They are getting ready together in the bathroom, Olivia having brought over her clothes and a bottle of champagne. Hilary is playing music, trying to get in the mood.

"So, you know," she says, "I'm going ahead with the adoption. With Julian."

Olivia pauses from applying foundation. "Oh?" she says. "That's great. How about David?"

"I'm going ahead without him, but I think I'm going to list him as a father. I think he won't mind."

"Really?"

"Well, I was going to have an agreement that he's not responsible at all for Julian. I just need him so they look favorably on the application."

Olivia raises an eyebrow. "You seem to have a surprisingly good opinion of David, considering all that's happened."

Hilary can't explain it, but she feels certain that he won't make a fuss. He'll yield to her on this.

"Are you ready for it?" Olivia asks. "He's not a baby, so it won't be the crazy change that is, and you won't have all the hormones, but it's still going to turn your world upside down. And schools! You have to get him into school! He's going to have to get fluent in English very fast!"

The talk of Hong Kong schools always turns rational women into hysterics.

"That's a ways down the road," Hilary says mildly.

"Oh, you don't know," Olivia says. "Everyone wants 'the best' for their child." She makes imaginary quote marks around the phrase. "You get crazy. People get crazy."

"Well, I have to make sure it goes through first. There's a lot that needs to happen." Hilary looks at Olivia. "Are there websites you go on?" she asks. "Like websites where people ask questions or for advice, stuff like that?"

Olivia considers. "Not really," she says. "There are a few groups on Facebook, if that's what you mean, and there are a few local sites where people go, but I don't spend much time on that stuff."

Hilary hesitates. "It's funny," she says. "I've been spending a lot of time online, because, you know, nothing to do, and I've been on these expat-forum sites. People talk about their helpers or their jobs or other things."

"Why on earth do you read about strangers' lives?" Olivia asks.

"It feels a little bit like living vicariously," Hilary says, embarrassed. "Like having a conversation with someone, and you don't even need to go out."

"You could be at a lunch but be in your pajamas."

"Exactly! It can be kind of addicting. But the weird thing is that someone on one of these forums knows about me and Julian and wasn't so kind about it."

"About you? Really? Hong Kong is too small. It's disgusting. What did they say?"

"That I was trying him on like a dress. That I was shopping for a child."

Olivia turns to Hilary. "Hilary, there are always going to be trolls. Especially on an Internet forum! What do you care what some anonymous coward says about you?" She turns back to the mirror, sweeps on blush. "The best thing about getting older," she says, "the absolute best thing, is that I don't give two hoots what anyone thinks about me."

"Come on!" Hilary protests.

"Okay," she allows. "I am working toward not caring one bit. I am on that path, and I am getting far along. I know you are too." Olivia's eyes meet Hilary's in the mirror. "Who cares?" she says. "It's all about them, not about you. They're motivated by jealousy or spite or their awful lives. It has nothing to do with you. Nothing."

"I guess," Hilary says doubtfully. "It seemed very personal."

"They're awful. The best thing anyone can do is just live her own life. You do that, and they should do that."

"It made me feel bad," Hilary says, almost childishly. Her eyes tear up.

"I'm sorry, darling," Olivia says. She sits down. "What can I say? There are awful people in the world."

"I know," Hilary says.

They sit in companionable silence.

"Well," Olivia says, "I'm with you. I'm here to help you. Whatever you need."

"Thank you."

They continue to get ready. Hilary remembers what her mother once said: You feel one age, and you see another in the mirror. She recalls nights in college, getting ready with her girlfriends before a frat party—not so different. What's staring back at them, two middle-aged women, is somehow foreign to her, although she thinks they might look better than they did when they were chubby college coeds.

"So who's going to be there tonight?" Olivia asks.

"The usual," Hilary says. "The TASOHK crowd. I'm sure there's very little overlap." TASOHK means ultra-American, soccer mom and corporate dad.

"Oh, good," Olivia says. "No one I know."

"You'll be slumming it with the suburbanites." Hilary laughs.

"Any handsome ex-football players?" Olivia muses. "I knew I should have married an American."

"Be prepared. There are going to be hundreds of them tonight."

"I'm ready," Olivia says.

Mercy

SHE'S WITH HER MOM at the gourmet supermarket in the basement of a big mall. Her mother's boss, Shirley, had texted, asking her to pick up a few last-minute things for the party, so they have big bunches of parsley for garnish, many lemons to cut into pretty shapes for used toothpicks from the canapés.

"I've only lived here a few months, but Shirley crazy to come to this market," her mother says. "The price here so high!"

"She just knows that if one of her customers complains, she can say she gets everything at the best supermarket. She can charge way higher prices this way, you know. Most of her food comes from wholesalers, but she gets the small stuff here." It drives Mercy crazy how her mom just doesn't get it.

Her mother shakes her head at the wasteful woman running a business this way. "This one lemon is eight dollars!"

"But it's a big one, from Tasmania. At the local market, they're small and not good. Anyway, it's not your money."

"Mercy, I want to help her," she says. "She is losing herself the money."

There are some seven or eight people ahead of them in the line. Late-afternoon Saturday is a busy time, with people picking up groceries for dinner.

There is a gradual commotion, in the way that minor disturbances come about. One, then two, then three people start to look at a woman, around forty, who is talking loudly in the way of the mentally ill.

"She's Korean," her mother whispers.

The woman is speaking Korean to the cashier, loudly and without stopping, even though the cashier is trying to respond.

"She must be crazy," her mother says. The cashier, who is Chinese, waves her hands and shakes her head, but the woman keeps talking.

"Sometimes when you are too lonely, you get like that," says her mother, who should know.

"There are a lot of Korean people from Korea here," Mercy says, using the peculiar way Koreans identify each other—Koreans from LA, Koreans from Queens, Koreans from Korea.

"Yes, I see them," her mother says. "Many in Taikoo Shing." A neighborhood with malls and lots of apartment buildings.

The cashier keeps ringing up the woman's items, items that suddenly look like the property of the insane: two oranges, a box of chocolates, a cabbage, and a six-pack of Japanese beer.

"*Gananhae,*" her mother says clinically. The woman is poor.

"How can you tell?" Mercy asks, curious for the first time.

"I can tell," her mother says. "Look at her shoes."

Mercy looks at the woman's shoes, a simple black pair of pumps with sensible two-inch heels, and considers, possibly for the first time, that her mother might have her own value system in which she lives and judges other people, namely Koreans. This makes Mercy feel adult.

"That's interesting, Mom," she says, and smiles. Her mother gives her a shy smile back. They both turn back to watching the woman and stand, listening, as she goes on and on, her manic delivery punctuated by her putting the items into a cloth bag. She pays, all the while chattering, signing the credit card slip, and walks out. The woman looks boldly at everyone, her gaze sliding over Mercy and her mother, stopping for a second. Koreans always recognize one another. Mercy looks away. The woman walks out, still talking.

People in the line exhale, shuffle their feet. The tension seeps out from the room.

"There was a crazy woman at church," her mom says. "Remember her? Haeri's mom, Mrs. Kim?"

"What happened to her?" Mercy remembers Haeri, quiet and studious, until ninth grade, when she came back from a summer program in Korea with permed hair dyed a startling orange, a predilection for blue eyeliner, and an equally changed attitude toward life. Her mother, a housewife, rarely left the house except to go to church, where she would sit and rock in the community room after service. The other women steered clear of her as her husband tried to talk to some of the other men. He was an unsuccessful import-export man, like her father. Haeri went wild after the Korean program, from which apparently three of the girls had gone home pregnant. Sent to improve their Korean and understand Korean culture, the teenagers had instead discovered that local bars would sell them anything and had hooked up with one another all summer long. This is what Haeri told the other girls at church after Sunday school.

"The hottest Korean guys are from Texas. They're so tall!" she had told them. "And there are no Asian girls in Texas, so they're so psyched. They're totally jealous that we live in New York, where there are so many Koreans."

At the program, there had been Koreans from Berlin, from Warsaw and the Canary Islands, and a few from South America and Africa. Their immigrant parents worried about their displaced children not knowing their homeland and sent them back through summer programs run by universities. Mercy's father had pooh-poohed the whole idea and asked where the money would come from. But Haeri's dad had come up with the money. Haeri said she was now called Hex—a new name for a new girl. It had stuck, strangely.

"What is Hex, I mean, Haeri"—Mercy corrects herself; the mothers still know her as Haeri— "what is Haeri doing now?"

"I don't know. They move away," her mother says. "Maybe Florida? I think she try to kill herself, the mom, and then they move."

They have a moment to consider the mentally disturbed mother, the wayward daughter, then they are called to the cashier and are shaken out of the reverie.

Margaret

THEY HEAD OVER in the car. Clarke's parents came over beforehand, and they had Essie take a photo of the whole group before they left. Then they decided to take one of just their nuclear family. Margaret stood behind Daisy and Philip in front of Clarke—the perfect family unit, a man and a woman with their boy and girl, their replacements in the cycle of life, Clarke turning fifty, with his entirely appropriate and attractive wife, their beautiful children. Margaret looks at the photo on her phone.

"So nice," she says to Clarke, handing it to him. "What a great photo."

"Love it," he says. He hands the phone to his parents. "Look, Mom."

"It'll be fun," Margaret says. A wish? A declaration? A vain hope, perhaps.

Daisy is fiddling around with her phone. "Can I Instagram the party, Mom?" she asks.

"Sure," Margaret says, uncertainly. She's seen Daisy's Instagram account, follows it as she's supposed to, and it still seems inexplicable to her—group pictures of girls flashing peace signs, photos of desserts.

"What does that mean?" Clarke asks.

"It's this thing that all my friends do. We post pictures, and people can respond. I have three hundred followers!"

"Nothing inappropriate, though, okay?" Margaret says.

"I've heard that girls get into terrible trouble these days with those things," Clarke's mother warbles.

Margaret and Clarke's mother are answered by an epic rolling of the eyes.

They get out of the car and ride up a creaky industrial elevator to find Priscilla rushing around clutching a clipboard, with reading glasses on a chain around her neck. She pauses to greet them and exclaim on how beautiful the children are. They look around and tell her what a marvelous job she's done. And she has. There are a million twinkling tea lights, and she has rigged up paper lanterns all over so the rather uninspiring original warehouse space has the look of a cathedral. She has arranged for a band from Manila to play cover songs and get the crowd dancing, and they're twanging through a sound check. There is a gorgeous long table set up and a mike in case anyone wants to make a toast.

"You have a lot of friends," Priscilla tells Clarke. "And such lovely ones."

What a pro, Margaret thinks, grateful.

"Kitchen's working hard," Priscilla continues. "We'll have some hors d'oeuvres for you soon. Want a glass of champagne?"

"Why not?" Clarke says.

It's a little after seven, and guests have been asked to arrive at seven thirty, so there's time to wander around. Daisy takes a few photographs of the family and herself against the backdrop of the party.

"Those are called selfies, right?" Clarke asks.

Daisy rolls her eyes again.

"What's with the eye rolling?" Margaret says. "Your eyes are going to roll up and never come down. I'm sorry we're so embarrassing to you."

"Can I see?" Clarke says.

Daisy shows him her phone, and Margaret looks at their two heads bent over the device. As staff bustle around them, lighting more candles, adjusting chairs, Margaret sits down. A waiter offers her a plate of chicken satay, decorated with a sprig of rosemary.

"No, thank you," she says.

The first guests come through the door, Charlie and Mel Gordon, and she gets up.

"Welcome to Clarke's birthday!" she says. "Thank you for coming!"

"We're so glad to be here," Mel says. "I haven't seen you in so long! You look well."

And so the party begins.

Hilary

OLIVIA INSISTS that they go early so she can get the lay of the land. It's 7:40 when they walk through the entrance, decorated with shimmering silver tinsel. Margaret and Clarke are standing near the front, with three other early birds.

"Hi, Margaret! This is my friend Olivia. I don't think you've met." They all cheek-kiss, bobbing back and forth. With them is a woman Hilary has seen around but doesn't know.

"I'm Hilary Starr," she says, introducing herself.

"I'm Melissa Gordon," the woman says.

"You look really familiar," Hilary says.

"Yes, I know! You do too!" They size each other up in a friendly way.

"TASOHK?" Mel ventures.

"No kids," Hilary says. "I know! We go to the same physio! From a few years ago."

"Dr. Chan! Above Pacific Coffee."

"Yes!" Hilary recalibrates. "You look really good," she says. Mel was much heavier then and less attractive.

The woman blushes. "Yes, my mom says she can't recognize me."

Some expat women thrive outside their native terrain. They are the trailing spouse, so they don't have to work. And they arrive and realize they can have someone else vacuum and make the beds and the lunch boxes and do the laundry, and so they take that found time and use it to improve themselves. Some who were stay-at-home mothers before go back to work; some become fluent in Mandarin;

some take up painting seriously, or whatever it was they used to want to do; and some become very fit and attractive.

This Melissa Gordon is someone Hilary used to see in the waiting room of the physio, pudgy in the way of many comfortable American housewives, but the knife-sharp planes and sleek brunette waves of the woman before her now make her almost unrecognizable.

"You lost a lot of weight," Hilary says. When she comes across someone who has gone through the same journey she had as a child, she doesn't feel kinship; she feels uncomfortable.

"Yes," Mel says. "I discovered CrossFit and Boot Camp!"

So she's one of the women down at Repulse Bay Beach weekdays, going through a circuit with an Australian trainer.

"Well, you look great." Hilary turns away. "This is my friend from college, Olivia."

Later Olivia will say that all the American people she met were unable to distinguish her from the waiters or other Chinese staff, a statement so patently ridiculous that Hilary is unable to stifle her bark of laughter, but for now Olivia graciously shakes Melissa's hand and exchanges niceties about the loveliness of the occasion. All that Hilary appreciates about Olivia has no currency here. Olivia does not watch the latest network shows on Apple TV; she doesn't go back to the United States every summer, or know what's going on with the NBA or the NSA or NASA. Instead, she talks about LegCo or the West Kowloon Arts project or other things that concern people who will make their life in Hong Kong forever. There are no people like that here. Everyone here is temporary. They all think of their stint in three-year increments. They have never considered politics in Hong Kong or China or the implications of raising the local minimum wage. Olivia is heard politely, then dismissed as foreign, ironically.

Now Olivia talks to Melissa, a light, meaningless conversation, and Hilary half-listens. Is it true that inevitably you end up with people like yourself? In college, everything is so idealistic, and you want to believe you can be anyone you want and be with anyone you want just because you both like early-twentieth-century French films or are both interested in cooking. When is it that you realize those are tenuous threads that are all too easily snipped by the stresses of daily life—work, money, children? She was someone different for David, and that wasn't able to sustain them for so long. If she looks around, the crowd is so homogeneous she can easily believe that the young are foolish indeed.

Mercy

THE KITCHEN is so hot she feels she's about to faint. Her mother sees this and hurries over.

"Do you need to sit down?" she asks.

"No, I'll be okay," she says.

"Get out of the kitchen, too hot!" her mother scolds, then hands her a tray of hors d'oeuvres. "Pass these if you are okay."

Mercy emerges out of the heat into a cool, temperature-controlled wonderland. Is there anything more than this party, right here, right now, that decisively underscores her jaundiced understanding of the world? There are the servers and the served. She knows this so well. As a waitress at her aunt's restaurant, in America, in an immigrant neighborhood, it was less stark, but here, oh, a wide, wide chasm divides the two. She thought an Ivy degree would help her bridge it, but here she is, in black pants and a white shirt, hair pulled back, wandering among the privileged, offering them a small, exquisite taste of cheese or prosciutto, being rebuffed as the women all give a slight shake of their head when she approaches, the men more welcoming, interested in her wares, as she proffers the tray.

She remembers the pastor at church laughing at her teenage self listening to Janis Joplin, the tinny music coming out of the speakers. "You want Mercedes, yes?" he asked. "Don't ask the Lord. You marry rich man!" Ever the callow teenager, she tried to explain to this sixty-year-old Korean man that Joplin was counterculture, singing about materialism, but he just laughed and joked that she had to be pretty to catch a good man.

It had been so close. She had almost gotten there. Charlie would have brought her to a party like this in ten years. She would have a modest diamond ring, a designer bag, a haircut from a junior stylist at an expensive salon—hard-won prizes but hers. David lives in this world, she's sure. Most of her friends are on a sure route to this place, this destination. The women are coiffed, their hair blown into silky waves. Their outfits are sparkly and shimmery; their skin is moist and toned. They radiate well-being and prosperity, the knowledge that someone cares about them enough to take care of them while they take care of the family. She doesn't want this exactly—she's never been purely materialistic, and money has never been her goal—but she wants something like it, maybe just an assurance that she won't fall by the wayside, that she won't become invisible.

She crosses the room, going from cluster to cluster, casting an anthropological eye on the crowd. Mostly American, 85 percent white, expats, most of whom will be here for less than ten years. Still, while they are here, Hong Kong is their oyster. She hears snatches of conversation about the best resort in Hoi An, the best airline to fly to Dubai, how someone had to fire her second helper for theft. These conversations are light and airy, buoyed by an unassailable sense of their place in the world, assured, secure in their corporate jobs and housing allowances.

A woman says loudly to her, "May I have a glass of sparkling water, please?" Mercy can tell that the woman thinks she's a local who can't speak English, and is speaking loudly and slowly so Mercy can decipher the foreign words. She tamps down the urge to reply, merely nods her head.

In the idealistic confines of college, she thought that all people had the same opportunities, but to be here, one of a throng of Asian servers serving a bunch of white people, is severely messing with her head. She knows that it's not the case, that in the media everyone is talking about Asian money and power and that everyone is rushing to get a piece, but today, this hour, this minute, when she has on a waiter outfit, with her bastard baby in her belly, and she's serving goat cheese puffs to some indifferent blonde from Charlottesville, she feels so despairing she thinks, why is she even considering bringing another girl into this world? For she knows her baby is a girl. She just knows. How could it not be? Given the arc of her mother and Mercy, of course she's going to have another luckless female. Isn't that some Korean folktale? To bring into the world another girl to suffer, carry on the story?

She's noticed too how she can tell that some women have only sons and some have only daughters. The women with boys are rangy and attractive, as if all that exposure to testosterone has honed them into a lithe, goddesslike receptacle for male worship. Women with girls look a little more beleaguered, as if already psychologically worn away. It's clear to Mercy, in the unspoken way in which some truths reveal themselves, that this girl will be her only child, another reason she's determined to keep it.

Crossing the room, she sees the banner for the first time. HAPPY 50TH, CLARKE!

An electric jolt goes through her body. Jesus.

She almost drops the tray.

It can't be.

Hong Kong is small, but it can't be that small. In the kitchen, no one mentioned the party's hosts. Her mother just said it was an American's fiftieth birthday and marveled at how dressed up the women were. She keeps walking, numbly, because she doesn't know what else to do, but now all the groups of people seem menacing, as if they might house one of the Reades, which they probably do. Her head expands in and out. White lights press in on her temples.

Of course, Hong Kong can be this small. For someone like her, with an excellent memory for faces and names, Hong Kong can be dizzying and claustrophobic. She will read about someone in *Time Out* or the *South China Morning Post* and meet them the next week or see them going up the escalator at the Landmark. It is a small, small pond.

Then, there, she spots a Reade. Philip, the middle child. He doesn't see her, because he's sitting down, playing with an iPad. She walks on. Again. There's Daisy. She scans the room. And there's Margaret.

Mercy retreats into a dark corner, puts the tray down and tries to calm the pounding of her heart, which threatens to beat right out of her chest. She puts her right hand on her chest to try to calm it.

Where is the other? Where is the other? Her mind repeats this phrase like an insane refrain. She is the other. She is the one who caused the injury, not the injured. She is the invisible. She's the one not mentioned in the magazine pieces and newspaper articles. She is the unforgiven, the unforgivable.

Mercy sinks down into a crouch. She hides.

Margaret

A WOMAN WHOSE NAME she can't remember is thanking her for not having a costume party.

"I mean, I found myself in a toga more often my first two years here than when I was in college!"

It is true that something about being an expat often means finding yourself in a cowboy suit, or a sari. Dress-up balls, or masquerade parties, are uncommonly popular here, which is usually credited to the British influence.

"If I have to buy another cheap polyester outfit in the lanes, I'll shoot myself," the woman says. "There's this Arabian Nights party at the American Club next month, and my girlfriends are going all out, getting dresses made, buying fake jewelry, and I just can't be bothered, you know?"

Margaret assents. Out of the corner of her eye, she sees Clarke stuck with someone from work she knows he doesn't like. "Excuse me," she says smoothly. "I just see someone. . . ."

The woman lets her go with a nod. What was her name? Shirley? Shelly? She was a mom at TASOHK whose daughter was in Daisy's class last year.

It's going better than she thought. She's had a glass of champagne and feels a little looser. No more, though, as she gets jittery after more than one. She wonders whether Clarke is having a good time. She walks over to him, places her arm on his waist.

"Hello, darling," she says. He is standing with Jack McMillan, someone who has been a thorn in his side at work ever since he arrived. He is a man who is almost good-looking, who aspires to surfer good looks but is just one or two degrees off. His hair is an expensive golden hue, which she is certain he highlights; he booms, "Here he is!" when someone comes into the room.

"Hey, Margaret," he drawls. He is in requisitioning or something. A Duke boy in China. Khaki pants in Guangdong.

"Hi, Jack," she says. "How are you?"

"Not bad, not bad. Can't believe the man here is fifty, you know?"

Jack must be forty-five.

"Age gets us all," she says.

"Hey!" Clarke protests. "Don't write me off. I've still got a few good years."

Jack made a play for Clarke's job when they were in Korea—a move that still leaves her breathless with wonder, that someone could be so ruthless. Still, here they are, being adult, smiling at each other. Conventions are not so easily thrown out, she's found.

"Are you dating anyone?" she asks.

"You know," he says. "Here and there. Actually, there." He points to a lissome twenty-something walking toward them.

Jack is known for turning up with the latest underage models off the plane from the Ukraine or Israel, the ones who were not quite tall enough for London or New York.

"This is Svetlana," he says when she arrives.

"Hello," Margaret says.

Svetlana has a heavy accent that Margaret cannot decipher. "Clarke," she says, "can you help me with something?" They escape and walk away.

"Thanks, darling," Clarke says, kissing Margaret. "What an asshole."

"Why do we always have to be the bigger person and invite people we hate?"

"I don't know," he says. "But better to be the bigger person, right?"

They are waylaid immediately by another group of people, eager to congratulate the birthday boy. Margaret stands a little apart, watching her husband talk to his friends, his business associates, wondering at him, at what a good man he is.

There is a ripple in the crowd. The children are about to do their performance.

Daisy and Philip stand in front of the crowd, shy and awkward, shifting their shoulders and looking down at the floor. From the side, Priscilla coaches them in a whisper.

"We've prepared a song," Daisy says. Priscilla hits play on an iPod.

They sing a sweet song about their father, set to the tune of "It Had to Be You." Philip's voice, not yet changed, rises in a sweet tenor; Daisy harmonizes with him. Waiters begin to distribute glasses of champagne. Clarke finds his way over to Margaret and puts his arm around her shoulders. She puts her hand around his waist and holds on, feeling the comforting solidity of his body. Of course, she cries, tears welling and running down her face in a constant stream. She cannot stand the empty space next to her two children, the way they are standing close so their elbows are almost touching, the fact that Priscilla, a stranger, arranged this because she could not. How to cope with all the new realities of her life, which shouldn't feel so new, so raw, still. How she feels she should be on the road to somewhere better but absolutely is not. All these emotions are drowning her, so she cries and cries, silently, hoping her children will not see.

They finish, and the audience claps enthusiastically.

"Speech, speech!" The crowd demands Clarke.

He lets her go—she can feel the warmth disappear from her when he departs—and goes to the front of the room.

Priscilla hands him a mike. He takes it and clears his throat.

"Thank you all for coming," he says. "It means a lot to me and Margaret." He looks at her, understanding. "Margaret and I moved here three years ago, and as we all know, Hong Kong can be a tough place to transition to, although it is a wonderful place. There are a lot of things to get used to: Work is quite different. I didn't have to drink snake liquor back in San Francisco to get anything done, and I've finally learned to call my assistant by her name without apologizing." A big laugh. "But the thing that has made our move here doable is the people."

He pauses.

"They often say that in expat life, your friends become your family. Because you don't have mothers and fathers and siblings nearby to count on, you grow close to the people around you. So many of you have come to our aid in so many ways. You have taken our children to birthday parties when we could not; you have brought us food when circumstances made it impossible for us to take care of ourselves; you have shown us unimaginable kindnesses. For this, Margaret and I are truly grateful. It's impossible to think that three years ago we did not know any of you. You are our family now, and I am so grateful that you are here to celebrate with us this birthday of mine, which I gather is quite a big one. Of course, I want to say thank you to my actual family, my mom and dad, here all the way from California, my gorgeous kids and Margaret, my amazing wife."

The crowd waits.

"And especially to my son G, wherever he is." His voice quavers. "We love you so much, G." He looks down, composes himself. Margaret holds her breath.

"To you, our Hong Kong family," he says.

Priscilla hands him a glass of champagne.

They all cheer and toast one another. The band strikes up again, and the space is filled with noise and cheer again. The moment has passed as lightly as it could. Margaret doesn't know if she's relieved or upset about this.

Is this all it is? Human beings have figured out that to celebrate and feel happy, you need certain elements—people, music, alcohol—and that's all it takes to create this feeling of celebration and acknowledgment of life and time passing. The rituals we make—the elaborate wedding, the twenty-first birthday—these all signal to the world outside the changes in one's life. And the funerals, to say goodbye to someone. The one she will never be able to do.

Hilary

HILARY HAS BEEN on pins and needles all night, waiting to see if David is coming. Olivia is well on her way to getting bombed, a combination of not knowing anyone at the party and not caring to know anyone at the party. Hilary knows most of the people here—they are on the American Club-TASOHK-Central circuit, and she is a card-carrying member of this group, even without children. She can be at this party and not feel a shred of social anxiety. The same cannot be said of Olivia, who both cares and doesn't care. If Hilary pressed her to be honest, the truth would be that Olivia feels superior to all the expats here. Hong Kong is her real home. She owns her apartment, her daughter goes to a local school and speaks Cantonese and English perfectly. To her, the expatriates are just visiting, naïve galoots who come and screech about the jade market and getting dresses copied in Shenzhen. Not for them the rarefied rooms of the Hong Kong Club or the Stewards Box at the Jockey Club on race day. They are temporary and best ignored or tolerated until they receive their orders to return home. She would usually live her life perhaps dining next to them at Otto e Mezzo or browsing alongside them at the bookstore, never having any real interaction. Olivia has granted Hilary an exemption due to their friendship in college, when Hilary acted as a tour guide to California and the rest of America.

Then she sees David walk through the entrance, looking around. She hasn't seen him in a long time. Not like him to be so late, but she guesses he's a new person now. He is alone, as far as she can tell. He looks good—a little thin, but good.

She taps Olivia on the shoulder. "David just walked in."

"Let's go say hi!" Olivia says.

"That's a terrible idea."

"Oh, come on," Olivia says, and drags her to David.

"Oh, hi, Hilary," he says uncomfortably. "And Olivia."

They stand awkwardly.

"How are you?" Hilary asks. "You've been traveling a lot?"

"Yes," he says. "A fair amount."

There's an awkward pause while Olivia sways, tipsy, beside them.

"I wanted to tell you something," Hilary says. "I was going to see if you wanted to get a meal, but I might as well tell you now."

"Okay," he says agreeably. Again she wonders where his calm is coming from.

"So I think I'm going to go ahead and adopt Julian," she says.

"Oh." A look passes over his face that she can't interpret. Not panic, not distress, something more complicated.

"I'm going to need your help, though," she presses on, although in the back of her mind something's telling her it's not a good idea. "They're so strict and picky here. I want to keep you on the forms as my husband, and we'll adopt him together, but it'll be purely a formality. You don't need to have any responsibility, and I can do a separate contract like that if you want."

"Jesus," he says. "That's a lot to drop on me right now."

Anger rises in her so quickly it feels as if her head is on fire. "Oh, you think?" she says hotly. "You think it's a lot? You . . . asshole. You think it was a lot for you to leave without any . . . any"—she cannot find the word—"any . . . notification," she says, using an absurd, businesslike word, "the day my mother came for her annual visit?"

"Calm down, Hilary," he says. "I'm not saying anything bad. I'm just saying it's a lot. And that's part of the whole problem, you know. When you bring this up, the fact that I left is more about that it was the day your mother was coming than the fact that I left. You have some messed-up priorities."

"What are you talking about?"

"You always, you always made me feel like I joined your family and not that you joined me, do you know what I mean?" He shakes his head. "This is not the place to be doing this."

They stare at each other, the hostility finally bubbling to the surface.

"I didn't come here for this," he says finally. "I'm going to go get a drink, and we can talk about this later, not at a party, not tonight." He walks off, shaking his head.

She looks at his receding back, trembling with anger. When had this man been her husband, someone she thought she might spend the rest of her life with? He seems like a stranger.

Olivia has been sobered up by the exchange. "Sorry, that didn't go well, did it?" she says, and puts her arm around Hilary, who is trembling a little.

"That's not how I imagined it," Hilary says. "I didn't expect him to be so . . . uncaring, or mean, even."

"Imagine where he is," Olivia says. "He's had to cut you off in his mind to be able to leave. Of course, he's not going to want to do the adoption."

"I just thought . . ."

"I know," Olivia says. "I'm sorry."

Mercy

ONCE SHE CROUCHES DOWN, she starts to plot her escape. She'll tell her mother she doesn't feel well, and she'll go down and get a cab home. But then everything stops for the kids' song and Clarke's speech. She listens to it all, feeling sicker with every word. When it's over, the crowd starts to buzz again, and she knows they're going to start the dinner service soon. It's buffet style, with open seating.

She gets up, then spots David.

Great. It's getting even better. She starts to walk and keeps her head down. He doesn't notice her, but then she bumps into someone.

"Oops," says a man in a tan suit. Mercy cannot breathe.

"Hey, you okay?" He looks at her, concerned.

She nods and keeps walking. Only ten feet to the kitchen now. She sneaks a look right and sees Margaret, looking right at her. She keeps walking, swings the kitchen door open, lets it close behind her.

Blessed cacophony of heat and activity inside. She needs to find her mother.

Margaret

SHE COULD HAVE SWORN she saw Mercy, walking to the kitchen, but it was out of the corner of her eye. Must have been someone who looked like her. What on earth would Mercy be doing at Clarke's party? She shakes her head as if she's seen a ghost and continues talking to Frannie Peck, who's had a few and is encouraging Margaret to do the same. They flag down a passing waiter for another glass of wine, which seems like a good idea at the time.

Hilary

A CIGARETTE. That's what she needs. She doesn't really smoke, but she could use a break. Olivia has a pack, and they take the industrial elevator down and walk through the parking garage to the street.

They light up in the street like teenage girls playing hooky. The smoke sweeps into her lungs, clarifying the moment.

"Why is smoking so bad if it feels so good?" Hilary asks. She feels light-headed, removed.

Outside, Aberdeen blinks and twinkles. It's an industrial warehouse zone, with a truly apocalyptic waterway running through it that is filled with a mysterious murky liquid. Around them, buildings encased in scaffolding emit ghostly light.

"It feels like a Batman movie out here," she says.

The elevator doors open again, and a young woman comes out. She looks pale and a bit unhealthy. She looks at them warily and then passes by.

"Do you want to leave?" Olivia asks. "It's kind of boring."

"I don't think we can," Hilary says. "It would be rude, wouldn't it?"

"No one cares," says Olivia.

"Cynic."

The young woman stands, waiting for a taxi. Hilary can tell, in that strange way that one can always tell, that she is listening to their conversation, which is odd, because she is dressed in a waiter's uniform and is probably local.

"So sad, isn't it?" Hilary says. "I don't know how you go on after something like that."

"If anything happened to Dorothy, I would kill myself, and I'm not being melodramatic," says Olivia. "She's the only thing I'm living for."

"We have to find more to live for," Hilary says.

"You're going to become a mother," her friend replies. "You'll understand. It's the only thing that matters."

Hilary ruminates on this, rolls it around her head, finds the thought pleasing. "I would like that to be true," she says. "I would like that very much."

Mercy

SHE FINDS HER MOTHER, tells her she's feeling unwell and has to leave. There's a flash of disappointment in her mother's face (Mercy, flaking again, if there's a verb for flaking in Korean), but it passes in an instant, and she nods her head and says, of course, go home.

Mercy grabs her purse and exits through the staff door. In the hallway, she jabs the button for the elevator, willing it to come quickly. Inside, a musty fan circulates dusty air in the fluorescent light. There's an old mirror on the wall, and she looks at herself. She looks normal. She looks fine. She's dodged a bullet. Margaret may have seen her, but she might not have recognized her.

Outside, two women are smoking, talking. She waits for a taxi next to them as they talk idly about maybe leaving the party. Then they bring up the Reades and their situation.

"You never get over something like that," the Asian woman says. "Most of those marriages don't make it."

"She was always perfect," says the white woman, not unkindly.

Mercy strains to hear. She wonders if they will bring her up, the guilty, the other, the never-mentioned. Before she can hear any more, a taxi passes, and she runs after it, arm aloft to flag it. She runs away and disappears.

Margaret

Margaret is drunk, for the first time since G was lost. Really drunk. It snuck up on her, like most drunken states, and by the time she realized, it was too late. Clarke keeps giving her sympathetic glances, and she feels ashamed before her in-laws.

She escapes to the bathroom and sits down on the toilet. She puts her palms on the opposite walls of the stall to try to stop the spinning. She tries to catalogue, as if that will make her feel better. She had a glass of champagne, a glass of wine after, and then another with Frannie Peck. There may also have been a shot of vodka, pressed on her by Clarke's colleagues, a hard-partying crew. She was feeling good, feeling buzzed, until all of a sudden she felt rotten.

And there is something else, a niggling feeling that she's missed something, or that something is wrong. She can't put her finger on it.

She gets up, stumbles as she tries to pull down her underwear. What a mess she is.

She pees, thickly, hoping that at least some alcohol is leaving her body.

What is the thing that is wrong? What is she missing?

Mercy.

She saw Mercy. Now she is sure of it.

She has not thought about the girl in so long. She put her out of her mind, because what was the point? Now she remembers the girl walking fast, head down, going to the kitchen. She was in a waiter's outfit, so she must have been working.

The white-hot hatred she felt toward the girl has cooled over the past year. When she thinks of her now, she can have moments of empathy. What is it like to have caused such a seismic change in someone else's life? What is she doing now? Has she moved on? She doesn't feel sympathy, but she doesn't feel an active enmity. She wished her dead for a long time, but Dr. Stein told her that was not a path forward.

She wishes she weren't so drunk.

She rises and walks unsteadily out the door to wash her hands. Someone comes in.

"Oh, hi," she says, trying to speak clearly. It's Hilary's friend, the elegant Chinese woman.

"What a wonderful party," the woman says. "Thank you for having me."

"Not at all." She wipes her hands on a paper towel and walks out to find Clarke. It seems imperative that she find him.

"Clarke!" she calls when she sees him across the room. "Clarke!"

He sees her and looks concerned. "Are you okay?" he says. "You should drink some water."

"I saw her," she says. "I saw her!"

"Who?"

"Mercy! I saw Mercy!"

"Mercy?" Clarke doesn't recall, and then his face changes when he realizes whom she is talking about. "What the hell are you talking about?"

"Mercy was here! She was working! She went into the kitchen!"

"What?" he says. "No, not possible. What would she be doing here?"

"I don't know, but I saw her! Do you think I should find her?"

"Why would you do that?" he asks.

"I don't know! I just want to know why she's here!"

Around them, people are listening with great interest. It's not often one gets a front-row seat to a full-blown family drama.

Clarke notices, takes her by the arm, and leads her away.

"You've drunk too much," he says. "I think you should sit down with my mother and drink some water."

"NO!" she shouts. "I'm going to find that girl and see why she's here!" She shakes him off and runs to the kitchen and flings open the door. "Mercy!" she shouts. "Mercy! Are you here?"

Hilary

PERFECT MARGARET READE is creating a spectacle. Hilary has never seen anything like it. She has clearly had too much to drink and is causing a commotion in the kitchen, yelling out the name of the girl, Mercy, the girl who was watching G when he disappeared. People have stopped talking and are watching Margaret scream and shout.

Clarke goes over and grabs Margaret and brings her to a chair, calming her down. She's crying and wailing quite loudly. He gestures to his mother to get the children away, as they are running toward their mother. He sits down next to Margaret and covers her with his jacket, talking to her quietly.

Hilary looks at Olivia, nods, and quietly they make their way out.

Part VI

Mercy

VISIBLY PREGNANT NOW, Mercy is the darling of all the elderly people she sees on the street. People coo at her, try to touch her belly, give her unsolicited advice in elevators. She never knew what a pass pregnant women get in society.

Her mother has been feeding her, both with home cooking and out at restaurants. She has been eating spicy *naengmyun*, mung-bean pancakes, plenty of kimchi, and she has developed an intense craving for the braised sea cucumbers at a small Szechuan restaurant in Causeway Bay. Her mother funds all this eating with the revelation of a second nest egg, kept hidden from her father. "I'm not stupid," she says. "I hide a lot."

Mercy looks down at her belly with wonder. She can feel the flutters now, small touches from inside her that are growing stronger. Apparently the baby will also hiccup and somersault in the womb.

Her mother has been here for a few months and has acclimated to Hong Kong life. She has found a Korean church and has been trying to get Mercy to go.

"You want me to go like this?" Mercy asks, pointing to her stomach. "Your unmarried daughter?"

"I don't care," her mother says. "God is for everyone."

Which is how she finds herself one Sunday attending a church that has set up in an office building in North Point. Most of the people her mother introduces her to are welcoming and nice.

"Columbia *joropseng*," says her mother proudly to everyone they see. Columbia graduate. Ivy League. Understandable in any language.

The place is filled with tacky calendars from small Korean busi-nesses and cheap ugly chairs, and while Mercy would have scoffed at it a year ago, it appeals to her now. It's so comforting. They sit down and listen to the sermon. Mercy's Korean is good, and she can un-derstand most of what the minister is saying. Today his sermon is about forgiveness. She looks around at all the Koreans in the room. She has spent so much time with the young American crowd it's a relief to see her other kind of people here. She recognizes these people—the middle-aged women with the perms and sensible shoes, the stylish young moms, the salaryman bankers. She knows them. They know her.

After the service, people gather for refreshments. She also knows this—the big urns of coffee and tea, the bowls of Coffee-mate and sugar cubes, Kjeldsens Butter Cookies in their white fluted paper cups. This could be a Korean church gathering anywhere on the globe. Ex-hausted from her time in the expatriate world, she eats biscuits and revels in the homely acceptance implied in this space.

Until a woman with a pinched face asks her where the baby's fa-ther is. It's a normal way in Korean to refer to one's partner, so she could be asking innocently, but Mercy's not so sure.

"Not here," she says, smiling.

"Is he working? What does he do?" The nosiness of Korean *ajumma* is unparalleled.

"Law," Mercy says. Nothing she has said has been a lie, although nothing is constraining her from lying either.

"Oh, lawyer. Great!" says the woman.

"How long have you lived in Hong Kong?" Mercy asks. The woman is short, and Mercy can see her scalp through the thin strands of hair she has dyed a purplish-black.

"Ten years," she says. "Have a daughter. She at Berkeley now."

"How wonderful," Mercy says. "Congratulations."

"She maybe become the dentist."

Mercy's mother appears by her side.

"*Heemduro?*" she asks. Are you tired? "Come sit down." She leads Mercy away. "Don't like that woman," she says. "Mrs. Lee. She always brag."

They sit by themselves, drinking hot tea with milk and sugar, surrounded by fellow Koreans in a foreign land. It's not so bad.

Margaret

Expat Hong Kong has emptied out in a long, wistful exhale. The families go back for home leave to see their parents and siblings, grill hot dogs, and drink beer on verdant lawns, experiencing the best of America.

There are several waves of migration. There's the mass exodus that happens as soon as school lets out, when eager mothers have all the bags packed and ready so that when the kids get home from their last day at school, they give them a quick snack, and then it's off to the airport for the flight to JFK or LAX and connecting on. There's another wave of people who have their kids do an immersion program in China or a session of summer school before heading out in mid-July for a month. Still others, mostly dual working parents, just carve out a week or two, fly home quickly, and come back again.

The American Club becomes a ghost town, lounge chairs sitting empty as a lone swimmer does laps, when just a few weeks ago, it was bustling with children taking tennis lessons, birthday parties, farewell dinners. On a Sunday, Margaret and Clarke sit, nursing coffees. Clarke has exercised in the gym this morning, and Daisy and Philip are in the teen area, watching movies and playing air hockey with the few remaining stragglers.

Margaret and Clarke stayed all last summer because she couldn't fathom leaving, but Clarke has broached the subject of going home to California for two weeks in July this year.

"You could see all your old friends," he says. "And we could see your mom and my parents. The kids haven't been back in a long time, and it's important for them to stay in touch with their old friends." This is what expats do, because they're always preparing for the inevitable return.

This is all out of the question for Margaret. She cannot leave Asia any more than she would ever think of giving up on G. How could he ever find her if she moves half a globe away? She feels guilty enough being a three-and-a-half-hour plane ride away.

But, her other children.

She doesn't say yes to going back for this summer, but she doesn't say no.

She's preoccupied with her dream, the one she keeps having, the one that woke her up this morning again, jittery. The apocalypse is coming. They have to get out. She has to pack. She has to think of everything her family might need and put it in backpacks. Water, food, blankets, can openers. What is necessary? What will help them survive? What shoes should they wear? In the dream, she is packing and packing, but her backpack keeps getting bigger and heavier, and she realizes she cannot carry it. So she takes things out. Then puts them back in. Considers what is important. Makes decisions and unmakes them. Packs and unpacks. A repetitive and anxious and crazy-making dream.

So she looks up what to store at home in case there is an earthquake or a nuclear bomb, and then buys everything. She has candles and gas ranges with extra fuel cans, water-purifying tablets, Cipro, containers of water, canned foods, a flint stone. There is a community of people she has found online who are preparing for the apocalypse, and they call themselves preppers. She has bought books off the Internet, and they come in brown paper packages tied with red twine, her address written in a shaky, unclear hand, an address that ends "Hong Kong, China, Japan," all three included for good measure. The books are often self-published and, unsurprisingly, not well-written, penned by paranoid recluses in rural areas. But the dream seems a sign. She doesn't want to leave anything to chance.

Besides, it feels good to have a project. And what better project than to maximize the chances of her family's survival in the case of an apocalyptic event? Clarke doesn't know, but she secretes everything in a closet off Essie's room, so Essie sees the growing supplies, grows fearful that something is happening that she doesn't know about. Margaret has a separate stash in her room in Happy Valley as well.

"I don't know," she says, noncommittal about going back to the United States. "Maybe."

After Clarke's party, she had woken up with a hell of a hangover and that dreadful shame that comes after a colossal bout of drunkenness.

She kept asking Clarke who saw her do what and what she had said, and he kept telling her to forget about it. She apologized to him, and he brushed it off, saying she deserved to tie one on, and then she had to go down for breakfast and face his parents. It took her a week to stop blushing involuntarily when she thought about what had happened.

But Mercy! She could remember that. Now she can't stop thinking about Mercy either. What she is doing, if she has a job, a boyfriend, a life. At her last session with Dr. Stein, she asked if it would be okay to contact Mercy, and the doctor asked why she wanted to.

"It's like an unfinished thing, and one that I can actually finish," she said.

"What do you think you will be able to 'finish' here?" Dr. Stein made air quotes around the word "finish."

" 'Cause I'll be able to talk to her," she replied lamely.

There is no resolution—there never is—but clearly Dr. Stein doesn't think it's a great idea. Clarke goes to shower in the locker room, and she picks up her phone. She Googles Mercy's name. It's common enough that there are several, so she adds in Columbia and finds a few hits. Mercy being quoted in an old article in the *New York Post* about Ivy League grads not being able to find work and doing temp jobs, an entry in a half marathon in Cambodia from several years ago, but nothing that is recent, nothing after what happened in Seoul. There is an old

Facebook page that hasn't been updated for two years and a Twitter account with no tweets.

Then she Googles G's story and finds, as always, page after page of Korean media, with his picture, with hers, with videos of their press conferences. She cannot read the articles, so she just goes through them looking at the photos.

And then she lets herself do what she allows herself to do only once every two or three months: She pulls up the album where there are videos and pictures of G, and she opens them up and loses herself in the pictures and the moving image of the child she no longer has.

It feels like looking at pornography, making her feel sick with guilty pleasure, knowing that she shouldn't be doing this, that she'll feel worse afterward, filled with an empty despair, but she watches the short clips, tears streaming down her face, letting herself remember his high-pitched voice, the way he clung to her leg, his first steps.

She hears someone behind her, quickly closes the window, and sits up straight. Luckily, it's not Clarke or the kids. She surreptitiously wipes at her eyes. She didn't have a chance to go in too deep, so she can recover relatively quickly.

She went to a talk on parenting at the end of the school year where the speaker had said that doing good things, charitable things, was actually a selfish act, because it made you feel good. She has been mulling that ever since. Should she do something selfless, something good? Should she reach out to someone who really needs her forgiveness? Would this make her feel better?

What would it be like to see Mercy again?

She starts typing an e-mail, ferociously, savagely, and hits Send before she can think about it any more. Doing something, anything, feels like progress. She puts down her phone and waits for Clarke to come so they can order breakfast.

Hilary

SHE HAS SAT through several sessions on adopting, started to process the paperwork, and otherwise gotten things rolling. And today she is meeting David for lunch to talk about what she had brought up at Clarke's party. Nothing too emotional—she e-mailed him to see if he would be free, and he replied. They agreed to meet at the sushi restaurant in the mall that houses his offices. Twelve thirty. His secretary e-mailed her an evite, which made her wonder how much Pansy knew. Probably all. Maybe Pansy was the girl. She was pretty.

Hilary showers, gets ready. A purple shift, a chunky silver bead necklace clasped around her neck. She wants to look professional, accomplished, a woman who can handle becoming a single mother. Sam drives her into town. She hasn't been in town in days, and she looks at all the efficient people striding around with purpose and drive. They carry briefcases or peck away at iPads in the coffee shops. They huddle, speaking urgently, or talk to the air on Bluetooth headsets curved around their ears. She has opted out, but she doesn't know when that happened, when she gave up the chance to become one of them.

It's partly the money in her family. While it doesn't seem as much these days, compared with all the hundreds of millions being minted by young men in tech, it's always been enough to know she doesn't have to work. After she got married, it wasn't as if she felt passionate about her job in PR, so it seemed natural to quit, to be able to travel with David on his business trips and wait for the family to start to form.

Except it hadn't. And then David was gone too. And now she's trying to find who she is in the midst of all that she is not.

She is early to the restaurant and sits down, orders green tea, peruses the menu. She sees David at the hostess station, pretends not to until he sits down.

"Hi," he says awkwardly.

"Hi," she says. "Thanks for coming."

"Probably overdue," he says.

She gives a surprised laugh. "Yes, probably," she manages. She studies his familiar face, trying to find the difference in him, now that he is no longer with her.

They talk about mundanities, the weather, what they will order, until they have sorted all those things out, called over the waiter, given him their desires. Then they pause.

"So," she says.

"Yes," he replies. "I know. You say your piece, and then I have something I need to share with you as well."

"Okay." She takes a deep breath.

"I want to adopt Julian. You know this. I'm sorry I brought it up in such an abrupt way and at the wrong place, but I was emotional at the time. I still am. It's a big decision." He is listening to her, with a kind look on his face.

"And after you left, I didn't know what had happened. David, I want you to know I don't understand what you did, but I don't hate you and I don't blame you. I don't think you were happy, and I wasn't that happy either. We were just coasting, seeing what would happen, and then you pulled the plug. Right?"

He nods.

"But I'd really like for you to support me on Julian. I really want this, and I think you might owe it to me."

He clears his throat as the waiter pours his Diet Coke. "Hilary, I want to apologize to you. I should never have done what I did in the way that I did."

She nods.

"I don't know why I did, but I was feeling like I didn't have much to lose, and I wanted to do something that I wanted to do instead of what I was expected to do, which I had been doing for so much of my life, and I was kind of sick of it. I thought, if not now, when? When am I going to live my life? I didn't want it to slip away without my noticing."

"Okay," she encourages.

"So I was a total bastard and just dropped out. And a coward, because you deserved much better. You deserved an explanation and a respectful way out of our marriage, and I didn't give that to you." He looks down at his drink, takes a sip.

"And I want to tell you that I'm fine with your adopting Julian. You can put me down. I actually don't even know what I want my role to be yet, so we'll work it out later."

The waiter sets down trays with salads and miso soup. Hilary starts to sip at her soup.

"But there's something else," he says. "Something I need to tell you that is going to be very difficult for you, and I wish it weren't."

He pauses, visibly nervous.

"Things happen that you never imagine, and I never . . ." He stops. "I'm worried you're not going to hear me out."

Dread washes over Hilary. "What do you mean?" she manages to ask.

"I never meant to hurt you. But I met this girl and . . ." He stops, unable to go on.

"Are you in love?" she asks. "Was it before you left?"

"No, no," he says. "The girl is not the thing."

"Then what is?"

At this crucial point, their main courses arrive—dishes filled with colorful sushi. He waits until they are alone again.

"Well. I guess I have to tell you that this girl is pregnant."

It's almost as if Hilary can hear the whistling of the bomb coming through the air and then landing, BOOM, right next to her. She feels as if the wind has been knocked out of her. She cannot breathe.

David looks at her, tries to grab the hand that is holding on to the edge of the table as if she might fall down without it. She clamps down even harder, not giving him anything to hold on to.

"Hilary? I'm so sorry. I didn't want it. I didn't even think it could happen, with our history, and I didn't think. I mostly took precautions too."

She shakes her other hand in front of his face to stop him from talking any more. She can't listen to any more words from him. She feels as if she is going partially deaf from the pressure building up in her head. The ambient noise of the restaurant disappears—all that remains is David's face, with his mouth grotesquely large, saying unsayable things. She breathes in and breathes out, as if this will save her life.

"Please," David's enormous mouth is saying slowly. "Please say something. I'm so sorry."

Hilary closes her eyes, to escape briefly into oblivion. She breathes in and out again.

"Okay," she manages to say. "Okay. Just give me a second."

David looks worried.

"You know," she says, "I don't think I've ever seen you look so concerned in our entire life together." But what he's said is still unfolding in her mind, and she goes silent again, trying to understand all the ramifications.

"So she's pregnant, and she's going to have the baby?" she says.

He nods. "I think she is. I didn't tell her what to do, not that I could have."

"No," she says.

Silence.

"What's her name?" she asks.

"Mercy."

"How did you meet her?"

"At a bar."

"Original," she says.

He shrugs his shoulders helplessly. "It just happened that way."

"And does she work? What does she do?"

"She doesn't work. She's between jobs."

"So is she living with you? Are you supporting her?"

He looks uncomfortable. "No, I haven't really seen her much since she told me. We definitely don't live together."

"What?" Hilary is outraged. "She's having your baby, and you haven't seen her since she told you? What's wrong with you?"

"It was such a surprise," he says. "I'm just figuring out what I should do. I told her to tell me whatever she needed, and I'm covering all the costs, of course."

"Why is she having the baby? Is she older?"

"Not at all. She's young, like twenty-seven." He understands what it sounds like. "She's smart. She went to Columbia, and she's American, Korean American, actually." He means, she's not some young bargirl.

"So why is she having the baby?"

"I don't know!" He throws up his hands. "As if I would ever be allowed to ask that question! You can't ask that question either, of all people!"

"How far along is she?"

"She said the baby's due at the end of October, so I think around halfway. It all happened really fast."

"So she doesn't have a job, and she's young. What is she going to do?"

"I have no idea," David says. "I really don't. I did not plan for this."

Looking at David, uncomfortable in his dark suit, sitting in front of her, suddenly Hilary pities David. She pities and despises him.

"Well," she says, "you've gotten yourself into a situation."

He grimaces. "You sound just like your mother when you say things like that," he says. Then, "Sorry. I don't know why I said that."

"It doesn't matter," Hilary says. She is still digesting the new reality. David will not stand in the way of her getting Julian. David has gotten a woman pregnant and will have a baby.

"Is she going to keep the baby, like raise it? She's so young."

"I have no idea, Hilary!" he says, exasperated. "I really have no idea. I haven't spoken to Mercy in weeks. This was all a big shock to me too."

"Don't you think you should?" she says. "Speak to her, I mean. You should be a good guy."

He pauses. "That's what she said too, that I should be a good guy."

" 'Cause it's true. Don't regret anything. Don't do anything you'll regret later. Be stand-up."

"I'm trying to be, Hilary," he says. "I was just trying to figure out who I could be, and then this happened, and it's been screwing with me. I didn't even have a few months for myself."

"You're not asking for sympathy, are you?" she asks, incredulous. "Please tell me you are not asking for sympathy."

"No, no, of course not," he says. "But . . . fuck it." He picks up his chopsticks and starts to eat. She stares at him for a moment, and then does the same. You have to eat to live, right? This is what goes through her mind.

Mercy

THROUGH THE CHURCH, her mother gets Mercy a job. One of the women she has befriended has a small shop in Tsim Sha Tsui where she sells Korean antiques, and she hires Mercy to help her out. Mercy takes the MTR to Tsim Sha Tsui every morning now and emerges into the crowded streets of Kowloon to make her way to the shop, in the basement of a small, run-down shopping mall. Their customers are tourists, mostly Americans, so the woman, Mrs. Choi, is pleased to have Mercy there to talk to them. She pays her a nominal amount, but she brings them both lunch every day, and Mercy is happy to have somewhere to go.

Is it really so easy? She has slipped into another life entirely, in the same city, in the same time. But here there is no pressure, there is no expectation. Nobody knows who she is, nobody knows what happened the past year, and she feels, hopefully, that even if they did, she would be forgiven, because it took place in another world. She still hasn't told her mother about G, but it seems so other, so foreign, she feels that even if she did, her mother wouldn't be able to understand. So instead she just lives in this new world, where everyone is Korean and no one expects you to go out and party and have a boyfriend, an amazing job, and a glamorous life. Here lives a different kind of expat. Mrs. Choi's kids, two boys, went to local school, and one graduated from Hong Kong University and one is at City U, local universities. They didn't have the money to even think about studying abroad, she said. Mercy has met them once or twice, when they came by the store. They are a little younger than her, but nice, shy. They speak fluent Cantonese and Korean, but their English is a little halting, inflected with a Hong Kong accent. She can tell she is exotic to them, sophisticated. They treat her respectfully, as if she is much older. What Charlie would be like if he hadn't gone to Columbia, she thinks.

It is June, and it is hot. She is starting to get bigger but is not ungainly yet. The rattle of the air conditioner in the shop is their constant background as Mrs. Choi watches Korean dramas on her laptop in the back office. Mercy sits up front, on a rosewood stool, waiting for customers.

This is where she is when she gets the e-mail.

Her blood freezes. Margaret Reade.

She shuts off the phone, reflexively, and slides it into her pocket. Can't be.

She gets the phone out and checks again. Yes, Margaret. The subject line is blank.

She gets up and tells Mrs. Choi she's going to get a soy milk and does she want anything? The answer is no, so she takes the escalator up to the street level. She wants to find a quiet corner to read the e-mail. She walks to a distant corner where there is a dusty jewelry shop and a hair salon, both not open yet. She sits on the low ledge. Heart pounding, she opens the e-mail.

Dear Mercy,

You must be surprised to hear from me. I'm surprised to be writing. I haven't seen or talked to you since Seoul. We have no news on G, although Clarke and I go regularly to check in. It is still very difficult, and my heart has been forever broken.

I'm not writing for any bad purpose. I'm just writing. I don't really know why. I haven't found a way forward yet. I wonder how you are doing. I have to be honest. I don't know if I want you to be doing well. I don't know if I could think that was fair.

But I am living my life. Mostly because of Daisy and Philip. They are doing okay.

I watched a documentary on texting and driving. In it, a young man killed someone's son because he was distracted at the wheel. The dead boy's father checks in with the man who has killed his child, and in the film, the man reads a letter that the father has written him. It was so beautifully written, and the father was so loving and forgiving, and I just cried and cried. Maybe this is why I'm writing you. I don't know. Maybe this is just a hand lifted up to see what is out there.

Margaret

Mercy can tell that this e-mail was written hastily. She reads it again. She doesn't know what she was expecting, but it was not this. She has no expectations of Margaret or Clarke. There is no rule book for relationships between people with their type of history. She knows she is expected to disappear, but she doesn't know if she's allowed to be happy or successful or whether she's supposed to live the rest of her life in repentance. She feels that the life she has now is acceptable, with the small pleasures she has recently acquired, but she can also see how a few years down the line, she might not be so tentative with her own right to happiness, how time might blunt her guilt even more. This is growth, she thinks, but it is still painful.

Margaret

SHE IS WALKING through IFC running errands when she is accosted by an Indian man.

"You are lucky," he says, "but you are sad. Can I tell you what will happen next?"

She looks at his eyes, and he smiles ingratiatingly. He is dressed in a cheap suit, the kind that makes you sad because the effort must be so great, like when she lived in New York City and once the Chinese deliveryman was dressed in a suit. To show you they are still hoping. She has heard of these men who accost you in public places, who offer to tell you your fortune and try to reel you in. She remembers reading about a court case where one woman had given her life savings to a psychic and then come to her senses.

"What do you think will happen?" she asks.

"I sense you are missing someone," he says. So vague it could apply to anyone, and yet. . . .

"Margaret!" she hears. It's Hilary Starr.

"Oh, hello," she says, turning to her.

"What are you doing?" She pulls Margaret away from the man. "Haven't you heard what these men do?" she asks, glaring at him. "Sometimes they blow some sort of gas in your face that makes you drowsy and susceptible. It's dangerous."

"Urban myth, surely," Margaret says, although she's not sure.

"This man is not the solution," Hilary says. "Do you want to get a coffee? I have to tell you the insane thing that just happened to me."

"Sure," Margaret says. They find a Starbucks and order lattes.

"I just had lunch with David," Hilary says. "I wanted to tell him that I'm going ahead with adoption. I don't know if you knew, but I've been having this boy come to my house for several months for piano lessons. He's seven, Julian, and I've decided I want to adopt him."

Margaret had heard vaguely about this and nods.

"That's wonderful, Hilary. Congratulations."

"But get this! So I'm telling him because I want to keep his name on the forms because it's easier to adopt as a couple, and then he tells me he's gotten some girl pregnant!"

Margaret claps her hand over her mouth. "Come on!" she says. "No way." It feels good to be having this conversation about other things, other people.

"Yes! And she's keeping the baby! She's young, some Korean American girl who went to Columbia." Hilary keeps talking, not realizing that Margaret has stopped reacting, gone white with shock.

Hilary stops after a while. "Are you okay?" she asks.

"Wait," Margaret says. "A Korean girl? From Columbia? What's her name?"

"A strange name. Mercy? Milly?"

As if she had summoned the girl into her universe again, just by writing the e-mail.

Margaret gets up abruptly, uncertainly, as if she is drunk, chair clattering to the floor behind her, and walks out, leaving Hilary agape in her wake.

Hilary

THE ODDEST THING. She ran into Margaret after leaving David, and full of the news, she asked her to coffee so she could tell someone, share with someone. Why does it not seem real until you've told someone?

But when she told her the news, Margaret got up and ran, like someone was after her. She left her latte steaming on the table.

Hilary let her go, then, thinking it over, it hit her.

Of course! The girl.

The girl who lost G. The nanny. David's girl. The same.

Jesus.

Mercy

SHE HAS TO WRITE BACK, of course. But what to write?

Maybe meet face to face? But the baby, her swollen stomach. She doesn't want to spring that on her.

She goes home that day, having sold an antique chest to a nice older couple from Indiana. She helps them fill out the shipping forms, and they pay with traveler's checks, something she hasn't seen in years. She feels useful, good, as if she has a place in the world.

At home, her mother is making *kimchi jjigae*, one of her favorites.

"Thanks, Mom," she says. "That smells really good."

"When I was pregnant with you, I always want the spicy food."

They sit down to eat at her tiny folding table, one of them on the bed, the other on the chair. Mercy wants to weep, because it feels so nice to be sitting here with someone who loves her unconditionally.

"Are you going to move?" her mother asks. "This place so small."

Mercy knows what her mother is asking. "I don't know," she says.

"Coming soon," she says. "Four months and you're going to be more and more uncomfortable."

"I know," she says. "But I don't know what I'm going to do."

"We could go back to New York," her mother says. "You can come home. Have more space. And baby can be born in America."

"I'm sorry, Mom," she says. "I have no idea what I'm going to do."

"I can help you, Mercy." Her mother moves over to sit next to her. Mercy can smell her familiar smell—the lotion she rubs on her hands after she finishes cooking, mixed with the scent of *doenjang*, a unique, pungent odor that brings her back to childhood.

Mercy's eyes fill with tears. "*Umma*," she says: Mom. And she breaks down.

She tells her mother everything, the whole story, with all her jobs and the unemployment and how she met Margaret and went to Korea with their family, and G—her mother breathes in sharply at this part but does not interject, just lets her keep going—and how she's been living, or not living, for the past year. She tells her about David and about Charlie and how she's messed everything up and how she thinks she always will be messed up. She tells her how she knows she's going to have a girl, and she's deathly afraid for her already. Mercy has been alone with all this for so long that, while she is telling it, she is so overwhelmed with gratitude and relief that someone is there to listen that she almost feels happy. She even tells her mother about getting the man to translate the fortune booklet when she was a teenager.

Her mother listens to all this and starts crying in the middle of it, so they are both weeping together, talking and listening, sitting on the bed in the tiny apartment.

"I love you," her mother says. "Don't worry. You are okay. How can you not tell me before? I am your mother. I fail you."

Mercy has watched enough Korean dramas to know that Koreans are used to tragedy and melodrama. It's in their blood. Mothers pretend to abandon their adored child rather than let them know some secret that would hurt them, or lovers don't tell each other the one thing that would unravel all their issues. It's a distinctly Korean way of being, and so she fits right in.

"It sounds like a drama," her mother says, as if reading her mind.

"I know!" she says, smiling through her tears.

"You shouldn't think you are unlucky forever," her mother says. "You can change your destiny. Look, I change mine by leaving your father. It reset. I don't know how it is going to be, but it's going to be different. It will be."

"But what should I do? Should I write her back?"

Her mother gets a fierce look on her face. "That woman cannot tell you you are not allowed to be happy. She is not in charge of you."

"But I ruined her life. Her family's life."

Mercy remembers something from her teenage years. She lost an earring at someone's house, and after searching for a while, she went to ask her mother for help. Her mother went and scanned the area where she had lost it. "When you want to find something small like this," she told Mercy, "you have to get down to the floor." She lay down on the carpet and put her eye to the ground. "Come down, Mercy," she said, gesturing. They lay on the carpet and scanned the floor at ground level. She was right: Things looked different from down there. Mercy found the earring immediately. "See," her mother said. "You have to get down to the level of the thing. Don't be too proud to do it." They lay there for a moment more, Mercy absorbing the lesson, the fact that her mother was there with her, willing to get down on the floor and find something with her, teach her something. She felt lucky.

Her mother speaks again now.

"That woman has responsibility too, Mercy. She choose you to help her, and these things can happen. It is not all your fault. You can live your life. You are allowed."

"I don't think she's telling me I can't be happy. I think she just wanted to reach out."

But people like Margaret are aliens to her mother. They are so far apart they will never be able to understand the other's motivations or predilections. To be her, to be Mercy, always traveling back and forth from these different kinds of people, is to be exhausted. To straddle all those viewpoints and be the translator and the mediator and never know what you yourself should be thinking.

"Thank you, Mom," she says. They sit with their simple Korean meal, spooning up the spicy stew, feeling it burn its way down their throats, nourishing them.

She will handle the Margaret issue by herself, but she does not feel alone anymore.

Margaret

IT HAS BEEN RAINING nonstop for a week. The sky opened up and never closed, and torrential, steady rain has been flooding the island. The mountains are crumbling onto the roads, where the concrete, swollen with moisture, has been caving in and creating soft, porous potholes. The sea is a muddied, swirling green full of sand and sediment; the beaches are a sodden, sorry mess.

Margaret comes across a book on the balcony, left behind by a forgetful Daisy. Now a bloated pulp of soft, tender paper, it smells rich and sweet and musty. She throws it in the garbage. The never-ending rain has made her feel hopeless but also secretly pleased that she doesn't have to go anywhere. She stays in, empties the dehumidifiers, and regulates the temperature of her house, as if she's in survival mode.

She enrolled Daisy and Philip in the first session of summer school with the promise that they might take a vacation after. They grumbled but acquiesced. So the summer days resemble school days a little, except slower, more soothing, the pressure let out.

Clarke e-mailed her a tentative itinerary that had them going back home in late July. He said he was going to book it unless she said no. She didn't respond, so she assumes he has booked it. He is learning.

Today is the day she is going to meet up with Mercy.

A few days after she sent her e-mail and then found out about the pregnancy from Hilary, she received a brief note back, thanking her for reaching out and suggesting that they meet in person. Mercy suggested a few days but could only meet after six, as she worked in

Kowloon now. Not a word about the pregnancy, although Margaret didn't really expect her to tell her over e-mail. They arranged to meet in Kowloon, close to Mercy's work.

She calls Clarke. "I'm going out tonight," she says. "Is it possible for you to come home early, since I have to leave by five?"

"Sure," he says. "What are you doing?"

"I'm meeting a group of girls for dinner," she says. If she keeps it general, he won't ask who.

"I'm really glad," he says. "It's good for you to go out and spend time with friends."

When she comes back through the kids' rooms on her way out, she comes upon Daisy sleeping, book splayed out next to her, unusual because she is too old for naps. It must be the rain. Daisy's hand is in the pocket of her hoodie, and it looks uncomfortable. When Margaret pulls it out, it's clutching a bead necklace. This girl. She can break Margaret's heart a million different ways.

If life is a continuum, and Daisy is at the beginning of an adult life and Margaret is the midpoint, where, what, is someone like Mercy? She seemed so unformed, so unknowing, a mere child still. For the first time, Margaret considers that Mercy has a family of her own, a mother, a father, possibly siblings. A family, a history, a background. All she saw before was someone in relation to herself, how Mercy could be helpful to her family, to her, for her. What Mercy did to her.

Margaret leaves to meet Mercy, wondering what, or who, she will find.

Mercy

WHEN SHE AND MARGARET see each other, she swallows, hard. Beautiful Margaret, still perfect looking, if a bit drenched from the rain. They sit down at the coffee shop, an out-of-the-way place in a touristy hotel. She places her hands under her belly. Margaret, always polite, doesn't say anything.

"I didn't know how to tell you," Mercy says.

"I knew," Margaret says.

"Really? How?"

"Hong Kong is so small," Margaret says. "You know that."

"It's due in October," Mercy says. "A Halloween baby."

"And what will you do?" Margaret asks. An open-ended question for a fluid situation.

"I don't know," Mercy says. "Jeez. This has gotten intense so quickly."

Margaret smiles. "Yes," she says. "Maybe we should order something."

"Don't you think it's funny," Mercy says, "that people always have certain rituals? We need to meet for meals or nourishment to mark certain occasions, and we have to observe certain customs before we get into what we really feel."

There she goes again, saying inappropriate and bizarre things at the worst times.

But Margaret smiles. "Yes, otherwise it would descend into chaos, I suppose."

"One small way for us to distinguish ourselves from the animals."

"You're very smart, Mercy," Margaret says. "I think you always have been."

"About everything but life," she says.

She hadn't known what to expect, but this is okay.

The waitress comes over, and she orders a chocolate milkshake while Margaret gets a coffee. "Cravings," she says apologetically.

"I know," Margaret says. "I had different ones with every child. With my first, it was BLTs with fries, all the time, and with mint-chip ice cream. I gained fifty pounds!"

"I think I'm well on the way to that," says Mercy.

They look at each other.

"So," Margaret says, "how have you been?"

Mercy is quiet. "Not good, obviously," she says. "But I don't want to talk about me when it's your family I've impacted so much."

"It's weird," Margaret says. "I've thought about you so much, but in a way, I've not thought about you at all. Only about G."

Silent again.

"I got a job," Mercy says. "Through my mom at the church. Oh, my mom came over, and she's living with me for a while." She feels that these are okay things to talk about with Margaret, virtuous, non-controversial things like mothers and churches.

"Oh? What kind of work?"

"Selling Korean antiques. One of the church ladies has this store. It's just down the street, and that's why I couldn't meet you earlier. I work there kind of as her sales assistant. She's nice."

Margaret's eyes fill with tears.

"Sorry!" Mercy says, stricken. "I'm so sorry."

Margaret shakes her head. "I'm sorry too."

"No, you don't need to be sorry!" Mercy says. "I'm the one. I'm the one to be sorry forever." As she says this, she realizes she has never apologized to Margaret, never seen her since what happened. There was the note, but that was it.

"I know," Margaret says. "I didn't know for a long time, but now I think I know."

"How are Daisy and Philip? And Clarke?"

"I think everyone is doing better than me. I'm the one dragging everyone down. They tiptoe around me."

"It's hard to move on," Mercy says.

"How did this all happen?" Margaret says, gesturing to Mercy's belly.

"Oh, this," she says. "It's complicated. It was unexpected, to say the least."

"I don't mean to pry," Margaret says. "Have you thought what you're going to do?"

"No," she says. "My mother wants me to go back to New York and have it there. The father's . . ." She doesn't finish the sentence.

"Okay," Margaret says. Another silence.

For a moment, Mercy considers telling Margaret about being the other, the unseen, the one not in the magazine article or the news story, but she can't see how she's going to explain it. "I couldn't eat for a year after what happened," she says instead. "I felt so guilty I couldn't do anything."

"I don't know what you went through," Margaret says simply. "What I was—what I am—going through is so intense I didn't have any time for anyone else other than my family."

"And I'm the reason! I'm the one to blame!" She feels she has to be out front taking the blame, telling Margaret, Here is your chance! Take your best blow!

Margaret doesn't, though. "I didn't know what it would feel like to see you," she says. "It's not as painful as I thought it would be."

"I don't know how you've survived," says Mercy, although right after she says it, she thinks it might not be the most helpful thing to say. At least she is talking about Margaret now and not about herself. She thinks that's probably the right tack.

"I wanted to erase you so badly," Margaret says. "I wanted you not to exist, because if you didn't, this never would have happened. But here you are, adding to the world. That's ironic, right?"

"I don't know if I can handle your being kind," Mercy blurts out.

The starts and stops of this conversation make Mercy feel as if she's having a series of seizures. "Do you know what the opposite of talking is?" she blurts out.

Margaret is taken aback. "No, what?"

"It's not listening. It's waiting."

Margaret processes, understands, then finally laughs. "Are you just waiting?" she asks. "Are you not listening to what I have to say?"

"No, no, no," Mercy protests. "It's just that this is a very weird conversation, and there are all these awkward pauses."

"I'm waiting for the massive wave of hatred to flood over me," says Margaret suddenly.

Mercy looks stricken. "I know," she says. "It should."

"I know it should. But I don't feel it."

They sit quietly. The waitress brings their drinks.

Mercy unwraps the straw. She shouldn't have ordered this. It makes her feel like a child next to Margaret. Shouldn't she be more strategic in every aspect of her life? She decides she must pick up the check when it comes, a forward thought that surprises her.

Margaret stirs cream into her coffee. "Were you at Clarke's party?" she asks. "I thought I saw you, but I didn't know why on God's green earth you would be there."

Mercy barks out an embarrassed laugh. "Um, I was. But I didn't know it was Clarke's party. I obviously wouldn't have gone if I had known. My mom has a job at that catering company, and she asked me to help out. Hong Kong is so small, you know. So sorry."

She wants to sink down into the earth. She wants this terrible and awkward encounter with this lovely and damaged woman to be finished. She wants to get up and leave.

But still she sits, they sit, drinking their coffee, their milkshake.

They are still bound by social convention. She supposes this is maturity, or adulthood, or life,

Mercy spoons up the melting ice cream in her milkshake and wishes, more than anything, to feel that at some point in the future, she might be happy. But she looks across the table and sees that the woman sitting there wishes for that even more desperately.

Margaret

LEAVING THE RESTAURANT, Margaret feels so unmoored she wanders for a while in Tsim Sha Tsui. It has finally stopped raining, and people are starting to emerge from indoors. TST is the type of neighborhood that gathers energy as the night descends, bustling and alive, with tailors calling out to hawk their services, brightly lit electronics stores blaring music, food stalls selling satay and pungent, bubbling curry.

She feels as if she's walking inside a bubble, watching everything happen around her. She doesn't know what she wanted out of seeing Mercy, whether it was supposed to have been cathartic or revelatory in some way, but she can't sort out what it was. It's too close. She remembers odd details from the past hour, like watching Mercy push back her hair with her hand, purse her lips around the straw of her drink—such utterly ordinary and quotidian gestures. Maybe that's the message, she thinks: that everything ultimately becomes ordinary. That Mercy is just another person, another human being. There is no answer to be found in her.

She walks as if in a dream. She remembers, in college, once seeing a woman carefully drop a coffee cup into a mailbox, as if it were a garbage can, and then walk crookedly away. Maybe, she realized later, the woman had had a stroke. She still feels guilty that she hadn't done anything, called after her to see if she was okay. But maybe that woman had been in a dream state so deep everything she did was unfamiliar and unconscious, and she had walked home and gone to bed, and then all was fine. Maybe this will happen to her.

Margaret walks down the steps to the MTR to take the subway

back to Hong Kong side. When she first moved to Hong Kong, she used to ride the train and get out at random stops, just to discover more of Hong Kong. Mostly it was disappointing, just blocks of apartment and office buildings and malls, with people pushing past her anonymously. The inside of the MTR jars in another way, all polished steel and bright blinking lights. It is clinical and clean, the pride of the government, as it transports its citizens back and forth, back and forth, with maximum efficiency.

Inside the car, she slides on the smooth steel bench, the compartment only half-full with drowsy commuters, young people chatting. It is past rush hour, so it is almost quiet, peaceful. Most people sit or stand, tapping at their phones, dozing off with earphones on their heads. She wonders at everyone, enclosed in their own little world. When her stop lights up on the panel, she gets off and walks, almost unconsciously, to her little apartment.

She gets off on her floor. A man is waiting for the elevator. Is he a waiter, a construction worker, a security guard? Around her are the sounds of people eating dinner, talking, listening to the radio or television, instead of the usual silence that surrounds her during work hours. She has never been here in the evening.

She opens the door to her sanctuary, walks in. She sits down on her bed, but all the sounds of the living around her are too distracting. It is no longer her place. And, she realizes, it never really has been. It was just borrowed, a place she used in the off hours, while the real residents were gone. She is an interloper.

Margaret opens the window to the sticky air and the outside noises. It has started to rain again, lightly. Below her is the vivid tapestry of Hong Kong: the bright, colorful wares of a fruit shop, a flower shop, the pungent odor of the butcher, the fishmonger pouring out the day's remaining ice onto the street with a muted clatter. Young couples wander under umbrellas, arms linked, eating sausages on sticks. Above, alone, she watches the world as the open window starts to streak with raindrops and a stray drop hits her cheek.

She used to wonder whether people were generally good or bad. She used to wonder whether she was a good person. She used to wonder whether bad things happened to good people more or less or if it was just random. And she used to look at people on the street and wonder what they were hiding or suffering from, or if they were that rarest of things: happy. She used to do all these things until she had to stop because her head was starting to ache.

Margaret closes the window, looks back into her tiny room, with its basic, elemental plan for living. She does not belong here, alone in an apartment building surrounded by strangers. She should go home, she realizes. She should go home to her family.

Part VII

Mercy

She's finally decided she's going to have the baby here in Hong Kong. Afterward, she and her mom have talked about maybe going to Korea or back to New York, or just staying in Hong Kong. She doesn't know, but she feels good knowing that she has someone with her.

She went to see Margaret one more time, at her house, with Daisy and Philip.

They all sat together, eating buttered toast and drinking tea, and it was okay. She wanted to say so many things to Margaret. Feeling ragged and emotional, she almost said something completely crazy.

"I want to give you something," she said. "I feel like I owe you so much. That I have taken so much, and I can't ever make it right. I even thought about—"

And then Margaret put her hand over Mercy's mouth, physically stoppered her. "Don't say it," she said. "Don't even think it."

She was grateful to Margaret for being so generous. That's what a mother is, she remembers thinking, someone who puts others' needs in front of hers, who takes the pain from others and swallows it herself. Her mother, Margaret: They are mothers. She thinks about that a lot as she puts her hands on her stomach to feel her daughter move fluidly inside her. This good person, this figure who is selfless and forgiving: This is who she needs to become.

Hilary

THE NEIGHBORHOOD of Repulse Bay is deserted. It is 5:00 a.m., late June. In the mornings, the sound of cicadas is a deafening backdrop to solitary men flagging down taxis to work, the coffee place is devoid of the usual Lululemon tribe, and the supermarket has a few desultory helpers buying groceries for one.

Hilary sits at her desk, replying to e-mails, filled with a serene yet overwhelming sense of well-being. She has deleted the forum websites from her computer and hasn't visited them for several weeks.

She has been assured by the most cautious of bureaucrats that her case seems very promising, that Julian will be with her in a time frame that they have gone so far as to allow might be less than a year. They are pleased that she would like to adopt an older child, a mixed-race child, a child who had less than promising prospects because of these factors. When asked about further access to him in the interim, they did not shut her down, merely suggested she wait a little. She has come to understand that this is all but a formality and a matter of time.

She is in her office, which she will convert into a bedroom for him. She looks around, tries to picture where the bed will go, the bureau, the desk. He will sleep here, across the hall from her bedroom. He will breathe through the night, whimper through nightmares, wake in the morning to find her staring at him. Her son.

She remembers a moment from the other day. She took him to a local diner for a snack. She texted Puri about something and then put down the phone. Julian took it from the table and looked up at her shyly. She nodded yes and tapped in her code for him. He became absorbed in the phone. This act, of a child taking his mother's phone and playing with it, an act that she had seen a hundred times before, filled her with an aching contentment.

For the first time, Hilary is considering leaving Hong Kong. She hasn't thought about it before, always assuming she would be here, with David, as he signed contract after contract. His law firm was happy for him to stay, and she didn't think otherwise. She was fine, not missing home, not minding where she was. But now, assuming that she gets Julian and she and David are done, there isn't much to keep her here. She would like to be closer to her mother as she becomes one, and so she's been thinking. She remembers that when she first moved here, a woman who had been in Hong Kong for six years had confided plaintively: "I feel like my real life is on pause. It's nice here, and I like all the help and the vacations, but I'm ready now. I'm ready to resume my real life, and now all I feel like I'm doing is waiting."

So if she moves back home, she'll start her life again, her new life with Julian. She doesn't want to traumatize him with too much change too fast, but she's thinking that after a few months, they will relocate. They can have a fresh start, together, as they begin their new life as a family. This seems right, that they'll both start anew.

Margaret

THEY WOKE UP this morning and impulsively decided to drive out to Big Wave Bay. Because the parking lot there has only some twenty spots, there is always a gambling element to the excursion (Will you have to turn back? Will you get a ticket or be towed?), and they are relieved to find a few spots still empty at nine thirty in the morning. Clarke pulls in, whistling, jaunty in a baseball cap. They pull out all the beach things from the trunk of the car and make their way down the short path to the beach, where they stand on the sand. It is still quiet and uncrowded.

"Hot!" Philip says. He hops from one foot to the other, grimacing. He clowns around, like a monkey scratching his armpits.

Margaret laughs. How lovely it is to see your children grow, develop personalities, become their true selves. Philip was a difficult baby and an obstinate toddler, but he is now bursting into a quirky and engaging child.

"Where should we set up camp?" Clarke asks.

They walk to a midpoint between the sea and the path.

"This looks like a good spot," Daisy says. She is lovely, this daughter of theirs, in her practical navy Speedo swimsuit, solid shoulders, and tousled hair. Margaret resists the urge to squeeze her delicious flesh. Daisy goes about making their temporary place, pulling out the mat and anchoring the corners, as Margaret unpacks the towels—women's work, Margaret thinks suddenly, without rancor. A man comes by to ask whether they'd like an umbrella, and they rent one for the day. Then the children run down to the water, excited, shrieking.

They splash and walk along to where there is a rock pool, looking for hermit crabs.

"Do you want anything?" Clarke asks.

There's a small canteen at one end of the beach that makes surprisingly good coffee. "Love a coffee," she says.

He wanders off, and she puts on a floppy hat and her sunglasses. Thus armored, she looks out at the flat line where the sea meets the sky and breathes in the warm morning air.

"Hooey" is what she thought when she first tried meditation and deep breathing. She went to a class at the gym she belongs to but felt so panicked and stressed she got up and left, eyes cast down so she wouldn't have to look at the teacher. She remembers thinking, Will the teacher think it's her and her teaching? Will she realize it's not about her? It's one of the things she's come to think about more and more: how everyone is stuck in their lives, thinking about what people are thinking about them, when actually nobody is thinking about them. Only you are thinking about yourself, usually. You or your mother.

Clarke comes back with a coffee for her and sits down next to her.

This is good, she thinks. Sitting here on the warm sand with the sun still low in the sky, water just before them, clouds puffy and white, children in their sights. This is a good thing. She feels his body next to hers, companionable, separate.

"I think I'll go to Korea before we leave for California," she says. "Just check in."

"Yes," he says. "That's a good idea."

They leave it at that, light, not too heavy, letting the intent pass over them.

"Want to swim?" Clarke asks.

"Mmmm," Margaret says. "Maybe in a bit. I want to get hotter before I go in."

"I'll get the kids to go in with me," he says. He rises and goes to their children, talks to them, and they wade in.

Scrolling through her Facebook feed this morning, Margaret saw someone post "Grief is the price you pay for love." She is a passive observer of this kind of social media, but she has seen how it's a kind of hive-mind, that it reflects the lives and mind-set of her peers, how posts about raising children, taking care of elderly parents, job stress have taken over the musings about finding your love, social occasions, newborns.

She thinks about that now. Is grief the price? Why does love have to be so costly? The benefits she has reaped from this love, have they been enough? When she had just Daisy toddling around, an older woman had said to her, "I think by the time they're two, kids have repaid their parents for everything. They give us so much joy in just those first two short years of their life. All the worrying and misery that might come after is just paying the piper." Margaret, then a frazzled, first-time mom, wondered what the woman was talking about. But now she thinks she knows. She's had those moments, a nestling child in her arms, a kiss and a deep inhale of the heady scent of a sleeping baby, a laugh of pure joy shared with her husband at something funny that has been said by an unknowing innocent—she has had so, so many of those moments. Her life has been rich with those moments. She is grateful for them. She wants to remember and honor them.

This is such a moment, she realizes. Sitting here, on the beach, with the warm sand beneath and the bright sun above, with Clarke and two of her children present, she feels something like a brief moment of contentment.

You don't win anything for being saddest the longest, Dr. Stein has said. There's no prize for being the most miserable. You are not betraying anyone by trying to live a better life. You are not giving up on anyone.

I'm not telling you to be happy. I'm telling you that it's okay to have moments when you're not sad. You can laugh, maybe once a month, maybe twice. It's okay.

Here's the thing. You think only one specific event, one miracle, will make things better, but actually, life will get better if you only let it. You have to let life get better. You have to for your family's sake, and for your sake. You don't think your happiness matters, but it does. It matters for your family. They can't be happy unless you see that you have the ability to be. Time will help. It can be agonizingly slow, but it always does.

Forward. Outward. Those are the directions she has to follow.

Remember this moment, she thinks fiercely. Hold on to it.

Epilogue

A BABY SLEEPS in a hospital bassinet, swaddled in a pink blanket. Mercy, exhausted, lies in bed, watching her. She has not slept for three days, for fear that the baby will stop breathing, a fear that has no foundation in reality save her own realization that she will die if her baby dies, that there is no way she can exist without this little one next to her.

No one told her how excruciating everything would be: the white-hot exhaustion, the fear of expelling anything, anything at all, from her shredded private areas, the way she woke up this morning with rock-hard melons on her chest that felt like they might burst at the slightest touch. She nods off and wakes up, goes to the bathroom to look at her drawn face, says to herself, "I'm a mother." She acknowledges her new self, tries to get used to it, all the while fighting the urge to run away, out of the room, to find her old world, her old self, which she knows is gone forever. Her belly is loose and flabby, missing its occupant. She has stared in the mirror at her naked body, lifted up the flesh of her abdomen, let it flop down, marveling at the difference.

Her mother is busy, pouring all her anxieties into cooking seaweed soup and bringing it to her in the hospital, insisting she have it fresh for every meal, so that means she is mostly alone, she and her baby, alone in a room that looks over the racetrack in Happy Valley. The baby is quiet, sleeping most of the time, so the room is eerily silent, save for some faint sucking sounds. So she spends a lot of time looking at all the windows in the apartment buildings and imagining the lives that are going on inside and marveling at the fact that every single one of those people was born, just like this baby.

The baby is such a scrap of a thing, with teeny hands and soft nails that are somehow also razor sharp. Her mouth purses into a rosebud, making Mercy's heart stop with love. At the birth, the baby didn't draw breath for a few beats, but then she inhaled and let out a good cry. Her Apgar scores were seven and eight, and Mercy was a bit indignant that already her daughter was being subjected to a standardized test.

This child is hers. When the baby stirs, moving her head a little, letting out a mewl, Mercy loosens her hospital robe so her chest is exposed, carefully unswaddles her baby, and sits down, leans back, and holds her baby, flesh to her flesh. Someone watching her might think it felt natural.

Sometimes she takes her sleeping baby in the rolling bassinet and perambulates through the halls, passes other mothers doing the same, all moving slowly, with their sore, weak gait, as if they are holding basketballs between their thighs. Most are accompanied by their partners or by their other children. They smile and nod, coo over one another's babies. Mercy likes to go to the nursery and see all the other babies, most sleeping, some sucking on pacifiers, all terrifyingly similar, with their old baby faces. She has not put her baby in the nursery, preferring to keep her with her in her room.

She has had no visitors except her mother, although David has indicated that he will come in the next few days—after she has had a few days to adjust, is how he put it in the e-mail. It is more for him to adjust, she thinks, but without too much resentment.

She sits there a moment longer, and then the baby mewls again.

Mercy sits up, moves so the baby's face is next to her giant breast. The baby's mouth opens but cannot get a hold of the rock-hard breast, and Mercy winces from the slicing pain that comes from the avid mouth. Milk starts to spray out from her nipple, and the baby's lips get wet and slippery, and suckling becomes even more impossible. Mercy closes her eyes in agony, the baby tries again, cannot latch, starts its thin, desperate cry. Mercy tears up in frustration.

A knock at the door. Usually it is a nurse to take her blood pressure or to give her some pills for iron deficiency or a doctor to check the clipboard.

Mercy looks up and cannot reconcile who is there. The woman who should hate her the most in the world, who should be the last person to see her with her own baby, to see her with anything good.

She cannot talk, cannot say hello, just gapes, and then, as the baby tries again to get a hold and fails, and starts to wail in earnest, she starts to cry herself.

"Oh, lord," says Margaret. "These are terrible days. I know. They say it's the best time of your life, but it's also the worst."

And then, behind her, Mercy sees another woman. She knows who it is immediately, although she has not met her. Another woman who should not be here, who should not see her with this baby, a bastard child from her own husband. Yet here these women are, bearing what she can see are flowers and food and gifts. So they are not here to torture or demand retribution. But how can it be?

She doesn't understand.

"She's hungry," Mercy says. "But my milk came in, and my boobs are so hard it's like she's trying to get on a flat surface. So she can't latch on. They didn't say anything about this in the books."

Margaret immediately goes out and gets a nurse and tells her she needs a breast pump. When the nurse wheels one in a few minutes later, Margaret brings it over and says, "When your breasts get like that, you have to pump off some milk so the breast becomes softer, and then the baby can latch on. May I?"

She gently moves the robe aside so the breast is exposed. She puts the pump over the nipple and starts the machine. Soon milk is spraying out from multiple ducts and collecting in the bottle underneath.

"I always thought that was so cool," Margaret says. "I used to love to watch the milk coming out when I was pumping."

Mercy can feel her breast softening. Relief floods her body.

"Okay," she says. "It seems pretty soft now."

They remove the pump, and she wipes off the milk on her breast and moves her baby toward her. The baby's mouth opens, and she clamps on. Mercy arches her back in pain.

"Oh, no," says Margaret. "You have to get her lower lip out, do you see? Otherwise, she's sucking directly on the nipple and it will be unbearable. Do you want to try again?"

Mercy shakes her head. "I just want her to eat right now," she says. There is a silence.

"Do you have a name?" Hilary asks.

Mercy cannot look her in the eye. "Not yet," she says. "It seems so impossible to name her, to give her that so soon."

"I know," Margaret says. "They're kind of like strangers in the beginning, although it's awful to say."

Another silence.

"Thank you," Mercy says. "I can't believe you're here. I can't believe that you would come."

"It seems like the right thing to do," Margaret says. "Becoming a mother is the most life-changing event in a woman's life."

Hilary nods. She grins suddenly. "But don't let your man know," she says.

Mercy looks down. Her baby is sucking, eyes looking up at her fiercely, as if to claim her.

"I remember with my daughter," Margaret says, "when she nursed, it scared me, because she was so primal about it. She looked at me, and it rattled me, because I realized she owned me absolutely and she was letting me know. It was life and death. It was real, and it was forever."

That Margaret is echoing Mercy's thoughts is unnerving.

"Has . . . David . . . come?" Hilary asks delicately.

Mercy shakes her head. The other women sigh, almost imperceptibly. They have all been disappointed in life, and this is just another instance.

"But he said he would," she says lamely, although she doesn't know why she feels the need. "I think in the next few days he will."

"Good," Hilary says.

They sit and listen to the baby suckle.

"Listen," Margaret says, "I know you must be uncomfortable on so many different levels, but I just wanted to come, and so did Hilary. No agenda."

Mercy nods. "Thank you," she says. "Thank you." She is overwhelmed with gratitude. Is this how new lives are born? she wonders. Is this how you make a new start? Not just her baby, not just her daughter. A new life for everyone, for herself maybe, where a simple but unimaginable act of kindness, of forgiveness, can hit the reset button, make everything seem possible, make hope reappear.

The women sit quietly in the sunlit room, each thinking her own impossibly complicated thoughts. The door opens. It is Mercy's mother, carrying a thermos of newly made soup for her child. She looks at the scene with confusion. All three women turn toward her, their faces open and expectant. They are all of them women. They are all of them mothers. They know who she is.

Acknowledgments

Writing a book is, among other things, an exercise in how much time you can spend alone, so it's crucial that when you emerge you are with people you like.

I like these people, for their friendship and advice: Mimi Brown, Ann Chen, Deborah Cincotta, Rachael Combe, Kate Gellert, Eunei Lee, Elaina Richardson, Katie Rosman, Gary Shteyngart, Pat Towers.

My agent, Theresa Park, is a marvel of efficiency and empathy, immediate with responses, soothing with assurances.

Abby Koons, Emily Sweet, Alex Greene, Andrea Mai, Peter Knapp, and Emily Owen are the dream team at the Park Literary Group who make my life better in so many different ways.

I thank the wonderful people at Viking Penguin for their unbelievable support of my work. They have made a dream home for me.

Kathryn Court is my wise and gracious editor; Lindsey Schwoeri, her able associate; Brian Tart and Andrea Schulz, crucial supporters; Kate Stark, Carolyn Coleburn, Lindsay Prevette, Lydia Hirt, Mary Stone, Meredith Burks, Emma Mohney, John Lawton, Christopher Dufault, Erin Reilly, Morgan Green, Phil Budnick, John Fagan, Kate Griggs, Candy Gianetti, Francesca Belanger, Paul Buckley, Nayon Cho, Victoria Savanh, Paul Slovak, and Clare Ferraro are all proof that publishing is full of people who love books and reading and live in a world inspired by these things. I sincerely apologize if I have inadvertently left someone out as I know so many people worked so hard to produce this book.

In the UK, Julian Alexander and Clare Smith have been long-standing and ardent supporters.

My former teachers Chang-rae Lee and Abby Thomas continue to light the way with their inspiring work.

Katherine Olivetti and Alia Eyres shared professional insights on psychotherapy and local adoption in Hong Kong. Any errors in interpreting the knowledge they were kind enough to dispense are my own.

Gratitude to my parents, my brother's family, and the extended Bae family.

And lastly and most, most importantly, BIG love and wonder for my family:

Joe, Owen, Daniel, Sarah, and James: Everything would be nothing without you.

Janice Y. K. Lee's *The Piano Teacher*
is also available from Penguin

Read on for the opening pages of . . .

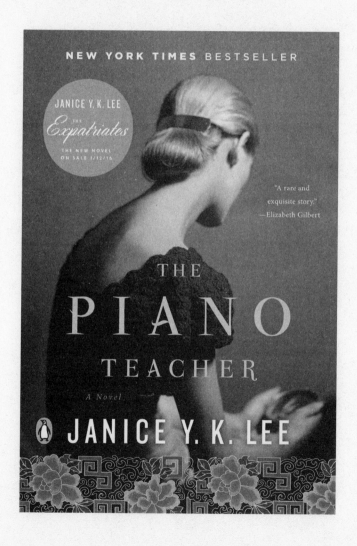

❖ Part I ❖

May 1952

IT STARTED as an accident. The small Herend rabbit had fallen into Claire's purse. It had been on the piano and she had been gathering up the sheet music at the end of the lesson when she knocked it off. It fell off the doily (a doily! on the Steinway!) and into her large leather bag. What had happened after that was perplexing, even to her. Locket had been staring down at the keyboard and hadn't noticed. And then, Claire had just...left. It wasn't until she was downstairs and waiting for the bus that she grasped what she had done. And then it had been too late. She went home and buried the expensive porcelain figurine under her sweaters.

Claire and her husband had moved to Hong Kong nine months ago, transferred by the government, which had posted Martin at the Department of Water Services. Churchill had ended rationing and things were starting to return to normal when they had received news of the posting. She had never dreamed of leaving England before.

Martin was an engineer, overseeing the building of the Tai Lam Cheung reservoir, so that there wouldn't need to be so much rationing when the rains ebbed, as they did every several years. It was to hold four and a half billion gallons of water when full. Claire almost couldn't imagine such a number, but Martin said it was barely enough for the people of Hong Kong, and he was sure that by the time they were finished, they'd have to build another. "More work for me," he said cheerfully. He was analyzing the topography of the hills so that they could install catchwaters for when the rain came. The English government did so much for the colonies, Claire knew.

They made the locals' lives much better but they rarely appreciated it. Her mother had warned her about the Chinese before she left—an unscrupulous, conniving people who would surely try to take advantage of her innocence and goodwill.

Coming over, she had noticed it for days, the increasing wetness in the air, even more than usual. The sea breezes were stronger and the sunrays more powerful when they broke through cloud. When the *P&O Canton* finally pulled into Hong Kong harbor in August, she really felt she was in the tropics, hair frizzing up in curls, face always slightly damp and oily, the constant moisture under her arms and knees. When she stepped from her cabin outside, the heat assailed her like a physical blow, until she managed to find shade and fan herself.

There had been seven stops along the month-long journey, but after a few grimy hours spent in Algiers and Port Said, Claire had decided to stay onboard rather than encounter more frightening peoples and customs. She had never imagined such sights. In Algiers, she had seen a man kiss a donkey and she couldn't discern whether the high odor was coming from one or the other, and in Egypt, the markets were the very definition of unhygienic—a fishmonger gutting a fish had licked the knife clean with his tongue. She had inquired as to whether the ship's provisions were procured locally, at these markets, and the answer had been most unsatisfactory. An uncle had died from food poisoning in India, making her cautious. She kept to herself and sustained herself mostly on the beef tea they dispensed in the late morning on the sun deck. The menus that were distributed every day were mundane: turnips, potatoes, things that could be stored in the hold, with meat and salads the first few days after port. Martin promenaded on the deck every morning for exercise and tried to get her to join him, to no avail. She preferred to sit in a deck chair with a large brimmed hat and wrap herself in one of the scratchy wool ship blankets, face shaded from the omnipresent sun.

There had been a scandal on the ship. A woman, going to meet her fiancé in Hong Kong, had spent one too many moonlit nights on the deck with another gentleman and had disembarked in the Philippines with her new man, leaving only a letter for her intended. Liesel, the girlfriend to whom the woman had entrusted the letter, grew visibly more nervous as the date of arrival drew near. Men joked that she could take Sarah's place, but she wasn't having any of that. Liesel was a serious young woman who was joining her sister and brother-in-law in Hong Kong, where she intended to educate Unfortunate Chinese Girls in Art: when she held forth on it, it was always with capital letters in Claire's mind.

Before disembarking, Claire separated out all of her thin cotton dresses and skirts; she could tell that was all she would be wearing for a while. They had arrived to a big party on the dock, with paper streamers and loud, shouting vendors selling fresh fruit juice and soy milk drinks and garish flower arrangements to the people waiting. Groups of revelers had already broken out the champagne and were toasting the arrival of their friends and family.

"We pop them as soon as we see the boat on the horizon," a man explained to his girl as he escorted her off the boat. "It's a big party. We've been here for hours." Claire watched Liesel go down the gangplank, looking very nervous, and then she disappeared into the throng. Claire and Martin went down next, treading on the soft, humid wood, luggage behind them carried by two scantily clad young Chinese boys who had materialized out of nowhere.

Martin had an old school friend, John, who worked at Dodwell's, one of the trading firms, who had promised to greet the ship. He came with two friends and offered the new arrivals freshly squeezed guava drinks. Claire pretended to sip at hers, as her mother had warned her about the cholera that was rampant in these parts. The men were bachelors and very pleasant. John, Nigel, Leslie. They explained that they all lived together in a mess—there were many, known by their companies, Dodwell's Mess, Jardine's Mess, et cetera, and they assured Claire and Martin that Dodwell's threw the best parties around.

They accompanied them to the government-approved hotel in Tsim Sha Tsui, where a Chinese man with a long queue, dirty white tunic, and shockingly long fingernails showed them to their room. They made an arrangement to meet for tiffin the next day and the men departed, leaving Martin and Claire sitting on the bed, exhausted and staring at one another. They didn't know each other that well. They had been married barely four months.

She had accepted Martin's proposal to escape the dark interior of her house, her bitter mother railing against everything, getting worse, it seemed, with her advancing age, and an uninspiring job as a filing girl at an insurance company. Martin was older, in his forties, and had never had luck with women. The first time he kissed her, she had to stifle the urge to wipe her mouth. He was like a cow, slow and steady. And kind. She knew this. She was grateful for it.

She had not had many chances with men. Her parents stayed home all the time, and so she had as well. When she had started seeing Martin—he was the older brother of one of the girls at work—she had eaten dinner at restaurants, drunk a cocktail at a hotel bar, and seen other young women and men talking, laughing with an assurance she could not fathom. They had opinions about politics; they had read books she had never heard of and seen foreign films and talked about them with such confidence. She was enthralled and not a little intimidated. And then Martin had come to her, serious, his job was taking him to the Orient, and would she come with him? She was not so attracted to him, but who was she to be picky, she thought, hearing the voice of her mother. She let him kiss her and nodded yes.

Claire had started to draw a bath in their hotel room when another knock on the door revealed a small Chinese woman, an amah, she was called, who started to unpack their suitcases until Martin shooed her off.

And that was how they arrived in Hong Kong, which was like nothing Claire had imagined. Apart from the usual colonial haunts—all hush and genteel potted palms and polished wood in white-washed buildings—it was loud and crowded and dirty and bustling. The buildings were right next to one another and often had clothing hung out to dry on bamboo poles. There were garish vertical signs hung on every one, and they advertised massage parlors and pubs and hair salons. Someone had told her that opium dens still existed in back-alley buildings. There was often refuse on the street, some-times even human refuse, and there was a pungent, peppery odor in town that was oddly clingy, attaching itself to your very skin until you went home for a good scrub. There were all sorts of people. The local women carried their babies in a sort of back sling. Sikhs served as uniformed security guards—you saw them dozing off on wooden stools outside the banks, turbaned heads hanging heavily off their chests, rifles held loosely between their knees. The Indians had been brought over by the British, of course. Pakistanis ran carpet stores, Portuguese were doctors, and Jews ran the dairy farms and other large businesses. There were English businessmen and American bankers, White Russian aristocrats, and Peruvian entrepreneurs—all peculiarly well traveled and sophisticated—and, of course, there were the Chinese, quite different in Hong Kong from the ones in China, she was told.

To her surprise, she didn't detest Hong Kong, as her mother had told her she would—she found the streets busy and distracting, so very different from Croydon, and filled with people and shops and goods she had never seen before. She liked to sample the local bakery goods, the pineapple buns and yellow egg tarts, and some-times wandered outside Central, where she would quickly find herself in unfamiliar surroundings, where she might be the only non-Chinese around. The fruit stalls were heaped with not only oranges and bananas, still luxuries in postwar England, but spiky, strange-looking fruits she came to try and like: star fruit, durian, lychee. She would buy a dollar's worth and be handed a small, waxy brown bag and she would eat the fruit slowly as she walked. There were small stalls made of crudely nailed wood and corrugated tin, which housed specialty shops: this one sold chops, the stone stamps the Chinese used in place of signatures; this one made only keys; this one had a chair that was rented for half-days by a street dentist and a barber. The locals ate on the street in tiny little restaurants called *daipaidong,* and she had seen three worker men in dirty singlets and trousers crouched over a plate containing a whole fish, spitting out the bones at their feet. One had seen her watching them, and deliberately picked up the fish's eyeball with his chopsticks and raised it up to her, smiling, before he ate it.

Claire hadn't met many Chinese people before, but the ones she had seen in the big towns in England were serving you in restaurants or ironing clothes. There were many of those types in Hong Kong, of course, but what had been eye-opening was the sight of the affluent Chinese, the ones who seemed English in all but their skin color. It had been quite something to see a Chinese step out of a Rolls-Royce, as she had one day when she was waiting on the steps of the Gloucester Hotel, or in business suits, eating lunch with other Englishmen who talked to them as if they were the same. She hadn't known that such worlds existed. And then with Locket, she was thrust into their world.

After a few months settling in, finding a flat and setting it up, Claire had put the word out that she was looking for a job teaching the piano, somewhat as a lark, she put it—something to fill the day—but the truth was, they could really use the extra money. She had played the piano most of her life and was primarily self-taught. Amelia, an acquaintance she had met at a sewing circle, said she would ask around.

She rang a few days later.

"There's a Chinese family, the Chens. They run everything in town. Apparently, they're looking for a piano teacher for their daughter, and they'd prefer an Englishwoman. What do you think?"

"A Chinese family?" Claire said. "I hadn't thought about that possibility. Aren't there any English families looking?"

"No," Amelia said. "Not that I've been able to ascertain."

"I just don't know . . ." Claire demurred. "Wouldn't it be odd?" She couldn't imagine teaching a Chinese girl. "Does she speak English?"

"Probably better than you or me," Amelia said impatiently. "They're offering very adequate compensation." She named a large sum.

"Well," Claire said slowly, "I suppose it couldn't do any harm to meet them."

Victor and Melody Chen lived in the Mid-Levels, in an enormous white two-story house on May Road. There was a driveway, with potted plants lining the sides. Inside, there was the quiet, efficient buzz of a household staffed with plentiful servants. Claire had taken a bus, and when she arrived, she was perspiring after the walk from the road to the house. The amah had led her to a sitting room, where she found a fan blowing blessedly cool air. A houseboy adjusted the drapes so that she was properly shaded. Her blue linen skirt, just delivered from the tailor, was wrinkled, and she had on a white voile blouse that was splotched with moisture. She hoped the Chens would allow her some time to compose herself. She shifted, feeling a drop of perspiration trickle down her thigh.

No such luck. Mrs. Chen swooped through the door, a vision in cool pink, holding a tray of drinks. A small, exquisite woman, with hair cut just so, so that it swung in precise, geometric movements. Her shoulders were fragile and exposed in her sleeveless shift, her face a tiny oval.

"Hello!" Mrs. Chen trilled. "Lovely to meet you. I'm Melody. Locket's just on her way."

"Locket?" Claire said, uncertain.

"My daughter. She's just back from school and getting changed into something more comfortable. Isn't the heat dreadful?" She set down the tray, which held long glasses of iced tea. "Have something cool, please."

"Your English is remarkably good," Claire said as she took a glass.

"Oh, is it?" Melody said casually. "Four years at Wellesley will do that for you, I suppose."

"You were at university in America?" Claire asked. She hadn't known that Chinese went to university in America.

"Loved every minute," she said. "Except for the horrible, horrible food. Americans think a grilled cheese sandwich is a meal! And as you know, we Chinese take food very seriously."

"Is Locket going to be schooled in America?"

"We haven't decided, but really, I'd rather talk to you about your schooling," Mrs. Chen said.

"Oh." Claire was taken aback.

"You know," she continued pleasantly. "Where you studied music, and all that."

Claire settled back in her seat.

"I was a serious student for a number of years. I studied with Mrs. Eloise Pollock and was about to apply for a position at the Royal Conservatory when my family situation changed."

Mrs. Chen sat, waiting, head tilted, with one birdlike ankle crossed over the other, her knees slanted to one side.

"And so, I was unable to continue," Claire said. Was she supposed to explain it in detail to this stranger? Her father had been let go from the printing company and it had been a black couple of months before he found a new job as an insurance salesman. His pay had been erratic at best—he was not a natural salesman—and luxuries like piano lessons were unthinkable. Mrs. Pollock, a very kind woman, had offered to continue her instruction at a much-reduced fee, but her mother, sensitive and pointlessly proud, had refused to even entertain the idea.

"And what level of studies did you achieve?"

"I was studying for my seventh grade examinations."

"Locket is a beginning student but I want her to be taught seriously, by a serious musician," Mrs. Chen said. "She should pass all her examinations with distinction."

"Well, I'm certainly serious about music, and as for passing with distinction, that will be up to Locket," Claire said. "I did very well on my examinations."

Locket entered the room, or rather, she bumbled into it. Where her mother was small and fine, Locket was chubby, all rounded limbs and padded cheeks. She was wider than her mother already, and had glossy hair tied in a thick ponytail.

"Hallo," she said. She had a very distinct English accent.

"Locket, this is Mrs. Pendleton," Melody said, stroking her daughter's cheek. "She's come to see if she'll be your piano teacher so you must be very polite."

"Do you like the piano, Locket?" Claire said, too slowly, she realized, for a ten-year-old child. She had no experience with children.

"I dunno," Locket said. "I suppose so."

"Locket!" her mother cried. "You said you wanted to learn. That's why we bought you the new Steinway."

"Locket's a pretty name," Claire said. "How did you come about it?"

"Dunno," said Locket. She reached for a glass of iced tea and drank. A small trickle wended its way down her chin. Her mother took a napkin off the silver tray and dabbed at her daughter's chin.

"Will Mr. Chen be arriving soon?" Claire asked.

"Oh, Victor!" Melody laughed. "He's far too busy for these household matters. He's always working."

"I see," Claire said. She was uncertain as to what came next.

"Would you play us something?" Melody asked. "We just got the piano and it would be lovely to hear it played professionally."

"Of course," Claire said, because she didn't know what else to say. She felt as if she were being made to perform like a common entertainer—something in Melody's tone—but she couldn't think of a gracious way to demur.

She played a simple étude, which Melody seemed to enjoy and Locket squirmed through.

"I think this will be fine," Mrs. Chen said. "Are you available on Thursdays?"

Claire hesitated. She didn't know whether she was going to take the job.

"It would have to be Thursdays because Locket has lessons the other days," Mrs. Chen said.

"Fine," said Claire. "I accept."